W9-DES-338

OUT OF THE ORDINARY

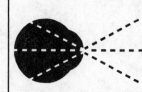

This Large Print Book carries the
Seal of Approval of N.A.V.H.

APART FROM THE CROWD

OUT OF THE ORDINARY

JEN TURANO

THORNDIKE PRESS
A part of Gale, a Cengage Company

Farmington Hills, Mich • San Francisco • New York • Waterville, Maine
Meriden, Conn • Mason, Ohio • Chicago

LIBRARY OF CONGRESS CIP DATA ON FILE.
CATALOGUING IN PUBLICATION FOR THIS BOOK
IS AVAILABLE FROM THE LIBRARY OF CONGRESS

ISBN-13: 978-1-4328-4631-2 (hardcover)
ISBN-10: 1-4328-4631-0 (hardcover)

Published in 2018 by arrangement with Bethany House Publishers, a division of Baker Publishing Group

Printed in the United States of America
1 2 3 4 5 6 7 22 21 20 19 18

For Paulette Tangelder
Because sometimes a person just needs
to be reminded they're appreciated!
Love ya!
Jen

CHAPTER ONE

June 4, 1883

Slipping through the crowd gathered on the upper deck of a most extravagant yacht, Miss Gertrude Cadwalader drew in a breath and adopted an air of what she hoped would be taken for nonchalance. Her greatest desire was that no one would realize she was anything but completely composed, even though something was horribly, horribly amiss.

Mrs. Davenport, the lady Gertrude was paid to be a companion to, had, regrettably, gone missing.

It wasn't that Gertrude was concerned her employer had fallen overboard, or that she'd suffered some manner of terrible accident. Circumstances such as those would have been much easier to handle than the reality Gertrude was facing — that reality being the unfortunate business of Mrs. Davenport having the propensity to go missing on a far too frequent basis.

On this evening, Mrs. Davenport had not been seen for over an hour. During that hour, Gertrude was all but convinced her employer had been pursuing activities that would be considered suspicious in nature by everyone except members of the criminal set.

Unable to help but shudder over that idea, Gertrude quickened her pace and reached a flight of narrow steps that led below-deck. Glancing over her shoulder, relief trickled through her when she realized all the guests who'd been invited to celebrate the recent engagement of Miss Permilia Griswold to Mr. Asher Rutherford were sufficiently occupied and not paying her the least little mind.

Keeping a firm grip on the railing because the unusually large bustle attached to her behind made traveling down stairs tricky, Gertrude reached the lower deck and took a second to peruse her surroundings.

To her left, she discovered a great many closed doors, a rather daunting sight, and when she looked to the right, she was less than reassured when she discovered just as many closed doors in that direction.

Knowing there was nothing left to do except get on with the disturbing matter at

8

hand, especially since the longer she lingered, the more mischief Mrs. Davenport could get into, Gertrude headed down the companionway to her right, stopping at the first door she encountered.

After she edged the door open, she found a delightful stateroom on the other side, paneled in gleaming wood. Set in the very middle of the room was a four-poster bed, complete with a canopy draped in blue silk. The bed was sitting high enough from the floor to where a person could very well slip underneath it if that person were trying to avoid detection.

Marching her way across the room, Gertrude stopped directly beside the bed and leaned over, stopping mid-lean when one of the wires used to create the monstrosity on her behind took that moment to jab though the delicate material of her petticoats and drawers. Wincing, Gertrude straightened even as she longed to rub a bottom that was now sore but impossible to reach past a bustle that seemed to be coming undone.

Deciding it would not benefit her to bend over again since she really had no liking for wires jabbing her, she cleared her throat and lowered her voice to the merest whisper.

"Mrs. Davenport, are you under there?"

When only silence met her ears, Gertrude

debated bending over again, but when the thought sprang to mind that there was a very good chance her bustle would only disintegrate further, jabbing her numerous times in the process, she abandoned that particular debate.

"Since I seem to be suffering some ill effects from a bustle you assured me had been crafted in a most expert manner, which, sadly, I'm learning was not exactly the case, I fear I'm beginning to lose all sense of a pleasant attitude," she began in a voice slightly louder than a whisper this time. "Because of that, and because I'm certain you, Mrs. Davenport, won't want my enjoyment in this lovely evening to be ruined because of an ill humor, I'm going to suggest if you are under the bed, you show yourself immediately. You must know that no good can possibly come from skulking around Mr. Harrison Sinclair's yacht."

When Mrs. Davenport did not come crawling out from underneath the bed, Gertrude made for the door, stopping a second later when she noticed a smaller door, one that might very well lead to a wardrobe. Knowing her employer had a great liking for wardrobes, and the space they provided a person when one wanted to go unobserved, Gertrude changed directions and strode across the room again, taking hold of the latch attached to the smaller door and giving it a pull.

She did not discover Mrs. Davenport lurking on the other side. Instead, she found a room she'd been told was called a "head" instead of a retiring room, one that came complete with a marble sink with gilded taps.

Unable to stop herself since her curiosity was now getting the better of her, she turned one of the taps, which immediately sent a stream of clear water spouting out of it.

Not wanting the fresh water to go to waste, she splashed some on her face, which had become heated during her searching endeavors, washed her hands, then stilled when she thought she heard footsteps in the companionway.

Turning off the tap, she reached for the fluffy towel that was hanging from a gilded hook, patted her face and hands dry, returned the towel to the hook, uncertain that was proper but not knowing what else to do with it, and then moved as stealthily as she could out of the head and through the stateroom. Opening the door ever so carefully, she stuck her head out and peered down the companionway.

At first, she thought she must have been imagining the footsteps, until she glimpsed the merest hint of a shadow disappearing around a corner. Hoping the shadow belonged to none other than the errant Mrs. Davenport, Gertrude hurried after it, coming to an abrupt halt when she rounded the corner and found herself facing two doors, one of which had been left slightly ajar.

"I've found you now." Pushing open that door, she discovered herself in a room that was devoid of Mrs. Davenport, but filled to the brim with leather-bound books, the scent of the leather reminding Gertrude of the library her father used to own, back in the days before he'd lost the family fortune and . . .

Shaking herself from thoughts she certainly hadn't expected to spring to mind, especially since she couldn't afford to become distracted, Gertrude headed farther into what turned out to be the yacht's library. She made short shrift of looking behind two chairs with tufted cushions upholstered in a navy and white fabric, disappointment stealing through her when she didn't uncover Mrs. Davenport crouched behind either chair.

Tapping a finger against her chin, she considered a small fainting couch that was positioned directly underneath a painting that, if she wasn't mistaken, might have been painted by Bouguereau. What such a painting was doing onboard a yacht, she couldn't say, but since Mrs. Davenport was often drawn to objects of an expensive nature, the small space located between the wall and the back of the couch certainly deserved further investigation. Moving to stand before the couch, Gertrude placed a knee on top of the cushion, peered over the back of the couch, and found absolutely nothing there.

Since there was little sense lingering in a room where her employer was obviously not, Gertrude began to straighten, but to her dismay, her bustle took that moment to shift, making her side-heavy. Before she could do more than let out a squeak, she wobbled to the left, the bustle shifted again, and before she knew it, the weight of it pulled her straight against the fainting couch. She was left reclining in an awkward and less than graceful pose between the high back of the couch and the cushioned seat.

When what felt like every wire that had been used to fashion the bustle — a bustle that was actually a sawed-in-half birdcage — began jabbing her in far too many places, Gertrude tried to push herself into an upright position. That decision turned out to be a grave error in judgment when she heard the fabric of her gown rip right before she became completely immobile.

Realizing that the wires of her bustle were keeping her firmly attached to the fainting couch, Gertrude knew she had no choice but to call for help. Before she could do so, though, footsteps sounded directly outside the library door.

Turning her head, the only part of her body she seemed capable of turning, she blinked and then blinked again when a lovely young lady dressed in a delightful gown of yellow tulle stepped into the room, paused, and then sent a frown Gertrude's way.

"I say, Miss Cadwalader, are you quite all right? I could have sworn I just heard a bit of a ruckus, but . . ." She waved a hand Gertrude's way. "There you are, completely at your leisure, although now that I think about it, you being at your leisure is somewhat odd. When I took note of you leaving the upper deck, I thought for certain you must be searching out a retiring room to fix your hair, since it is, as I'm certain you're aware, looking downright frightful at the moment."

For the briefest of seconds, Gertrude

could only stare at the young lady known as Miss Clementine Flowerdew — a member of the fashionable set and a lady Gertrude rarely conversed with, and certainly wasn't looking forward to conversing with at this inopportune time.

That Miss Flowerdew was looking very well indeed, there could be no question. Strands of jewels were woven into the young lady's perfectly styled flaxen hair, the style of that hair drawing attention to the graceful curve of her white neck. Encircled around that neck were additional jewels, set in numerous strands that ended in a glitter of diamonds nestled directly in the very center of Miss Flowerdew's charms.

A flicker of what felt exactly like envy took Gertrude by surprise, brought on, no doubt, by the thought that any charms *she* might possess were tucked away beneath a gown that was made of yards and yards of hideous green fabric.

Even though she wasn't a lady who held an overt interest in fashion, which made her the ideal companion for a woman who considered herself a designer but had no true talent for design, she did occasionally wish Mrs. Davenport would refrain from using her as a subject to try out her more outlandish creations. Refraining from that behavior would have allowed Gertrude to attend the engagement event that very evening without wearing a curiously designed bustle, one that was now responsible for keeping her a prisoner on the fainting couch.

The idea for that bustle had come about when Mrs. Davenport had overheard a conversation between Gertrude and her very good friend Miss Permilia Griswold. Permilia was the guest of honor this evening and a woman with a keen eye for fashion. As such, she was always up to date on the trends fashions were expected to take. Those trends were now suggesting that bustles were to expand in size by numerous inches. Evidently wanting to embrace the idea that bustles were to become larger than ever, Mrs. Davenport had set about creating the largest bustle anyone had probably ever seen, resorting to using a real birdcage to obtain the size she'd decided she needed.

That size was directly responsible for the yards and yards of fabric Gertrude was wearing, since Mrs. Davenport had longed to create what she called a waterfall effect that would cascade gracefully from Gertrude's backside. While Mrs. Davenport claimed the green color was her inspiration for creating that waterfall, something to do

16

with rushing water, Gertrude had the sneaking suspicion her employer had used the green because it was the only color available that came with so many yards of fabric to the bolt, the availability of that bolt a direct result of no one with any sense of style wanting to be garbed in such an awful color.

Sadly, there was no disputing the idea that the gown Gertrude was wearing did not show to advantage next to Miss Flowerdew's frothy creation of yellow tulle, which left . . .

"Oh dear, I do hope I haven't hurt your feelings with the frightful hair remark, Miss Cadwalader. I did so want to get off on the right foot with you. Clearly, though, since you've yet to respond to my statement, you weren't aware that there's something gravely amiss with whatever that is you currently have fashioned on your head."

Raising a hand, Gertrude patted the right side of her head and then patted the left. "Everything seems to be in order" was all she could think to say.

Miss Flowerdew walked closer, shaking her perfectly coiffed head in a rather sad sort of way. "You look as if you've attached two golden baker buns to either side of your head — a look that is neither fashionable nor appealing."

"Mrs. Davenport told me *she* was told by a society matron who just returned from Europe that *this* particular style was all the rage this season."

Miss Flowerdew bit her lip. "Perhaps that style may be well-regarded in some obscure European country, one that's far, far away, but I didn't witness a single lady wearing that look when I was over in Paris a few weeks back."

Taking a second to rub at a kink in her neck that was becoming more knotted by the minute, Gertrude released a sigh. "And that right there, Miss Flowerdew, is why one should never trust a lady of a certain age who is looking far too innocently back at you, while she's styling your hair in what you believe is a questionable manner, but she insists is not."

"I beg your pardon?"

Gertrude stopped rubbing her neck and waved Miss Flowerdew's comment aside. "It's of little consequence, simply a touch of pondering about finding myself in somewhat peculiar circumstances at times. However, now is hardly the time for me to descend into a state of self-reflection. May I assume you're searching for a retiring room and that is why you were following me? As you can see, there's not a retiring room here in the library. I do know that you can find a well-appointed one on the aft deck, right behind the sitting salon, where people are currently taking their leisure to get out of the stiff ocean breeze."

To Gertrude's surprise, Miss Flowerdew gave a delicate shrug of her shoulders before she smiled, walked across the room, then made quite the production of lowering herself into a chair, smoothing out the folds of her skirt before she lifted her head. "I didn't follow you because I was searching out a retiring room, Miss Cadwalader. I followed you because I'd like to speak with you privately." She nodded to the chair adjacent to her. "It would be easier to enjoy our conversation, though, if you'd join me over here."

Gertrude took the briefest of seconds to contemplate her current dilemma.

Miss Flowerdew, being of the fashionable set, was a woman who would probably not understand how it had come to be that Gertrude was currently wearing a birdcage on her bottom. But if she didn't explain her unusual situation to Miss Flowerdew, she'd continue being stuck. That could lead to someone stumbling upon Mrs. Davenport and whatever it was Mrs. Davenport was up to, which could very well turn disastrous for her employer.

The sense of loyalty she held for Mrs. Davenport, a woman who was undoubtedly odd, yet provided Gertrude with a more than generous wage, had her lifting her chin.

"As curious as this is going to sound, Miss Flowerdew," she began, "I'm afraid that it's impossible for me to join you since I've gotten myself into a tricky situation, one that I can't seem to correct by myself."

Miss Flowerdew leaned forward, pursed her lips, then, curiously enough, smiled. "You need a favor from me?"

"I don't know if I'd go so far as to call it a favor, more on the lines of a smidgen of assistance."

If anything, Miss Flowerdew's smile brightened. "Assistance that would leave you in my debt?"

A trace of unease began tickling the back of Gertrude's neck, mixing with the knot that was still there. Summoning up a smile of her own, she nodded toward the door. "Upon further reflection, I truly don't want to put you out, nor do I want you to miss any of the festivities currently taking place topside. If you'd simply be so kind as to tell Miss Permilia Griswold that I could use *her* assistance when you return to the top deck,

I'd greatly appreciate it."

"Appreciate it enough to where you'd be willing to agree to do *me* a little favor?"

"You're very tenacious with this idea about me owing you a favor, aren't you?"

Instead of replying, Miss Flowerdew rose to her feet and moved closer, her gaze traveling over Gertrude with eyes that were far too sharp for Gertrude's liking.

"You've landed yourself in a pickle, haven't you?"

"I don't know if I'd go so far as to claim I'm in a pickle."

"You're obviously stuck to the couch, which certainly constitutes being in a pickle."

"I suppose it does," Gertrude admitted.

"How fortuitous," Miss Flowerdew chirped before she began pacing back and forth in front of Gertrude, seemingly sizing up the situation. Stopping, she arched a delicate brow Gertrude's way. "How did it happen?"

"I lost my balance trying to get a . . . ah . . . closer look at the painting hanging above this very couch. Then, to add insult to injury, my bustle broke, evidently from the force of my fall, and pieces of it pierced the couch. I don't want to move because I'm afraid I'll ruin the upholstery if I do."

Tapping a toe against the floor, Miss Flowerdew looked from Gertrude to the painting hanging behind the couch, then back to Gertrude again right as her eyes widened. "Forgive me, Miss Cadwalader, but I must tell you that your current situation seems to be more ominous than curious. Why, the only reasonable explanation that springs to my mind to explain why you would have needed to peruse that painting so closely is that you're a thief but got foiled in your attempt to steal that painting by gravity."

"Good heavens, Miss Flowerdew, get ahold of yourself. That's a completely ridiculous conclusion, especially since it would be next to impossible for anyone to make off undetected with a painting of that size."

"So you *were* considering the matter."

Gertrude's brows drew together. "No, I wasn't, I was . . . oh, never mind. Allow me to simply say that I'm not a thief, nor was I attempting a heist on Mr. Sinclair's yacht."

Ignoring everything she'd just said, Miss Flowerdew began pacing again, stopping a few seconds later to look Gertrude's prone form up and down. "Do you have so much fabric making up your skirt because that's where you stash your ill-gotten gains?"

"Of course not, especially since, again, I don't spend my time as a thief but only as a companion to Mrs. Davenport. If you must know, she's responsible for the gown I'm wearing, and she used extra yards of fabric because of the questionable bustle she designed for me."

Miss Flowerdew released a sniff. "A ridiculous explanation if I ever heard one."

"It may be ridiculous, but it's true. And, it's also an explanation I'll be able to prove once I get unstuck from this couch. I'll then be able to show you the bustle in question, and then you'll be extending me an apology, one I richly deserve since you've now taken to questioning my integrity."

Turning her back on Gertrude, Miss Flowerdew walked across the room and retook her seat. Considering Gertrude with narrowed eyes, she finally gave a short jerk of her head. "Very well, let me see this so-called questionable bustle."

"I can't very well show it to you since, if you've forgotten, I'm stuck. You'll have to assist me with getting unstuck first, and then I can prove my innocence."

Miss Flowerdew suddenly smiled. "Which brings us directly back to the beginning of our conversation, one that, if *you've* forgotten, dealt with you being in my debt. I'm perfectly willing to assist you, however, it *will* come with a cost — that cost being your agreement to assist *me* in the foreseeable future with a little matter that's very dear to me." Her smile turned smug. "Since the question has arisen regarding your reason for being on the couch in the first place, a question that I'm sure you're going to want to keep hush-hush, I suggest you agree to my terms."

"That sounds a little like blackmail."

Miss Flowerdew tapped a gloved finger against her chin. "It does at that, doesn't it?"

"I'm not one to give in to demands, Miss Flowerdew, especially since I've done absolutely nothing to warrant a blackmail demand in the first place."

Wrinkling her nose, Miss Flowerdew settled back into the chair. "Has anyone ever told you that you're far too cheeky to fit the expectations of a wallflower?"

"Has anyone ever told you that there's not actually a society known as the wallflowers — it's simply a derogatory name for a group of lovely young ladies who aren't considered as fashionable as society wants them to be?"

Miss Flowerdew completely neglected to respond to that, choosing to beam another bright smile Gertrude's way instead. "My goodness but we do seem to have gotten distracted from the business at hand. And since we are missing out on the festivities that are occurring above board, allow me to redirect our conversation to the important matter I need to broach with you."

Sitting forward in the chair, Miss Flowerdew suddenly looked far too earnest. "I'd like you to personally introduce me to the oh-so-delicious Mr. Harrison Sinclair, and then I want your promise that you'll do whatever is in your power to convince him to offer me a proposal of the matrimonial type."

Chapter Two

For a brief second, Gertrude forgot she was attached to the fainting couch and tried to sit forward, stilling when another ominous rip met her efforts. Refusing a sigh, she quirked a single brow Miss Flowerdew's way. "Forgive me, but why in the world would you think I have the type of influence with Mr. Sinclair that would allow me to sway him in the matter of marriage to you?"

Miss Flowerdew folded her hands primly in her lap. "Don't be coy, Miss Cadwalader, it does not become you. Surely you must realize that talk is rampant throughout society regarding your recent association with Mr. Sinclair. In all honesty, talk of the two of you was heard in the very best salons all the way over in Paris last month." She smiled. "The recent adventures you've evidently shared with the gentleman are common knowledge. And because of those adventures, and because you've been seen in Mr. Sinclair's company quite often as of late, you're the perfect person to convince Mr. Sinclair that I would make him a more than suitable wife."

Gertrude blinked. "I'm currently the subject of the gossips within society?"

"Indeed, which is quite the boon for you if you ask me." Miss Flowerdew's smile widened. "Why, society is all agog over your association with such a dashing gentleman. But tell me, is it really true you were trundling around the city dyed an unusual shade of orange?"

Gertrude gave an airy wave of a hand. "While I know it must seem downright riveting that a person can become orange, it wasn't nearly the intrigue society is apparently making it out to be. My companion, Mrs. Davenport, was curious about what would happen if she applied a certain stain to my skin, and unfortunately, instead of giving me a sun-kissed look, it turned me orange."

Miss Flowerdew settled back into the chair. "Which is peculiar to be sure, but lends credence to the idea that you and Mr. Sinclair must enjoy a true friendship since he evidently wasn't bothered by your condition and was perfectly willing to be seen out and about with you."

"I suppose we do enjoy a friendship, but —"

"Is it also true that Mr. Sinclair saved your life from that madman who was trying to do in Mr. Asher Rutherford?" Miss Flowerdew interrupted.

"I suppose he did intervene on my behalf and save me from a nasty death, but simply because a gentleman saves a lady's life, that doesn't mean that particular lady is then in a position to encourage said gentleman to begin courting another lady."

Miss Flowerdew's smile faded as her lips formed an *O* of surprise. "Good heavens. Why didn't I see this at once? You've grown fond of Mr. Sinclair, what with all the time you've spent with him, and are reluctant to agree to assist me because you want to secure his romantic affections for yourself."

An immediate denial formed on Gertrude's tongue, but for some reason, she couldn't get that denial past her lips.

While it was true she'd spent time in Mr. Harrison Sinclair's company of late, what with them having mutual friends in Mr. Asher Rutherford and Miss Permilia Griswold, she'd not actually allowed herself to dwell on the affection she *might* have begun holding for Harrison.

That he was a fascinating gentleman, there

was no question, but he was not the type of gentleman an ordinary woman such as herself should ever view in a romantic fashion.

Harrison Sinclair was a man possessed of rakish good looks and a wonderful sense of humor. He was also in possession of an extensive fortune, one that was responsible for New York society deciding he was soon to become the most eligible gentleman in New York, especially since Mr. Asher Rutherford was now engaged to Permilia and firmly off the . . .

". . . and while I do hope that I won't hurt your feelings, dear, you must realize that a man of Mr. Sinclair's caliber might be a touch out of your . . . ah . . . well . . . no need to go into specifics since I'm sure you're only too aware of what I'm about to point out."

Shaking herself from her disturbing thoughts, Gertrude opened her mouth, but was spared a response when Miss Flowerdew hitched another smile in place and continued speaking in a rapid manner, as if she'd realized she might have insulted the very woman she was hoping to coerce into helping her.

"Do know that I completely understand and sympathize with the tender affections you've apparently formed for Mr. Sinclair, because he is a most delicious gentleman. But you seem to be a most practical sort, and that practicality, Miss Cadwalader, is exactly why I feel comfortable broaching this subject." Miss Flowerdew smiled her brightest smile yet. "Mr. Sinclair has become quite fashionable of late, even given his somewhat unusual fashion sense, which means he has the attention of diamonds of the first water." With that, she stopped talking and batted expectant lashes Gertrude's way.

"And I'm not a diamond of the first water?" Gertrude finished for her when Miss Flowerdew remained silent.

A tinkle of laughter greeted that response before Miss Flowerdew clapped her hands. "I knew you would catch my meaning without me having to spell it out for you. Now that we've gotten that pesky business settled, may I dare hope you're in a more accommodating frame of mind and are now willing to pave my way toward a more intimate association with Mr. Sinclair?" She smoothed a wrinkle out of her skirt. "In all honesty, I'm doing you a favor since I'm certain other society ladies will soon be seeking you out, pestering you relentlessly to convince you to assist *them* with becoming better known to Mr. Sinclair."

Before Gertrude could respond to that bit of nonsense, Miss Flowerdew rose ever so gracefully from her chair and began strolling about the room, stopping in front of a bookshelf filled with leather-bound books. Trailing a finger down one of the spines, she turned. "I must say, Mr. Sinclair certainly does have a well-appointed library, filled with what are obviously expensive objects. Makes me wonder if his wealth is more substantial than anyone knows."

As soon as those telling words spilled from Miss Flowerdew's lips, Gertrude understood exactly why she was reluctant to agree to the lady's request.

Miss Flowerdew didn't want to pursue Harrison because he was a commendable gentleman, but instead only longed to attach her name to his because he could offer her a life of luxury, one she could then flaunt to other members of society. Simply put, Miss Flowerdew was proving herself to be anything other than a pleasant young lady — which meant she did not deserve a gentleman like Mr. Harrison Sinclair.

Harrison, even though he was one of the most handsome gentlemen of the day, possessed a kind nature, one not often found in men with such dashing good looks.

That kindness, aided by the fact that he had not a hint of vanity in him, was incredibly appealing, and certainly wasn't meant to be spent on ladies who cared more for his fortune and handsome face than his caring attitude and willingness to befriend a wallflower who just happened to be orange the first time he met her.

"Do you suppose Mr. Sinclair would be agreeable to suggestions pertaining to his wardrobe?" Miss Flowerdew asked, pulling Gertrude immediately back to the disturbing conversation at hand.

"You don't care for how Mr. Sinclair dresses?"

Miss Flowerdew waved off the question. "His sense of style is somewhat peculiar, given that he pairs the most unusual colors together. I also believe he'd look more refined if he visited a barber on a weekly basis, which would take care of the windblown look he seems to favor with that overly long, dark hair of his." She smiled. "I will admit that Mr. Sinclair looks very refined this evening in his formalwear, something I'll be certain to point out to him later in the hopes it will encourage him to adopt that style more often."

Gertrude's lips began to curve. While Harrison was presently looking well turned out, she was all but convinced that was a direct result of Mr. Asher Rutherford, owner of Rutherford & Company, providing Harrison with clothing for the night. Asher had also provided Harrison with a length of black ribbon to secure his unruly locks, that ribbon pulled from one of Asher's always-well-stocked pockets after he'd realized his friend had used a scrap of fabric from someone's petticoat — most likely a scrap that had belonged to one of his three sisters — to tie a bow at the nape of his neck.

In all honesty, even with Harrison resembling a most dashing man-about-town this evening, Gertrude was slightly disappointed he wasn't wearing so much as a hint of purple, pink, magenta, or any other vivid color he was known to favor. His fondness for unusual color combinations frequently raised a few eyebrows, but in Gertrude's opinion, she found that idiosyncrasy charming since it suited Harrison's true character.

"Ah, Gertrude, there you are. I was getting worried when I noticed you missing from the festivities and realized that Mrs. Davenport was missing as well, a sticky situation to be sure, but . . . goodness, *Miss Flowerdew*, what in the world are you doing down here?"

Turning her head toward the door, Gertrude found Miss Permilia Griswold walking into the library. She was looking beautiful, garbed in an exquisite gown of delicate lavender silk trimmed with small feathers. Her red hair was twisted in a sophisticated knot on top of her head, and a diamond choker encircled her neck, one her father had sent her from Paris a few weeks before, a token of apology for his being unable to attend her engagement festivities.

With only a small frown sent Gertrude's way, Permilia continued walking across the library, not stopping until she was directly in front of Miss Flowerdew, who was in the process of retaking her seat.

Miss Flowerdew, unfortunately, was already cocking her head to the side and regarding Permilia in a far too considering fashion. "Did you just say that Mrs. Davenport has gone missing? And, if that is indeed the case, why, pray tell, hasn't everyone been alerted to the situation? If you've forgotten, we're on a ship, Miss Griswold, in the ocean at that, and if the poor dear has fallen overboard, well, she's probably done for by now."

Instead of answering her, Permilia moved to the chair beside Miss Flowerdew and sat down, taking a long moment to rearrange her skirts. She finally lifted her head and smiled.

"It's so refreshing, Miss Flowerdew, to learn you're the type of young lady who worries about the well-being of others, but rest assured that Mrs. Davenport has not fallen overboard. She occasionally suffers from a small state of confusion, that state soothed, or so I believe, by, er . . . wandering. I'm sure she'll turn up soon, just as I'm sure she's probably in the galley since I have found her moseying around kitchen areas before when she's suffering from, er, confusion."

Miss Flowerdew leaned forward. "I've never taken Mrs. Davenport for one of those dear, dotty ladies who suffer from confusion."

"Since I've never observed you spending much time, if any, in Mrs. Davenport's company, I'm not surprised," Permilia replied sweetly. "But, enough about that. I don't believe you ever answered my question regarding what you're doing down here. I would have thought you'd want to spend your evening topside, enjoying the festivities along with the other guests, one of whom, if you've forgotten, is your delightful cousin, Miss Temperance Flowerdew."

Pursing her lips, Miss Flowerdew settled

back into the chair. "Temperance and I rarely spend time together at events unless I have need of her assistance. She's more of a chaperone to me than a relative. If you weren't aware of this, she's my very distant cousin, and we're hardly on friendly terms with each other."

Pursing her lips right back at Miss Flowerdew, Permilia tilted her head. "Cousin or not, she still saw fit to bring you tonight as her guest. That was incredibly generous of her, particularly since you and I know you would not have been as generous toward her if you'd received my invitation to this celebration instead of Temperance."

"Since you're evidently trying to get me to leave the library, Miss Griswold, what with your veiled insults that I assure you I've noted, I'll return topside before words are passed between us that I'm sure we'll both regret." Rising to her feet, Miss Flowerdew began marching across the room, turning when she reached the door to catch Gertrude's eye. "Do say that you've come to your senses and are willing to assist me with that little matter we were discussing before Miss Griswold interrupted us."

Gertrude frowned. "Since you've yet to assist *me,* Miss Flowerdew, and I'm clearly still in need of assistance, I don't understand why you still believe I owe *you* a favor."

"If you want me to remain silent about that painting hanging over your head, then yes, you do owe me a favor."

"You know full well I was never intending to make off with it."

"So you say." With that, Miss Flowerdew turned abruptly and vanished through the doorway.

"What in the world was that all about?"

Gertrude groaned. "She wants me to introduce her to Harrison."

"She was introduced to Harrison, along with everyone else I might add, when she boarded the ship."

"True, but she wants to be *introduced* to him, if you know what I mean."

Permilia shook her head. "Ah, of course she does, but . . . was she threatening to blackmail you with a ridiculous story about you trying to steal a painting?"

"She was."

Permilia leaned forward. "You weren't trying to *return* the painting to the wall and she walked in on you in the process, were you?"

"No, although I have almost been caught doing exactly that before — not that I was the one responsible for taking the painting in question, although . . ." Gertrude stopped talking and frowned. "How long have you known about my curious habit of returning items to their proper places?"

"I spent two years as an anonymous society columnist. That means I know what most people in society are up to, including Mrs. Davenport, so I've had my suspicions about your curious habit for quite some time now." Her eyes suddenly sharpened on Gertrude as she leaned forward. "Forgive me for not inquiring about this before, but is there a reason why you're lounging on that couch in a way that appears to be less than comfortable?"

"I'm stuck."

"Honestly, Gertrude, you should have said so straightaway." Rising to her feet, Permilia was soon standing right beside the couch, her brows drawn together as she looked Gertrude up and down. "It's the bustle, isn't it?"

"It broke when I lost my balance after I was checking behind the couch to see if Mrs. Davenport was hiding there."

"You really are going to have to have a stern talk with your employer, Gertrude, because her antics are beginning to take a turn for the concerning, and I'm not simply talking about her less than legal pursuits at society events. Making you wear a bustle the size of which I've never imagined is hazardous to your health."

Gertrude sighed. "I've been meaning to sit down with her for months to discuss her increasingly peculiar behavior, although I keep putting it off because she's a lady far more fragile than the woman she presents to the world. She suffers from acute melancholy, but curiously enough, that melancholy seems to be held at bay when she's creating her peculiar designs. She takes immense pleasure in turning out one new fashion after another. And having to wear her peculiar creations seems a small price to pay to see her happy, even if some of those creations are less than safe or comfortable to wear."

"How uncomfortable *is* that bustle you're wearing?"

"I would have to say extremely uncomfortable since numerous wires have come undone and are digging into my skin."

"Then I say further discussions of your employer must wait until we get you more comfortable." With that, Permilia bent over and began moving yards of fabric out of the way, her lips twitching with every yard of fabric she shoved aside. "How have you even been able to walk with all this wrapped around you?"

"It has not been without difficulty, but do have a care before you try to tug me free. I don't want to ruin Harrison's couch."

"Harrison would not want you to remain in such an uncomfortable situation simply because of his couch. He considers you a friend, which means he, if he were present, would encourage me to do whatever it takes to set you free, no matter the damage that might occur to the upholstery in the process."

"Speaking of my friendship with Harrison, Miss Flowerdew mentioned that society has taken to remarking on that."

Permilia looked up. "I'm afraid Miss Flowerdew is right. I've had numerous young ladies approach me at the store of late to inquire about Harrison, now that they all seem to be arriving home from Paris and are stopping in the city to run a few errands before they travel to their summer homes. They've also been asking me about you, which means . . ."

"Ladies are going to become annoyingly friendly toward me in order to get closer to Harrison," Gertrude finished for her.

"He won't notice their attempts to attract his attention."

"Which will only make him more of a challenge to them."

"A challenge he'll ignore since I'm of the belief he's turned an interested eye your way."

"An interested eye because he enjoys my company as a *friend.*"

"I imagine that friendship could turn into much more if you'd let him know, subtly of course, that you would welcome his affections, and not affections of strictly the friendship sort."

Gertrude smiled. "I've heard rumors about people who've recently found the love of their life. Those rumors have it that love-struck couples soon turn their thoughts to securing love matches for anyone in their direct vicinity who may not be otherwise engaged. And, while it is very sweet of you to even think Harrison would welcome the idea of a relationship other than friendship with me, I'm a realist at heart, and that realist knows that a gentleman like Harrison is far above my reach."

"Of course he's not."

"Have you *seen* him?"

Permilia grinned. "I see him on an almost daily basis since he's so close to Asher, and because of that, I've gotten to know him well. That is why I think the two of you would suit each other admirably. He's a very giving man, you're a very giving woman, and together, well, you'd make a charming couple."

"I am not the type of lady to attract the attention of a gentleman like Harrison. My face is nothing special, my figure is a touch plumper than is considered fashionable, my hair, while a somewhat nice shade of gold, is usually ridiculously styled, a victim of Mrs. Davenport and her handy curling tongs, and . . . I have no wealth to speak of, which makes me less than a prize — all things Miss Flowerdew was trying to bring to my attention in a less than subtle way."

"Your generous heart makes you more of a prize than any of the beauties of the day, but just so you know, your face and figure are quite pleasant. Why, if you'd simply allow *me* to style you, you'd look very fashionable indeed."

"That would hurt Mrs. Davenport's feelings. You know she fancies herself a stylist."

Instead of looking bothered by the refusal, Permilia smiled. "And that right there proves my point about your generous heart. Harrison, if you haven't noticed, is not concerned with matters of fashion, beauty, or anything of that nature. He also seems to enjoy spending time in your company, asks about you frequently, and even told me you'd promised to go sailing with him at some point this summer, a promise he recently mentioned you hadn't bothered to keep."

"He only asked me to go sailing because it's an offer that's expected of a man who owns an entire fleet of ships."

Permilia shook her head. "You need to have more confidence in yourself. Harrison adores you and not simply as a friend."

"He might rescind his friendship if I don't find Mrs. Davenport soon, especially if she's up to her usual shenanigans."

Permilia blinked. "Goodness, I somehow managed to forget all about Mrs. Davenport being missing. How long has she been out of sight?"

"Over an hour."

Straightening, Permilia squared her shoulders. "Which is undoubtedly concerning and means we have to get you unstuck sooner rather than later. And, while I'm certain you're not going to like what I'm about to suggest, I don't see that we have another alternative to your dilemma."

"That sounds ominous."

"I'm afraid it is, because the only way I believe we're going to get you free is for us to strip you straight out of that dress and abandon that bustle once and for all."

CHAPTER THREE

Being herded into the small confines of a storage closet, while over a hundred guests mingled on the aft deck of his yacht, was not exactly what Mr. Harrison Sinclair had been expecting when his sister Margaret had insisted they remove themselves from the crowd to have a little chat. However, since Margaret was not a lady to stoop to such dramatics unless that drama was warranted, he pushed aside the argument he longed to make regarding their surroundings, and waited to hear the matter of great urgency she needed to discuss.

As the seconds passed and Margaret didn't bother to speak, he leaned closer to where he thought she was standing, not that he could see her in the total darkness that surrounded them, releasing a grunt when his head connected with the top of hers.

"Ouch! Honestly, Harrison, that hurt," Margaret said in a voice that was no louder than a whisper.

Lowering his voice as well, even though he thought that might be taking the whole cloak-and-dagger routine a little far since they were well removed from where the guests were gathered, he rubbed his smarting forehead and straightened.

"Forgive me, Margaret, but if you hadn't insisted on having your chat with me in this storage room, we wouldn't currently be sporting throbbing heads. Was there something wrong with any of the other rooms on the yacht, such as the library, perhaps, or the cardroom?"

"I couldn't take the chance of us being overheard."

"Don't you believe it may draw undue attention if someone observes us slinking out of the closet after we're done with our chat?"

"We'll simply say we were looking for a broom."

"I'm not certain that's a credible explanation. The guests onboard tonight are not the type who'd go off looking for a broom on their own, especially when there are members of the crew available to do such mundane tasks."

"That type of thinking is exactly why I don't care for society, but I doubt we'll be observed since everyone seems to be having a delightful time of it topside. Because I know you won't want to miss seeing everyone's reaction to the surprise you arranged when the *Cornelia* arrives at West Brighton Beach, I'll make this as quick as I can. Someone, I'm sorry to report, seems to be up to nefarious purposes on this very yacht even as we speak."

"Nefarious purposes?" Harrison repeated.

"Indeed. A member of the crew sought me out in the wheelhouse to inform me that someone's been skulking around on the lower decks. Shadows have apparently been spotted where shadows are not supposed to be, the result being that the crew is now walking about on pins and needles, looking over their shoulders every other minute."

Harrison blinked even though the blinking did absolutely nothing worthwhile since sheer blackness still surrounded him. "Skulking around? That sounds a little . . ." He blinked again. "Wait a minute — before we get into the skulking business, *you're* still supposed to be *in* the wheelhouse, minding the wheel no less."

"Don't be so overly theatrical, Harrison. It's hardly as if I abandoned the wheel and left the yacht deprived of a steady hand. Adelaide took over for me."

Without bothering to reply to that disturbing statement, Harrison tried to squeeze past his sister to get to the door, releasing a pent-up breath when he realized Margaret had stepped directly in front of that door and was blocking his way.

"I would suggest you let me by," he said, not surprised when his most menacing of tones didn't move his sister a single inch. *"Please,"* he added for good measure, which still did not sway his sister at all since she staunchly held her ground.

"Adelaide's perfectly fine guiding this ship," Margaret said.

"She's barely more than a child, and if you've forgotten, Margaret, our family is currently responsible for the lives of over a hundred people who are on board this yacht. Allowing our baby sister to take over the helm is probably not the best way to be responsible for those lives."

"Adelaide's twenty, not a baby, and she's more competent at the helm than most weathered captains I know given that she learned how to hold the wheel before she learned how to talk."

"She'll always be a baby to me."

"Yes, well, I wouldn't go out of your way to mention that to Adelaide. She's a little sensitive about her age since everyone is constantly remarking about how young she looks. Why, to hear Adelaide tell it, God did her a grave disservice by bestowing abnormally round cheeks and baby blue eyes on her at birth. Evidently her face has become a trial for her because she's not taken seriously within the shipping industry, what with the veterans of the industry constantly pointing out her overly feminine attributes."

"While I would love nothing better than to discuss the abysmal plight of women and the unfortunate disregard for their many abilities by industrialists, I'm not certain this is the proper time. As for Adelaide and her disgruntlement with being born with a face that can only be described as arresting, she's simply going to have to learn there's nothing she can do about that other than to accept the sad burden of being beautiful."

Margaret let out what might have been a sigh. "Your friend, Mr. Asher Rutherford, made the mistake of telling Adelaide earlier that her face would be a welcome sight in all the fashionable magazines and catalogs. He even went so far as to ask her if she would be willing to become the new 'face' of Rutherford & Company."

Harrison wasn't quite able to suppress a wince. "That wasn't well-done of him."

"Indeed, especially since Adelaide has now sworn off shopping at Rutherford & Company and is also refusing to come out of the wheelhouse. That state of affairs is distressing Edwina no small amount, who wants exactly the opposite of what Adelaide wants, and has taken to pestering Adelaide about joining her on the upper deck in the hopes that Asher will offer *her* the opportunity of becoming the face of Rutherford & Company. She, unsurprisingly, is more than anxious to have her face seen throughout New York, believing, or so she said, that becoming the fashionable face of the day will aid her in becoming accepted in all the right society circles."

Harrison's brows drew together. "While Edwina has mentioned a time or two that she wouldn't be opposed to entering society, I didn't realize she'd become so determined. However, if she truly wants to have Asher include her in a few print campaigns, I'm sure he'd be only too happy to do so. She does have the same face as Adelaide. And, now that I think about it, I wonder if Asher got the twins confused again, especially since I know I've remarked over the years how Adelaide has no interest in fashion, whereas Edwina does."

"He might have done exactly that, which will soothe the put-out attitudes of both twins. But their tender feelings have nothing to do with our dastardly situation at hand. We need to discover who is skulking about and put a rapid end to it. I'm afraid talk below-deck is beginning to turn to ghosts."

Harrison smiled. "I can't claim to be surprised about that considering seamen are a rather superstitious lot, but . . ." His smile faded straightaway. "Why do I get the impression the whole *we* business really means me?"

"Because it's more than likely that the person doing the skulking is one of Asher's friends. Since he is *your* friend and I don't mingle well with people, you'll have to handle the situation, and do so in as discreet a manner as possible."

Before Harrison could voice a single protest, Margaret opened the door, slipped through it, and left Harrison behind.

"I'd start in the engine room. That's where the crew first noticed something odd," she called over her shoulder before she disappeared up a short flight of stairs that sat between an intricate balustrade made of wrought iron designed by Tiffany Studios.

Knowing there was nothing to do but investigate the odd happenings on his yacht, even though there was the distinct possibility the peculiar situation was due to the overimagination of his crew, Harrison stepped from the storage closet. Nodding at a server who was making his way toward the very stairs Margaret had just used, he pretended not to see the curious look the man sent him. Helping himself to one of the stuffed mushrooms the server was carrying on a silver tray, Harrison thanked him and headed off down the companionway, making a note to seek out more of the delicious mushrooms just as soon as he finished his mission.

Walking down a different flight of stairs, he reached the deck that housed the engine room, galley, quarters for the crew, and storage areas for the coal they used to create the steam that powered the ship.

Pulling open the heavy metal door that led to the engine room, Harrison caught the attention of a few crew members, having to shout to be heard over the hissing and clanging of the machinery that was keeping the yacht moving at a fast clip.

By the time he was done asking his questions, he was hoarse from the shouting and didn't have much to go on. The only consistent concern he'd heard from everyone was that shadows had been seen throughout different rooms, but when anyone of a brave nature went to investigate those shadows, nothing had been found.

After reassuring the crew that the shadows could not have been caused by any ghosts since the *Cornelia* was only a few years old and not a single person had ever died on board, which lent credence to the idea that there was no reason for the ship to be haunted, Harrison left the slightly relieved crew to their business.

He gave the galley only a cursory look because it was filled with servers and chefs he'd brought in for the night's festivities, before moving on to the quarters where the crew slept. Not finding anything suspicious, he reached a flight of stairs that led to the staterooms, stopping dead in his tracks when a flicker of a shadow captured his attention from halfway up the stairs.

"Is someone there?" he called, peering up the stairs, which, unfortunately, were completely empty.

He was heading up the stairs, taking them two at a time, when he heard the distinct sound of footsteps above his head. Reaching the next deck, he headed down the companionway, stumbling to a stop when a very feminine form plowed directly into him, one belonging to none other than Mrs. Davenport — a well-regarded society matron, and the woman who happened to be the employer of Miss Gertrude Cadwalader.

The mere thought of Gertrude had his lips curving into a smile.

She was a lady he found to be undeniably delightful. Unlike many ladies he'd recently become acquainted with, Gertrude was a very sensible sort, possessed of a wonderful sense of humor and ability to accept the peculiarities life sent her way with a smile on her lovely face.

The first time he'd met her, she'd been dyed an interesting shade of orange, a circumstance he'd found rather puzzling, especially since he'd been suffering from a blow to the head and had, at first, thought he'd been hallucinating.

Once he'd regained his sensibilities, he'd discovered he'd not been hallucinating at all, but had truly encountered a lady who resembled a sunset. The reasoning behind Gertrude's unexpected color had been surprising to say the least, especially when he learned she'd willingly allowed Mrs. Davenport to coat her with an unknown concoction that was supposed to give her a weathered appearance to coincide with her milk wagon–driver disguise. To say the disguise did not turn out as planned was an understatement, but fortunately Gertrude's color faded back to normal after a few weeks. While she'd been orange, however, she'd kept a wonderful sense of humor about her condition.

The very idea she'd not been bothered about being orange spoke volumes about her true character. And when Harrison had learned that she often allowed Mrs. Davenport to practice what that lady referred to as her *artistic muse,* that practicing having Gertrude traveling around society looking rather curious more often than not, Harrison had come to believe that Gertrude possessed a tremendously kind heart along with a most generous nature.

That he'd also concluded Gertrude's employer, Mrs. Davenport, was not your typical society matron, there was no question, which made the very idea that she was currently standing in front of him, on a deck where guests were not assembled, a cause for concern.

"Mrs. Davenport," he finally said, reaching out a hand to steady the woman when he realized she was wobbling on her feet. "Are you all right?"

Taking a second to shake out the folds of her skirts, the shaking causing something to jingle on her person, Mrs. Davenport flashed him a pleasant smile and nodded a head that possessed unusually dyed black hair styled in a manner that one would expect on a lady half her age. Ringlets bobbed with the nodding she was doing, and the tiny jewels that were woven into the dark strands winked here and there in the faint light coming from the lamps spread through the companionway.

When she finished nodding, she began regarding him out of eyes that were framed by lashes that had certainly been darkened by some substance, and eyes that were currently widened in what almost seemed to be a far too innocent way.

"I'm very well, thank you for asking, Mr. Sinclair, but what of you? You seem to be on some type of urgent mission. Dare I ask if something has gone horribly, horribly wrong with your charming boat and we're about to find ourselves swimming with the fishes?"

Having never once heard anyone describe his three-hundred-foot yacht as a "charming boat," especially since it was considered one of the most lavishly equipped yachts to have ever been built, Harrison felt his lips quirk into a grin as he took a hand he'd just then noticed Mrs. Davenport was holding out to him.

Raising that hand to his lips, he placed

the expected kiss on it.

"You may rest easy, Mrs. Davenport. This *charming* vessel is in fine working order. I was just down in the engine room and all the machinery is performing exactly as it is intended."

Withdrawing her hand, one that Harrison just then realized was missing its glove, although her left hand was still covered in white silk, Mrs. Davenport tilted her head. "Is it common for the owner of a yacht to inspect the engine room while a celebratory event is occurring, Mr. Sinclair? I would have thought that would be a job for the captain, or a member of the crew."

Having the uncanny feeling that Mrs. Davenport was attempting to ferret information out of him, Harrison settled for a smile and a shrug. "Since it is my yacht, I'm often found in many of its nooks and crannies for one reason or another, but enough about that. Why aren't you enjoying the celebratory atmosphere of the upper deck? There's not much to entertain a person on this level."

Mrs. Davenport batted dark lashes Harrison's way. "I've come to find Gertrude, of course. I believe she came down here to, ah, find a spot of quiet in the . . . um . . . library." She suddenly began regarding him in a very considering fashion. "But, speaking of Gertrude, I was hoping you and I would have a moment to speak privately this evening, because, well, we have matters to discuss regarding my companion."

An odd tingling began forming at the very base of Harrison's neck, a tingling he normally felt when the skies were as clear as could be but he knew a storm was brewing just past the horizon. Rubbing a hand over the tingling, he frowned. "We do?"

"Indeed."

"And what about Gertrude?" he pressed when Mrs. Davenport took that moment to become distracted with the folds of her skirts, twitching them to the right, which caused an unexpected tinkling sound from beneath her skirts. Her twitching came to an immediate end as she began taking an absorbed interest in the floor.

"Is there something I can assist you with, Mrs. Davenport?" he finally asked to break the curious silence that was now settled between them.

"What a darling gentleman you are to inquire, but no, I'm fine," she said with a breezy wave of her hand as she lifted her head. "Now, where were we before I got distracted? Ah, yes, my companion." She leveled a stern eye on him. "I'm not sure if it was a slip on your part, but you just called Gertrude by her given name. I was unaware the two of you had become so overly familiar with each other."

"I don't know if I'd go so far as to say we've become *overly* familiar with each other. We're friends, of course, and it has been my experience that friends frequently abandon formality to embrace a more, well, familiar attitude."

"Oh dear . . . that simply will not do at all."

The tingling on the back of his neck intensified. "Forgive me, Mrs. Davenport, but I truly do not understand why you seem so put out with my claiming a friendship with Gertrude."

Mrs. Davenport nodded. "I'm not surprised you're confused. You are a man after all, and men do tend to have difficulties grasping the subtle nuances of a situation."

"There's a situation?"

"Too right there is." Mrs. Davenport leaned toward him. "Gertrude has become rather dear to me, Mr. Sinclair. In fact, she's the best companion I've ever employed, and as such, I feel it is my responsibility to look after her best interests, and you, my good man, are a distinct threat to her."

Harrison blinked. "I'm a threat to Gertrude?"

"Certainly, especially since you've been in her company often of late, and I do fear that during that time you may have very well given Gertrude the wrong impression."

"I'm definitely not grasping whatever subtle nuances you may be trying to get me to grasp."

Mrs. Davenport released a bit of a sigh. "You are a handsome gentleman, Mr. Sinclair, possessed of a substantial fortune and adventurous attitude. You would turn even the most seasoned of heads, but paying attention to a young lady of Gertrude's limited experience is not well-done of you. To be perfectly blunt, I'm afraid your association with her, one you just claimed was a mere friendship, may very well be setting her up with false expectations, which you and I both know will never come to fruition."

Harrison stiffened. "I assure you, Mrs. Davenport, I have done no such dastardly deed. I have the utmost respect for Gertrude and would never do anything to harm her. I certainly haven't behaved in an untoward manner with her, nor have I ever gotten the impression she viewed me as anything other than a friend."

"Far be it from me to point out the obvious, but it's a well-known fact that you're somewhat oblivious when it comes to the ladies and how much attention they try to send your way."

Opening his mouth to refute that statement, Harrison was denied a response when Mrs. Davenport lifted her chin and continued speaking before he could get a single word out of his mouth.

"Gertrude is not the type of young lady who draws much attention from gentlemen, Mr. Sinclair. Because of that, and because you're a dashing gentleman, one who draws attention wherever you go, no matter that you neglect to realize that, she's susceptible to your charm. That right there is why I'd like your word right here and now that you will begin distancing yourself from my companion so that her tender feelings will not be trampled to pieces in the end."

Harrison frowned. "I would imagine Gertrude draws more than her fair share of attention from gentlemen. She's a delightful young lady, possessed of her own adventurous attitude. Perhaps you simply have not taken note of that attention because it's a circumstance you would rather not acknowledge."

"Are you suggesting I'm not an observant sort?"

Refusing a wince because he was usually far more careful in how he spoke to members of the feminine set, especially since he'd grown up with three sisters, Harrison summoned up a smile. "Forgive me, Mrs. Davenport. I did not mean to offend. What I'm sure I meant to say was because you're so very fond of Gertrude, and just recently claimed she's the best companion you've ever had, you may avoid thinking about the gentlemen who pay attention to her since you don't want to lose her companionship to one of those . . ."

Harrison stopped talking when Mrs. Davenport began looking more offended than ever.

"I'm sure I have no idea what you may be implying," she said with a sniff.

Inclining his head, he blew out a breath. "Apparently, I have no idea what I might have been implying either, so perhaps it might be for the best if we simply change the subject before we find ourselves at odds with each other."

Mrs. Davenport inclined her head as well. "A prudent choice, my boy." She held out her arm. "You may take my arm."

The corners of Harrison's lips began to

twitch as he offered her his arm. Turning her in the direction of the library, they began to move down the companionway, making it all of three feet before Mrs. Davenport stopped in her tracks. She sucked in a sharp breath, her eyes widened, and then a thud sounded from somewhere beneath her skirts.

With no more than a blink of an eye, she released his arm, nodded toward the library, and then shooed him on his way.

"I'll join you in a moment" was all she said as she made a shooing motion again and then sent a pointed look toward the library.

Unused to being shooed, or faced with a society matron who seemed to be behaving in a slightly suspicious manner, Harrison didn't take so much as a single step away from her. "Are you certain you wouldn't like me to assist you with whatever trouble you're currently experiencing — trouble that apparently has landed by your feet?"

"You're far more perceptive than I've given you credit for," he thought he heard her mumble before she squared her shoulders and wagged a finger at him. "My dear boy, while I've always been a lady who appreciates chivalry in a gentleman, I'm afraid now is not the moment for me to accept your chivalrous offer. If you must know, I was trying to spare you from a slightly embarrassing problem I'm experiencing, but since you seem to be an inquisitive sort, allow me to simply say that the tapes holding my bustle in place seem to be coming undone, unless it's the garters that are holding up my stockings. Whichever catastrophe I'm experiencing does seem to suggest I'm falling apart where I stand, which means I need a spot of privacy to set my person to rights if you please."

Even though the back of his neck was once again tingling merrily away, Harrison knew there was nothing to do but allow Mrs. Davenport her privacy, especially since her garters had been brought into the conversation. He was of the sneaking suspicion she'd brought up her garters to distract him, and while she'd certainly done exactly that, he was quite willing to do as she asked and continue to the library without her if only to discourage further talk of unmentionables.

"I'll just nip on into the library and see if Gertrude's there," he said, earning a smile of approval from Mrs. Davenport. Striding down the companionway at a pace that was almost a run because he hadn't missed noticing Mrs. Davenport was already twitching her skirts about, he hesitated right outside the library door, leaning closer to that door when another thud reached his ears, this one coming from inside the library.

When the thud was immediately accompanied by what sounded like a yelp, Harrison pushed open the door and stepped into the room. He froze on the spot, though, when his gaze went directly to Gertrude, who was standing in the library, rubbing a backside that seemed to be devoid of the expected clothing.

Chapter Four

For what felt like an eternity, Harrison was incapable of getting his feet into motion. For the life of him, he could not comprehend what was unfolding in front of his eyes, but felt as if he'd entered some peculiar world — one where ladies talking about their unmentionables, or frolicking about in those unmentionables around his library, appeared to be the order of the day.

Clearly, something of a peculiar nature had caused Gertrude to abandon the frock he knew she'd been wearing the last time he'd seen her, but what that event was, he truly had no idea. He also had no idea why Gertrude, along with Permilia Griswold, was now laughing uproariously, both ladies clutching their sides as their peals of amusement bounced around the room, until . . .

"Good heavens, it's Harrison!" Gertrude practically roared right before she jumped over the fainting couch, while Permilia scrambled to stand in front of that very couch, spreading her arms wide in an obvious effort to hide a barely covered Gertrude from his view.

"I do beg your pardon" was the only thing he could muster up as he spun around and headed for the door, his exit blocked by none other than Mrs. Davenport.

She'd apparently gotten herself put back together, but the smile on her face was soon replaced with a frown as she tried to peer over his shoulder.

"What is all the ruckus about?" she demanded.

"Ah . . . well . . . as to that," he began, relieved when Permilia apparently took pity on his less than stellar attempt to explain the situation and spoke up.

"Gertrude had a mishap with her bustle, Mrs. Davenport, but not to worry. We've successfully gotten her parted from that bustle and from the couch, although we had to part her from her clothing to achieve that success. Besides suffering a few scrapes from a bustle that appears to be crafted from an honest-to-goodness birdcage, she's in fine form — if you discount that she's not exactly dressed for company since her gown, along with the bustle, are still stubbornly attached to the fainting couch."

Mrs. Davenport took a single step backward and pinned Harrison under a stern eye, as if he'd somehow contributed to the mayhem in his library. "Do not tell me you got a peek at Gertrude while she's in a state of, shall we say, dishabille?"

"I always thought the term *dishabille* was reserved for describing a lady when she was at her leisure," Harrison said, those words sounding somewhat ridiculous even to his own ears. "If you ask me, Gertrude is anything *but* at her leisure," he continued even as Mrs. Davenport began to watch him as if he'd taken leave of his senses. Not wanting to prove her right, he pressed his lips together and vowed to not say another word unless he was certain that word could not be considered ridiculous.

"*Dishabille* means scantily dressed," Mrs. Davenport finally said, reaching out to pat him on the arm in what could almost be called a motherly fashion. "And while I'm sure you *were* taken by surprise when you walked in on Gertrude, I'm afraid the rules are clear about what must happen next." She paused and eyed him expectantly.

"Ah . . . what must happen next?" he forced himself to ask.

Mrs. Davenport took a second to tuck a strand of black hair that was escaping its pins behind her ear before she patted his arm again. "You'll have to marry her."

Harrison's mouth went a little slack. "Marry . . . her?"

"Quite right. And by my encouraging you to marry Gertrude, I hope this puts to bed the idea I've somehow dissuaded other gentlemen from pursuing her to keep her as my companion."

Harrison shook his head ever so slightly. "I don't recall suggesting that you purposefully dissuaded anyone."

"I distinctly recall you did," she countered.

Feeling quite as if he'd lost all control of a conversation he was having difficulty following, Harrison opened his mouth, relief flowing through him when Gertrude took that moment to clear her throat — loudly.

"I'm certain you're merely suffering a misunderstanding with Harrison, Mrs. Davenport, because he's not a gentleman prone to suggesting opinions that would distress a lady." She cleared her throat again. "As for the matter regarding him having to marry me, I'll not hear another word on that. Harrison is not to blame for stumbling on me dressed in such an unforeseen manner, because one hardly expects to find a woman parted from her gown during an engagement celebration due to a mishap with a bustle."

"I thought that part about the bustle was simply a jest," Mrs. Davenport said before she brushed past Harrison and marched her way across the library.

The next sound to reach him was a bit of rustling before Mrs. Davenport gasped. "On my word, it would seem as if this bustle was not as sturdy as I believed. I'll make a note to myself at a later date to reinforce the cage with stronger metal on my next attempt to avoid such a disaster in the future."

"You'll make a note to never try your hand at one of those monstrosities again," Gertrude countered. "But since we're on the subject of that bustle, I need to point out that I'm afraid the upholstery is ruined on the couch. Do know, Harrison, that I will send you the funds to cover the cost to replace it tomorrow, and do accept my most fervent apologies for damaging your delightful piece of furniture in the first place."

Resisting the urge to turn to her, Harrison kept his attention focused on a bug that was crawling slowly up the wall of the companionway. "You'll do no such thing, Gertrude. In all honesty, I've never liked that fainting couch, finding its putrid yellow color far too dull for my tastes."

"It's a lovely peach color, filled with

delightful daisies sprinkled throughout the upholstery," Permilia said, causing Harrison to jump ever so slightly when she materialized right next to him.

He fought the urge to turn again, even though he was beyond curious to inspect a couch he was all but convinced didn't sport so much as a single daisy on it. "Peach, you say, with daisies?"

Permilia grinned. "Yes, it's peach, a color remarkably similar to orange if you didn't know."

"I like orange," Harrison said right as an image of Gertrude sprang to mind, an image from the time she'd been dyed orange.

Pretending not to see the sudden knowing look Permilia sent him, although why she was looking that way, he had no idea, he gestured to her dress. "Would I be correct in saying you're wearing a delightful gown of blue?"

"It's lavender, but because I've come to the conclusion you don't see colors like most people see colors, you may call my gown blue if you so desire."

Harrison smiled. "That's very kind of you. Now if we can only convince your soon-to-be husband that there's simply no hope I'll be able to match up my clothing choices to his satisfaction, he'll spend less time grimacing and I'll spend less time defending what he considers my peculiar fashion sense. But, speaking of Asher, we seem to have neglected to remember this evening is a celebration of your engagement. And I've planned a surprise for the two of you, with the help of a good friend of mine, Mr. Gilbert Cavendish."

Permilia's eyes sparkled. "What kind of surprise?"

"It would hardly be a surprise if I told you." He pulled out his pocket watch and took note of the time. "According to my calculations, we should almost be to our destination, which means we need to repair to the upper deck as soon as possible."

"There's a destination?" Permilia asked.

"Indeed."

"How lovely, but I'll need to see to Gertrude first."

"You go on ahead, Permilia," Gertrude called. "You can't miss your surprise. Besides, I can't very well join everyone because I now have nothing to wear. And, not that I want to disclose this next little bit because I have been embarrassed sufficiently enough tonight, but . . . I'm afraid I may be stuck again. This time between the couch and the wall."

"Perhaps you should simply push the

71

couch out of your way, dear," Mrs. Davenport suggested.

"I've tried that. It won't budge."

Harrison swallowed a laugh, caught Permilia's eye, saw that they'd begun to twinkle, and couldn't resist a grin. "I'm afraid the couch is bolted to the floor, as is most of the furniture onboard, Gertrude, which is why it won't budge."

"Which makes perfect sense, but is not exactly what I wanted to hear right about now," she called. "Would you have any suggestions regarding how I should get unstuck?"

"We could try butter," Mrs. Davenport said before Harrison could reply. "I've been itching to discover whether butter can be used to assist a person getting in and out of small spaces. Shall I go to the galley and fetch some?"

Harrison wasn't certain but he thought Gertrude let out a most unladylike snort. "We're not slathering me up with butter. And why in the world have you been contemplating such an unusual use for butter in the first place?"

"Who says I've been contemplating that?" Mrs. Davenport asked.

"You did, just now," Gertrude said.

"It's not a difficult task to unbolt the

couch, Gertrude," Harrison called, effectively ending the debate the two ladies were still having about butter. "And while I'd be more than happy to unbolt the couch for you, because of your unusual predicament, I think the most prudent option would be for me to fetch one of my sisters and have her do the deed. I'll also inquire as to whether one of them may have something stashed onboard the *Cornelia* that is suitable for you to wear. I have to imagine, given Edwina's love of fashion, she'll be the one who'll have an extra gown, or twelve, lying about."

In a blink of an eye, Mrs. Davenport was standing right beside him again, having practically knocked poor Permilia out of the way to resume her recently abandoned spot. She then flashed a delighted smile at him, looking exactly as if Christmas had come early.

"On my word, I've heard about those sisters of yours — beauties of the day if the talk about the city is accurate. But, tell me this, dear — why is it that none of your sisters has been brought out into society yet? Could it be they lack the proper connection, as in an established society matron, to introduce them into the highest circles?"

"Oh . . . dear . . . this is going to turn

problematic," Gertrude called, the vague nature of her voiced concern being completely ignored by Mrs. Davenport, who was evidently pretending she'd gone deaf and hadn't heard a word her companion had just spoken.

Taking a firm grip of Harrison's arm, she began drawing him down the companionway, turning her head and nodding to Permilia as she did so. "Be a dear, Permilia, and close that door for Gertrude. I don't believe she'll need you to stay and keep her company, what with her considerate nature and not wanting you to miss your own engagement celebration. Besides, I'll be back in no time at all, and hopefully in the company of Harrison's sister *Edwina* — the young lady I'm now all in a dither to meet, especially since it would appear as if she and I share a great love of fashion."

Before Harrison could do more than nod to Permilia, who was already turning to head back into the library because she evidently was not keen to simply leave her friend stranded in his library while less than appropriately dressed, and stuck behind the fainting couch at that, he found himself moving at a surprisingly fast clip down the companionway.

"I do hope you'll encourage your sisters

to seek me out if they have any need of my position within society to see them well-settled," Mrs. Davenport said as she pulled him up a narrow flight of stairs, releasing a little huff when she soon discovered they couldn't fit up the stairs moving side by side.

Instead of releasing his arm, she simply readjusted her hold on it, stepped forward, and then proceeded to pull him up the stairs behind her, almost as if she was concerned he'd get away from her if she let go of his arm.

Once they reached the aft deck, her grip on his arm didn't falter, although she did pause after taking only two steps and turned to him, completely disregarding the curious looks they were receiving from some of the guests. "I'm afraid I have no idea where we'll find your sisters."

"I imagine they're in the wheelhouse."

"Ah, wonderful." Sending the curious crowd what amounted to a regal inclination of her head, Mrs. Davenport started toward the wheelhouse, leaving him with the distinct notion she was remarkably familiar with his yacht — almost too familiar with it, now that he considered the . . .

"I know you told Gertrude you wouldn't accept compensation for your couch, but do know that I will send you the funds to cover the damage since I was responsible for it being ruined — inadvertently of course through the malfunction of what I thought was a well-crafted bustle."

Harrison shook the remnants of his interesting thoughts aside and smiled. "Accidents happen, Mrs. Davenport, and as a gentleman, it would be an insult to my honor to take money from a guest of mine, or that guest's companion, because of an accident." He slowed their pace and caught Mrs. Davenport's eye. "If it makes you feel better, do know that I will donate the couch to a church I support in the Lower East Side, one that is always thankful for donations."

"You go to church in the Lower East Side?"

"I do. Not all the time, mind you, since I am frequently on one of my ships, sailing one sea after another. But, when I'm in town, I enjoy the authenticity of being around people I've known since I was a child."

Mrs. Davenport came to a complete stop and tilted her head. "I had no idea you grew up in the Lower East Side."

"Born and raised on the docks down there." Harrison gave her arm a squeeze.

"And while I'd love to delve into the unusualness of my past . . ." He gestured out to sea, where lights could now be seen, marking the New Iron Pier that led to Brighton Beach. "Those lights you see are where we're headed. And because we're drawing near to the pier where everyone will need to depart the yacht, stories of any type will need to be put on hold."

Ushering her directly up to the wheelhouse, he paused with his hand on the knob. "Before we go in here, I should probably warn you about my sisters."

"You sisters come with a warning?"

"I'm afraid so, and while there are many warnings I could give you pertaining to my sisters, the one that is the most pressing is this — Adelaide, one of my younger sisters, is somewhat out of sorts this evening, so whatever you do, do not remark on how beautiful her face is. And, if you do happen to remark on Edwina's face, which is beautiful as well, do not do so in earshot of Adelaide."

For the briefest of seconds, Mrs. Davenport seemed to consider what he'd told her, and then, to his surprise, she simply nodded, and with a "Will do," gestured to the door.

Turning the knob, he held the door for

Mrs. Davenport, followed her into the wheelhouse, then took her arm, knowing a little extra support was occasionally needed when a person was faced with meeting his sisters for the very first time.

Unfortunately, before he could perform the expected introductions, Margaret, who'd been manning the wheel, looked up, smiled in clear delight, then gestured Adelaide forward to take over the job of steering the yacht right before she turned her smile his way.

"On my word, Harrison, you've done it! You've captured the culprit. And how thoughtful of you to bring her here, evidently realizing that now I can finally fulfill one of my deepest desires — that being tossing someone directly into the brig."

CHAPTER FIVE

"I really believe we should wait for one of Harrison's sisters to arrive and unbolt the couch instead of having me attempt the difficult feat of prying you from that tight space," Permilia said, even as she stood on the fainting couch and tightened her grip on Gertrude's upper arms.

Gertrude shook her head. "Did you not hear Mrs. Davenport make that remark regarding butter?"

Permilia's grip slackened ever so slightly. "I did, but if you'll recall, you nipped that idea in the bud rather sufficiently, so I'm not certain I understand your meaning."

"Mrs. Davenport, bless her unusual heart, is not a lady to easily brush aside ideas when they strike her fancy. You mark my words, she'll be trying to convince one of Harrison's sisters that it'll be easier to butter me up than unbolt the furniture. That right there is why I need you to try your best to set me free. If you've forgotten, you were the one who managed to get Wilhelmina Radcliffe unstuck from underneath that chair a few months back. Because of that experience, I have every confidence in your ability to get me unstuck as well. I've been mortified enough this evening, thank you very much, and am convinced that an experiment with butter, with me being the subject of that experiment, will finally part me from the small shred of dignity I've managed to retain."

Permilia grinned. "I can't claim that the image of you covered in butter isn't an amusing one. However, since I do seem to have experience getting ladies unstuck, which seems downright odd now that I think about it, brace yourself because this might demand some determined tugging on my part."

With that, Permilia set to work, but no matter how hard she tugged, Gertrude didn't budge so much as a single inch.

"I'm really going to have to begin abstaining from all those pastries I enjoy," Gertrude muttered as Permilia swiped a hand over a perspiring brow.

"You have a lovely figure, Gertrude. It simply wasn't meant to be stuffed in such a tiny area." Drawing in a breath, Permilia readjusted her balance while readjusting her hold on Gertrude, muttered what seemed to be a prayer under her breath, and reared backward. What sounded exactly like a pop met her efforts, and before Gertrude could do more than yelp, she found herself, along with Permilia, tumbling up and over the couch, landing hard on the floor of the library.

At first, the only sound to be heard was their labored breathing, but a second later, snorts of amusement replaced the breathing, replaced a second after that with howls of laughter.

A full minute passed before Permilia released a last hiccup of laughter, pushed herself into a sitting position, waited for Gertrude to do the same, then grinned.

"I'm pleased to say that my reputation as a rescuer of stuck ladies remains firmly intact."

Gertrude returned the grin. "Let us hope that particular talent of yours won't be needed on my behalf ever, ever again." She rose to her feet, rubbed an elbow that was smarting dreadfully, then held out a hand to Permilia and helped her friend off the floor.

She gestured to the door. "Now that I'm free, I must insist you rejoin your engagement celebration. A lady usually only gets one of those, and I don't want to you to tarry longer because of my unusual circumstances."

A crease immediately marred Permilia's forehead. "I'm not going to leave you here all by your lonesome, Gertrude. I'll rejoin the celebration after we get you properly dressed and able to come with me."

"You'll do no such thing. I'm fine, and I have little fear anyone else will stumble upon me, what with Harrison probably gathering everyone on the top deck to divulge his surprise. He can't very well do that divulging, however, without both of the guests of honor, so go. Again, I'll be fine and I'll join you just as soon as I'm able."

Permilia rolled her eyes. "Fine, I'll go, but if you're not above deck directly, I'll be back." Snatching up a blanket from a basket beside one of the chairs, Permilia wrapped it around Gertrude's shoulders, gave her a lovely hug, then hurried from the room.

When the door closed behind her friend, Gertrude walked over to a chair and sat down, rearranging the blanket so that it afforded her a small amount of modesty. Leaning her head back, she drew in a breath, heat settling into her cheeks when everything that had recently transpired began whirling through her mind.

She'd gotten stuck to a fainting couch. And while that was certainly a most embarrassing situation, having Harrison walk in on her while she'd been cackling like mad and less than sufficiently dressed was without a doubt *the* most mortifying experience she'd ever had in her life.

It was almost too much to comprehend, especially with his being a gentleman she held in high esteem, that feeling certain never to be returned on his part after he witnessed her making a true cake of herself and . . .

Gertrude sucked in a sharp breath as truth, and an unexpected morsel of truth at that, took that very second to burrow deep into her soul.

She'd vehemently denied Miss Flowerdew's accusation that she was romantically attracted to Harrison when, in all honesty, Miss Flowerdew's assessment of the situation might have been spot-on.

The very idea she'd somehow allowed herself to develop affections of the romantic sort for Harrison lent credence to the idea that she, Gertrude Cadwalader, a normally no-nonsense and practical sort, was in actuality a complete ninny.

Harrison Sinclair was afforded the attention of diamonds of the first water, as Miss Flowerdew had pointed out, and, sadly, Gertrude knew full well she would never rise to that particular status in life, not with her being anything other than ordinary.

Ordinary ladies did not garner the affections of gentlemen of Harrison's caliber.

Rubbing a hand against a head that felt as if it might burst, Gertrude tried to summon up the practicality she was known to embrace. Unfortunately, nothing of a practical nature sprang to mind. Instead, an odd longing to procure a more sophisticated attitude took hold of her and wouldn't let go.

If she possessed even a smidgen of sophistication, she would have been discovered by Harrison reclining gracefully on the fainting couch, reading a Jane Austen novel in one hand while nibbling at a sugar cookie with the other. Her stockings, which she hadn't failed to notice were pooled around her ankles, would have been in fine form, and her hair would have been fashioned in a manner that one wouldn't need to travel to a country far, far away in order to find other ladies wearing a similar style.

She certainly wouldn't have been discovered standing in a private library garbed in her unmentionables, nor would she have then taken to leaping over a couch where she'd promptly become stuck due to the fact that her figure was not what anyone could call svelte.

Blowing out a breath, Gertrude dropped her head and folded her hands in her lap, stilling when she realized she was considering lifting up a prayer request, one that revolved around asking God to send her a small dollop of sophistication.

The absurdity of such a prayer sent additional heat to her cheeks.

God, she was fairly certain, had far more important matters to attend to other than to grant her the ridiculous request of becoming sophisticated, especially since she truly only wanted to become sophisticated in order to impress Harrison.

Given that Harrison was a gentleman who did not notice the interest of *the* most fashionable and sophisticated sort, her prayer was ludicrous. Besides, considering her relationship with God had certainly suffered ever since her mother died, a circumstance she took full responsibility for, He was hardly likely to bestow any amount of grace on her, let alone answer a frivolous prayer.

Annoyance with herself had her abandoning her chair and walking over to the bookcase, hoping to find a distraction from her disturbing thoughts. She pulled out a leather-bound book about sea routes, flipped to the first page, and began reading, pausing when a knock sounded on the closed door.

Lifting her head as the door began to open, Gertrude blinked when what could only be described as a whirlwind entered the room. Replacing the book, she watched one of the most beautiful ladies she'd ever seen in her life breeze across the library in her direction, dragging a large satchel behind her with one hand and holding a bowl of something in the other.

Gertrude was hardly put at ease when the lady stopped directly in front of her and held out the bowl — one that was filled to the brim with *butter.*

Accepting the butter because she couldn't think of a good reason not to, Gertrude's lips curved as the lady dropped the handle of the satchel to the floor and smiled Gertrude's way.

"Ah, Gertrude, what a clever lady you seem to be, getting yourself unstuck from a situation I was led to believe was nothing less than dire. We'll have no need for the wrench Harrison told me to fetch after all." The lady fished a wrench out of the bodice of her lovely blue traveling gown and tossed it in the direction of the fainting couch before she turned back to Gertrude and immediately began looking her up and down. "My brother wasn't exaggerating your current dilemma, though. You do seem to have taken leave of your clothing, and while I applaud your resourcefulness with a plot that appears to be downright ingenious, do know that the other members of my family might not be as approving as I am about that plot."

Gertrude tightened her grip on the bowl of butter. "I'm afraid you have me at a disadvantage, Miss . . . ?"

The young lady blinked, then shoved aside a raven-black curl that was obscuring part of her face, revealing features that suggested she might very well be one of Harrison's sisters. "Oh, do forgive me. I'm Edwina Sinclair, of course, and you're Miss Gertrude Cadwalader, a very *dear* friend of my brother's if I'm not much mistaken." Her smile dimmed. "But good heavens, I'm sure I've taken you completely aback by calling you Gertrude when I first entered the room, although it does seem rather silly to call you anything else, especially since I have every hope that you and I will someday be related. However, according to the etiquette books I've been gobbling up of late, young ladies of the proper kind are not supposed to address each other informally, not until they've gotten permission to do so, that is."

Finding herself charmed by the very earnest Miss Edwina Sinclair, Gertrude set aside the bowl of butter. "While I'm not exactly sure how we'd come to be related, do feel free to use my given name. Your brother and I do share a friendship, and because of that, it does seem silly for us to adopt a formal attitude."

Edwina clapped her hands together. "Ah, how lovely, and you must call me Edwina. I knew you and I were destined to become fast friends, and I feel as if we're friends already since my brother has spoken so highly of you and on a frequent basis at that." She sent Gertrude a wink. "As for the matter about how we'll be related, should I assume you're simply being coy until an announcement is made — one that I'm certain will be made soon now that my brother has apparently spent time in your company while you've been less than appropriately dressed?"

Gertrude frowned. "I fear you're under a grave misimpression, Edwina. Harrison did not spend any significant time in this library with me, having merely stepped into the room before stepping directly out of it again."

Edwina's forehead furrowed. "It wasn't intentional, having Harrison discover you in your unmentionables?"

Gertrude's forehead took to furrowing as well. "I should say not."

"And here I thought you'd decided to take matters into your own hands, hastening my brother's decision to marry you, but no matter." She sent Gertrude another wink. "With my help, you mark my words, you'll be married to Harrison before the summer has a chance to end."

"Ah . . . well . . . ah . . ."

"Save your appreciation until you're about to walk down the aisle," Edwina interrupted, although it wasn't much of an interruption since Gertrude couldn't think of anything else to say. "We have important business to attend to, that being getting you into tip-top shape." She turned on her heel and marched back to the door, reappearing a moment later, towing none other than Temperance Flowerdew, Clementine's distant cousin, beside her.

"Temperance has agreed to help me get you more presentable," Edwina said as she pulled Temperance across the library. "Although I'm not certain why she was lingering out in the hallway. She, from what little conversation we've shared while fetching you some clothing, and the butter of course, lent me the impression the two of you are friends."

Temperance shot a look to Gertrude even as her lips twitched. "I was lingering outside to allow you an opportunity to become acquainted with Edwina. I assumed my presence would only add confusion to what was certainly going to be an unusual introduction, and I do believe I was quite right about that." She nodded to the garments that were cascading over her arms. "Now that we've gotten that out of the way, shall we get you properly dressed once and for all?"

Before Gertrude could respond, Edwina let out a ripple of laughter. "My introduction to Gertrude pales in comparison to the introduction you and I shared, Temperance — what with all that yelling that was taking place at the time." She turned to Gertrude. "Temperance and I decided we needed to quit the wheelhouse lickety-split when some heated words began to fly." She gave a sad shake of her head. "Poor Temperance was looking quite like a deer caught in the coach lights when her cousin, a dreadful woman if I've ever met one, burst into the wheelhouse, dragging poor Temperance along with her. That dreadful woman then threw herself into the argument Mrs. Davenport was engaged in with my sister Margaret, adding a great deal of drama to a situation that was rapidly turning concerning."

Glancing to Temperance, who, in Gertrude's opinion, was once again looking exactly like a deer caught in the coach lights, she turned back to Edwina. "I'm sorry, but did you just say that Mrs. Davenport was engaged in an argument with your sister?"

"Indeed, and it was a juicy argument at that, one with all manner of accusations being thrown around, most of them having to do with some type of skullduggery being perpetuated on board this very yacht."

Chapter Six

With her legs turning ever so wobbly due to the troubling information Edwina had disclosed, Gertrude moved back to her chair and sat down. "Should I ask what manner of skullduggery Mrs. Davenport was being accused of, and . . ." She frowned. "Why in the world would Clementine throw herself willingly into an argument between two ladies I don't believe she's overly familiar with, and why would she have gone into the wheelhouse in the first place?"

"While this is embarrassing for me to admit," Temperance began as Edwina looked over the gowns she was carrying, "I fear Clementine was lying in wait for Harrison on the aft deck, and after she saw him disappear into the wheelhouse, there was no stopping her from following him." Temperance shook her head. "She insisted I accompany her, and I must tell you now, Gertrude, my cousin seems most put out with you. She kept muttering something about not gaining your cooperation, which might have been the incentive behind her making some ridiculous claim about you and a painting Clementine apparently saw you admiring."

Pulling a dress from Temperance's arms, Edwina held it up, eyeing it even as she nodded. "From what little I was able to gather, Clementine was trying to suggest you were contemplating making off with the painting hanging in this very room, but I'm afraid I don't know what happened after that since everyone started shouting and Temperance and I decided to hightail it right out of there." Holding out the dress, she walked toward Gertrude. "Luckily for you, Harrison had already told me about your unfortunate predicament, which gave me a reasonable excuse to leave the wheelhouse when events began turning tricky. I'm still a little confused about why Mrs. Davenport shouted that bit about you needing some butter, but . . ." She changed directions, set the dress she was holding on a chair, bent over to the satchel, rummaged around in it, then pulled out what appeared to be a loaf of bread wrapped in cloth. Gliding over to Gertrude, she handed her the bread.

"The only conclusion I could make about

the butter was that you must be hungry and needed a snack before dinner is served. That's why I had the men in the galley include a loaf of bread, because, well, I've never known anyone to enjoy butter by itself."

For the briefest of seconds, Gertrude simply allowed all of Edwina's words to settle into her mind, but then, after they'd settled, she couldn't help but laugh. Once she started, she couldn't stop. As tears of mirth began leaking out of her eyes, she accepted the handkerchief Edwina handed her, pretending not to notice that Harrison's sister was now looking at her with concern.

Waving aside the bread that Temperance had evidently buttered for her while she'd been in the throes of hysterics, Gertrude swallowed a last laugh, grinning when Temperance shrugged and began eating the slice of buttered bread.

"This is delicious, although I do beg your pardon, Gertrude, for not inquiring whether you wanted to share your snack," Temperance said after she swallowed the bite of bread and looked somewhat guilty.

Gertrude waved the apology aside. "I'm not hungry, Temperance, and curious as this is going to sound, Mrs. Davenport didn't suggest the butter as a snack, but more as an alternative way to get me unstuck from behind the couch."

"I *knew* I was going to like that woman," Edwina said, pausing in the act of shaking out the gown she'd been considering. "What an intriguing idea, using butter to get a person unstuck. Mrs. Davenport must be a most resourceful sort. Did I mention that she was holding her own with Margaret, a woman who has been known to make grown men shake in their boots?"

Gertrude leaned forward. "Speaking of that, we need to get me dressed sooner rather than later. Mrs. Davenport is not a woman to abandon an argument, and I shudder to think what she may say if she fears your sister is getting the best of her."

Edwina shook her head. "As I said, Mrs. Davenport was holding her own, and you're not leaving this room until I have you looking your best." She nodded to the bread Temperance was in the process of buttering up again. "While I'm perfectly capable of dressing you quickly, it might be uncomfortable for you, what with all the lacing and pulling and buttoning up I'll need to do. It may be prudent for you to have a small snack to fortify you for the mission ahead."

"While I thank you for such a considerate suggestion, Edwina, I'm certain the last thing I need to do is indulge myself with bread and butter. I have no desire to ever become stuck again due to my figure, which means I need to start being mindful about what I eat."

"Harrison told me you have a delightful figure," Edwina said, eyeing Gertrude up and down. "And, from what I can tell, even with you sitting down, he was quite right about that."

Something warm and delightful began thrumming through Gertrude's veins. "Harrison actually said that?"

"Indeed, although it wasn't said in a forward manner if that is a concern. The subject of your figure was broached when he was trying to describe what type of dress I should search out for you." Edwina leaned closer to Gertrude. "In my humble opinion, Harrison taking notice of your figure is telling indeed since he's not a gentleman who usually pays such a marked attention to such matters."

Straightening, Edwina held out the gown she was still holding. "But no time to delve into the intricacies of my brother's mind, we need to get you ready. I'll have that blanket if you please, and after we get you dressed, well, we simply must do something about your hair."

Realizing there was little point in balking because she couldn't very well leave the library until she was suitably dressed, Gertrude rose from the chair, parted ways with the blanket, and soon found herself taken well in hand by Harrison's sister. Before she knew it, her laces were being pulled in an entirely too enthusiastic manner — so enthusiastic, in fact, that she was finding it difficult to breathe.

"You may need to loosen those laces just a touch," she said in a breathy voice, the only type of voice she was capable of making since air was difficult to come by.

"I'm afraid I can't do that," Edwina said, panting ever so slightly as she gave the laces one last pull. "You're rather larger than I am in the bosom area, which means tight laces are the only way we'll get you into my gown." She made short shrift of tying the laces before nodding to Temperance, who was on her third piece of bread and butter. "I don't believe we'll have the same problem with the gown of mine that you're going to wear, Temperance. You have exactly the opposite figure from Gertrude, being so slender and willowy."

Temperance paused with the bread halfway to her mouth. "I'm sure there's no need for me to borrow one of your gowns. If you've neglected to notice, the one I'm wearing is perfectly respectable."

Edwina immediately narrowed her eyes on Temperance. "While that gown certainly does the job of covering you, Temperance, it does not show you to advantage. It's at least five seasons out of date and doesn't fit you properly, leaving you looking as if you've missed far too many meals instead of simply being slender." She gestured to the pile of dresses that were now on the fainting couch. "Any one of those would look darling on you, and I promise if you allow me to style you this evening, you'll not regret it."

Stuffing a piece of bread into her mouth, Temperance chewed, swallowed, and then shook her head. "While it's very kind of you to offer to style me, Edwina, although not the part where you pointed out that my gown does not show me to advantage, I think I'll just leave you to work on Gertrude. In all honesty, I need to check on my cousin. It was not well-done of me to abandon her the way I did, even with her making a cake of herself by barging into that argument."

Edwina's expression turned stricken. "Do forgive me, Temperance. I certainly didn't mean to insult you. I fear etiquette books are sorely lacking at times with providing a lady with the knowledge needed to traverse that pesky field known as manners. But that's certainly not an acceptable excuse for my blurting out observations that shouldn't be spoken aloud."

Temperance smiled and moved up next to Edwina. "That was a lovely apology, Edwina, and one that would have done any etiquette book proud. I accept your apology, and as a woman who grew up attending the finest finishing schools and was taught to always consider every word that slips past my lips, I find myself oddly envious of your ability to speak your mind. There are certainly times when I think saying exactly what one longs to say is beneficial, but it is not something I've had the courage to do of late."

Edwina returned Temperance's smile. "You're very gracious, and do know that I will try to mind my manners from this point forward. Although . . ." She cocked her head to the side. "This will probably come out rather forward as well, but if you've attended the best finishing schools, why is it that . . ." Her words trailed away as she looked Temperance over and winced.

Temperance laughed. "See, you're doing better already at minding your manners, although I know full well you were about to ask why I look so dowdy. But, since you have decided we're to be great friends, and I could certainly use more of those, I'll tell you why. My parents died a few years back, and unfortunately, I've now become a poor relation, something that has done wonders for allowing me to embrace a humble attitude."

"But wouldn't you enjoy abandoning that humble attitude, along with that hideous dress you're wearing, if only for this one night?" Edwina pressed.

Temperance frowned. "You're very tenacious, aren't you?"

"It's another flaw I've been trying to work on."

"Not having much success with that flaw either, are you?"

Edwina grinned. "I'm afraid not, but do say you'll let me fix you up. It'll be my way of making up for my serious lack of manners."

Temperance returned the grin. "I suppose it wouldn't hurt to see what you can do with me. Although, as a confirmed wallflower and poor relation, I'm afraid any efforts on your part will be for naught since I doubt I'll draw any notice even if I am fashionably dressed."

"A lady, when fashionably dressed, always

draws attention, be she a wallflower or not." Edwina gestured to her person. "I am, undoubtedly, not a member of the society set, nor am I a wallflower. But I never step foot out of the house without looking my best, which allows me to embrace my days with confidence."

With that, Edwina returned to the business of getting Gertrude dressed, proclaiming her ready to go within a remarkably short period of time.

Because Gertrude felt quite like a stuffed sausage and knew she might have a tough time of it rising from a chair if she took a seat, she remained standing as Edwina threw herself into the process of dressing Temperance.

Fluffing up the skirt of the gown she'd pulled over Temperance's head, Edwina stepped back and nodded. "There. Perfection. Now the two of you will blend in seamlessly with the crowd at the Manhattan Beach Hotel."

"We're going to the Manhattan Beach Hotel?" Gertrude asked.

"*You* and *Temperance* are going to the Manhattan Beach Hotel," Edwina corrected. "I have not been invited."

Gertrude wrinkled her nose. "I'm certain

you must be mistaken about not being invited."

"I'm certain I'm not. Harrison neglected to extend an invitation to me or my sisters."

"Then allow me to do so now, Edwina." Gertrude held up her hand when Edwina immediately began protesting. "As one of Permilia's closest friends, I can assure you that she certainly wouldn't mind you joining us, nor would Mr. Asher Rutherford mind for that matter. In all honesty, I'm sure Harrison simply assumed you and your sisters realized you were expected to attend the event at the hotel, but being a gentleman, he forgot to mention it."

Edwina shook her head. "He didn't include us because he knows my mother would be most put out with him if he did. My sisters, Adelaide and Margaret, are not ladies who care for balls, dinners, or dressing in glamorous fashions, so they are not put out in the least by the idea that they've not been invited. I, on the other hand, would love nothing more than to be given an opportunity to mingle with society members, a notion my mother finds appalling. That is exactly why I know for a fact she's made Harrison promise to keep a watchful eye on me while she's away."

"Why is your mother so against society

events?" Gertrude asked.

"She abhors society and the pretense she feels goes hand in hand with it." Edwina heaved a long-suffering sigh before she, surprisingly enough, grinned. "But since you've been so gracious as to extend me an invitation, it would be churlish of me to refuse, so I'll be delighted to join you at the Manhattan Beach Hotel."

Gertrude smiled. "Wonderful, but aren't you worried that accepting my invitation will put you at odds with your brother?"

Edwina's grin widened. "Harrison is not a man who is comfortable disappointing ladies. He's not immune to pouting, or a few sniffles here and there, which I admit, I've put to good use on numerous occasions throughout my life. He'll not be put out with me at all if I summon up a few tears. Quite honestly, I think he's been coming around to the belief that while my sisters are content to immerse themselves in the family business, I have another life to lead, one that won't see me building ships year after year."

Temperance paused in the act of pulling a lovely silk glove up her arm that she'd retrieved from Edwina's satchel. "You know how to build ships?"

"I know everything about shipping, although I'm not nearly as mad about the industry as the rest of my family." She nodded to Gertrude. "A word of advice about that, though. If you truly want to win my family over, do at least pretend an interest in the business. That will help you pave the way into their hearts."

"You and I are really going to have to have a little chat about the delusion you seem to be under regarding my relationship with your brother."

Edwina completely ignored that statement. "You'll also endear yourself to my mother if you mention how much you adore children. My mother is longing for a grandchild, so do be certain to bring children into the conversation as often as you can once Harrison brings you around to meet her."

"I don't believe Harrison has any plans to bring me around to meet your mother," Gertrude said slowly.

"Well of course he doesn't have immediate plans to do that since my mother isn't currently in New York."

Gertrude fought a grin. "Did you ever think that perhaps your mother has taken to hinting about having grandchildren because she'd like to see you or your two sisters wed in the near future?"

Edwina waved that aside. "Margaret has

vowed never to wed. And as for me, I'm all for finding a nice gentleman, but one doesn't find nice gentlemen down on the docks, which is why I'd like to join society."

"What about Adelaide?"

"She's determined to spend her life as the captain of a ship, so I don't believe she'll be getting married anytime soon, unless she meets a pirate." Edwina smiled. "Adelaide has always been keen on pirates."

Temperance laughed and shook her head. "That would certainly draw your mother's attention away from you wanting to enter society if your sister showed up with a pirate on her arm."

"Mother likes pirates, especially since my father began his career as one, clear back in the day, although he was more of a privateer than pirate."

"What an interesting lady your mother seems to be," Gertrude began. "But I'm afraid that after she discovers I invited you to the Manhattan Beach Hotel, she'll not be keen to make my acquaintance."

"Her desire for a grandbaby will more than appease her annoyance with you in the end."

Gertrude drew in a breath and tried again. "I'm not certain you're aware of this, but your brother has recently moved to the top of a very elite list — one that is titled *Most Eligible Gentlemen in New York.* I'm confident Harrison will be able to be incredibly discerning when it comes to choosing a future bride. That right there will allow your mother to persuade him to choose a woman whom she doesn't find annoying."

Edwina, instead of looking contrite, smiled rather knowingly. "My brother has never been one to single out a lady before, but he certainly has taken to singling you out and bringing you into conversations often, although . . ." Her smile faded. "Since you are associated with Mrs. Davenport, and that lovely lady is currently at odds with my sister, what with all the yelling they were doing, we might have a bit of difficulty convincing Margaret to embrace the idea of you now."

"Which isn't as concerning as you believe because your brother has never given me cause to believe he wants to further our association past the friendship stage," Gertrude began, pretending she didn't see Edwina roll her eyes. "However, returning to the subject of Mrs. Davenport, now that Temperance and I are suitably dressed, and before we leave this library, perhaps it would be for the best if you could explain in a little more detail exactly what she was arguing about with your sister."

Edwina stuffed a box of pins she'd been using back in her satchel. "Margaret wanted to throw Mrs. Davenport into the brig."

"Throw her into the brig?" Gertrude repeated.

"Indeed, but there's no need to look so nervous. We don't have a brig on board the *Cornelia.* And besides, since I'm sure Mrs. Davenport wasn't truly involved in any shenanigans, being an esteemed society matron from what I've gathered, there's nothing to worry about." She tossed a glance to the painting behind the fainting couch. "Unless that does go missing. Then everyone will need to worry because that is the first piece of artwork my parents bought after they began making a success out of the shipping business they'd struggled to build for years."

Gertrude glanced to the painting in question. "Strictly out of curiosity, and because you did say your father was once a bit of a pirate, what do you think your family would do to a person if they happened to make off with a prized possession from this yacht?"

Edwina fastened the latch on the satchel and straightened. "I fear we'd deal with the culprit most severely. My family has toiled long and hard over the years to build up our business. That means we have little tolerance for thieves. Why, I have to imagine if someone did try to make off with anything from this ship, that someone might very well be forced to walk the plank."

CHAPTER SEVEN

Raking a hand through hair that had escaped the confines of a ribbon he would have never bought for himself, Harrison couldn't help but wonder how he always seemed to be caught up in one feminine drama after another.

It wasn't that he had anything against the lady set, especially since he'd grown up surrounded by members of the feminine sort. But, in all honesty, he had no true understanding of the female mind. He also didn't have the slightest idea how to sort through all the drama ladies seemed to embrace with such enthusiasm, even though they always seemed to expect him to know how to go about doing exactly that.

Holding his hair out of his face with one hand while placing his other on the ship's railing when the *Cornelia* took that moment to dip due to the surging tide, Harrison settled his attention on Miss Mabel Huxley and Miss Henrietta Huxley.

Those two ladies were currently making their way unaided down the plank that led to the New Iron Pier, having refused his offer of assistance. Why they'd refused him, he wasn't certain. But since he wasn't overly familiar with the sisters, having only made their acquaintance a few months before when they'd decided to take Permilia under their collective wings, he could only imagine that he'd phrased his offer of assistance in a manner Miss Mabel and Miss Henrietta found lacking. In his defense, though, he'd only told the ladies they should take his arm because they were of an age when breaking a fragile neck should be of great concern. For some unknown reason, they'd immediately gotten up in arms.

When faced with two ladies who'd begun sending him sniffs of clear disapproval, he'd abandoned any attempt at assisting them. He was now holding his breath as the ladies marched their way toward the pier, hoping the slippery nature of the plank wasn't going to see them suffering a dip into the sea.

Quite truthfully, he was contemplating the idea of remaining mute for the rest of the night because every time he did open his mouth, one lady or another took exception to all the words he allowed to escape.

At present, he was certain numerous ladies on board the *Cornelia* were suffering from acute cases of annoyance, the cause of which being attributed directly to him.

The most annoyed of the bunch was certainly Margaret. She'd been more than vocal with her disappointment that he had not allowed her to tie Mrs. Davenport up and toss her in the brig. Although why his sister had suggested a brig was puzzling since they didn't have a brig on the *Cornelia* in the first place.

Next up on the list of being annoyed with him would have to be Mrs. Davenport. She'd taken issue with the idea that he'd neglected to insist Margaret apologize to her for what she proclaimed were nothing less than *"unfounded, nasty accusations."* And, while it wasn't that he believed Margaret didn't owe Mrs. Davenport an apology, he'd never been a gentleman to order ladies about. That meant he didn't believe it was his place to insist his sister apologize, but when he'd tried to explain that to Mrs. Davenport, she'd sent him a snort, of all things, and immediately took to presenting him with her back.

To make the situation even more uncomfortable, Miss Clementine Flowerdew had rendered a most outlandish tale concerning

Gertrude and a painting in the library. And then, after she was done with her rendering, she'd smiled a lovely smile his way even as she began batting her lashes, quite as if she'd gotten something in her eye.

When he'd made the unfortunate decision to inquire if she needed his assistance with the troubling eye business, Margaret released a grunt and immediately launched into a somewhat scathing lecture, informing Clementine in no uncertain terms that it was not a moment for a touch of frivolous flirting.

Before Harrison could wrap his mind around the idea Clementine Flowerdew was evidently flirting with him, Clementine stuck her pert nose straight into the air, told Margaret she didn't appreciate such an uninviting atmosphere, and glided for the door, turning to send him one last smile.

Evidently, he'd made another mistake when he'd returned that smile, even though he was of the belief that not doing so would have been a serious neglect of basic manners.

Margaret and Mrs. Davenport immediately began casting less than friendly gazes his way, and faced with such blatant feminine animosity, Harrison had done the only thing he could think of. . . . He'd fled the wheelhouse and taken refuge behind one of the four imposing cowl vents that were stationed at the front of the ship.

Waiting until Margaret steered the *Cornelia* over to the pier and his crew had secured the yacht with ropes to that pier, he'd then lurked behind the cowls until Adelaide, being a most sensible sort, organized the departure of the guests from the ship.

"Didn't I tell you, Mr. Sinclair, that Mabel and I were perfectly capable of reaching the pier without the strong arm of a gentleman to assist us?" Miss Henrietta suddenly called, drawing Harrison's attention. "It's not as if either one of us is at our last prayers just yet."

Having no idea exactly the age of Miss Henrietta, as she preferred to be called, and not being quite brave enough to ask her since she was known to be a somewhat peculiar and unpredictable lady, Harrison decided the prudent response would be one that ignored the whole last prayers business altogether. With his lips quirking into a grin, he leaned over the railing. "I had no idea you were so put out with me because you were of the belief I was making a disparaging implication regarding your age. I assure you, that was not my intent at all. Did it never cross your mind that I was simply insisting on offering you my manly assistance because I wanted everyone to witness me arriving at Brighton Beach with two lovely ladies in my company?"

Even though there was a good deal of distance separating them, and the sun was beginning to set over the Atlantic Ocean, Hamilton could have sworn Miss Henrietta rolled her eyes. "Even though I'm not immune to the charm of a handsome gentleman, do know that I am immune to nonsense when I hear it." With that, Miss Henrietta spun on her heel, took hold of her sister's arm, and began marching down the pier at a brisk pace.

"Miss Henrietta certainly is a delightful lady, possessed of such an unassuming nature, but oddly enough, she and her sister have begun to grow on me."

Straightening, Harrison found Mr. Asher Rutherford, his very good friend, guest of honor that evening, and supplier of ribbons, coming to a stop beside him. "The sisters do seem to have a rather curious type of appeal," Harrison agreed as he nodded toward the retreating sisters in question. "Which is fortunate for you since Permilia seems to enjoy their company so much."

Asher blew out a breath. "Life is curious

at times since I would have never imagined the Huxley sisters becoming such an integral part of our lives. But because they do share a past with Permilia's father, George, and Permilia is missing her father at this important time in her life, the sisters have filled a void for her in a way that I find endearing. They treat her as if she's their own daughter, something Permilia's stepmother never did, and for that, the Huxley sisters will always have my deepest regard."

"Does it bother Permilia that George has decided to remain over in Paris to try and mend his marriage with Ida instead of returning to the States for his daughter's engagement celebrations?"

"Since his remaining in Paris has Ida remaining there as well, I'm going to have to say no." Asher frowned. "I'm still not convinced George will be able to mend his marriage to Ida, what with him revealing he only married her to help usher Permilia into society, and Ida revealing she only married him for his money. Permilia, on the other hand, seems to be hopeful they *will* be able to mend their relationship in the end. If that mending comes with the price of them not being in New York for our wedding in a few months, she seems to be fine with that idea as well."

"It'll certainly make that day brighter for both of you if Lucy, the dreaded stepsister, isn't around on your happy day," Harrison added. "She and Permilia don't share what anyone could call an affectionate bond."

Asher smiled. "Since we've recently learned that Lucy has abandoned her interest in Mr. Slater, it'll make the day brighter for you as well since rumor has it around society that the ladies have decided you're the gentleman to pursue at the moment." His smile widened. "Lucy, from what I understand, is very susceptible to matters like that, which means you may have become her next target had she returned from Paris to attend her stepsister's engagement celebration and then subsequent wedding."

Harrison leaned closer to his friend. "There's not really talk like that about me making the rounds, is there?"

"Of course there is."

"A disturbing idea to be sure, and one that proves exactly why I'm not keen to enter society, no matter that society seems keen to welcome industrialists into their hallowed midst these days."

"I would think since you are a gentleman who isn't growing any younger, and you have been quite diligent in regard to growing the family shipping business, you'd relish the idea of ladies finding you to be a most excellent matrimonial choice."

Harrison quirked a brow Asher's way. "Do not tell me you're turning into one of *those* gentlemen, are you? The ones who've found their true love and now believe everyone needs to do the same?"

Asher quirked a brow right back at him. "I've recently come to the conclusion that love is a state that mustn't be neglected, and a state that everyone should have an opportunity to embrace."

"Since when have you taken to turning poetic, and in a Byronic manner at that?"

Asher, instead of looking even a smidgen embarrassed, looked rather smug instead. "I recently began enjoying the work of Lord Byron, finding myself pleasantly surprised by the depth of emotion he put into his work. I daresay I never gave that esteemed gentleman his due, what with believing his poems regarding love to be a touch unrealistic, if you will. But, since I've now had the pleasure of gaining Permilia's charming affections, I find Lord Byron's work to be delightfully educational and strongly suggest you pick up a few of his works in order to aid you in acquiring the affections of your own charming lady."

"You're worse off than I imagined," Harrison muttered right as Asher suddenly began looking far too determined.

"Because you are one of my closest friends, Harrison, I've decided I owe it to you to move your life along in the proper direction. That means I'm going to assist you with procuring your own happily-ever-after."

Harrison began inching backward. "I don't believe that's necessary, especially since I'm perfectly happy as it is."

"You work almost all the time except for when you join me for lunch at one of my clubs a few times a week."

"I enjoy working and building up my shipping business, and it's not as if my only social activity is joining you for lunch a few times a week."

"What else, pray tell, do you do?"

"Well, to refresh that obviously faulty memory of yours, I ride my horse in Central Park."

"With me, and after we've enjoyed our lunch. That doesn't count."

"I'm perfectly content with my life."

"You need a lady."

Harrison's brows drew together. "How in the world did you surmise that from me saying I'm perfectly content?"

"Gentlemen always say they're perfectly

content when they're really longing to spend their time with a lady. I'm sure I said exactly the same thing before I met my Permilia, but now I know I was hardly content, which is why I've decided to offer you my assistance in finding you a lady of your own."

"I'm surrounded by ladies all the time, because, in case you've forgotten, I have three sisters and a mother — all of whom seem to enjoy spending an enormous amount of time in my company."

"You need a lady who can be your true companion." Asher leaned closer to Harrison. "I've come to the conclusion Gertrude is perfect for you."

Harrison completely forgot he'd been trying to inch away from his friend and froze on the spot. "Why in the world would you have concluded that?"

"Because you pay attention to her."

"I pay attention to all my friends."

"You don't look at Gertrude the way you look at your other friends."

"Of course I wouldn't look at Gertrude the way I look at you. That would be curious indeed especially since I do try to smile more at my lady friends than I do at the gentlemen I know."

"You're being obtuse, and on purpose I think."

Harrison grinned. "Too right I am because I'm not used to you taking an interest in my romantic life, or lack thereof. And while Gertrude is a charming lady, one whose company I enjoy immensely, I'm simply not in the market for a wife. I have a business to continue growing and that business demands all of my attention these days."

Asher, annoying friend that he apparently was, completely ignored Harrison's protest. "Permilia told me you stumbled in on Gertrude when she was dressed in her unmentionables. If word of that gets out, you do realize you'll have no choice but to offer the lady the protection of your name, don't you?"

"How in the world do you imagine word of that incident getting out? It's not as if we were entertaining a large crowd while she was standing around in her unmentionables. Besides, I barely stepped into the room before I realized it was a place I shouldn't be, which had me turning directly around and presenting Gertrude with my back."

Ignoring all that as well, Asher suddenly narrowed his eyes on Harrison before he stuck his hand into his formal evening coat and pulled out another black velvet ribbon from the apparently unending supply he kept on his person. Handing it over to Harrison, he gave a sad shake of his head. "You're looking the part of a pirate at the moment, which won't do at all. And, since you evidently lost the first ribbon I gave you, I'm sure you'll now understand why you need a lady in your life, one who would be capable of keeping you well put together."

"And you believe Gertrude would be up for that task — the same Gertrude who had orange skin when I first met her and drifts through the city dressed in fashions that are more curious than some I've been known to wear?"

Asher's lips twitched at the very corners. "You've actually noticed the curious fashions Gertrude adopts upon occasion?"

Unwilling to address that somewhat telling remark, since he knew full well he was considered a less than observant gentleman, Harrison hitched another smile into place even as he took a moment to tie back his hair with the ribbon Asher had just given him. He couldn't help but notice as he slipped his fingers through his tangled hair that he did seem to have lost the first ribbon altogether. That was a sad sort of circumstance if there ever was one, and a circumstance that had no doubt happened while he'd been in the midst of one troubling lady event after another.

"Have I ever mentioned how disconcerting I find it when you always seem to have some random item someone needs at the ready?" Harrison asked in a blatant attempt to change the subject. "You're quite like a magician in that regard, and truth be told, I've always found magicians to be a somewhat sketchy lot."

"Don't think I haven't realized you're trying to distract me from the Gertrude topic, but to address your disconcerting statement, Harrison, I'm the owner of a department store. I'm expected to have random items at my disposal. I'll have you know that because I'm always in possession of spare handkerchiefs, smelling salts, glue, hair ribbons, and a wide variety of other essentials such as stockings and garters, profits at the store have continued to increase on a steady basis, especially over the past few months." He smiled. "Customers enjoy knowing a merchant is prepared for any situation, and that right there is exactly why they've become so comfortable shopping at Rutherford & Company."

"While I find myself beyond curious as to why you'd carry around glue, and concerned that you just admitted you often have spare garters on your person, as well as stockings, you must know that your profits have increased lately because you were fortunate enough to convince Permilia to come on board as your vice president. Given that she seems to have an uncanny ability to discover artistic talent in the oddest of places, such as Five Points, your profits are only certain to continue increasing with every new designer she brings to the store, something that should have that merchant heart of yours going pitter-patter. Add in the notion that society has now decided you and Permilia are the most riveting couple of the year, even more riveting than the soon-to-be Mr. and Mrs. Edgar Wannamaker, well, I wouldn't be surprised if you don't have to resort to hiring on additional staff members in order to control the crowds that are flocking to your store in order to get a glimpse of your riveting faces."

Asher smiled and leaned on the ship's railing. "I am a fortunate gentleman, aren't I?"

Joining him at the railing, Harrison returned the smile. "You are, but before you turn annoyingly poetic again, allow me to point out that the evening is quickly getting away from us. We really should be making our way over to the Manhattan Beach Hotel. Most of the guests, if you've neglected to realize, have already departed for the hotel and will be waiting for you, the guest of honor, along with your fiancée."

"I'm sure all of our guests will be quite comfortable being looked after by the staff at the hotel, which are rumored to be exceptional in their execution of their various duties. Having said that, I can't leave the ship yet. Permilia went to check on Gertrude's progress and hasn't returned."

Harrison opened his mouth with an offer to track down Permilia and Gertrude on the tip of his tongue when the sound of laughter suddenly rang out across the deck. Turning from the railing, his attention was captured by the sight of Gertrude walking toward him. She was laughing at something Edwina was saying and had her arm entwined with Edwina's, quite as if she'd known his sister for years. On Gertrude's other side were Permilia and Temperance Flowerdew, both of whom were laughing as well. What they were laughing about, though, Harrison had no idea, because an odd buzzing noise had settled in his ears, making it difficult to hear.

The only idea he seemed to have left in his head was that Gertrude, now wearing a rather fine dress of palest blue, or at least he thought it was blue, was looking very delightful indeed.

Tilting his head, he considered her closely, unable to help but wonder if she was looking so delightful to him because she'd done something different with her hair. It was no longer parted into two buns anchored directly over her ears, but was now drawn up in a knot on top of her head, with little wispy bits of golden curls tumbling out of that knot that were caressing what he just then noticed were very delightful-looking cheeks.

As the most curious feeling began churning through him, Harrison found himself rooted to the spot, wondering if his captivation with Gertrude was some odd result of Asher suggesting he should consider viewing her in a more romantic light.

His pondering on the subject was interrupted when Asher took hold of his arm and began prodding Harrison forward in a somewhat determined fashion.

"And so it begins," Asher said with a distinct trace of amusement in his voice.

"So what begins?" Harrison managed to get out of a mouth that was now unusually dry.

"Your transition into a poet, of course."

With that, Asher released a bit of a laugh and increased their pace, ushering Harrison straight in Gertrude's direction.

CHAPTER EIGHT

Dashing at eyes that were watering due to the laughter she was sharing with her friends, Gertrude lifted her head and found Harrison standing a few feet away from her, the sight of him causing her to swallow the laugh she'd been about to release.

It wasn't that she'd lost the ability to laugh because she was faced with a most dashing gentleman — because there was no question that Harrison aptly fit that description. Having spent so much time in his company over the past few months, she'd grown accustomed to his appearance, but what did have her slowing her steps, and then coming to a complete stop, was the manner in which he was watching her.

There was something curious in his eyes, something she couldn't quite put a finger on, but it almost seemed as if he'd taken to watching her as if he'd never seen her before in his life.

Truth be told, she couldn't help but wonder if he was considering her so closely to discern whether she had the look of a thief about her, or wondering when she was planning to make off with the prized painting hanging in the library, an idea she knew Clementine had planted in his head.

As her cheeks began heating, even with a sea breeze sending its cooling mist over her face, Gertrude squared her shoulders and tried to sort through thoughts that had taken to jumbling every which way. She wasn't certain what she should say, but a hushed atmosphere was now settled over the small group assembled on the deck, broken only by an occasional clearing of a throat coming from Asher that, oddly enough, seemed to be tinged with a hint of amusement.

Lifting her chin, Gertrude managed to get an impressive "Ah . . ." out of her mouth, but then found no other words seemed to want to follow, which left her floundering again.

Fortunately, Edwina, who was standing directly by her side, did not seem to be floundering in the least. She stepped forward, marched her way across the small space that separated her from her brother, and poked Harrison in the arm.

"What in the world is the matter with you, Harrison, and why are you standing there with your mouth gaping open and looking as if you've just spotted a ghost, or . . ." Edwina drew back her arm and sucked in a rather loud breath of air. "Where is Mrs. Davenport? Do not tell me that Margaret won the day in the end and threw her in some type of makeshift brig, or worse yet, sent her and that annoying Clementine Flowerdew adrift in one of our dinghies. I mean, granted, Clementine does seem to be a bit of a nightmare, but she's well connected socially from what I've been able to gather, and I'll never be invited to another society event if you've allowed her to be cast out to sea."

Harrison blinked, blinked again, and then, surprisingly enough, grinned. "Surely you must realize that I would hardly be standing here having a little chat with you if Margaret had cast those two ladies adrift."

Edwina reached out and poked her brother again, then apparently decided that wasn't enough poking, so she did it again. "Margaret was completely put out with the situation, Harrison, and you know she's not one to deal gently with society members. I could easily believe she would cast two annoying society members adrift. And if they

128

haven't been sent out to sea, where, pray tell, are they?"

"Adelaide, being a most sensible sort, saw to it that they were escorted from the yacht after we drew up next to the pier."

Edwina narrowed her eyes. "Why did Adelaide have to do such an unpleasant task?"

"Because she's a kind soul?"

Edwina's eyes narrowed to mere slits. "You made a great escape from the wheel-house, didn't you?"

"Since you did the very same thing, I don't think you should be pointing out the error of my ways," Harrison shot back. "And . . . what did you mean, you'll never be invited to *another* society event?"

Waving that straight aside, Edwina tilted her head. "Are you quite certain Mrs. Davenport and Clementine were seen safely to the Manhattan Beach Hotel?"

"Since Adelaide assured me that she personally saw those two ladies into one of the many carriages the hotel sent to the pier to pick up our guests, I can say with relative certainty that they made it safely to the hotel. And —" he held up his hand when Edwina opened her mouth — "given that my very good friend, Mr. Cavendish, has been assisting me with pulling off the event at the hotel, and because he is known to be a most charming gentleman, I would imagine he personally escorted Miss Flowerdew and Mrs. Davenport into the ballroom we'll be using this evening. He's probably even gone so far as to see them well settled with a refreshing glass of wine. So, that's that, and with Mrs. Davenport's and Miss Flowerdew's exposure to Margaret limited, I'm going to declare here and now that there was little harm done."

Another poke in the arm was Edwina's first reaction to that before she began speaking again, this time in a voice that had risen by a good octave. "Little harm done? You can't treat society members so willy-nilly. And while I admit that Mr. Cavendish is a delightful gentleman, and well connected, it would have eased the troubling situation tremendously if *you* would have personally escorted Mrs. Davenport and Miss Flowerdew from the ship and into a carriage because that would have certainly gone far in soothing their tender society feelings."

Before Harrison had a chance to respond to what was clearly a tirade on his sister's part, Temperance stepped forward, although she was looking quite unlike her usual self. If he wasn't much mistaken, she was also wearing one of Edwina's gowns, and had apparently benefited from his sister's skill with styling hair since Temperance's dark hair was no longer pulled into a severe knot on the back of her neck, but was styled almost identically to Gertrude's.

"I'm very much afraid, Edwina," Temperance began, "that if your brother had escorted Clementine to the hotel, it could have turned his world topsy-turvy. He would have been woefully unprepared for the assault I fear Clementine has decided to wage to win his affections."

Harrison took a single step backward. "Your cousin wants to assault me?"

"Not a physical assault," Temperance returned. "An assault more along the lines of *using every feminine ploy* she has at her disposal, one where fluttering lashes, breathy sighs, and even a few carefully planned damsel-in-distress scenarios will most certainly be directed your way."

"Any suggestion on how I might avoid this assault?" Harrison asked.

Temperance bit her lip. "I have no idea except to perhaps suggest you make plans to travel extensively over the summer and hopefully in a different country."

Harrison frowned. "That seems a little excessive, and isn't actually feasible because I do need to oversee production of numerous ships currently being built down at the

New York City docks."

"Perhaps you should simply find a lovely young lady and proceed to court her, which will sufficiently take care of the problem of several ladies trying to pursue you once and for all," Asher suggested, sending Gertrude a bit of a wink, one that left her with the distinct feeling Permilia wasn't the only newly-in-love person who seemed to be embracing a matchmaking attitude.

Harrison, fortunately, missed that wink, but then he shook his head, that telling motion sending an unexpected wave of disappointment coursing through Gertrude's veins.

"As I keep saying, I'm perfectly content with my life, and unwilling to change that life simply because rumor has it I'm soon to be in demand."

"That is hardly embracing the spirit of a poet," Gertrude thought she heard Asher mumble before he exchanged a look with Permilia. He evidently read something in her look, because he then smiled a charming smile and nodded to the group at large.

"While pondering Harrison's dilemma is certainly a most riveting way to spend an evening, we do have guests awaiting our arrival at the Manhattan Beach Hotel. Shall we get on our way and see what other exciting entertainments we may encounter this evening?"

Edwina was the first to move, striding across the deck toward the plank. She looked over her shoulder. "No time to linger. There are amusements waiting for us."

Harrison took a step toward his sister. "I wasn't aware you were accompanying us, Edwina."

Edwina turned and sent her brother a lovely smile. "Gertrude issued me an invitation. She was under the misimpression it was a simple oversight on your part that I wasn't invited, even though you and I know that isn't the truth." She narrowed her eyes at Harrison. "However, since all the etiquette books I've recently read suggest it's bad form to refuse an invitation that's so graciously offered, I had no choice but to accept." Edwina darted a look to Temperance. "I am right about that etiquette business, aren't I?"

Temperance smiled and joined Edwina, taking hold of her arm. "Very nicely done, Edwina, and now, before your departure is thwarted with some argument on your brother's part, we should go, and quickly." With that, Temperance, a lady who appeared to be coming out of the meek and reserved shell Gertrude had always known her to embrace, sent Harrison a cheeky grin before she practically ran toward the plank, Edwina matching her every step.

"Wait for us!" Permilia called, pulling Asher after them and disappearing down the plank behind Edwina and Temperance a moment later.

Left all alone on the deck with Harrison, Gertrude turned his way, finding him looking somewhat bemused. Shaking his head, he caught her eye.

"Why do I get the distinct feeling I've just lost a battle I wasn't aware I was fighting?"

"Your sister is adorable, and I'm quite certain because of that you're often on the losing side of whatever battle she decides to wage against you."

Harrison smiled. "She does know a thing or two about thwarting me, although I must say I'm still a little taken aback by all the other battles that are apparently being waged against me, especially the ones pertaining to matters of pursuit, and . . ." He suddenly stopped talking when someone called out to him from across the deck.

Glancing toward where the voice had sounded, Gertrude discovered a lady heading their way from the direction of the wheelhouse. She was dressed all in black and gesturing wildly toward the plank, even while her mouth moved furiously. It was anyone's guess, though, what she was saying, since the wind was whipping her words right out to sea.

"It's my sister Margaret, and she's not looking happy," Harrison said. "Take my hand."

A second later, with her hand held firmly in Harrison's, Gertrude was pulled into a run, in the opposite direction of the plank for some curious reason, while his sister began calling his name in a voice loud enough now for everyone to hear.

"Whatever you do, don't let her know we've seen her."

"Don't you think she's probably figured that out since we're running away from her?" Gertrude managed to ask even though she was developing a stitch in her side that was making running and talking a little tricky.

"Excellent point, but we can't stop now because, well, she'll catch us for certain."

"She might have a more difficult time catching us if we weren't still on the boat," Gertrude said, drawing in a painful breath, the pain a direct result of her suddenly remembering she was laced far too tightly into her corset and didn't have much room for extra air.

"Another excellent point, but I was trying to confuse her," Harrison said before he slowed ever so slightly and caught her eye. "Why are you grimacing?"

"Stitch in my side" was all Gertrude had to say before Harrison stopped moving completely, cast a look over his shoulder, then turned and scooped her straight up into his arms.

"Goodness," she managed to say in a voice that sounded rather faint even to her ears as he brought her directly against a finely muscled chest. He tightened his grip on her right before he broke into a run.

As his feet pounded against the boards of the deck, Gertrude couldn't help but notice that they were traveling at a remarkable rate, that rate not laboring his breathing in the least. She found that state of affairs to be incredibly impressive, especially since she knew full well she'd never been what anyone would have considered a waif of a woman.

Glancing up, she found her attention mesmerized by the sight of a strong jaw that was only inches away from her face, but before she could truly appreciate the sight, Harrison turned a corner and then they were running down the plank.

As he whisked her off the yacht, pursued

by a now furious-sounding woman, Gertrude grinned when a most peculiar thought sprang to mind.

With his dark hair escaping the confines of his ribbon, Harrison had the look of a pirate about him, one who was absconding at breakneck speed with a fair damsel he'd decided to capture and make his own.

Even knowing that idea was completely ridiculous because pirates were unlikely to abscond with an ordinary woman, Gertrude allowed herself to enjoy the moment, knowing there was little chance she'd ever experience the thrill of being whisked off a yacht in the arms of a dashing man ever, ever again.

CHAPTER NINE

As he reached the New Iron Pier, Harrison flashed a smile to all the people who were gawking as he ran past them. Given the looks of astonishment on their faces, it was clear they were surprised to witness a man dashing away from a ship with a woman clutched in his arms. Odd as it seemed, he couldn't help but wonder if they were now expecting him to disclose something of a dastardly nature that would explain such an unusual occurrence.

If that were the case, he had no explanation readily available because it certainly wasn't as if it was a normal happenstance to haul a young lady off one of his ships in his arms, but truth be told, he simply had not been able to help himself.

The mere sight of Gertrude in what could only be described as a state of distress, what with her wheezing and gasping for breath, along with proclaiming the unfortunate

138

news that she'd developed a stitch in her side, which everyone knew could be incredibly painful, had brought out a surprisingly strong sense of protectiveness in him. That protectiveness had then prompted him to sweep Gertrude up into his arms, rather like he imagined one of the heroes would have done in the romance novels his sisters were so fond of reading.

That he'd read a good many of those romances was not something he'd ever shared with his sisters — or anyone for that matter. But because he had read them, and had done so to discern if he could possibly gain a small measure of understanding about women in the process, he'd concluded that because the sweeping incidents happened frequently between the pages of those books, ladies seemed to enjoy that particular action.

Gertrude, he hadn't neglected to notice, had not let out even a peep of protest when he'd snatched her up. That right there had him wondering if she, perhaps, might possess a more romantic nature than he'd expected to discover in a woman who seemed to be a most practical sort. Although why he'd suddenly turned his thoughts toward romance was a little disconcerting, especially since he was in the midst of an unusual situation that had him whisking a woman down a . . .

"While I willingly admit that this is a most thrilling and unexpected way in which to depart from a ship, Harrison," Gertrude suddenly said, pulling him abruptly from his thoughts, "I should probably tell you that the stitch in my side has disappeared, which means you should probably set me down before you injure yourself due to my, er, weight."

Harrison stopped dead in his tracks. Dipping his head, he caught her eye and found that the words he'd been about to say, something having to do with it being laughable he'd injure himself simply from carrying her, evaporated straight from his mind. That, unfortunately, left him with nothing whatsoever to say as he suddenly found himself mesmerized by Gertrude's eyes.

It wasn't that most people would consider her eyes to be extraordinary, since they were a very ordinary shade of green, or at least he thought they were green. But mixed in with that color were little flecks of what might be gold, which he found utterly fascinating. Leaning closer, he stilled when he heard her suck in a sharp breath, realizing in that moment he was hardly behaving in an acceptable manner since anyone who was watching them would surely conclude he was considering kissing her. In all honesty, now that he thought about it, that idea was curiously compelling.

Blinking that type of thinking away because he'd only recently proclaimed that he was not interested in forming a romantic association with any lady due to his demanding schedule and work obligations, he rustled around his scattered thoughts, summoning up an impressive, "You have very nice eyes," which promptly earned him a rolling of those nice eyes in the process.

"One could almost make the case that you have a tongue for flattery when you utter phrases like that," Gertrude said as her lips curved. "However, glib tongue aside, you have yet to release me, which is hardly going to aid our escape from your sister. If you've neglected to notice, we've allowed your sister plenty of time to close any distance that may have separated us. Frankly, I'm somewhat surprised she hasn't already caught up to us, which only increases the sense of dread I'm experiencing because she's now had far too much time to compose what she wants to say."

Turning back toward his yacht with Gertrude still held in his arms, a circumstance he knew he was continuing if only to prove to her that he was perfectly capable of holding her for an infinite amount of time, he noticed he'd managed to travel quite a distance from the *Cornelia.* He smiled when he caught not so much as a glimpse of Margaret.

"If I were to hazard a guess, I'd say Margaret has abandoned the chase, probably because there are other boats behind the *Cornelia* that are waiting to deposit their passengers."

"I thought the *Cornelia* would stay in that spot until we returned from the hotel."

"While that would be very convenient, I'm afraid that's not how it's done. The New Iron Pier was built to provide a landing spot for ships carrying passengers heading to Coney Island for an afternoon or evening of fun. However, those ships have to depart somewhat quickly since there are always other ships waiting to let their passengers disembark at the pier."

"Where will your ship go?"

"Margaret will steer her out to sea and drop anchor. She and Adelaide will then keep watch for my signal after we're finished at the Manhattan Beach Hotel. Once they see my signal, which is simply flashing a light out to sea with a code we've devised, they'll return and we'll be on our way back to the city."

"Is that why you didn't bother to issue an invitation to your sisters to join in the festivities at the hotel — because they're expected to mind the ship?"

Harrison frowned. "Not at all. I didn't issue an invitation to my sisters because Margaret and I discussed it earlier. And we decided that withholding an invitation from Edwina would allow us to avoid annoying our mother in the end." He sighed. "It might have been beneficial if my mother had bothered to explain how determined Edwina was becoming in her quest to enter society when she asked me to keep a watchful eye on my sister. That would have allowed me to be better prepared for Edwina's unexpected attack. Although, now that I consider the matter, Margaret might have been my mother's true confidante in this, because while Margaret is known to have a bit of a temper, she normally doesn't bother to chase after me to take me to task."

Gertrude cleared her throat. "I was wondering if perhaps your sister was chasing me, not you. She was told I'm considering making off with that painting of your mother's, and pair that with the argument I understand she had with Mrs. Davenport, well, she probably feels she has just cause to seek an audience with me."

Harrison rested his chin on top of Gertrude's head, a convenient place to rest since he was still carrying her and her head was positioned in exactly the right place. "I'm sure Margaret didn't believe Clementine's accusation since she rarely puts much stock in anything a member of the fashionable set says. But I will admit that I shudder to think what would happen if that particular painting did go missing since it's one of my mother's prized possessions."

"Perhaps you should consider hanging it in a more secure place than on a ship. Ships do tend to sink, if I'm not mistaken."

"An excellent point, but since the *Cornelia* is named after my mother, and since she was thrilled to learn I wanted to name my yacht after her, she decided one of her prized possessions had to have a place of honor on board my yacht, for luck if you will." He smiled. "If you haven't heard, we of the shipping sort do tend to hold our superstitions fast to us at all times, and good luck symbols are to be taken very, very seriously."

"Then let us hope your fine yacht always remains above the water, and that no one of the criminal persuasion ever targets your ship for plunder."

"Once word gets out about Margaret and her desire to throw someone in the brig, I doubt anyone of the criminal set will bother stepping foot on our ship. My sister has a reputation down on the docks for being somewhat frightening, and once our crew spreads this latest tale around, the one regarding Margaret and Mrs. Davenport, I imagine that will be quite enough to keep thieves away."

Gertrude seemed to stiffen in his arms, right before she let out a little laugh. "And thank goodness for that. However, matters of thievery aside, I do think it might be for the best for you to finally set me down. We're attracting a lot of attention, and while I know you're a most intimidating gentleman, there's a group of men over there watching us rather closely. I would hate for them to come to the conclusion you're up to nefarious purposes, which might end with you embroiled in a brawl."

Lifting his head, Harrison narrowed his eyes on the men in question, men who were considering not him but Gertrude, and considering her in a way that was far too intense for his comfort. Setting her to her feet, he drew himself to his full height, returned his attention to the men, then quirked a single brow their way.

Being a gentleman who was more than capable of holding his own in a fight, even when the odds were not in his favor, he stepped in front of Gertrude and clenched his hands into fists. Before he could take another step forward, though, Gertrude was right by his side again, holding on to his arm with one hand while waving cheerfully at the men now smiling and waving back at her in response.

"While I certainly appreciate you being willing to defend my honor," she said, continuing to smile, "they're not bad men, Harrison. They simply were trying to ascertain whether I needed their assistance or not. And since I've now shown them I'm fine, let us be on our way."

Without allowing him a second to do more than send another scowl to the waving and smiling gentlemen, Gertrude somehow managed to get him turned around and striding down the pier, her pace so rapid she began wheezing a moment later.

"I would have been able to hold my own," he said, glancing over his shoulder to make certain they weren't being followed, which they weren't. "Although I do thank you for trying to keep me from harm."

Gertrude stopped walking and turned to face him. "I wasn't worried about you."

"Oh" was all he could think to respond as the last vestiges of temper he'd been feeling immediately disappeared. "Well, right then."

She tugged him back into motion, and feeling much more charitable with the world at large, he spent the rest of their walk down the pier pointing out items of interest. After explaining what little he knew about the two pavilions that sat on both ends of the pier, and stopping for a brief moment to enjoy the music of the regimental brass band that was hired each season to entertain visitors to Coney Island and the pier, they reached the end of the pier. Helping her to the boardwalk, he watched her eyes widen as she took in the sights.

"Forgive me, Gertrude, but I neglected to realize that you've evidently never been to Coney Island before. That seems rather odd because you're clearly a lady possessed of an adventurous nature, and nothing screams adventure quite like Coney Island."

Gertrude swung her attention back to him. "Where in the world did you get the idea I'm a lady possessed of an adventurous nature?"

"You're a companion to Mrs. Davenport. You'd have to be an adventurous sort if only to keep up with her."

Her brows drew together. "I suppose I

never looked at it quite like that, but I'm afraid I'm not widely traveled. Mrs. Davenport is content to remain in the city except for when we repair to her cottage in Newport. And while she does mention going to Paris to take in the sights and visit the designers there, I'm afraid that simply mentioning Paris is as close as we've gotten to that intriguing city." She looked away. "Which way to the hotel?"

Smiling, he turned her in the right direction and began walking again. He kept a firm grip on her arm, making certain she didn't stumble, while also keeping her well away from the many men who kept turning to stare at her as they continued down the boardwalk.

Needing a distraction so he wouldn't be tempted to threaten those men with bodily harm since Gertrude had proven herself to be overly concerned for gentlemen she apparently found harmless, but he found nothing of the sort, he cleared his throat and forced a smile. "While I can't sail you all the way to Paris this summer because I have so many business matters to attend to in the city, I'm planning a trip back to Long Island next week. I'd enjoy bringing you and Mrs. Davenport with me. We could attend this charming little country church, the Flatbush Reformed Dutch Church to be exact, where a friend of mine, Reverend David Sturgis, always gives a wonderful sermon. After that, we can share a small adventure of taking a picnic lunch to a wonderful cove I've put anchor in many times before, and . . . we could even enjoy a swim in the water if you enjoy swimming."

"I do enjoy swimming," Gertrude said, "although I haven't been in the ocean for years. But tell me more about this church. I've never heard of the Flatbush Reformed Dutch Church."

"It's one of the oldest parishes on Long Island. Because I have a house on Long Island, although it's on the farthest end, I enjoy taking the train on Sunday mornings to hear Reverend Sturgis's sermons."

"You have a house on Long Island?"

"I do, as well as in New York, and a few other places scattered around the world."

"Goodness, I can't imagine owning one house, let alone several." She released a bit of a sigh. "But returning to the idea of a day spent with you on Long Island, and joining you at what sounds like a delightful little church, I'm afraid Mrs. Davenport is a bit peculiar when it comes to churches. She only attends Grace Church in the city and doesn't bother with church at all when we travel to her cottage in Newport."

"Would she be opposed to you taking a day off to travel to Long Island with me? She wouldn't need to be concerned about propriety because my sisters would be with us as well."

Gertrude shook her head. "It's not that she would oppose the idea, it's more that I wouldn't be comfortable leaving her behind to attend services at Grace Church on her own. Mrs. Davenport can occasionally become, well, I don't know how to explain it except to say that there have been times when she's become overwrought during a service, which is why I make myself available to her every Sunday."

"Overwrought because she's so moved by the words of the sermon?" Harrison asked.

Gertrude waved his question aside as she nodded to a man who'd just tipped his hat to her. "She barely listens to the sermon, spending most of the time searching for someone."

"And that someone would be . . . God?"

The corners of Gertrude's lips twitched. "That would be the logical assumption to make, but no, I don't think she's looking for divine intervention, although exactly who she's searching for, well, that's anyone's guess."

"You've never asked her about it?"

"I'm Mrs. Davenport's companion, Harrison. I'm not her confidante."

Wanting to question her further, but having spotted one of the Manhattan Beach Hotel's carriages that he'd arranged to transport all the guests from the *Cornelia* to the hotel, he led Gertrude over to it, nodding at the driver, who immediately stepped forward and held open the door.

Helping Gertrude up and into the carriage, Harrison followed, taking a seat opposite her.

"I do hope you know that even though I have to regrettably turn down your offer of a lovely summer excursion, I do appreciate the invitation," Gertrude said as the carriage lurched into motion.

Harrison smiled. "I'm sure we can find another outing that would be suitable for both you and Mrs. Davenport. Perhaps I can take you down the coast. I have numerous business matters to attend to up and down the coast, and I can't recommend the beaches strongly enough."

Considering him for a long moment, Gertrude tilted her head. "You're a good friend to me, Harrison. And while I know I'd enjoy visiting different beaches, I don't believe it would be prudent for us to go off on an adventure together, even with Mrs. Davenport accompanying us. The gossips have evidently begun remarking on the friendship we share, and I fear that gossip would increase tenfold if word got out we'd begun taking trips together."

Harrison opened his mouth, but paused when Gertrude held up a hand.

"You're a very kind gentleman, Harrison, and I will not abuse that kindness by making you the subject for wagging tongues. It would only ruin our friendship in the end."

Not wanting to distress Gertrude further because he thought he detected just a trace of moisture in her eyes, Harrison settled for nodding, even though he was less than willing to accept her refusal. He knew she spoke nothing less than the truth — but that truth was not sitting well with him.

"Besides," Gertrude continued as she summoned up a smile and turned his way, "I don't know if you are aware of this, but I've recently begun teaching classes in deportment at Miss Snook's School for the Education of the Feminine Mind. Even though school is not yet back in session, due to Miss Mabel and Miss Henrietta generously donating their very large mansion off Broadway to Miss Snook as the new location for the school, I fear my spare time this summer will be spent making that mansion more hospitable for the young ladies who are soon to begin taking classes there."

"I would be more than happy to lend my assistance to the school if you need someone who happens to be somewhat competent with building things," he heard himself say before he could stop himself.

Gertrude blinked. "That's a very generous offer, but I was under the impression you have limited time at your disposal."

Realizing he was acting rather curiously, what with his being so tenacious about trying to secure Gertrude's company through one invitation after another, Harrison felt a bead of sweat form on his forehead and begin sliding down his face.

Dashing it aside, and wondering what in the world was wrong with him, he forced a smile when he noticed Gertrude was watching him somewhat warily, then breathed a sigh of relief when the carriage suddenly turned onto the drive that led to the hotel. With that turn, Gertrude stopped watching him, turned to the window, then let out a bit of a gasp as she pressed her nose to the glass.

"Good heavens, I had no idea the Manhattan Beach Hotel would be so very fine, nor did I imagine I'd see such a wonderful manicured lawn leading up to the hotel. Why, even though it's quite dark outside, I would have to imagine that grass takes hours to tend to, and . . . goodness . . . I do believe I see a croquet field, and . . . on my word, it looks like there are guards up ahead, and . . . are they stopping the carriage?" she asked right as the carriage began slowing down.

Harrison looked out the window. "Those aren't simply guards, Gertrude. They're Pinkerton detectives."

Gertrude drew in a sharp breath and pressed her nose against the glass again. "Why in the world would Pinkerton detectives be lurking around the outside of the Manhattan Beach Hotel? Has there been some type of disturbing incident that requires their presence here?"

Moving over to join her on her side of the carriage, Harrison reached for her hand. "There's no need for such concern, Gertrude. The owner of the hotel regularly hires Pinkerton men to protect it. I've been told that man feels it's well worth the cost because it gives his cherished, and need I add wealthy, guests peace of mind."

If anything, his disclosure had Gertrude looking less than peaceful as she began smoothing out the folds of her skirt in what could only be described as an agitated manner.

"Is something the matter?" he finally asked when she started muttering under her breath, something having to do with another disaster in the making.

Looking up at him, she summoned a smile that looked less than convincing. "What could possibly be the matter? It's a lovely evening. I'm attending an engagement celebration of one of my dearest friends, and I'll be safely guarded while I'm enjoying that celebration by what sounds like an entire brigade of Pinkerton detectives."

"Why does the presence of the Pinkerton detectives seem to concern you so much? They're here for your protection."

Gertrude's smile faltered, but then she hitched it back into place and gave an airy wave of a hand. "Of course it doesn't concern me. If you've forgotten, I'm well acquainted with the Pinkerton agents, or at least the ones Asher hired only a few months back when his life was threatened, especially Agent McParland." Her eyes suddenly widened. "Now, that would really put me at ease if he was on duty here tonight. He seems to be a most competent sort, and . . . understanding."

Harrison heard nothing after Gertrude

mentioned a Pinkerton by name. "You remember that Pinkerton's name?"

"Of course. He was a lovely man. . . ." Gertrude said almost absently as the carriage began slowing before it came to a complete stop directly in front of the main entrance. Barely turning her head to send him a nod, which Harrison found somewhat curious but didn't question since he was still pondering the Pinkerton disclosure, Gertrude then pushed open the carriage door and disappeared through it before he, the driver, or even the doorman had an opportunity to assist her to the sidewalk.

Not quite understanding what had caused her to behave in such an unexpected fashion, even as the unwelcome thought sprang to mind that Gertrude may have decided she was anxious to discern whether Agent McParland was present at the hotel that evening, Harrison slid across the seat to the carriage door. He then simply sat there and watched Gertrude trundle up the walkway, calling over her shoulder to him about needing to see to her hair.

Whatever else she said, he didn't catch since the wind took that moment to gust around the carriage, taking the rest of Gertrude's words with it.

Ducking through the carriage door that

was now being held by a very confused driver, Harrison exchanged a commiserating smile with the man before he lifted his head and settled his attention on Gertrude again.

She'd almost reached the entrance, and if he wasn't much mistaken, she seemed to be moving at a pace that was practically a run. That curious state of affairs, and coming so quickly after she'd suffered a troubling bout of debilitating stitches in her side, left Harrison wondering if he'd somehow managed to miss a clue regarding why Gertrude was suddenly behaving as if something was horribly, horribly amiss.

CHAPTER TEN

Pressing a hand against a side that was developing another stitch, Gertrude vowed there and then she was going to have to make a diligent effort to participate in more vigorous activities, especially since it did appear as if a pattern was evolving — one that kept seeing her dashing hither, thither, and yon on a far too frequent basis.

She was also going to have to find a moment to seek out a retiring room, and once there, pray that someone would be around to loosen the laces of her corset just a touch. Otherwise, she might very well become the classic portrait of a swooning lady, falling to the ground with a hand fluttering over her forehead. Truth be told, it was quickly becoming apparent she was not a lady who could exist for an extended period of time without a normal amount of air.

Managing a nod to the doorman at the main entrance to the hotel, an impressive four-story wooden structure built in the Queen Anne style, Gertrude hurried over the threshold and then moved across an entranceway that had been built to impress even the most jaded of guests.

Crystal chandeliers hung from the arched ceiling of the lobby, and thick oriental rugs covered large areas of the marble floor, where the bits of marble showing were polished to such an extent that they gleamed in the light cast from the chandeliers. The furniture was upholstered in pastel colors, most of those colors being different hues of yellow paired with a good deal of white, and plants that reminded a person they were enjoying a holiday at the seaside were placed in a charming fashion around the room.

A stone fireplace was flanked by floor-to-ceiling glass doors on the far side of the lobby, ones that unquestionably led to the covered verandas Gertrude had glimpsed as she'd gotten out of the carriage. On the wall adjacent to the fireplace was a long wooden counter. Standing behind that counter was a gentleman formally dressed in a well-cut navy suit, lending him the appearance of a gentleman in authority.

Gertrude made a beeline for that gentleman, then soon found herself ushered through the hotel by a member of the staff.

That man, Mr. Jackson, informed her he'd been employed as a bellhop from the very day the hotel opened, and he turned out to be a very talkative sort.

"Is this your first time to the Manhattan Beach Hotel, Miss Cadwalader?" he inquired as he walked with her down a long hallway, gesturing with his hands time and again to areas of the hotel he thought she'd find interesting.

Gertrude nodded. "I must admit it is, and do know I'm suitably impressed with my surroundings."

"I'll be certain to pass along your praise to the owner, Mr. Austin Corbin."

Before Gertrude had an opportunity to ask a single question about Mr. Corbin, Mr. Jackson launched into a speech about the hotel and its owner, a speech Mr. Jackson had obviously delivered many, many times since he recited it in a voice that might be described as rehearsed.

". . . and then, after he'd purchased this very land we're standing on, although it really was nothing more than a swamp at that time, Mr. Corbin used his influence as the president of Long Island Railroad to construct the New York and Manhattan Beach Railroad, which has brought the seashore to within one hour of uptown New York."

"How ingenious," Gertrude said when Mr. Jackson stopped talking and sent an expectant look her way.

"Indeed, and if you'll believe this, Mr. Corbin was then able to get former president Ulysses S. Grant to attend the grand opening of the hotel on July 4, 1877, which was my very first day escorting guests and their luggage about the hotel."

"It sounds as if you truly do enjoy your position."

"I do, and —" Mr. Jackson continued with barely a breath taken — "I've been privileged to escort Mrs. Astor to her room, as in *The* Mrs. Astor. And I've even carried the luggage of Mr. Ward McAllister, earning a bit of praise from that gentleman when he proclaimed himself delighted that I'd not banged up his favorite traveling trunk while whisking it off to his room."

"Mr. McAllister is known to be rather stingy with his praise, so you should take great satisfaction in having gotten that out of him."

Mr. Jackson motioned Gertrude down another hallway before beaming a smile at her. "Oh, I do take satisfaction in that, Miss Cadwalader, although I do wish high society would spend more of their summer at our resort instead of only dropping by for a day or two." His smile faded ever so slightly. "Do you believe, being a member of that society, there will come a day when Long Island is considered just as fashionable as Newport?"

"Since Newport society is incredibly selective regarding who it'll allow into their hallowed midst, I see no reason for Long Island to not become increasingly fashionable as more of the nouveau riche descend on this part of the country," Gertrude said. "Although, because race tracks have begun taking a firm hold on Long Island, there will be some members of the more established Knickerbocker set who will never embrace this location because they are vehemently opposed to gambling, race tracks, and all that comes with those pursuits."

"Speaking of the race tracks, did I mention to you that the Jockey Club uses this hotel as their summer headquarters?"

"You did not, but what a lovely hotel for the Jockey Club to have at its disposal," Gertrude said before she frowned. "However, on a different note, why did you assume I'm a member of high society? I don't recall saying anything that implied as much."

Mr. Jackson waved away her question. "Your name, of course, Miss Cadwalader. Everyone knows the Cadwalader name is well-regarded throughout New York." He slowed his pace, much to her relief since the stitch in her side had yet to fully disappear, and smiled. "I do hope we here at the Manhattan Beach Hotel can now count on you to sing our praises to your family, which I would have to believe will go far in convincing them to visit this fine, fine resort."

Unwilling to admit to the overly earnest gentleman smiling so expectantly her way that she wasn't on what anyone would consider overly familiar or good terms with her extended relations, Gertrude settled for simply sending Mr. Jackson a nod before she turned the conversation right back to talk of the hotel.

Mr. Jackson was more than happy to speak further on that subject, which allowed Gertrude to remain silent as he rattled off one interesting tidbit after another. In the process, Gertrude found herself possessed of knowledge that now included that the Manhattan Beach Hotel possessed over one hundred and fifty guest rooms, numerous shops that sold a wide variety of goods, and restaurants to tempt every palate; for those guests who enjoyed taking a dip in the salty sea, the hotel provided over twenty-five hundred single bathing huts that were located at the edge of the ocean. For the guest who preferred to bathe in the ocean with his or her friends, the hotel also had additional bathing huts that could accommodate up to six guests at a time.

As they turned down yet another hallway, Gertrude felt just a smidgen of relief when Mr. Jackson finally came to a stop, especially since she was getting a bit winded from trying to keep up with his long-legged pace, that pace having increased with every new tidbit that passed his lips.

"Here you are, Miss Cadwalader," he said with a flourish of his hand toward a door before them. "You'll find your friends in that ballroom, and I do hope you enjoy your evening and come back and visit us soon."

Presenting her with a bow, Mr. Jackson turned and walked away without another word, leaving Gertrude smiling fondly after the man who'd imparted what seemed like the hotel's entire history in the span of time it had taken them to reach their destination. Heading for the room she'd just been shown, Gertrude nodded to another staff member who stepped forward and held the door for her, finding herself a mere moment later standing in a lovely ballroom.

It was not an overly large setting, which leant it a welcoming atmosphere, that atmosphere aided by the chandeliers that were responsible for the soft light flickering around the room. Gazing around, she found round tables draped in fine linen set up along the very edge of a parquet floor, those tables set to perfection with crystal glasses and highly polished silverware. A breeze tinted with the scent of the sea glided in through open doors that faced the ocean.

Mixed in with the scent of the sea was a hint of the meal that was undoubtedly soon to come, one that would certainly be nothing less than delicious. Given the tightness of the laces that were squeezing her somewhat relentlessly, though, she was resigned to the idea she'd be able to do nothing more than merely nibble her way through a portion of that delicious meal, even if she could find someone to loosen her laces a little.

Craning her neck, Gertrude resorted to standing on tiptoe as she tried to find Mrs. Davenport, but before she got so much as a glimpse of her target, she was distracted by the sight of Clementine marching her way, smiling far too brightly.

"There you are!" Clementine exclaimed, surprising Gertrude when she pulled her into an unexpected hug, the surprise disappearing straightaway when Clementine began whispering urgently in Gertrude's ear.

"May I dare hope that your tardiness is a direct result of you having a little chat with Mr. Sinclair — one that revolved around me and my desire to have that gentleman turn his affections my way?"

"Ah" was all Gertrude seemed capable of summoning up, which had Clementine taking a telling step away from her as her smile dimmed and her eyes turned hard.

"You didn't even bother to broach the topic of me to Mr. Sinclair, did you?"

"I do think your name was broached, but . . ." Gertrude released a breath. "I'm afraid I must tell you some most distressing news — Mr. Sinclair proclaimed himself uninterested in forming an attachment with any lady at the moment, stating that he's far too consumed with matters of business to be distracted with matters of the heart, or . . . er . . . something similar to that."

Clementine's mouth dropped open for a second before she pressed her lips together, then nodded before she drew in a breath and moved closer to Gertrude again. "Am I supposed to believe that you told Mr. Sinclair that I was interested in procuring his affections, and then he said all that instead of proclaiming himself delighted to learn of my interest?"

"I wouldn't say I was quite that specific with Harrison," Gertrude began. "It was more a case of the crowd gathered with us speaking in a general manner about ladies and attachments, and then he proclaimed himself currently uninterested in those very attachments."

Clementine gave a sad shake of her head. "You were hoping he'd declare himself interested in you, weren't you? And now you're trying to convince me that the gentleman is not interested in ladies in general, which, in your twisted spinster mind, must have you believing you still stand a chance with him."

"I don't recall mentioning anything about me hoping he'd declare himself. But speaking of twisted . . . why in the world would you have told Harrison that I was intending to steal his painting? You know I was intending nothing of the sort, and besides, do you really believe that was a prudent move with you still apparently wanting me to help you?" Gertrude asked, annoyance sliding through her when she realized Clementine wasn't listening to a word she was saying because she was absorbed with something over Gertrude's shoulder.

"Ah, there he is now," Clementine all but purred as she raised a hand and smoothed it over hair that was not out of place. Lowering that hand a moment later, she sent Gertrude a nod. "If you'll excuse me, it's now become remarkably clear that *if* I'm going to secure Mr. Sinclair's affections, and secure those affections before the summer season begins in earnest, I'll need to do that myself." Turning on her heel, Clementine glided away without another word, straight in the direction of Harrison, who'd just walked into the ballroom.

A moment later, Clementine was clutching the arm Harrison had extended to her, looking for all intents and purposes as if she was the cat who'd been given a very large dish of cream.

Unable to help but notice that Harrison seemed to be less than affected by the great deal of lash fluttering sent his way from a now beaming and slightly smug-looking Clementine, Gertrude felt her lips twitch before she turned back to the crowd that had assembled in the ballroom. Glancing over the guests who seemed to be enjoying themselves as they sampled delicacies from the many trays being offered to them by members of the staff, Gertrude set about the daunting task of trying to run Mrs. Davenport to ground yet again. She could only hope that during the time Mrs. Davenport had been at the hotel, she'd not yet delved into any mischief.

"There you are, Gertrude," Permilia exclaimed, walking up to join her. "But where's Harrison?"

"He's being entertained by the oh-so-delightful Clementine Flowerdew, who practically accosted him the moment the poor man stepped into this room."

Permilia's brows drew together. "Did the two of you have a falling out on the way here?"

"Of course not. Why would you assume that?"

"Because it seems unusually cruel of you to throw Harrison to the wolves that way, or in this case, throw him to Clementine, especially considering Temperance disclosed to us how determined her cousin is to secure a proposal from him."

Gertrude looked around, then leaned closer to Permilia and lowered her voice. "I'm afraid there was no choice but to leave Harrison to his own devices after I learned the Pinkerton detectives are prowling around this very hotel."

Permilia reached out and gave Gertrude's

arm a bit of a rub. "Allow me to set your mind at ease. Mrs. Davenport has not been wandering about on her own. She was waiting for us in the lobby, and while I will admit she did seem to be slightly interested in the guests who were wandering about, most of whom were dripping in jewels, she abandoned that interest the moment I introduced her to Edwina." Permilia nodded to where a small orchestra was setting up. "They've tucked themselves away behind the musicians and are having a lovely chat even as we speak."

Instead of being put at ease, Gertrude felt a distinct trace of alarm run over her. "It's never a good sign when Mrs. Davenport tucks herself away, even if she is in the presence of another lady."

"There's relatively little trouble she can find back there, Gertrude. Which is why I'm going to encourage you to relax your vigilance in keeping an eye on your companion, at least for the moment, which will then allow me to introduce you to a lovely gentleman by the name of Mr. Gilbert Cavendish."

Before Gertrude knew it, Permilia was holding fast to her hand, pulling her across the ballroom floor at such a fast clip Gertrude was once again finding herself winded.

Digging in her heels when she began feeling distinctly light-headed, she caught Permilia's eye when her friend finally stopped and sent her a quirk of a brow.

"Do you not care to meet Mr. Cavendish?" Permilia asked.

"Not if I have to gallop across the room in order to become introduced to him since, if you've neglected to notice, I'm having difficulty breathing. And," she continued when it looked to her as if Permilia was trying not to grin, "even though it's troubling, not being able to breathe, I actually find it more troubling that you seem to have turned yourself into a matchmaker, first with Harrison, and now with this Mr. Cavendish."

"Mr. Cavendish, or Gilbert, as I'm sure he'll insist you call him, is a most charming man, possessed of a handsome face and pleasant disposition, along with being suitably ambitious, and" — she nodded somewhat smugly — "I've been told he's related to the Earl of Strafford, as in a living and breathing aristocrat over in England."

"You do realize there'd be little point in remarking on that relation if that aristocrat *weren't* breathing, don't you?"

Permilia patted Gertrude's arm. "Now you're simply being difficult. It wouldn't hurt for you to at least meet Gilbert. As I mentioned, he's charming."

"Would you really point out anything to the contrary since it appears you're anxious to see every wallflower married?" Gertrude asked, craning her neck in a futile attempt to locate her employer. "And, while it is sweet you're so determined to marry me off, although I do believe you're delusional, I really must go find Mrs. Davenport."

"She's fine."

"Or so you keep claiming, but she won't be fine with the Pinkerton men lurking about. She abhors men of that ilk, and I shudder to think what may happen if one of the detectives stumble upon her acting shifty."

"She's with Edwina, which should dispel your fears because I do think Mrs. Davenport, given the excitement she showed when I introduced her to Harrison's sister, has pushed aside any thought of skullduggery, if only for this evening."

Something unexpected began slithering down Gertrude's spine, something she refused to contemplate. "Why do you think Mrs. Davenport was *so* anxious to become acquainted with Edwina?"

"I believe Edwina proclaiming after she was introduced to Mrs. Davenport that she would be forever in that woman's debt if

Mrs. Davenport might consider bringing her out into society had something to do with the enthusiasm Mrs. Davenport is now displaying."

Gertrude rubbed at the stitch in her side. "And that enthusiasm, which has the makings of disaster written all over it, is exactly why I need to run Mrs. Davenport to ground."

Striding through the ballroom again, Gertrude ignored that her rapid pace was making her light-headed again, but she was forced to a stop before she reached the orchestra when Permilia stepped directly in front of her, blocking her forward momentum.

"I get the curious feeling you're worried about something more than Mrs. Davenport's propensity for shenanigans." And with that, Permilia took a firm grip on Gertrude's arm, and without a by-your-leave, she marched Gertrude over to the far side of the ballroom. Pushing her through a door that led to a wooden veranda, she dropped her hold on Gertrude's arm and lifted her chin.

"So . . . out with it," she said.

"I already told you, I'm just out of sorts because you and I both know this is not an atmosphere Mrs. Davenport behaves well in. There are shiny jewels all over the place, and it's only a matter of time until something catches her interest, and then, well, with the Pinkerton men here, there's every chance she'll get caught before I'm able to make things right for her."

"Mrs. Davenport travels to public places within the city often, and I've never gotten the slightest hint from you that she behaves poorly in those places. From what I've observed, she restricts her unusual habit to private parties and dinners."

"There's always a first time for everything."

"What's really bothering you?"

"You're very annoying."

Permilia's only response to that was a quirk of a delicate brow.

Throwing up her hands, Gertrude moved to the veranda railing and leaned against it. Taking a moment to gather thoughts that turned out to be rather disturbing, she finally turned back to Permilia and released a bit of a sigh.

"It concerns me that Mrs. Davenport is taking such an interest in Edwina because she's never taken an interest in sponsoring a lady before, at least not since I've been in her employ. I simply don't understand why she'd take that interest now, and what it may mean for my continued employment with her."

Permilia's forehead furrowed. "I would have to imagine, what with the attention Harrison has shown you, no matter that ridiculous proclamation he made regarding not having time for ladies, that Mrs. Davenport is now concerned that you may soon leave her employ. Because of that, it's logical to assume her interest in Edwina is an attempt to fill a void she may soon find in her life — that void being the absence of you."

Gertrude drummed her fingers against the railing. "No, I don't believe that's it. It's more likely she's growing bored with me and finds Edwina far more fascinating. In all honesty, I can't say I blame her since Edwina is such a darling lady. But because she's so darling and not boring, I'll soon find myself out on the streets, seeking new employment."

"Surely you must know you're not meant to continue indefinitely as a paid companion, don't you?"

Because Permilia's tone was now edged with disbelief, Gertrude felt her lips begin to curve. "Even though you are my dearest friend, Permilia, you seem to be suffering from a little touch of delusion of late. And, while I realize an unusual pattern seems to be developing — one that has wallflowers, you and Wilhelmina Radcliffe to be exact, turning their backs on their walls and being whisked directly into new, romance-filled lives — that is not a circumstance I ever see happening to me. That means I fully intend to continue as a paid companion, but am now faced with the idea that I might need to start looking for a new lady to be a companion to."

"That's not a good plan at all, especially since I don't see any reason for you not to enjoy a romance-filled life," Permilia argued. "Romance, as can be seen in my case, is not simply for the fashionable set. You, my dear friend, are a delightful lady, and that is why you will find romance in your future, as well as your own very special gentleman."

"I'm ordinary, Permilia, and a realist. That means I've become content living my life in a less than exciting fashion, knowing there is little chance I'll ever make a match of it with some special gentleman. As far as I'm concerned, there's absolutely no reason to believe that I'll ever be anything *but* a paid companion, supplementing my income by teaching a few classes at Miss Snook's School for the Education of the Feminine Mind."

"You're not meant to live an ordinary life, Gertrude."

"As friends, allow us to agree to disagree on that."

Permilia shook her head. "I most certainly will not agree to that, but because we are friends, I'm going to beg a moment more of your time to explain why I'm right and you're wrong."

"Since this is your night, there's really no need for you to beg. It's not as if I'm going to bolt for the door to avoid whatever argument you're about to make, especially since air is a commodity I'm currently in short supply of, which makes even the thought of bolting somewhat prohibitive."

Leaning back against the railing, Permilia smiled. "And that makes you my captive audience, so without further ado, allow me to tell you about a sermon Asher and I had the privilege of listening to in a small church located in Five Points."

"You've been attending church in Five Points?"

"Some of the students at Miss Snook's school spoke highly of this particular church, or more specifically, of Reverend Mingott's refreshingly simple sermons."

"Since this Reverend Mingott's church is in Five Points, may I assume his sermon dealt with accepting the hand God has given a person and being grateful for that hand?"

Permilia laughed. "One would think that would be an appropriate topic for Reverend Mingott's congregation, but no." She immediately sobered. "His message that day centered around the notion of being ordinary and living an ordinary life."

"Which I would imagine is a state of living he encourages his parishioners to embrace since they live in the worst part of the city."

"On the contrary," Permilia countered. "Reverend Mingott encouraged just the opposite, although he began the sermon about an ordinary man who believed he was living life in a contented manner. Reverend Mingott then continued on by explaining that the man participated in ordinary activities, worked an ordinary job, visited every so often with people who embraced the same liking for ordinary experiences, and ended with how the man felt he was doing everything that God would expect of him since he was living a life that might not be exceptional, but was far from dismal."

Permilia smiled. "Reverend Mingott then made one of the most poignant points I've heard in years. He looked out over the congregation and said that even though this man believed he was living a life God would find pleasing — an ordinary life if you will — he was doing nothing of the sort because . . . God doesn't expect His children to live ordinary lives, but extraordinary ones."

"Not everyone is capable of living those extraordinary lives, Permilia," Gertrude pointed out.

"Well, no, not unless a person is willing to give up living an ordinary life on her own and hand that life over to God, trusting Him to lead the way to the path of extraordinary." Permilia moved to Gertrude's side. "That, my dear, dear friend, is what I know God expects and wants for you."

Blinking away tears that had taken her by surprise, Gertrude drew in a breath and forced a smile, unwilling to tell Permilia exactly why she was certain God wanted nothing of the sort for her. She and God had been at odds for years, though she was not a woman who'd turned her back completely on her faith. But because of what she'd endured with her mother years before, along with what had happened to her father, she was not one to put much stock in the belief that God had anything of an extraordinary nature for her to experience in her life. Nor did she believe she deserved a life of anything other than ordinariness since she'd surely disappointed God with the way she'd handled her mother, a woman who'd descended into melancholy to such an extent that she'd —

"Ah, ladies, there you are," Mrs. Davenport called as she stepped onto the veranda, her arm firmly entwined with Edwina's. "I've been sent to fetch the both of you, or at least you, Permilia, because a most charming gentleman by the name of Mr. Gilbert Cavendish has just announced that dinner will be served soon. He also asked me to tell you that before that dinner is served, he's arranged to have the orchestra play a special melody for a special dance, one he chose specifically for you and Asher."

"I wonder if Mr. Cavendish mentioned to Asher that he and I would be opening up the evening with a special dance?" Permilia asked no one in particular before she headed for the door, mentioning something about needing to make certain the special dance wasn't a quadrille.

Smiling after her friend, Gertrude was soon joined at the railing by Mrs. Davenport and Edwina.

"Isn't this a most splendid evening?" Mrs. Davenport began as she stopped directly in front of Gertrude and smiled.

"It's been an interesting one," Gertrude said, not caring for the sudden glint that stole into Mrs. Davenport's eyes or the way she squared her shoulders, which was something Mrs. Davenport always did right before she divulged news of the concerning type.

"I suppose it is interesting at that, but I know you'll find your evening much improved by what I'm about to disclose — that I've decided to . . ." She paused, drew in a breath, but before she could speak, Edwina, looking as if she were about to burst, spoke up.

"Hester wants to repair to Newport for the summer instead of staying in New York," Edwina exclaimed. "And . . . she's offered to introduce me into Newport high society."

"Who in the world is Hester?" Gertrude asked slowly.

Edwina's smile faltered as she glanced to Mrs. Davenport. "Did I mishear you when you encouraged me to use your given name?"

Mrs. Davenport sent a quick glance Gertrude's way before she looked back at Edwina and smiled brightly. "Not at all, dear. My name is Hester."

"I thought your name was Agnes, not that you ever encouraged me to use it," Gertrude said as a temper she'd not been expecting crawled through her veins and her cheeks began to heat. "And, if you'll recall, you and I agreed, *Mrs. Davenport,* that I, being your very weary companion after an eventful winter social season, deserve to spend the summer in New York, far away from society events and obligations."

Edwina raised a hand to her throat, looking rather horrified. "On my word, do forgive me, Gertrude. I had no idea you'd find this news distressing. Do know that I certainly will not press Mrs. Davenport to still take me to Newport because, clearly, you have no desire to go there."

Mrs. Davenport, to Gertrude's annoyance, beamed an even brighter smile Edwina's way. "Of course we'll go to Newport. We've simply taken Gertrude by surprise." She leaned closer to Edwina and lowered her voice, although it was not so low Gertrude couldn't hear her. "Gertrude does not care for surprises, you see, but mark my words, once she has time to grow accustomed to the idea, she'll be pleased with our decision."

Gertrude lifted her chin. "I won't grow accustomed to this idea."

"Think of how fresh the air always is in Newport, and think how delightful it'll be for you to go to the Newport Casino and actually have someone to play tennis with, because Edwina's already mentioned to me she enjoys that activity." Mrs. Davenport nodded. "It'll be a pleasant time for both of you."

"It'll be exhausting for me, as you very well know."

Mrs. Davenport's bottom lip began to quiver, which barely moved Gertrude at all. But when an honest-to-goodness tear leaked out of her eye, Gertrude threw up her hands.

"Fine, we'll go to Newport."

Dashing the tear straight off her face, Mrs. Davenport clapped her hands in delight. "Wonderful! And now that we've settled on that, do know that we'll need to be on our way by the end of this week."

Chapter Eleven

"Who would have ever thought I'd receive such timely assistance from an editor from the *New York Sun*?" Harrison asked, stopping directly in front of Asher as he snagged a glass of champagne from a passing server and took a sip. "There I was, about to lose all feeling in my arm due to the surprising strength of Miss Flowerdew's grip, when from out of nowhere, Mr. Charles Dana joined us. It was a fortuitous arrival to say the least, especially when he began questioning Miss Flowerdew about society intrigues and she was only too happy to throw herself into that nasty business, allowing me the opportunity of making an inconspicuous escape."

Asher frowned. "One would have thought after learning Miss Flowerdew is anxious to become better acquainted with you, you'd have given her a wide berth for the rest of the evening."

"That's a little tricky to do when a young lady is determined to waylay a gentleman, and takes said gentleman by surprise the second he enters a room."

"Women can be tricky."

"Too right they can," Harrison agreed, reaching out to give his friend a hearty and commiserating clap on the back.

Unfortunately, it quickly became clear that clapping a man on the back when he'd just put some tasty tidbit into his mouth was not a particularly good idea because it resulted in a bad case of choking.

Wheezing for breath, Asher's color went from red to purple, which had alarm coursing through Harrison as he stepped close to his friend and gave his back a sound pounding. That pounding came to a rapid end, though, when Asher went from wheezing to sputtering and took an unsteady step *away* from him.

"I'm fine, Harrison, or somewhat so, which means you may feel free to put any additional thoughts of pummeling aside, if you please." Asher fished a handkerchief out of his pocket and began dabbing at his now watering eyes, stilling when his gaze happened to land on Harrison again. Heaving what sounded exactly like a long-suffering sigh, he slid his handkerchief into his pocket before pulling out another length of velvet ribbon. Handing it to Harrison, Asher shook his head.

"I don't have an unlimited supply of those, so do have a care with that one. Far be it from me to point out the obvious, but you wouldn't even have need of the ribbons if you'd simply allow me to introduce you to my barber."

Setting his champagne on a high round table beside him, Harrison took the ribbon and made short shrift of tying his hair back. "If I did get introduced to your barber, I'd then be forced to visit him often to keep my hair looking presentable. Then I'd have to abandon something else in my tight schedule, such as riding my horse in Central Park, which would lead to Rupert, my horse, becoming plump as a partridge. And," he continued as Asher looked ready to argue that very valid point, "if I would agree to the barber, I would then imagine it would only be a matter of time until you'd start badgering me to visit your store on a regular schedule to improve the state of my wardrobe."

"There's nothing wrong with adopting a fashionable attitude," Asher said, gesturing to the formal suit Harrison was wearing. "You're looking very well turned out this evening, and because you used the services of Rutherford & Company's personal stylist, it barely cost you any of your precious time."

Harrison brushed away a small bit of lint from the well-cut sleeve of his jacket. "And while I appreciate you affording me such a dapper appearance this evening, I've just realized that being well turned out is probably why Miss Clementine has been so keen to cling to me. It's your fault she's now got me in her sights, and to avoid similar circumstances in the future, I do believe I'll have to be more hesitant with allowing your stylist to dress me."

For a second, Asher simply considered Harrison, then frowned. "You don't actually dress so outlandishly to dissuade young ladies from pestering you more than they do now, do you?"

Harrison thought about that for a good few seconds. "What an interesting idea, but I'm sure that's not why I choose to pair stripes with plaids. However, my clothing taste, or lack thereof as you strongly believe, aside, have you seen Gertrude of late? I'm afraid I got parted from her when we arrived at the hotel."

"I would have thought you'd do your best to remain firmly attached to Gertrude's side after learning Clementine Flowerdew is intent on securing an offer of marriage from you," Asher said.

"And I would have been content to do exactly that if Gertrude hadn't bolted from the carriage almost before it stopped at the entrance to the hotel. She disappeared from sight before I had the opportunity to catch up with her."

"You didn't do something to annoy her, did you, hence the reason for the bolting?" Asher asked.

"While I would normally proclaim outrage at such a suggestion because I've never been one to annoy the ladies, I've been wondering if I was mistaken in my belief she enjoyed the way I got her safely off the *Cornelia.*"

"Is there more than one way to get off the *Cornelia*?"

"Not usually," Harrison admitted. "But I opted to carry Gertrude down the plank and then down a good stretch of pier, so she might have taken issue with that, although . . . she did proclaim it a thrilling way to depart from a boat, so now that I think further on that, no . . . I don't believe I did anything to annoy her."

"Which is lovely to hear, but getting back to this carrying business — what possessed you to carry Gertrude off your ship in the first place?"

"She was suffering from a stitch in her side and wheezing somewhat dreadfully, brought about no doubt because Margaret was chasing us."

Shaking his head, Asher grinned. "And that right there is why I'm perfectly comfortable not having sisters."

"Indeed, but because I have those sisters, I've been privy to inside information pertaining to the lady world. And that world seems to enjoy gentlemen sweeping young ladies up into their arms when they're in distress, hence the reasoning behind my gallant gesture to Gertrude."

Asher's brows drew together. "Your sisters told you ladies enjoy being swept up into a gentleman's arms?"

"Don't be daft." He leaned close to Asher and lowered his voice. "I got that from reading a few, or perhaps more than a few, romance novels my sisters keep tucked away in the oddest of places."

Asher looked around, then lowered his voice as well. "That's a brilliant strategy, my friend, and one I might have to investigate because I certainly could use some additional insight into the feminine mind, what with me about to be married. But tell me this, besides the sweeping a lady up, have you uncovered any other gestures written between the pages of those books that a lady might find to be swoon-worthy?"

"There are always a few instances of the hero riding to the heroine's rescue on a horse. But I'm not certain I agree with the hero then plucking that heroine straight up and onto the back of his horse. Such an abrupt action makes me wonder if the lady would be left sighing in pleasure or screaming in fear for her very life."

"That is a question to ponder, but tell me this — if Gertrude wasn't annoyed with you for carrying her, why do you imagine she bolted into the hotel?"

Harrison picked up his champagne again and took a sip before he nodded. "Curious as this may sound, her bolting might have had something to do with Agent McParland."

"The Pinkerton detective I hired a few months back?"

"The very same. I think she may fancy him, because after learning that Pinkerton detectives are hired by this hotel, she brought him up in the conversation and then evidently went off to find him, leaving me behind." Harrison shrugged. "Or at least that's one of the reasons I've come up with as to why she dashed into the hotel."

"And here you almost had me convinced you weren't interested in her," Asher said with a shake of his head, but before he could expand on that, they were suddenly joined by Mr. Gilbert Cavendish.

Gilbert was one of Harrison's closest friends, and he'd proven himself worthy of that title over the past few weeks, not hesitating to offer his assistance to Harrison when it became known that Permilia's stepmother had decided to remain in Paris instead of returning to the States to organize Permilia's engagement celebration.

"Gentlemen," Gilbert began with a nod all around, "forgive me for interrupting, but I'm afraid we really do need to get the festivities underway. We're a few minutes from becoming off schedule, and then, well, everything will be cast into disarray."

Harrison blinked. "I'm sure a few minutes won't lead to complete disarray."

Gilbert raked a hand through brown hair that was less than carefully maintained, an unusual circumstance that lent credence to the disarray theory. "I realize that you, Harrison, being a more casual sort, do not understand the distress a gentleman of my sensibilities suffers when events don't go as planned. However, because I did share my

191

schedule with the very temperamental chef who is currently wielding a very large knife back in the kitchen, while making threats to anyone who happens to duck their head into that kitchen to check on the status of dinner, he's expecting everyone to take their seats within the next thirty minutes. That means we really need to get the special dance we've planned for Permilia and Asher underway with all due haste."

Asher choked on the sip of champagne he'd just taken. "You've planned a dance for me and Permilia?" he managed to ask after he caught his breath.

Gilbert frowned. "Surely I mentioned that to you."

"I'm afraid not."

Wincing just the slightest bit, Gilbert nodded and summoned up a charming smile. "Well, I'm telling you now, but there's no need to fear. Harrison told me all about Permilia's lack of interest in performing quadrilles, so I've chosen the delightful Ticklish Water Polka for the two of you to enjoy."

Asher's face turned a somewhat concerning shade of white. "If memory serves me correctly, and I assure you, I do believe it's currently serving me very well, my charming fiancée once maimed a gentleman while performing that particular polka. Because of that disturbing incident, perhaps we should simply forgo the dance, which would then appease what sounds like a very temperamental chef since we won't be late sitting down for his dinner."

Raking his hand through his hair again, Gilbert shook his head. "Absolutely not. Permilia will certainly expect a special gesture on your part, and swirling her about the room while everyone looks on is just such a gesture." He summoned up a smile. "Being the magnanimous friend I am, I give you leave to claim the idea of the dance as your own. That, my dear Asher, will allow you to remind your bride twenty years from now of your thoughtfulness when you take to annoying her by chewing your food too loudly, or . . . by breathing."

"I don't believe Permilia is the type of lady to become annoyed by breathing," Asher said.

"That's because you haven't known her for twenty years," Gilbert countered before he craned his neck and looked over the room. "And, even if she does take to maiming you while you swirl her about the room, something I must say I wouldn't be opposed to watching since I've never seen a person maimed while dancing before, you'll then have *that* memory to pull out and use when needed, something I daresay you'll be thanking me for someday." He stopped craning his neck and took to nodding at something in the distance. "Maiming aside, I've just spotted a fine-looking young lady over there. Would either one of you be so kind as to formally introduce me to her before we sit down to dinner? I have yet to find a partner for the meal, and . . . she is lovely."

Craning his neck as well, Harrison felt his lips curve when he noticed that the lady Gilbert was interested in was none other than Miss Clementine Flowerdew.

"I will certainly introduce you to her, Gilbert, but I'm not sure your charming mother will approve of this particular introduction. The lady you've cast your eye on is a member of New York society, and you know how your mother feels about society."

Gilbert flashed a brilliant smile. "Mother, bless her far too opinionated heart, is currently over in India, having traveled there with my stepfather to finalize an exportation of spices we've recently purchased. She's not expected to return for months. Besides, she's more opposed to English society ladies than she is to American ones. And because she's recently begun bemoaning the fact that she has no grandchildren, she'll be more agreeable to any lady I might set my sights on."

Asher handed his empty champagne flute to a passing server, then returned his attention to Gilbert. "Doesn't your half brother over in England have children?"

"He does not, and even if he did, they wouldn't be of any true relation to my mother since she was only his stepmother and didn't hold that position long because my father died before I was even born. That unfortunate situation had my mother abandoning London, a city she loathed from the start, and abandoning a fully-grown stepson who was only too anxious to assume my father's title of Earl of Strafford."

Asher tilted his head. "I readily admit I'm not well versed in the way the aristocracy works in Britain, but if your brother has no children, won't you eventually inherit his title and all the land that goes with that title?"

Gilbert shrugged. "Even though my half brother, Charles, is considerably older than I am, he's recently married again after his first wife died a few years back. His new wife is incredibly young, and I have every hope she'll provide him with an heir — and hopefully, a spare."

"You don't care to assume the title?" Asher asked.

Gilbert shook his head. "Because my mother returned to the States directly after my father died, I consider myself to be an American, although I can claim the honorary title of Lord Cavendish simply because of my birth."

"Disclosing you're the son of an earl might go far in securing Miss Clementine Flowerdew's attention." Harrison nodded Clementine's way. "Especially since I know for a fact that society ladies, and ladies in general, do seem to enjoy the idea of spending time with an aristocratic —"

"I'm sorry, but did you say that young lady's name is Miss Flowerdew?" Gilbert suddenly interrupted, even the mere idea of him interrupting a person taking Harrison so aback that he could only manage a nod in response.

"Flowerdew's not a very common name I would have to think," Gilbert said, more to himself than anyone else. "Which begs the question whether this Miss Flowerdew would know an old friend of mine — Miss Temperance Flowerdew."

"Clementine and Temperance are distant cousins," Asher said.

Gilbert's eyes widened. "You're familiar

with Temperance?"

"She's friends with Permilia, and she's in attendance tonight." Asher nodded to the other side of the ballroom. "If you'll look over there, she's currently engaged in a conversation with Miss Mabel Huxley and Miss Mabel's sister, Miss Henrietta."

"I must go pay my respects to her" was all Gilbert said before he turned and strode away without another word.

"That's an interesting turn of events," Asher said right as the sound of a violin rang out.

"It is indeed, but speaking of interesting events, the orchestra seems to be warming up, which means another interesting event is about to take place — the Ticklish Water Polka."

"You don't need to sound so enthusiastic about what could very well turn into my suffering a maiming from my less-than-proficient-polka-dancing fiancée."

Grinning, Harrison took hold of Asher's arm and steered him across the ballroom floor, ignoring that his friend was certainly dragging his feet.

CHAPTER TWELVE

Watching Asher trying to guide Permilia through the steps of the Ticklish Water Polka was, curiously enough, going far in diminishing the abysmal state of mind Gertrude had been in ever since Mrs. Davenport had clearly bested her by bringing out the tear. That single tear was directly responsible for why Gertrude would now be repairing to Newport for the summer.

It wasn't that she had anything against Newport, if one forgot that it was teeming with society members, which meant it was also brimming with society events. Those events were certain to draw Mrs. Davenport's attention — and not for strictly entertainment purposes. That right there was one of the reasons Gertrude was less than pleased with her employer.

She'd been promised a summer of rest, one she felt she deserved after dealing with Mrs. Davenport's shenanigans all winter and spring, and yet that promise had been blithely cast aside.

Apparently, the treat of sponsoring a young lady into the social set was all it took for Mrs. Davenport to abandon her promises. Add in the notion that Edwina seemed genuinely interested in every word that sprang out of Mrs. Davenport's mouth, and there was little hope left that Mrs. Davenport's mind could be changed about their new plans since she clearly relished Edwina's attention.

To add even more aggravation into the mix was the pesky notion that Mrs. Davenport was encouraging Edwina to address her as Hester — a courtesy Gertrude had never been extended in what now seemed to be far too many years working for the woman.

It was little wonder she was beyond annoyed with her employer, and that was without counting the troubling business of Mrs. Davenport becoming overly interested in a tiara worn by one of the guests at the Manhattan Beach Hotel. That guest had made the unfortunate choice of joining them on the veranda, wanting to share the beautiful sight of the moon casting its rays over the ocean. However, because the moonlight had also drawn attention to the sparkly tiara nestled in the lady's hair, she'd attracted Mrs. Davenport's interest, which was never a fortuitous event.

Gertrude had been forced to resort to brute strength to tow Mrs. Davenport off the veranda and away from temptation. However, because her employer was incredibly resourceful when she set her mind to it, Gertrude knew she was going to have to be extra vigilant in keeping track of Mrs. Davenport, especially with Pinkerton detectives roaming around the —

"I daresay Asher wasn't expecting that move."

Glancing to her left, Gertrude found Harrison standing next to her. He was grinning from ear to ear, and when she looked toward what had captured his attention, she discovered that while she'd been distracted with unpleasant thoughts, mayhem had come to visit the ballroom in the form of Permilia.

Somehow, and Gertrude couldn't say exactly how, her friend appeared to have steered, or perhaps knocked, poor Asher directly into the orchestra stand. That unexpected state of affairs seemed to have caused the members of that orchestra to scatter every which way, some of them even tumbling out of their chairs and sprawling on the floor in an obvious attempt to avoid the chaos.

Turning to Harrison, Gertrude wrinkled her nose. "I remember Permilia mentioning she once injured a gentleman while attempting this polka. On my word, who would have ever thought she'd surpass that record by not only abusing her partner, but taking out half an orchestra as well?"

Harrison's eyes crinkled at the corners. "And here I thought I was being so diligent by cautioning Mr. Gilbert Cavendish, my partner with arranging the festivities tonight, against having the orchestra play a quadrille because of the trouble Permilia experienced trying to perform the Go-As-You-Please Quadrille during Alva Vanderbilt's ball."

Pulling her attention from Harrison's delightful grin when she realized she was becoming somewhat mesmerized by his lips, Gertrude shook herself ever so slightly and nodded to where Permilia was now helping a violinist to his feet. "It's fortunate Permilia approaches life with such a wonderful sense of humor. There aren't many ladies who'd cause such mayhem and yet face it with a smile and a helping hand up."

"Or be willing to throw themselves back into a dance, but that's exactly what she seems about to do, because the orchestra members are picking up their instruments again."

"That's brave of them."

"Indeed," Harrison said before he extended Gertrude his arm. "Nevertheless, since I do believe you are a lady of bravery as well, shall we join our friends on the floor to distract the crowd from Permilia's . . . unusual exuberance for dancing?"

Far more pleased than she should have been that Harrison thought her brave, even though she couldn't fathom how he'd come to that conclusion, Gertrude accepted his arm and fell into step beside him as he drew her onto the ballroom floor. Facing him, she heard the first note of a new song ring out and then she was twirling around the room, dancing as she'd never danced before, and to a waltz instead of a polka.

"The orchestra seems to be trying a new tactic," Harrison said with a grin.

Gertrude looked over his shoulder and found Asher and Permilia gliding along, Asher evidently having more success guiding his fiancée in the steps of a waltz.

"I think she might have just trampled his foot, though, because Asher's wincing again," Harrison said before he suddenly pulled her close and spun her around, the action leaving her slightly breathless.

Looking over his shoulder again, she smiled as she realized he'd resorted to the spin to protect her from a collision with Permilia. Her friend, for some unknown reason, was attempting a flamboyant twirl, one that certainly took Asher by surprise since he was now standing without a partner.

She couldn't help but grin when Asher suddenly dashed after his fiancée, presented her with a bow, then took her arm and off they went again toward the opposite side of the ballroom, where no guests were standing.

"He's trying to minimize the damage," Harrison said before he swept Gertrude into a perfect twirl, his proficiency with the steps taking her by surprise.

"I never knew you were such a wonderful dance partner," she managed to say after she'd sucked in the largest breath her tightly laced corset would allow.

"My mother insisted I learn the basics when it became clear that to grow our business, I, being the only son, would need to mingle with society gentlemen on occasion. I wouldn't go so far as to claim I'm a wonderful partner, though, since I just now realized you've begun wheezing. Shall we sit the rest of the dance out?"

Gertrude waved that aside, unwilling to abandon the first time she'd ever taken to the floor with such a compelling gentleman. "A little wheezing isn't going to kill me, Harrison. But to distract me from my condition, tell me more about your dance lessons. Did your sisters take them with you as well?"

"I had a private instructor, whereas my two younger sisters learned to dance at a school for young ladies that catered to families not of society, but of industry. Edwina, I'm sure you won't be surprised to learn, feels that school did an inadequate job of teaching her proper etiquette, which is why she's often seen perusing numerous books dedicated to that very subject."

"And what of your older sister, Margaret?"

Harrison pulled her close to him again to avoid Permilia, who was now practically galloping in their direction, sending Gertrude a cheeky grin as she passed while Asher flashed a smile before wincing yet again.

"Margaret received her education through numerous governesses, but she was a nightmare for those women, preferring to study science over the feminine arts — and she was quite vocal about her preferences. My mother finally relented and brought on board a tutor after Margaret scared off governess number seven. But then, when she came of age, she decided she wanted to have a debut, although not within highest society. Even though my mother was somewhat taken aback by the idea because Margaret had never shown an interest in anything most young ladies of the same age did, she arranged for Margaret to be brought out, even holding a few balls at our home.

Unfortunately, word was getting around the city, unbeknownst to my parents, that marrying into the Sinclair family was certain to be financially beneficial to the gentleman able to win Margaret's hand. She soon found herself courted by not one but two fortune-hunters, and when their duplicity was finally revealed, Margaret swore off gentlemen forever, vowing to spend the rest of her life immersed in the family business." He shook his head. "I think her preference for wearing black is somehow symbolic of her vow, but don't quote me on that since Margaret's always been an unpredictable sort."

"Margaret was the victim of two fortune-hunters?"

"I'm afraid so, and that right there is why my mother is so suspicious of society members, because those fortune-hunters were actually from somewhat respectable society families."

"And explains why Edwina has yet to achieve her goal of becoming introduced to society."

"Exactly, but enough about my family. Tell me something about you."

"There's not much to tell."

Harrison pulled back and caught her eye. "I'm sure that's not true. I imagine there's quite the story behind how it is *you're* so proficient at dancing, because in case you've neglected to notice, you've not stepped on my foot even once."

"There's not much of an interesting story there except to say that while I attended boarding school, I was told time and time again it's beyond the pale to trample a gentleman's foot while taking the floor with him."

Harrison frowned. "You attended boarding school?"

"I did, sent there by my relatives after my parents died."

Twirling her effortlessly past the orchestra, Harrison's brows drew together. "How old were you when your parents died?"

"My father died when I was seven, and then my mother followed him about three years later. My relatives then stepped in and

206

arranged for me to attend Miss Porter's School, located in Farmington, Connecticut."

He brought them to an immediate stop. "Am I to understand you were sent away to boarding school directly after you suffered the loss of both of your parents?"

Urging Harrison back into motion with a bit of push, Gertrude smiled. "My Cadwalader relatives are not what one could ever call the overly warm or sentimental type. And I enjoyed boarding school and was thankful to my relatives for arranging my education at Miss Porter's. It was pleasant there, with plenty of people to speak to whenever I wanted, something I missed after my father died."

"You didn't speak with your mother?"

"My mother descended into a state of severe melancholy after my father, God rest his soul, lost all of his money due to a bad investment."

"He lost all of his money?" Harrison repeated.

"He did, and while my mother was devastated to discover she'd been rendered a pauper, I think she was more upset by the gossip that swirled around town due to that status because —" Gertrude sucked in a small breath of much-needed air — "my father took the advice of a lady who was not my mother, and *that* advice is what led to his financial disaster."

Harrison's fingers tightened around her hand. "How did you learn about this lady and her bad advice?"

"She came to pay us a visit after my father suffered an apoplectic fit and died in this woman's arms in a house of . . . ill repute, and . . ." Gertrude's feet refused to move another inch, which had her lurching to a stop. "I have no idea why I disclosed that to you especially since I've never told anyone that before, and . . . goodness, but this doesn't exactly seem like the perfect moment to have brought up my family's most scandalous secrets."

Harrison dipped his head closer to her. "You disclosed it because we've become good friends, Gertrude. And you disclosed it because it's obviously been weighing heavily on you." He smiled. "If you haven't noticed, I have broad shoulders, so do know that you can use those shoulders whenever you need to relieve some of the weight you've been carrying."

Tears welled in her eyes, and not caring to allow those tears to dribble down her cheeks, Gertrude blinked, and then blinked again, trying to hold them at bay. She was not, nor had she ever been, a lady prone to weeping, but at this very moment, while in the presence of a gentleman who was the kindest man she'd ever met, she found it difficult to keep her emotions in check.

"Forgive me, Gertrude, I did not mean to distress you," Harrison all but whispered in her ear, the tickle of his breath against her neck sending shivers down her spine.

Straightening that spine, Gertrude drew in a ragged breath and forced a smile. "You've not distressed me, Harrison. I fear I'm simply unaccustomed to being offered a strong shoulder. However, since our dance is clearly over, and Permilia and Asher are even now accepting the applause of the crowd, let us go and join them, as well as congratulate Permilia for performing one of the most unusual versions of a waltz I've ever witnessed."

For the briefest of moments, Harrison simply considered her, but then he nodded, took her arm, and began steering her in the direction of Permilia and Asher. Stopping directly in front of her friend, Gertrude soon found herself pulled into Permilia's enthusiastic embrace.

"Wasn't that delightful?" Permilia said, stepping back before beaming an affection-ate smile Asher's way. "Why, I imagine before too long, I'll be known as one of the most accomplished dancers in the city, all due to the efforts of my charming soon-to-be husband."

"Of course you will," Asher returned as he beamed a smile right back at his soon-to-be wife. "Although I am going to suggest you have one of your designers create a softer shoe for you, my dear. The pointed toes on the delightful shoes you're currently wearing have left a definite indentation on my shins."

Permilia laughed, but before she could respond to that telling remark, they were joined by a man Gertrude had yet to meet, one who was handsome in an unassuming way, and one who was accompanied by a smiling and laughing Temperance.

The very sight of Temperance laughing with the man took Gertrude so aback that she simply stood there for a moment, gawking, until she realized that Temperance had turned to her and was regarding her curiously.

"I say, Gertrude, are you quite all right? I don't mean to bring attention to this, but you're a rather unusual shade of pink, and . . ." Temperance removed her arm from the gentleman's and stepped closer. "You're wheezing."

Since Temperance was not a lady Gertrude was accustomed to seeing on the arm of any gentleman, nor had she ever seen Temperance smiling in quite the way she was smiling now, she found herself at a loss for how to respond, because while she'd been gawking, she'd forgotten what Temperance had said. Thankfully, Harrison cleared his throat somewhat loudly, breaking through the state of muteness that had apparently overtaken her.

"Do forgive me, Temperance," she finally got out of her mouth. "I fear the exertions from that waltz have left me feeling rather out of sorts, especially since my laces seem to have . . ." The rest of Gertrude's words trailed away when she realized it was hardly appropriate to bring up the cause of her labored breathing in polite company.

"I say, Gilbert, have you made Miss Gertrude Cadwalader's acquaintance yet?" Harrison asked, smoothly inserting himself into the conversation, which sent what felt like butterflies rolling about her stomach.

She was not accustomed to anyone intervening on her behalf, and that the intervention came from Harrison made it all the more delightful, although . . . having butterflies in her stomach was a concerning turn of events, especially when the only reason for that . . .

"I have not," Gilbert returned, presenting Gertrude with a bow. "Mr. Gilbert Cavendish at your service, Miss Cadwalader." He leaned forward. "May I say it is delightful to make your acquaintance, especially since I've always been fond of ladies with a brave nature, and taking to the floor at the same time as our dear Permilia, well, you may call me impressed."

"I'm never going to live down the small incident with the orchestra, am I?" Permilia asked, but before anyone could answer that question, she took hold of Asher's arm, saying something about checking on the welfare of the violinist she'd knocked over as she tugged Asher away.

"Is it my imagination or are the orchestra members fleeing as if their very lives are in danger?" Temperance asked, which had everyone turning their attention to where the orchestra members were, indeed, nodding to Permilia even as they scrambled backward, clutching their instruments in front of them.

Gilbert smiled. "I'm certain they're simply quitting their places because I told them dinner is soon to be served." He nodded to Gertrude. "And forgive me for cutting our introduction short, but I'm currently being held accountable for the evening's schedule by a most temperamental, and quite honestly, frightening chef. Because of that, Harrison and I need to get on with matters — the next matter on my list being Harrison giving what I'm certain will be a most sentimental speech regarding Asher and his lovely Permilia. Once Harrison is done giving what I do hope is a quick rendition of that speech, we'll toast our friends in style with a selection of champagne I brought back from Paris and then sit down to dine."

Gilbert turned to Temperance. "You'll find no seating chart here this evening, a circumstance I take full responsibility for, although the reasoning behind that lapse is a result of having so little time to pull this evening together. That's also why there will be limited dancing offered after the meal because the Manhattan Beach Hotel was unable to secure us enough staff members to host this event for more than a few hours."

He drew in a breath and smiled. "Having said that, I wanted to make certain you'll save a seat for me so that we may catch up further during dinner. I also hope you'll afford me one of the three dances that are to be held after the meal is finished."

Temperance's cheeks turned a lovely

shade of pink. "Of course I'll save you a seat, as well as dance with you." She nodded toward where the orchestra had once been assembled but were now nowhere in sight. "You'd best hurry though, since it almost looks as if Permilia's about to deliver a speech, and that's not really how these things are done."

"Too right you are," Gilbert said, taking hold of Harrison's arm and ushering him in the direction of Asher and Permilia.

"Save me a seat for dinner as well, will you, Gertrude?" Harrison called over his shoulder.

With her lips curving into a smile, Gertrude was just about to nod Harrison's way when she happened to catch a glimpse of Clementine standing on the opposite side of the room from her. She was staring far too intently at Temperance with lips Gertrude could tell were pursed even over the distance that separated them. When Clementine then switched her attention to Gilbert and tilted her head, Gertrude narrowed her eyes.

"Harrison, a moment if you please," she called, hurrying to catch up with him.

Harrison turned and waited for her to join him. "Have you changed your mind about sitting with me?"

"For a woman who rarely has an opportunity to dine in the company of a gentleman under the age of eighty, I would be delighted to join you for the meal. And given that you and I seem to share conversation easily, another circumstance I rarely experience, dining with you would make for a most pleasant event. However . . ." She blew out a breath and lowered her voice. "Temperance seems to be enjoying herself this evening, something I do not recall ever witnessing, but I just noticed Clementine watching her cousin as well as perusing Gilbert, and . . ."

"You want me to dine with Clementine so that Temperance can continue enjoying herself," Harrison finished for her.

Gertrude blinked. "And here I've been under the impression you're somewhat oblivious when it comes to understanding the feminine mind, but you didn't even hesitate with understanding where I was going with that."

"I'm afraid you're giving me far too much credit, Gertrude. But, my mostly oblivious nature aside, I'll certainly do as you ask, although who will you dine with tonight?"

"I'll join Mrs. Davenport and your sister, which might be a prudent choice anyway since I have a feeling those two are rapidly moving forward with their plans to repair to Newport."

"My sister is going to Newport with you and Mrs. Davenport?"

"That does seem to be the case. Mrs. Davenport is thrilled to have a young lady to sponsor into Newport society, so thrilled in fact she's encouraged Edwina to use her given name — Hester."

"I didn't realize Edwina was quite this determined, but . . ." Harrison frowned and considered her closely. "Your feelings have been hurt by this, haven't they?"

Not particularly caring to discuss her feelings, hurt or otherwise, Gertrude gestured to where Gilbert had joined Permilia and Asher. "I'm fine, truly I am, but by the expression on Gilbert's face, you won't be fine if you delay your speech much longer."

Harrison leaned toward her. "You'll save a dance for me after dinner?"

Gertrude's heart gave a bit of a flip even as she forced herself to shake her head. "You and I have already shared a dance. Because there are limited dances this evening, you should ask some of the other ladies in attendance to take to the floor with you." She grinned. "Besides, since I've confided that I'm suffering from laces that are far tighter than I'm used to, by not dancing with me, you'll be helping me maintain an adequate supply of air."

He returned the grin, and after bowing over her hand while placing a kiss on it, he turned and strode across the room, leaving her feeling more than a little light-headed, and this time not due to a lack of sufficient air.

Realizing she was beginning to draw attention from a few of the guests, probably because they'd caught her watching Harrison far more closely than she should have, Gertrude turned on her heel and walked to the side of the ballroom, craning her neck as she tried to find Mrs. Davenport.

Panic began trickling through her when she found not so much as a glimpse of her employer. The panic quickly increased when she realized that, even though she'd vowed to keep a close eye on Mrs. Davenport, that vow had all but been forgotten while she'd danced with Harrison.

Knowing there was no help for it but to go in search of her missing employer, Gertrude began moving through the ballroom, hoping with all her heart that Mrs. Davenport had not seen fit to use Gertrude's distraction with Harrison to get herself into any troubling shenanigans.

CHAPTER THIRTEEN

Pushing aside the panic that threatened to overwhelm her, Gertrude drew in a large breath, regretting that action a second later when she began wheezing, her lungs apparently not having enough room to accommodate so much air. Just when she began feeling decidedly light-headed again, though, someone began pounding her on the back, the pounding immediately diminishing her wheezing, although it set her eyes to watering.

Lifting those eyes, she found Mrs. Davenport standing beside her, watching her with clear concern.

"Goodness, dear, what in the world is wrong with you?"

"She's obviously suffering from having her laces tied too tightly," Edwina said, stepping around Mrs. Davenport before she reached out and pressed a handkerchief into Gertrude's hand. "I take full responsibility for your unfortunate state, and do know that from this point forward, I'll not dismiss claims of not being able to breathe so easily."

Gertrude dabbed at her eyes. "We would have never gotten me into this gown if not for your efforts, Edwina. I simply need to remember that gulping in air is not a luxury I can afford for the rest of this evening."

"I fear you won't be able to eat anything either," Edwina said.

"Which will make it easier for me to get into smaller sizes in the future." Gertrude tucked the handkerchief into the sleeve of her gown. "But enough about my unusual condition. Tell me, what have the two of you been up to while I've been occupied?"

Mrs. Davenport's smile was far too innocent. "Nothing of any consequence. We've simply been discussing fashions and what Edwina will need to bring to Newport."

"And you were discussing those fashions the *entire* time I was occupied?" Gertrude pressed.

Mrs. Davenport's smile dimmed. "I did use the retiring room at one point, but that's hardly a matter of interest to anyone."

"Did you encounter anyone of interest in the retiring room?" Gertrude asked.

Mrs. Davenport, to Gertrude's concern, waved that aside. "There are always interesting ladies in a retiring room, but what I find more interesting is how much time you've spent with Harrison this evening."

"Dancing with a gentleman at a ball is scarcely interesting, Mrs. Davenport, especially since dancing is expected when one attends a ball."

"But not every lady is fortunate enough to take to the floor with a gentleman such as Harrison. You should know that your dance was remarked on by numerous guests, all of whom have been interrupting my time with Edwina to inquire about your relationship with the man."

Gertrude forced a smile. "From what I understand, my friendship with Harrison has been remarked on frequently of late, so I wouldn't put much store in any additional remarks made this evening."

Mrs. Davenport lifted her chin. "I have no idea why you're being so annoyingly obtuse. I'm not blind to what's transpiring between you and Harrison, although I do hope you'll afford me a small measure of notice before you decide to leave my employ." She sent a fond smile Edwina's way. "At least I can console myself with knowing I'll not be completely abandoned."

Gertrude fought the urge to roll her eyes. "There's no need for any consoling because I have no intention of abandoning you. However —" she gestured across the ballroom floor — "since Mr. Gilbert Cavendish does seem to be encouraging everyone to find their seats, let us repair to a table and banish further discussion on this ridiculous subject."

Mrs. Davenport tossed an injured look to Gertrude, then entwined her arm with Edwina's, releasing an honest-to-goodness sniff if Gertrude wasn't much mistaken.

"Shall we find a table, dear?" she asked, and then, without bothering to see if Gertrude was going to follow, led Edwina toward a grouping of tables, missing the silently mouthed apology Edwina sent Gertrude.

Smiling in response, with a silent "You have nothing to apologize for," Gertrude fell into step behind the two ladies, vowing then and there to pay extra attention to Mrs. Davenport, who was clearly suffering from some imagined slight, especially since such imaginings normally caused Mrs. Davenport to embrace a melancholy attitude.

"Ah, Miss Henrietta, Miss Mabel," Mrs. Davenport began, coming to a stop beside a table where the sisters were standing. "Would you mind if we join you?"

"How delightful," Miss Henrietta exclaimed as Miss Mabel nodded in clear agreement. "It's a rare occasion indeed when my sister and I get the company of two ladies who aren't past their prime."

Shuddering just a touch when Mrs. Davenport began swelling on the spot to what she obviously took as an insult to her somewhat advanced age, Gertrude breathed a small sigh of relief when a server approached them carrying a tray filled with champagne flutes, right as someone began tapping one of the flutes to draw everyone's attention. Turning toward the sound, Gertrude was happy to see Harrison lifting up his champagne flute and smiling in a way that Gertrude couldn't help but notice had more than one young lady — and even a few of the older ones — sighing.

By the time Harrison was finished telling everyone exactly how fortunate Asher was to have found such a lovely lady to soon call his wife, Permilia and Asher were both dabbing at their eyes with handkerchiefs Asher produced from his well-stocked pockets. Even Miss Henrietta and Miss Mabel, two ladies who weren't known to be overly emotional sorts, were sniffling into their own handkerchiefs, although what Miss Henrietta meant by muttering something about finally finding her true calling in life, Gertrude couldn't say.

Taking the chair to Mrs. Davenport's right while Edwina took the chair to Mrs. Davenport's left, Gertrude pushed aside the disappointment that stole over her at the sight of a smiling Clementine being escorted into a chair by Harrison. Needing a distraction from that, she turned and found that Miss Henrietta was sitting in the chair directly beside her, regarding her far too closely for comfort.

"It speaks highly of your character, dear, what you did for Miss Temperance Flowerdew. There aren't many ladies who'd forgo sitting down to dine with that oh-so-delicious Harrison Sinclair simply to help a friend," Miss Henrietta said.

Gertrude frowned. "Forgive me, but neither you nor your sister were anywhere near me when I suggested Harrison dine with Clementine."

"We didn't need to be," Miss Mabel chimed in, leaning forward in the chair next to her sister. "As I'm sure you well remember, Henrietta and I have spent decades observing people, and during that time, we've become proficient at reading lips."

"How . . . disturbing."

Miss Henrietta winked. "Quite, but it does allow us to be well informed about even the most mundane of topics." She spread a white linen napkin over her lap. "Our keen prowess with observation is exactly how we're aware of the deplorable treatment that Miss Temperance Flowerdew receives at the hands of her distant relatives. And that is exactly why I've decided to include her, along with you if there was any question, into my new quest of taking wallflowers in hand and improving their lots in life."

Gertrude blinked. "Is that what you were referring to when you muttered something about discovering your true purpose in life?"

"Ah, so you've a talent for observation as well," Miss Henrietta said with a nod. "And yes, that's what I meant."

"Don't you find assisting Miss Snook with her school to be rewarding enough?" Gertrude asked.

Miss Henrietta tilted her head. "While it's very rewarding to know that a house Mabel and I never enjoyed is now to be used as a school dedicated to educating women of the working class, I also find myself drawn to assisting ladies of the wallflower set." She smiled. "Because I'm privy to the many intricacies that unfold within society, as well as being privy to the nuances within the industrialists, I believe I can offer ladies such as yourself invaluable information and connections that will see you well-settled in the end."

"Oh . . . I don't believe there's any need for you to offer such assistance to me," Gertrude began. "I'm perfectly content with my lot in life."

"Of course you're not," Miss Mabel said, leaning across her sister again and lowering her voice to the merest whisper. "You're employed by a most curious lady and are expected to attend to business you've no business attending. Henrietta and I are going to do our very best to see you out of that situation."

"How would you go about that?" Gertrude couldn't help but ask.

"Get you married off to Harrison, of course," the sisters said together, their words drawing Mrs. Davenport's attention.

"I told you your time with Harrison was being remarked upon" was all she said before she turned back to Edwina and launched into a discussion of bustles, one that seemed to center around creating a bustle that would not make the wearer bottom-heavy.

"Don't pay her any mind," Miss Henrietta

said as two servers approached the table carrying tureens of soup. "She's worried she'll soon be without a companion, and is probably only now realizing exactly how much she depends on you and your discretion."

Having no idea what to say to that, Gertrude settled for saying nothing at all, attending to the soup one of the servers was placing in front of her.

Thankfully, Miss Henrietta and Miss Mabel were distracted with the many courses of the meal, and the conversation soon turned to the dishes they were sampling. Miss Henrietta enjoyed the terrapin, tongue, red mullet, and roast saddle of mutton, while Miss Mabel preferred the mayonnaise of chicken, quail, and compote of cherries.

Gertrude, on the other hand, only enjoyed the soup because with her laces being so tight, she didn't have room for much food.

After the lemon ices were served, along with a glass of sparkling wine, servers stepped forward to clear off the tables as the orchestra members began retaking their seats.

"Returning to the subject of taking you in hand," Miss Henrietta suddenly said, laying aside her napkin after she blotted her lips.

"Do know that I have every confidence my sister and I will be successful with that. You only have to look to Permilia to see the proof of our success because, modesty aside, it was due to mine and Mabel's observational skills that she ended up engaged to Asher."

Gertrude blotted her own lips, using the time to compose a reply to what was a very unusual conclusion regarding Permilia and Asher's courtship. "While I do find that an interesting notion, being under the impression Permilia secured Asher's affections because they were immediately drawn to each other, I must state most emphatically that there's no need for either you or your sister to take me in hand."

"There's every need, because without our assistance and expertise in these types of matters, you're certain to miss a prime opportunity and lose the affection of . . ." Miss Henrietta stopped talking and smiled brightly at someone Gertrude couldn't see.

When the fine hair on the nape of her neck stood to attention, she knew exactly who'd joined them, and after turning her head, she wasn't at all surprised to find Harrison standing there.

"How was your meal?" he asked.

"The poor girl barely ate anything," Miss

Henrietta said before Gertrude could respond. "But I enjoyed my meal, as did my sister." She nodded to Gertrude before returning her attention to Harrison. "Have you come to beg a dance from our charming Gertrude?"

Warmth settled over Gertrude, but she was spared further embarrassment when Harrison flashed a grin to Miss Henrietta. "Gertrude has, unfortunately, already informed me she's unavailable for further dances with me because of the limited number of dances being offered. That's why I'm here to beg a dance from you, Miss Henrietta, one I'm hoping you'll grant me."

With cheeks turning pink, Miss Henrietta was on her feet and grinning as she took the arm Harrison extended her. They made it all of three feet before she stopped, set her sights on Mr. Charles Dana, the editor from *The Sun* and the gentleman who had been Permilia's editor when she was working as an anonymous society columnist, and nodded his way.

"I believe you were intending to ask Miss Gertrude Cadwalader to dance, weren't you, Mr. Dana?" Miss Henrietta all but barked. "She's sitting right there." She nodded in Gertrude's direction.

Mr. Dana's eyes widened, but then, apparently not wanting to cross swords with Miss Henrietta, he practically jumped from his chair, and the next thing Gertrude knew, she was on the ballroom floor, smiling at Mr. Dana as they waited for the music to begin.

"You could have told her no," she whispered right as the first note rang out.

"I think not," Mr. Dana whispered back, and then they were dancing.

Gertrude soon found herself taking on the unusual position of leading when Mr. Dana, after trying to steer her in the wrong direction twice, admitted he wasn't much of a dancer and was perfectly agreeable with her taking the lead.

Once she got them moving somewhat smoothly over the floor, they settled into a friendly conversation, Mr. Dana even broaching the idea of bringing her on as a new Miss Quill, since his readers were writing daily to the paper, bemoaning the loss of the column Permilia once penned.

"I'm afraid I'm kept busy with my position as Mrs. Davenport's companion," Gertrude said. "But why don't you approach someone like Miss Clementine Flowerdew? She's accepted in all the right circles and is privy to the latest news of the day."

Mr. Dana stopped counting his steps and

shook his head. "I approached her earlier, and while I'm sure she does know more than her fair share of the scandals traveling around society, I didn't get the impression she's a lady who enjoys responsibilities." His brows drew together. "Perhaps I should approach that cousin of hers, the other Miss Flowerdew. She's a wallflower from what Miss Clementine told me. And I have to say from personal experience that wallflowers are known to be quite knowledgeable about society matters, given the amount of time they spend languishing against the walls instead of . . ." His voice trailed off to nothing as if he'd just realized he was dancing with a wallflower and might have insulted her.

Taking pity on Mr. Dana, who was red in the face and trying to cover up his slip by resuming his counting of steps, Gertrude smiled. "Wallflowers are notoriously underestimated, Mr. Dana, but since I'm personally known to Temperance, I'll ask her if she'd be interested in doing a column for you here or there. She's known to be rather shy at times, which is why I won't encourage you to ask her yourself."

Mr. Dana looked over Gertrude's shoulder, brought her to a stop, and then gestured to where Temperance was dancing with

Gilbert Cavendish, laughing at something he'd said and looking anything other than shy. "I believe she may have found a reason to come out of her shell."

"You may be right," Gertrude said as the music slowed to a stop and she walked with Mr. Dana off the floor, where he immediately found himself badgered into asking Edwina to dance by Miss Mabel, who'd apparently just agreed to partner Harrison next.

Sinking into the chair beside Mrs. Davenport, and claiming exhaustion when Miss Henrietta began casting her beady gaze around for another partner for her, she looked to her employer and found Mrs. Davenport watching her somewhat sadly.

Knowing it would take next to nothing to send Mrs. Davenport into a bout of melancholy that would not bode well for anyone, Gertrude began chatting about bustles, and before even a minute passed, Mrs. Davenport was smiling and explaining how she was going to improve on her latest bustle design, her smile widening when Gertrude offered herself up as a model for that design.

When the last notes of the last song faded away, Gertrude helped Mrs. Davenport to her feet, then waited as Gilbert rushed around with a pad of paper in his hands.

That pad listed the carriages the guests were assigned to, and even though she was disappointed to not find herself in Harrison's carriage since he was staying back to settle the hotel bill, she was relieved that Mrs. Davenport had abandoned any sign of melancholy.

Making their way through the hotel, she and Mrs. Davenport, with Edwina joining them once again, were about to enter their assigned carriage when Gertrude was hailed from behind by Clementine.

"You're supposed to ride with me, Miss Cadwalader," Clementine called, and even though Gertrude was certain that was not the case, but not wanting to cause a scene with so many guests watching her, she assured Mrs. Davenport and Edwina she'd be fine, and walked over to join Clementine.

Taking her arm, Clementine gave it a good pat. "I must say you've surprised me, Miss Cadwalader, but in a most delightful way."

"I've surprised you?" Gertrude repeated.

Clementine leaned close. "You suggested to Mr. Sinclair that he dine with me this evening." She patted Gertrude's arm again. "I truly thought you were opposed to assisting me with capturing his affections, but do know that your unexpected suggestion to him about dinner will not be overlooked by me. Rest assured, I will, from this point

232

forward, consider you a friendly acquaintance of mine, and . . ." She smiled. "I'll see to it that I make certain to acknowledge you when we attend the same functions, which will go far in elevating your status within society."

A prickle of temper took Gertrude by surprise. "You seem to be under the misimpression that my asking Harrison to partner you for dinner was a sign I've decided to help you secure his affections."

Clementine's smile slid directly off her face. "Why would you have suggested it then?"

"I'm sure I have my reasons, none that need concern you, though. But in the interest of avoiding another one of your very condescending and completely unacceptable gestures of friendship, or 'friendly acquaintance' business as I believe you called it, do know that I have no intention of furthering your cause with Harrison, nor do I care whether you acknowledge me out in public or not."

Clementine dropped her hold on Gertrude's arm and narrowed her eyes to mere slits. "I make a far better friendly acquaintance than enemy, Miss Cadwalader. But since you evidently don't care to become one of my friendly acquaintances, consider yourself warned."

Spinning on her heel, Clementine stalked away and disappeared into a waiting carriage, leaving Gertrude behind.

CHAPTER FOURTEEN

Two days later

"Gertrude, be a dear and trot back to the attic and see if you can locate one or two more traveling trunks," Mrs. Davenport said, pulling Gertrude from a lovely daydream she'd been having about Harrison and the dance they'd shared at the Manhattan Beach Hotel. "I want to put my best foot forward this season in Newport, and I can hardly accomplish that if I don't take the proper accessories with me." She bit her lip. "Now that I think about it, fetch three traveling trunks. I don't believe I'll be able to fit all these reticules in the trunk I'm packing now, and we've barely started assembling the wardrobe I'm going to need as I go about the daunting task of ushering Edwina into the folds of high society."

Setting aside the hat she'd been wrapping in paper, Gertrude quirked a brow at the large pile of reticules that were waiting to be packed, a pile that was significantly larger than it had been five minutes before. Reminding herself for what felt like the millionth time that it would not bode well for her to balk at what was yet another unreasonable request from a lady who was being more contrary than usual, Gertrude summoned up a smile.

"While I'm more than happy to *trot* up to an attic that seems miles and miles away from this room, I would like to point out that the summer season in Newport has a limited number of days, which means . . ."

"They'll be filled to the brim with marvelous society events, so perhaps you should bring down four trunks instead of three," Mrs. Davenport finished for her.

Unable to help but feel as if she'd landed smack-dab into the midst of some odd type of test she had no idea how to pass, or why she was being tested in the first place, Gertrude turned around and began counting silently under her breath, stopping when Mrs. Davenport began *tsk*ing under *her* breath.

"I know you're counting again, dear, a clear sign of a troubled mind if there ever was one. However, I must point out that if anyone should be troubled, it's me. Why, I'm taking on the daunting task of launching a young lady who is very nearly a spinster, and believe me, that will be no easy feat." She released a dramatic sigh. "Every eye will be upon us, remarking on the fashions we're wearing, and that right there is reason for concern. I'm kicking myself for not suggesting you and I travel to Paris months ago to secure a summer wardrobe for me, a mistake that now leaves me at a disadvantage, unless . . ."

She sucked in a sharp breath of air. "On my word, why didn't I think of this before? I'm simply going to pack a few of the designs I've been fiddling around with of late." She fanned a face that was quickly turning pink with the reticule she'd plucked from the large pile. "You mark my words, Gertrude, once Newport sees how flattering a larger-than-life bustle can be for a lady's figure, I'll be granted the title of society matron extraordinaire — the one lady in society everyone will be clamoring to embrace. Why, it wouldn't surprise me if, after our time in Newport, I become known not only as the society matron to seek out if one wants to launch a young lady with less than perfect credentials into society, but also an innovative designer of truly unique fashions."

Gertrude frowned. "It almost seems as if

you're contemplating taking on a more visible role within society, abandoning the idea you've always embraced about maintaining a life best kept out of the spotlight."

Mrs. Davenport waved that aside with a flick of a wrist. "I've decided to branch out a little because keeping out of the spotlight gets lonely after a while — not to mention boring."

"You must know that branching out is not a good idea, particularly because of the questionable activities you enjoy pursuing."

"I'm sure I have no idea what you could possibly be implying," Mrs. Davenport said with a sniff before she waved a hand toward the door of her bedchamber. "However, before you and I get completely at sixes and sevens with each other, I do believe I hear the attic calling you."

Swallowing the hundred or so reasons that were on the very tip of her tongue in response to Mrs. Davenport's decision to *"branch out a little,"* or the thousand or so responses she could make about the denial Mrs. Davenport had voiced pertaining to her *"questionable activities,"* Gertrude folded her arms over her chest and shook her head. "Since you've decided we need four trunks fetched from the attic, it will be a more effective use of our time if we send a footman up to the attic instead of me. That way I can remain here with you, packing up the choices you've made, which will ensure our unpacking will go much smoother once we land in Newport, a landing that has now been pushed up considerably since you want to depart with the tide tomorrow."

Mrs. Davenport's expression turned stubborn. "I don't know why you seem so cross about changing the date of our departure. I told you, we have no choice but to leave tomorrow because Edwina simply can't miss Mr. Ward McAllister's picnic. Everyone who is anyone will be at that event, and I'll enjoy better success of seeing her well launched if I do that initial launching with Mr. McAllister's support. You know he'll take one look at Edwina's stunning face and give her his blessing, something that will immediately guarantee her inclusion with the most fashionable set." Mrs. Davenport settled a stern gaze on Gertrude. "Surely you must understand why I'm insisting on keeping to such a tight schedule, even if it might require a touch of extra work for you. I'm sure Edwina would do the same for you if your roles were reversed."

Throwing her hands up in defeat, and feeling just a little resentful that Mrs. Davenport was so keen to assist Edwina even if it meant working her trusty companion to the bone, Gertrude spun around and headed for the door. "Far be it from me to point out the obvious, but sending a footman instead of me to fetch additional trunks would go far in allowing me plenty of time to see us packed."

"You recently vowed to embrace a more active attitude to diminish the number of stitches you've been experiencing of late," Mrs. Davenport called after her. "I imagine traveling to the attic a few times a day is extremely beneficial to a lady's constitution."

Gertrude stopped in her tracks and turned. "I've already been up to the attic at least seven times today. I think my constitution has suffered enough, thank you very much. In all honesty, four more trips to the attic — and hauling four more trunks out of that attic — could very well do me in."

"Or provide you with improved physical stamina," Mrs. Davenport said with a nod. "Besides, I don't trust anyone but you to visit the attic, so sending a footman up there is completely out of the question."

"Since when have you not trusted anyone but me to visit the attic?"

Mrs. Davenport turned back to her pile of reticules, pretending an absorbed interest in them while she neglected to answer Gertrude's question. Knowing it would be easier all around to give in and trot back to the attic — four times at least, from the sound of it — Gertrude lifted her chin and marched from the room.

Striding down the long hallway of the second floor of Mrs. Davenport's brownstone, Gertrude drew in a deep breath, the corners of her mouth curling when the odd thought sprang to mind that at least she could draw in a breath today, a circumstance she was never taking for granted again. Drawing in an even deeper breath simply because she could, she reached the flight of stairs that led to the third floor and began climbing.

As she climbed, she reminded herself how ridiculous it was for her to get her feelings injured simply because Mrs. Davenport was treating her exactly how one was expected to treat a paid companion.

Paid companions, as everyone knew, occupied a curious position within most households. They were not as lofty as the butler, or as essential as the housekeeper, but they were considered above the footmen and maids, even ladies' maids. They were also given the privilege of attending society events, but while they did enjoy a certain elevated status, they were still the paid help, something she'd apparently begun to forget.

Reaching the landing to the third floor, Gertrude set aside thoughts that were leaving her somewhat depressed, an attitude best left abandoned when faced with the task of ambling around a gloomy attic filled to the brim with abandoned odds and ends. Walking to a door that led to the narrow steps of the attic, she picked up the candle she'd left on a table in front of the door because the attic was not attached to the gas that was used to light the rest of the house. Striking a match, she lit the candle, headed through the door, and began navigating her way up the stairs.

Once in the attic, she took a single step forward, then froze in place when what sounded exactly like flapping wings greeted her arrival. When something flew directly over her head, she let out a shriek, ducked, then dropped the candle, shrieking again when the attic descended into blackness as the flame sputtered out.

Crawling on her hands and knees, she headed for the far side of the attic, hoping she'd eventually run into the wall where a curtained window was located, praying all the while that while she crawled, the mad creature now whizzing over her head wouldn't attack. Wincing every other minute as she ran into one pile of abandoned objects after another, she finally reached the wall, knowing without a shadow of a doubt she was now certainly the worse for wear.

Her head was throbbing from running into something unmovable, her knee was bleeding from dragging it over something sharp, and her entire body was trembling, a direct result of the terror that was flowing through her because she had no idea what type of creature was running amok in the attic. Worse yet . . . was it in possession of fangs?

Reaching out a hand to guide her in the blackness, Gertrude finally found the curtain she was searching for, and giving it a good yank to the side, she squinted against the sunlight that immediately flooded the room. Struggling to her feet, she fiddled with the window latch, pushed the window open, then dove for the floor again when fluttering wings sounded directly behind her. A second later, a small bird flew over her head and out the window, chirping merrily away in what Gertrude thought might be appreciation.

Leaning against the sill as the bird flew away, Gertrude drew in a gulp of fresh air, wondering how it would feel to be like the bird that had just escaped — free from the confines of an unforeseen prison, or in her case, free from the responsibility of maintaining a position where her best work was never appreciated and unreasonable demands greeted every new day.

When her vision began to blur and her mood began turning maudlin, an attitude that would not help her complete the many tasks demanding her attention, Gertrude brushed aside the lone tear that was trailing down her cheek and stiffened her spine.

There was no point languishing in a state of self-pity, especially when she'd seen firsthand the harm such languishing could do to a person.

Lifting her chin, Gertrude began moving through the objects scattered and stacked throughout the room. She finally spotted a trunk and headed straight for it, setting the old blanket that covered the top of it aside before she reached for the latch. Tracing her finger over an ornate *J* that was worked into the brass of the latch, she opened the lid. To her surprise, the trunk was practically empty except for an old Bible sitting on an aged child-size ivory gown, adorned with what looked to be expensive lace and row upon row of faded bows.

Curious now, Gertrude plucked the Bible out of the trunk, picking her way once again across the room until she reached the window. Using the faded ribbon that was marking a place, she opened the Bible and found that one of the passages had been circled on the page.

It was a passage from the Psalms.

" 'When my father and my mother forsake me, then the Lord will take me up,' " she read out loud. Lifting her head, she looked out the window, not really seeing the clouds drift by as she wondered about the person who'd circled that passage, and if that person was also the owner of the ivory gown still nestled in the trunk.

Flipping to the front of the Bible in the hope the owner's name would be found there, Gertrude frowned when she found the pages that normally tracked the lineage of a family missing, ripped out, or so it appeared, because there were jagged bits of thin paper left behind.

Sympathy for the owner of the Bible was immediate, especially since she knew from personal experience what type of anger could cause a person to rip out their family history from the front of a Bible. She'd done the very same thing years before, hoping that the ripping would ease some of the anger she'd held against everyone during that dark time. But, truth be told, she was still angry with God, that anger beginning not long after her father had died.

It was directly after her father suffered his fatal apoplectic fit that Gertrude had begun making a journey to church every day. Once there, she'd spent hours praying, not asking God to return her father to her since she knew that wasn't possible, but to step in and diminish the shame she and her mother were experiencing due to the tawdry circumstances surrounding her father's death.

When the level of gossip increased instead of decreasing, Gertrude had no choice but to conclude that God was evidently disappointed with her, hence the reasoning behind not granting her request. Wanting to appease God, Gertrude threw herself into being the best daughter possible to her mother in order to win back God's favor. However, when her mother descended into a state of deepest melancholy, brought about by their lack of finances and continued shame, Gertrude decided that God clearly didn't care for her family. And after her mother's melancholy turned deadly, Gertrude abandoned the idea God was a loving and compassionate God, and embraced the idea that He was a distant deity.

Throughout the years since her mother's death, there'd been times when she'd all but abandoned her faith, even with her attending church regularly and knowing people who believed in God and the love He held for everyone. But for her, God was not a daily part of her life, nor . . .

"Gertrude, are you still up there?"

Closing the Bible that had brought about such disturbing thoughts, Gertrude picked her way across the attic again and peered down the narrow staircase. Peering back up at her was Mrs. Davenport.

"What in the world is taking you so long?" Mrs. Davenport asked.

"Have you seen your attic in the last decade or so? Because if not, do know it's a maze up here and somewhat difficult to navigate through."

"You haven't found *any* trunks?"

"I found one."

"Then bring it down and you can worry about finding others later, after you get back from running a little errand for me."

The hair on the back of Gertrude's neck stood to attention. "What errand?"

"I'll explain while we enjoy tea and those delicious shortbread cookies you love so much. Did I mention I asked the cook to bake us some so they'll be fresh out of the oven?"

"You only ask for shortbread cookies when you're feeling guilty about something," Gertrude said.

"Don't be silly. I'm just rewarding you for making so many trips to the attic."

Before Gertrude could respond to that nonsense, Mrs. Davenport disappeared from sight, the sound of her retreating footsteps fading rapidly.

Abandoning the urge to stay in the attic for the rest of the day, which would allow her to avoid whatever errand Mrs. Davenport needed her to complete next, one that would certainly turn out to be more strenuous than trotting up to the attic every other minute since shortbread cookies were being used as a bribe, Gertrude moved back to the trunk, dropped the Bible into it so she could peruse it later at her leisure, then shut the lid. Grabbing the handle, she began dragging it behind her, yelping under her breath after she reached the stairs and the trunk kept banging into her legs as she pulled it down step by painful step.

By the time she reached the second floor, she was perspiring more than slightly and looking forward to a good cup of tea and numerous shortbread cookies, her vow of watching her figure put aside on this all-too-trying day.

Wheezing ever so slightly from her exertions, even though the wheezing was not going to persuade her to forgo her treat, she tugged the trunk into Mrs. Davenport's sitting room, let go of the handle, and dusted her hands together.

"I think this will be large enough to hold the rest of your reticules, and . . ." She glanced at Mrs. Davenport, who was staring with wide eyes at the trunk, and frowned. "On my word, is something the matter? You're looking quite as if you've seen a ghost."

Mrs. Davenport pulled her gaze from the trunk, drew in a ragged breath, then smiled an overly bright smile. "I'm fine, dear, although I've just decided we should have our tea in the drawing room. The atmosphere down on the first floor will be much less chaotic since we won't be surrounded by so many memori . . . I mean, items still needing to be packed."

The next thing Gertrude knew, and before she could ask a single question, Mrs. Davenport practically dragged her from the sitting room, muttering something about the past and how unexpectedly it could come back to haunt a person.

CHAPTER FIFTEEN

"There's nothing quite like a cup of tea to restore one's humor, is there?" Mrs. Davenport asked, lifting a cup made of delicate bone china to her lips while apparently ignoring the fact that her hands were trembling like mad.

Gertrude set aside her tea and sat forward on the dainty green-striped chair that flanked the one Mrs. Davenport was sitting in. "You need to tell me what's troubling you."

"Nothing's troubling me. I'm simply a little out of sorts due to the strenuous nature of packing for our spur of the moment holiday. I'll be fine just as soon as I finish my tea."

"Whose trunk was that?"

"I'm sure I have no idea. It must have belonged to some long-lost ancestor."

"An ancestor who had a name beginning with *J*?" Gertrude pressed.

Mrs. Davenport gulped down her tea, even though doing so had her eyes watering, probably because the tea was still rather hot. Setting her cup down on the small table beside her, she picked up a shortbread cookie and stuffed the entire cookie into her mouth. That made it all but impossible for her to respond, although she might have bitten off more than she could chew because she made a great show of turning to look out the drawing room window as she spit some of the cookie into a napkin.

Swallowing a laugh, Gertrude reached for a cookie as well, put a small piece into her mouth, and simply enjoyed her treat, deciding her best option was to wait Mrs. Davenport out because her employer was not a lady prone to keeping silent for any great length of time.

To her surprise, Mrs. Davenport did not break her silence in a timely fashion, although she wasn't perfectly silent since she kept stuffing one cookie after another into her mouth. Finally, after a good five minutes had passed, she turned from the window with a face that was somewhat green, eyed the empty cookie platter, and gave the smallest of shudders.

"Shall I ring for more?" Gertrude asked, reaching for the small bell sitting by the empty platter.

"I wouldn't want to impose on the kitchen," Mrs. Davenport said weakly, lifting her napkin and taking an inordinate amount of time to dab cookie crumbs from her lips even as she, if Gertrude wasn't mistaken, let out a bit of a belch.

Sitting back, Gertrude switched tactics. "Did I mention there's an old Bible, along with an ivory dress with some exquisite lace and numerous bows, stored in that trunk?"

Mrs. Davenport shuddered again, mumbled something about it being "time for a distraction," and then lifted her head and smiled brightly Gertrude's way.

"Did *I* mention how delighted I am that matters seem to be progressing nicely with you and Harrison?" Mrs. Davenport leaned forward to pour herself another cup of tea with hands that barely trembled when she picked up the pot.

Gertrude summoned up a smile of her own. "I don't know where you got the idea that there are any matters to progress with Harrison. You know perfectly well I haven't even seen that gentleman since he saw us home from the *Cornelia* two nights ago."

"It's always very telling when a gentleman makes a point to personally escort a guest home," Mrs. Davenport stated with a knowing nod. "And it didn't escape my notice that he sent a note around for you yesterday, although I must admit I've been disappointed that you didn't see fit to share the contents of that note with me."

Since Gertrude wasn't comfortable divulging that Harrison's note revolved around his wanting her to keep an eye on Edwina while he was away on business, because that would have Mrs. Davenport believing all sorts of conspiracies were afoot to keep her from presenting Edwina to society, Gertrude settled for a shrug. "Harrison simply wanted me to know he'd been called out of the city on business."

"Clear proof of his affections for you, if you ask me. I have to imagine he wanted you to know he was out of the city so you wouldn't worry his interest in you was anything less than earnest."

Even though that was a lovely thought, Gertrude knew it wasn't the truth, but before she could deny Mrs. Davenport's statement, her employer suddenly sat on the very edge of her seat, pinning Gertrude under a sharp gaze.

"Returning to the subject of disappointments, I have to say I was also disappointed you did not see fit to mention the very unusual circumstance of Harrison sweeping you into his arms and whisking you straight off his boat." Mrs. Davenport saluted Gertrude with her cup. "While I admire your ingenuity in setting up a situation where being swept up into Harrison's arms was a possibility in the first place, I'm hurt you didn't share such a milestone with me."

Gertrude's forehead furrowed. "My landing in Harrison's arms wasn't intentional, although I am curious as to where you got that little tidbit."

"I heard it from Edwina, who heard it from her sister Adelaide, who heard it from the eldest sister, Margaret."

"Then I suppose you also heard that Harrison's reason behind the sweeping stemmed from Margaret chasing us. During that chasing, I developed a stitch in my side and was wheezing somewhat dreadfully as we tried to outrun her."

Mrs. Davenport tapped a finger against her chin. "I'm afraid I neglected to hear that pertinent detail. However, not that I care to appear smug, but you've evidently been suffering from wheezing often of late. Makes me wonder why you've been protesting your trips to the attic when they will strengthen your lungs, making you less prone to wheezing in the future."

Gertrude wasn't certain if she should

laugh or bang her head against the wall. "To refresh that obviously faulty memory of yours, Mrs. Davenport, the main reason I was wheezing the night of the engagement celebration was because I had to borrow a dress that was two sizes too small for me from Edwina. The reason behind that borrowing, if you'll recall, was because the bustle you created and demanded I wear that night was not what anyone could call practical, and . . . well . . . there's really no need to revisit the horror that happened to me while I was wearing that creation."

Mrs. Davenport pursed her lips. "There's no cause to be so snippy."

"There's no cause to embarrass a person either, but that didn't stop you from sending me off to a formal engagement celebration wearing a birdcage attached to my behind."

"It was only half a birdcage."

"True, although I must say here and now that birdcages really have no place being turned into bustles — no matter that gossip has it the size of bustles will continue to increase. However, because we are short on time and arguing is not going to help the tight schedule we're currently under, if you'll excuse me, I'm off to pack up all the reticules you've decided we can't leave behind."

To Gertrude's concern, the color that had recently returned to Mrs. Davenport's face drained immediately as she began biting her lip and looking almost nervous.

"If you're concerned I'm going to make use of that mysterious trunk, do know that I'm planning on hauling it straight back up to the attic, where it can continue to molder forever if that's what you wish," Gertrude said.

Mrs. Davenport's eyes suddenly seemed suspiciously bright. She blinked, blinked again, then let out a sigh. "You're very kind, dear, too kind to me in fact, and I fear what I have to disclose next will do a grave disservice to that kindness you've always afforded me."

Gertrude lowered herself back into the chair she'd just begun to vacate. "Have you decided you don't need to take all of those reticules with you to Newport, and you're worried I'm going to be annoyed with you because I'll need to put them away?"

"No, that's not it at all, although what I have to explain does revolve around reticules, or rather one particular reticule, the one I might have, quite unintentionally mind you, misplaced . . . on a yacht . . .

that might happen to belong to Harrison."

For what felt like an eternity, Gertrude simply sat on the chair, wishing she had not heard the words Mrs. Davenport had just uttered. When her employer shifted on the seat and smiled a less than genuine smile, the temper Gertrude always fought to keep in check no matter the ridiculousness of Mrs. Davenport's request took that very moment to break free. Heat coursed over her as her fingers clutched the arms of the chair, her mind whirling with retorts she knew she would never voice, no matter the fury she felt toward her employer.

"May I dare hope the contents resting in that particular reticule are not of a questionable nature?" she finally managed to ask.

Mrs. Davenport's smile dimmed. "They're perfectly ordinary items, Gertrude, items often found in a lady's reticule."

"But do they belong to you?"

"Ownership is so tricky to explain at times."

Gertrude lifted her chin. "It's not, and you're stalling. What's in the reticule?"

Mrs. Davenport winced right before she began to tick items off on her fingers. "Two strands of pearls, one silver spoon, a lovely gold locket encrusted with diamonds that has a lady's portrait in it, and a ring that fits my left ring finger to perfection."

With anger now thrumming through her every vein, Gertrude rose to her feet and stalked to the window, leaning her forehead against the cool pane of glass as she tried to regain her composure. It would not benefit her situation to rail at Mrs. Davenport, but at this particular moment, she simply could not understand how it had happened that she'd come to be employed by a woman with a distinct propensity for helping herself to items that did not belong to her.

Why had she never confronted Mrs. Davenport or demanded an explanation for behavior that was completely beyond the pale?

Mrs. Davenport was a wealthy woman who could purchase whatever item caught her fancy, and yet, from the very first week Gertrude began working for her, she'd been expected to return items that Mrs. Davenport pilfered from one society member after another.

Diamond bracelets, rings, jeweled combs, and even snuffboxes were simply a few of the items Gertrude had been expected to return discreetly. But in all those years, she and Mrs. Davenport had never discussed the matter. The one and only time Mrs. Davenport had even broached the subject was three days after she'd hired Gertrude. That broaching consisted of Mrs. Davenport mentioning she'd accidentally picked up a diamond ring from Mrs. Livingston's soirée and needed Gertrude to return the ring posthaste, although return it as stealthily as possible.

Instead of demanding a more reasonable explanation, though, Gertrude simply hopped in the hansom cab Mrs. Davenport suggested she hire, directed that cab to Mrs. Livingston's four-storied brownstone, paid her respects to Mrs. Livingston, and then, in a move that would have impressed the most seasoned actress on stage, dropped the ring as inconspicuously as possible to the carpeted floor. She'd then waited all of a few seconds before she'd released a rather dramatic breath and then pointed out the ring nestled in the carpet, earning Mrs. Livingston's most earnest appreciation.

It had not been an experience Gertrude enjoyed, and she'd sworn to herself that she'd never do such a thing again. But then, when a diamond bracelet had shown up on a table the day after another society event, she'd found herself traveling through the city in a different hansom cab, returning it without demanding so much as a single explanation from Mrs. Davenport before-hand.

But when she'd met up with Mrs. Davenport after completing her unpleasant task, she'd tried to discuss the situation with her employer.

The discussion had not gone well.

Mrs. Davenport seemed to shrink in size and age right before Gertrude's eyes. She'd also looked fragile and forlorn, reminding Gertrude exactly how her mother looked before she'd died. Because of that, and because Gertrude knew what could happen to a person when they descended into a despondent attitude, she'd immediately stopped her questioning about Mrs. Davenport's troubling habits and they'd never spoken about it again.

A pointed clearing of a throat pulled Gertrude from her memories. Forcing herself to turn from the window, she found Mrs. Davenport watching her warily.

"Are you still cross with me, dear?" she asked.

Gertrude arched a brow. "I think *cross* might not be the word I'd choose to describe what I'm feeling toward you now."

"Disappointed?"

"Try again."

"Vexed?"

"Not even close."

"Does this mean you're going to refuse to retrieve my reticule for me?"

Swallowing the *yes* she longed to release, Gertrude walked back to her chair and sat down.

Regarding Mrs. Davenport for a long moment, so long in fact that her employer began fidgeting, Gertrude finally threw up her hands in defeat. "Fine, I'll do it. But how, pray tell, do you expect me to know who to return all those pilfered items to that are lurking in that reticule? It's not as if we were in a society member's house that night. We were on a yacht, out to sea, and while I'm beyond curious to learn how you managed to relieve some of those guests of their possessions, I'm even more curious to learn how you're going to suggest I return those items without unwanted questions being asked."

"You'll be relieved to learn I didn't take any of those items from the guests, dear. I took them from a stateroom on the *Cornelia.*"

"You did not," Gertrude breathed.

Mrs. Davenport winced. "I'm afraid I did, but everything came from one stateroom, and it wasn't Edwina's room, if that makes you feel better."

"How could that possibly make me feel better?"

"Well, you said that Margaret was chasing you, and I'm fairly certain the items that accidentally landed in my reticule came from her stateroom."

"Enough of the 'accidentally landed' business, Mrs. Davenport. You helped yourself to items that didn't belong to you, but this time, you've placed me in a very tenuous position. Harrison is a friend of mine, and I'm appalled that you would abuse his hospitality, and abuse me in the process, by helping yourself to his sister's possessions and then expecting me to make everything right."

"I've behaved badly, haven't I?"

"Too right you have, but since I don't believe you'll do well in jail, I'll try to fix your latest incident of questionable behavior." Gertrude stood up and lifted her chin. "However, do know that this is the last time I'm intervening on your behalf, because as of today, I'm rendering my notice — effective as soon as I complete this last unpleasant task for you."

CHAPTER SIXTEEN

Not allowing herself to dwell on the tears she'd seen in Mrs. Davenport's eyes, nor allowing herself to return to the drawing room to withdraw her tendered notice, Gertrude continued down the front hallway. She stopped to fish out a few coins from a jar on the entranceway table to pay for a hansom cab, tucking them into her reticule before she lifted her chin and marched toward the door.

Nodding her thanks to the butler already holding the door for her, Gertrude stepped outside. She made it all of three feet before her path was blocked by a lady climbing the few steps that led to the front stoop.

"Temperance!" she exclaimed. "This is a lovely surprise."

Looking up from where she'd been watching the steps, Temperance Flowerdew lifted a hand and pushed back the brim of a very large hat, one that was a bit worse for wear and sported a fabric flower on it that had certainly seen better days. Reaching the last step, she moved directly to Gertrude's side, and then, to Gertrude's astonishment, Temperance pulled her into a very firm hug before she released her hold and took a step back.

"I do beg your pardon for descending on you with no notice, Gertrude."

"No notice is needed, Temperance, although . . ." Gertrude stared at Temperance's cheek. "What in the world happened to your face?"

Tugging the brim of her hat lower, Temperance shrugged. "It's of little consequence. I merely got in the way of Clementine's hand when she was in the midst of a tantrum."

"Clementine struck you?"

"I'm afraid she did, but I assure you, it looks worse than it feels. I've always marked easily, a disadvantage of being born with pale skin." She patted the large bag she was carrying. "I have rice powder and a horsehair brush in here that will set me to rights again, or at least hide the results of Clementine's temper."

Gertrude's own temper began to flare. "Does she hit you frequently?"

"She misses more often than not, and she

would have missed today, but I fear she took me unaware. There I was, putting freshly laundered clothing into her wardrobe, and the next thing I knew, she was attacking me."

"Good heavens."

"Indeed, but allow me to spare you the grim details of what happened next. You're clearly on your way out, so I won't keep you."

Gertrude looked over her shoulder, saw a shadow flicker past a window by the front door, and blew out a breath. "I'm afraid if you're here to visit with Mrs. Davenport, she's currently, ah . . . indisposed and in no position to receive callers."

Temperance's eyes widened. "She's not having a tantrum as well, is she?"

"Mrs. Davenport isn't the tantrum type. She embraces a more attack-you-with-guilt strategy, something that, in my humble opinion, is just as effective as physical violence."

"Too right you are," Temperance agreed. "My cousin's wife, Fanny Flowerdew, married to Wayne Flowerdew if that was in question, is a master with using guilt. Why, if I had a penny for all the times she reminded me that it's because of her generosity I have a roof over my head, I'd be a rich woman and wouldn't need to accept their charity."

"We wallflowers do seem to bear some difficult burdens at times."

"I wish I could disagree with that, but no truer words have ever been said." Temperance readjusted her hat, tugged the wide strap that was attached to her bag higher on her shoulder, and sent Gertrude a nod. "I won't keep you. And no need to worry that I'll bother Mrs. Davenport. I was actually here to speak with you, but it's not a matter of grave importance, so perhaps we can make arrangements to meet at a later date."

"Since you've never sought me out before, you obviously have a matter of *some* importance to speak with me about, so perhaps you'd care to walk with me to the nearest hansom cab. I'm more than happy to share my cab with you if you need a ride back home."

Entwining her arm with Temperance's, and not wanting to linger another second on the front stoop because she didn't want Mrs. Davenport to burst outside and deliver a speech she'd probably already composed — one that would undoubtedly be filled with emotional pleas to cajole Gertrude into remaining her companion — Gertrude steered them down the steps. It wasn't until they reached the corner, though, that she realized Temperance seemed to be dragging her feet.

"Am I walking too fast for you?" Gertrude asked, slowing her steps.

"Your pace is fine, it's just that I don't have funds with me to pay my share of a hansom cab," Temperance admitted.

"How did you get here then?"

"I walked, and before you look more horrified than you do right now, know that I enjoy walking. It's very good for a lady's constitution."

"A notion I should take to heart since I've recently decided I need to pursue more active endeavors, but for today, and because it will allow you an opportunity to tell me why you sought me out, we'll enjoy a hansom carriage, the fare paid for by Mrs. Davenport." Gertrude smiled. "It's the least she can do for all the trouble she's causing me."

Not allowing Temperance an opportunity to argue, Gertrude tightened her grip on Temperance's arm and plowed forward, keeping up a brisk pace until they reached the next block. To her relief, especially since she was becoming a little winded, an entire line of hansom cabs came into view.

"Doesn't Mrs. Davenport keep a carriage in the city?" Temperance asked as Gertrude directed them toward the cabs.

"She does, but this is one of those occasions where I feel drawn to use a public form of transportation. Mrs. Davenport owns somewhat distinctive carriages, barouches, buggies, and even a delivery wagon or three, and because of their distinctive characteristics, it's for the best if I'm not seen exiting one of those today."

Temperance stopped walking. "You do realize you're being annoyingly vague, don't you, and somewhat mysterious now that I think about it."

Gertrude took a second to rub a stitch that was forming in her side, brought on, no doubt, by practically galloping down the street. "Forgive me, I know I'm not being very forthcoming. However, the reason why I can't use Mrs. Davenport's carriages would be best left unexplained. In all honesty, the less you know about where I'm going, or the tricky task that's ahead of me, the better."

Temperance flipped up the brim of her hat, narrowing her eyes at Gertrude. "I'm far less delicate than you think."

Gertrude could feel the very corners of her mouth begin to curve. "Are you, now?"

A jerk of her head was Temperance's first response before she drew herself up. "I realize you're only familiar with the meek and timid Temperance Flowerdew, but I was not always timid, and certainly not meek. I've recently decided to abandon my mantle of meekness and resume the demeanor I once possessed, one that allowed me to experience a life of adventure. That right there is exactly why I'm going to insist you allow me to travel to whatever destination you've got in mind, no matter how tricky the situation may turn out to be."

Gertrude's lips stopped curving at once. "You'll do no such thing. I would never be comfortable involving you, even with that past life of adventure you claim to have led, into what amounts to nothing less than a bit of skullduggery on Mrs. Davenport's behalf."

The second those words left her mouth, Gertrude longed to call them back. Temperance was looking more determined than ever, and she was striding off in the direction of the hansom cabs.

"I'm definitely coming with you now," Temperance called over her shoulder right before she broke into a run, reached the first hansom cab, then jumped inside before the driver could get down from his seat and get the door for her.

Wondering what Temperance would do if

she simply chose another cab and left her friend behind, Gertrude's wondering came to an abrupt end when Temperance leaned out of the still-open door.

"If you'll recall, Gertrude, I'm currently without funds, so unless you want me to end up in debtor's prison because I can't pay the fare for this cab, you'll put all thoughts of leaving me behind aside."

"The world's gone mad," Gertrude mumbled before she walked over to the hansom cab, assured the driver she was in possession of funds, gave him directions to the docks, then climbed into the cab and took a seat directly beside Temperance because the cab only offered one bench seat. Taking a firm hold of the strap above her head, she held on tight as the cab lurched into motion.

"This is so exciting, my first adventure in what feels like forever," Temperance said, folding her hands demurely in her lap as the cab trundled down the road. "However, since I did insinuate myself into your situation against your wishes, do feel free to withhold the location of our final destination." She smiled. "That will be my punishment for being so forward."

"Since we're traveling in a hansom cab that has windows on either side, it's not going to come as much of a surprise to you when it pulls to a stop down on the docks. Although, just so we understand each other, you will remain in the cab while I go about the daunting business of dealing with a most delicate matter, and on that point I will hear no argument."

"You can't go strolling about the docks on your own."

Gertrude rolled her eyes. "I'm not going to be strolling the docks. It's more a case of my returning to a certain ship and retrieving something Mrs. Davenport apparently left on board the other night."

Temperance's mouth dropped open. "Good heavens. Do not tell me that you're about to try and retrieve, or rather make off with, that painting Clementine's been going on and on about, because . . ." She raised a hand to her chest. "That'll get you a direct ticket to jail. Talk of that painting going missing has already been bandied about, thanks to dear Clementine, and if it goes missing now, the first person the police will interrogate will be you."

For a second, Gertrude could only stare at Temperance, having absolutely no words at her disposal to respond to what was a farfetched deduction, until a thought struck that had her mouth moving again. "Do not tell me you suffered a slap from Clementine because you were arguing with her about my suspicious behavior."

Temperance waved that directly aside. "Of course not. Clementine slapped me because I hadn't disclosed to her that my very good friend, Mr. Gilbert Cavendish, is the half brother of an honest-to-goodness earl, and as such, he could, although it's highly doubtful, inherit an earldom over in England." She drew in a large breath before she continued. "She's also annoyed that I never mentioned I was good friends with Mr. Gilbert Cavendish, grew up in a house right next to his, and . . . I certainly never bothered to disclose that Gilbert, as the son of the Seventh Earl of Strafford, possesses the honorary title of Lord Cavendish, which Clementine evidently finds very appealing."

"I thought Clementine was intent on securing Harrison's affections?"

"Oh, she is, but Clementine's nothing if not greedy. I do believe she's now interested in securing the affections of both Harrison and Gilbert, and will then choose the gentleman who can give her the greatest advantages within society in the end."

Gertrude's brows drew together. "She certainly doesn't seem to lack any confidence about her appeal to members of the gentlemen set."

"Quite, although she's a lady who doesn't believe in taking any chances when she sets her sights on something she really wants. She's intolerant of anyone thwarting her plans, which is why I set out to speak with you today because —" Temperance paused — "Clementine has apparently decided I'm standing directly in the way of something she may want to acquire, that something being Gilbert. And to make certain that my standing in the way doesn't continue, she's convinced her father, Mr. Wayne Flowerdew, that I'm going to ruin her chances of securing a happily-ever-after. That means I've been given one month to secure employment and remove myself from the Flowerdew residence."

"You're being kicked out of your home because Clementine believes you're her competition?"

Temperance grinned. "I didn't think of it like that, but yes, apparently, she does believe I'm competition. How lovely." Her grin faded. "Although that's hardly going to be of comfort when I'm cast out on the streets in a month with not a penny to my name."

Gertrude took hold of Temperance's hand. "While I do know that Mrs. Davenport is now in need of a new companion, I'm afraid I'm not comfortable referring you to her. She's a peculiar woman, prone to unusual habits, but . . ." She smiled. "Miss Henrietta Huxley recently remarked that she would like to add you to her list of wallflowers she wants to take in hand, so she may have some suggestions for you on how to proceed with your life."

Temperance's eyes widened. "The very idea that Miss Henrietta Huxley longs to take me in hand is downright terrifying. However, returning to the far more troubling matter you mentioned first, do not tell me Mrs. Davenport has released you from service?"

"I haven't been fired," Gertrude said. "I tendered my notice because I've finally had enough of her questionable antics. Not to delve too deeply into the matter because the less you know the more believable you'll be if I run into unforeseen circumstances, she's now put me in the undesirable position of tidying up a mess that may ruin my friendship with Harrison, along with his entire family."

Temperance looked out the window for a second, then nodded, just once. "It seems to me as if the only acceptable option is for you to divulge all to me, and then I'll take over and tidy up Mrs. Davenport's mess. That way you won't be in danger of ruining your chances with Harrison, and I'll be able to say I was of great importance in assisting you to the altar."

Gertrude blinked. "I'm afraid you may be suffering from inaccurate information. Making it to the altar, let alone walking down it with Harrison waiting for me at the end, is highly unlikely. He enjoys my company as a friend, but that is as far as our relationship will ever go."

Shoving the brim of her hat away from her face again, Temperance peered at Gertrude for a long moment. "How is it possible you haven't realized Harrison holds you in the highest esteem?"

"I know he holds me in esteem, but it's of the *friendship* variety, and certainly isn't the type of esteem where one expects a proposal."

Thankfully, the hansom cab took that moment to turn down Twenty-Eighth Street, jostling Gertrude and Temperance in the process, but unfortunately, Temperance shoved herself upright and pinned Gertrude with a far-too-knowing gaze.

"I do not claim to be an expert on gentlemen, but I am a wallflower. That means I'm observant as *most* of us are, and I've observed Harrison regarding you with more than friendship lingering in his eyes."

Something that felt very much like hope slithered up Gertrude's spine. "You truly believe he fancies me?"

"Indeed, but because I've also observed that he's somewhat obtuse when it comes to feminine matters, I do believe you're going to have to take the lead with him, delicately of course, and allow him to know you fancy him as well."

Gertrude raised a hand to her chest. "I could never."

"You can if you don't want him to eventually end up with one of the many society ladies rumor has it are about to descend on him in hordes."

"I wouldn't know how to go about that type of business."

Temperance smiled. "I'm afraid I won't be much assistance, what with my limited knowledge of gentlemen, but perhaps Miss Henrietta Huxley will have some suggestions. She did proclaim an interest in taking some wallflowers in hand, didn't she?"

Before Gertrude could do more than grimace at that thought, the hansom cab pulled to the side of the road and came to a stop. Glancing out the window, she felt her nerves begin to jingle.

"It seems we have arrived," she said, reaching for the reticule that was tied to her wrist. She opened it and pulled out the note Harrison had sent her the day before.

"Have you written down instructions on how to proceed?" Temperance asked, holding out her hand.

"No, which means there's no need for me to hand this over, nor is there a need for you to try and take it so that you can bolt out of the carriage and proceed in my place. This is simply a note Harrison sent me yesterday, asking me to look after Edwina. I'm going to use it to get on board the *Cornelia,* saying I'm supposed to meet Edwina on the yacht."

"What are you going to say when you're told Edwina isn't on board, or . . ." Temperance's eyes widened. "What are you going to do if Edwina *is* on board?"

"She's not on board, because Mrs. Davenport told me Edwina is spending the day shopping."

"But what if one of the other sisters is on board?"

"Then I'll simply tell them I've come to see about Mrs. Davenport's reticule. But I'm hoping I won't have to address that situation because I have no idea how I'd explain why that reticule ended up in one of the rooms by the library, or why it was stuffed into the very back of a desk in that room."

"Should I not inquire as to how Mrs. Davenport's reticule got stuffed into a desk?"

"Probably not, nor should you inquire about the contents that may or may not be lurking in that reticule."

Leaving Temperance with her mouth slightly agape, Gertrude drew in a breath, reached for the door, and stepped from the cab. Telling the driver she'd be back directly, Gertrude squared her shoulders and walked toward the dock, her feet dragging the closer she got to the *Cornelia.* Heading up the plank that had, thankfully, been left down, she reached the deck, drawing the immediate attention of the few members of the crew who were polishing brass fixtures.

"May I help you with something, miss?"

Clearing her throat while praying she would be able to get a reasonable answer out of her mouth, Gertrude directed her attention to the man who'd posed the question. "I do hope so," she began, holding up the note. "I've been asked by Mr. Sinclair to keep an eye on his sister, Edwina, while he's away, and I'm supposed to meet her here this afternoon."

The man frowned. "I'm afraid Miss Sinclair is not here."

"I'm sure she's simply running a little behind schedule," Gertrude said, stepping closer to the man and waving the note from Harrison so that he could see Harrison's signature scrawled across the bottom. "Would it be permissible for me to wait for her in the library? I noticed the other evening that it's very well stocked, which will allow me to pass the time quite pleasantly while I wait for Edwina."

The man looked at the letter Gertrude was still fanning herself with, then smiled and nodded. "That will be fine. Would you like me to escort you there?"

"That's very kind, but I do remember the way, and I wouldn't want to disrupt your work."

Not allowing the man an opportunity to argue, Gertrude began walking, her heart beating so rapidly she was all but certain the men still polishing the brass could hear it. Breathing a sigh of relief when she looked over her shoulder and found no one following her, she increased her pace. Once she reached the stairs, she hurried down them to the next level, then walked through the companionway, pausing when she reached the library.

Because Mrs. Davenport had been somewhat rattled when she'd followed Gertrude out of the drawing room after Gertrude had given her notice, the location of the missing reticule was less than clear. All Mrs. Davenport could remember with any certainty was there'd been a desk in the room she'd darted into to get rid of her reticule after Harrison heard her jingling, a room that was in the near vicinity of the library.

Knowing there was nothing to do but get on with the daunting matter at hand, Gertrude started with the door closest to her, finding herself in a storage area with no desk in sight.

Moving on to the next door, she found no success in that room either, but when she opened the door to the third room, she smiled. Bolted to the floor was a lovely desk, one with large drawers. She strode over to it and made short shrift of pulling out the drawers, her smile widening when her fingers closed around a beaded object that could only be Mrs. Davenport's reticule. Tucking it under her arm, she walked out of the room, then froze on the spot when she encountered a woman in the hallway — a woman who'd frozen as well, and a woman Gertrude had the sneaking suspicion just might be related to Harrison and his sisters given that she had the distinct look of a Sinclair about her.

"Well, well, well," the woman began in a voice as cold as ice. "What *do* we have here?"

CHAPTER SEVENTEEN

Harrison gave the new shipping proposal he was working on one last glance, then pushed it aside, leaning back in his office chair and raising his arms above his head to help relieve the knot that was developing in his back.

Contract proposals were not his favorite way to spend an afternoon, but since Adelaide, who adored working on contracts and had an unusual affinity for figures, was preparing to depart from New York with Margaret to deliver a new ship down the coast to a client, it was up to him to complete the proposal.

Yawning, he glanced out the window, took a moment to enjoy the sight of a beautiful sunny day, and wondered if Gertrude might be available to take a sail around the coast with him later that evening.

Even though she'd been adamant about the idea that being seen with him would cause the gossips to come out in droves, he'd missed her while he'd been away delivering an engine part his father needed, and . . .

"Harrison, thank goodness you've returned. I was worried you'd decided to take a small holiday after parting ways with your father, but here you are, back at the office, and as I already mentioned, thank goodness for that."

Setting aside his thoughts of Gertrude, along with the notion that he'd missed her, which was rather curious because he'd never missed a lady unrelated to him before, Harrison rose to his feet as his mother, Cornelia Sinclair, swept into his office. She was looking lovely in a sensible walking dress of what he thought might be yellow, although why she'd chosen to wear a red hat that was at distinct odds with the yellow, he couldn't say.

He walked around his desk, met his mother in the middle of the office, then bent down and kissed her cheek.

"You're looking very well today, Mother. That's a delightful yellow gown."

Cornelia patted his cheek. "It's green, dear, to match my hat, which is a shade darker, but green all the same."

Harrison tilted his head and considered

the hat in question. "Is it really?"

"Indeed, however . . ." Cornelia took a step away from him, looking him up and down. "That's an interesting ensemble you have on today, darling. Overly bright some might say, and I'm not sure the pink jacket should be worn with . . ." She bent over and began examining the print of his trousers. "What an interesting choice some tailor made to create trousers out of periwinkle blue, and are these small designs supposed to be clovers scattered about the fabric?"

"I thought my jacket was orange," Harrison began, "and no, I don't have clovers on my pants."

"I'm afraid you do, and I'm afraid I should mention that your jacket wouldn't be any less bright if it was actually orange." Cornelia straightened and shook her head. "I keep hoping Asher's formidable fashion sense will eventually rub off on you. But since that hope is beginning to dim, you might want to consider reaching out to your friend and *accepting* his assistance. A well-dressed gentleman is far more appealing to ladies than an unusually dressed one, and you must remember that I would enjoy being presented with a few grandchildren before I'm at my last prayers."

"You're nowhere near to being at your last prayers, Mother. And to address your suggestion about seeking fashion advice from Asher, according to reliable sources, society ladies have recently gotten me into their matrimonial sights, unusual fashion sense or not. They, apparently, don't seem to be bothered by pink jackets paired with . . . er . . . flowered trousers, so there's no need for me to bother Asher."

In a blink of an eye, Cornelia turned from an indulgent mother to a highly indignant one. "Society ladies are casting their attention your way?"

Harrison refused a wince. "That does seem to be the talk around the city."

"There's *talk* of you around the city, and not simply business talk?"

"How was your trip to see your sister?" Harrison asked as he took his mother's arm and ushered her as quickly as possible across the room to where two battered chairs flanked an old wooden table. Waiting until she took a seat, not that he was allowing her much choice in the matter since he'd delivered her directly in front of the chair and helped her into it, Harrison strode over to the pot of coffee he always kept in his office and poured his mother a cup. Walking back to her, he handed over the cup and smiled expectantly.

Taking a sip, and then proving she was the best kind of mother because Harrison knew the coffee was lukewarm at best and yet she took another sip before setting the cup on the table, Cornelia raised her head.

"I won't be distracted by your charming manners."

"Forgive me, Mother, but I don't believe you're capable of becoming distracted when you've got something on your mind," he said, lowing himself into the other battered chair.

"But that doesn't stop you from trying," Cornelia pointed out. "However, since you are a charming scamp, and I have missed you while I've been away, allow me to simply say that my visit with my sister was aggravating to say the least. That is why I've returned to the city sooner than expected."

"Is Aunt Beatrice still of the belief you should abandon your interest in the family business and spend your days attending one social event after another?"

"Of course, but that's not the reason I found her so taxing this visit. It was her many and vocal opinions regarding my darling girls that set my teeth on edge. She's convinced all three of them are going to become confirmed spinsters, and she's laying the blame for that squarely on my shoulders."

"In all likelihood, she was just making polite conversation," Harrison said. "You know you and your sister don't share many interests. I imagine she believes you enjoy speaking about your daughters, which is why she must bring them into your conversations so often."

"She believes I'm a horrible mother and have ruined all chances my daughters have of making formidable matches by not presenting them to society." Cornelia shuddered. "One would think that after what happened to Margaret and her experience with two fortune-hunters, my sister would be more sympathetic to my desire to keep my girls firmly out of that cesspool known as the socially elite."

"Not all society gentlemen are fortune-hunters, nor are all the ladies only interested in landing a gentleman of wealth."

Cornelia quirked a brow. "This from a man who just admitted he's become interesting to eligible society ladies, none of whom seem to have an issue with the fact that you possess not even a smidgen of style, but . . . you do possess a far too intriguing fortune."

Harrison raised a hand to his heart. "Now,

that hurts."

"I highly doubt that," Cornelia said with a roll of her eyes. "But returning to the reason I'm here, it's about —"

"Edwina," Harrison finished for her, knowing it would be best all around if he simply owned up to the idea that he'd lost all control over the situation with his younger sister.

Unfortunately, it soon became clear his mother was not aware of that particular situation because she abandoned the cup of coffee she'd picked up again, sat forward on the chair, and pinned him with a glare that was downright terrifying.

"What about Edwina?" she demanded.

"You haven't seen her since you've returned?" Harrison countered, the only plausible question that sprang to mind while his thoughts began sorting through any and all explanations that might not find him the victim of his mother's wrath.

"You're stalling. Out with it. What has she done now, and why, pray tell, weren't you there to stop her?"

Harrison's forehead furrowed. "Perhaps you have me confused with your other son, Mother. If I need remind you, I've never been able to stop my sisters with any of the mad schemes they've contemplated over the years."

"Very funny as I don't have another son, but . . . what mad scheme is Edwina contemplating?"

"I'm afraid she's traveled past the contemplation phase and embraced a plan of action."

When his mother began tapping a shoe against the floor, Harrison knew there was nothing left to do but disclose all, no matter the trouble that it was certain to bring him, as well as Edwina.

"She may have decided to give society a whirl, and because she's a most resourceful lady, a lovely trait she inherited from you . . ." He tossed a smile his mother's way, not reassured when her lips pressed into a thin line and her toe-tapping increased.

He cleared his throat. "Yes, well, you see, she's become acquainted with Miss Permilia Griswold, Asher's fiancée, a lovely young woman I know you'll adore since you adore Asher. Add in the idea that Permilia seems to be the love of Asher's life . . ."

"No distractions if you please. Edwina . . . society . . . her resourcefulness."

"Quite right. I've taken to digressing, haven't I?"

Cornelia sat back, crossed her arms over her chest, and began a tactic he'd seen her use often throughout the years, a tactic he and his sisters affectionately referred to as *waiting them out.*

Drawing in a breath, he crossed *his* arms over *his* chest, then made the instant decision now was not the time to attempt to beat his mother at her own game.

"Besides making the acquaintance of Permilia Griswold, who is a member of society, although was regulated to the wallflower section, Edwina also became known to a delightful young lady, another wallflower no less, and because of that introduction —"

Cornelia sucked in a sharp breath, stopping Harrison mid-sentence. "You never refer to ladies you know as delightful. Could it be possible that you've been purposefully withholding information about this delightful young lady because you've developed an interest in her, and yet don't want me to interfere in your courtship?"

"I don't have time to court any lady, Mother, as you very well know. Our business is booming these days, and because of that, I need to give it my full attention. From what I understand, courting a lady takes effort and flowers and . . . well, I could go on and on about the courting rituals I've

290

read about in . . . well, never mind about that. Suffice it to say that now is not the time for me to pursue any lady, but do know that I certainly will seek out your counsel when the time is appropriate for me to set my attention to matters of courting."

"Matters of the heart, dear, rarely wait for an appropriate time to strike."

"Duly noted, but —"

Interrupting whatever he'd been about to say with a wave of her hand, Cornelia tilted her head. "What courtship books have you been perusing?"

"I have no idea how we've become so distracted from the subject of Edwina, but returning to my darling yet oh-so-troublesome sister, she's making arrangements even as we speak to travel to Newport and become introduced to society by a society matron, Mrs. Davenport."

Instead of the outrage he was expecting that statement to elicit, even though he knew he should be slightly embarrassed about tossing his sister under the carriage wheels for the sheer purpose of distracting his mother, Cornelia turned her head to the window, taking a long moment to study the people on the sidewalk before she turned back to him. "You haven't been reading your sisters' novels again, have you?"

"You know about my deepest and darkest reading secret?"

The corners of Cornelia's lips twitched. "Of course. I'm your mother. And as your mother, I know exactly why you decided to read stories with a strong romantic thread to them. You're the only male in the family, except for your father, and because you've been surrounded by females your entire life, reading novels that were penned by the likes of Jane Austen, Emily and Charlotte Brontë, and even Mary Shelley, was a brilliant way for you to get a small understanding of how the feminine mind works."

"I think you may be affording me far too much credit, Mother."

Cornelia shook her head. "You're less obtuse about women than what you present to the world, darling, even if you've yet to understand that."

"I think you may have just insulted me."

"I have done no such thing, although one could hardly blame you for adopting an obtuse attitude. In all honesty, I've always believed you've done so as a means of self-preservation, a way to survive to adulthood, if you will, while surrounded by so much femininity."

Harrison smiled. "I used to believe it was a normal occurrence for rooms to have legs hanging from the rafters."

Cornelia returned the smile. "Your sisters have always been less than selective about where they hang their stockings, especially when we're traveling at sea. But those types of experiences have allowed you to witness more of the feminine world than most gentlemen of the day, which will eventually serve you well if you're blessed to have daughters of your own." Her smile suddenly faded. "But speaking of daughters, I'm suddenly returned to the idea that one of mine is running amok, and . . . forgive me, but you didn't mention something about a Mrs. Davenport earlier, did you?"

"I did. She's the society matron who has enthusiastically agreed to sponsor Edwina into society, and the last I heard, she's invited Edwina to spend the summer season with her in Newport."

Cornelia gripped the arms of the chair. "May I dare hope that Davenport is a common name amongst the New York society set?"

"Why would you dare hope something like that?"

Cornelia released a sigh. "I've somehow managed to become so distracted with all the talk of ladies, your sisters, and novels that I've yet to explain the true reason for seeking you out at the office."

With that, she rose to her feet and strode across the office, picking up a bag she'd abandoned by the door. She rifled through it, then pulled out what appeared to be a lady's reticule, one that looked as if it was meant to be used at formal events. Holding it up to Harrison, she arched a brow.

"Does this look familiar to you?"

The back of Harrison's neck began to tingle. "I can't say it does."

Cornelia opened the reticule and pulled out a strand of pearls. "Do these look familiar to you?"

"I'm sorry, but all pearls look the same to me."

Heaving a breath, Cornelia reached into the reticule again and pulled out a locket. "What about this?"

The tingling increased. "Is that Margaret's locket?"

"It is, the one with a miniature painting of your grandparents inside it." She dropped the locket back inside the reticule. "There are other items in here as well, but what is truly concerning to me is that I discovered these in the possession of a young lady I found sneaking around the *Cornelia,* a lady who claimed she was a paid companion to none other than a Mrs. Davenport."

A sense of dread descended over him. "This young lady wouldn't happen to go by the name of Miss Gertrude Cadwalader, would she?"

Cornelia blinked. "Good heavens. You know Miss Cadwalader?"

"She's that *delightful* lady I mentioned before, and a very dear friend of mine."

Cornelia blinked again before she lifted her chin. "Perhaps you really are far more obtuse than I've imagined, because Miss Gertrude Cadwalader is not delightful in the least. She is a confidence artist and a thief. And as such, she deserves to remain in jail, which is exactly where the authorities I summoned took her."

CHAPTER EIGHTEEN

"Surely you must realize it'll go easier on you, Miss Cadwalader, if you simply make a full confession while also providing me with a complete list of your associates."

Resisting the urge to bang her head against the scarred wooden table in front of her because she'd been asked to confess and divulge names of her associates for the past four hours, Gertrude lifted her chin.

"We've been over this about a million times, Officer Huntington. I don't have any associates. I'm simply a paid companion, not a professional criminal."

Officer Huntington looked up from the notes he'd been compiling. "That's what all criminals say, Miss Cadwalader. Now, tell me, who exactly is this Mrs. Davenport you mentioned to Mrs. Sinclair when she found you in possession of items that didn't belong to you, and what part does Mrs. Davenport play within your criminal organization?"

"Mrs. Davenport is not a criminal. She's a respected member of New York society."

Officer Huntington removed his spectacles, wiped the lenses with a handkerchief he pulled from his pocket, returned the handkerchief, and then pushed the spectacles back over his nose. "Why would a respected member of New York society bother to associate with someone of the criminal persuasion?"

"I'm *not* of the criminal persuasion. I'm a paid companion who was running an errand for my employer, which, unfortunately, did not turn out quite the way I'd expected."

"Ah, so Mrs. Davenport has no idea she employs a thief?"

"I'm *not* a thief."

"Why were you caught red-handed with possessions that didn't belong to you?"

"That's a little tricky to explain, but allow me to simply say that those possessions were never taken from the *Cornelia,* so in actuality, they'd never been stolen."

"Only because you were caught before you were able to leave that ship."

Gertrude leaned back in her chair. "Which is a valid point, Officer Huntington, but again, I wasn't trying to leave the ship with items that didn't belong to me. I was only trying to return them to their proper place."

"Which is an odd thing for a thief to do, but it implies that someone took those items to begin with. However, here's what I believe happened. You slunk around the ship looking for valuables while attending what sounds to me like a night of frivolity. Then you returned when you thought the coast was clear, using an excuse that'll be easily dismissed once Miss Edwina Sinclair is located, that claim being rather flimsy since you and I both know there were no plans for you to meet Miss Edwina Sinclair today."

"Fine," Gertrude admitted, knowing Officer Huntington was right in claiming she'd been slightly less than honest. "I didn't have plans to meet Edwina on board the *Cornelia,* but I didn't travel to the yacht to rob it. I truly was only there to fetch that reticule and return items that were inadvertently stashed inside the reticule to their proper owner."

"You do realize that sounds completely mad, don't you?" Officer Huntington asked before he bent his head over his pad of paper and began jotting down a few notes. Raising his head as his hand stilled over the page, he caught Gertrude's eye. "If you'll just give me a few names, I promise I'll have the judge go easy on you."

"Why do I feel as if I've suddenly been deposited directly into a dime novel, one complete with an overenthusiastic detective and a dupe of a suspect who seems to be destined to spend the rest of her life behind bars in some derelict jail?"

Officer Huntington simply stared at her for a good long moment before he began writing in a rather forceful fashion.

Drumming her fingers against the table, a nervous habit she'd developed after her father died, Gertrude stilled when Officer Huntington lifted his head and sent her a scowl. Placing her hands in her lap, she cleared her throat.

"Could I perhaps send a note to Mrs. Davenport, asking her to send me an attorney or some type of counsel?" she asked, earning another scowl from Officer Huntington in the process.

"If this Mrs. Davenport *was* somehow involved in this heist, and if she's truly a society matron," Officer Huntington began instead of answering Gertrude's question, "should I assume she lost all of the money that has allowed her to travel within society and has resorted to theft to maintain appearances?"

For the briefest of seconds, his question gave Gertrude pause, until she recalled that her employer never kept any of the items she stole, and she paid everyone on her staff a more than generous wage. She also, now that Gertrude considered the matter, never had creditors pounding on her door seeking payment for accounts past due.

Gertrude shook her head. "Mrs. Davenport's finances seem to be in fine order, sir, not that she discusses such matters with me, her paid companion."

"How did she come by her fortune?"

"Ah . . ."

"Where's *Mr.* Davenport?" he shot at her before she'd had a chance to fully think about the first question, not that she knew where Mrs. Davenport had gotten her money. She also didn't have the least little idea what had happened to Mr. Davenport except to think he'd died sometime in the distant past. Mrs. Davenport never spoke about that man, leaving Gertrude with the impression it was a painful topic for the woman.

"I believe Mr. Davenport is dead," she settled on saying.

"And he was a wealthy gentleman who left his fortune to his wife?"

"I would assume so, but again, I'm the paid companion, not a confidante."

Officer Huntington nodded in a satisfied

manner before he bent his head and began scribbling furiously on his pad of paper.

"What could you have possible gotten that was worthy of being written down from what I've just disclosed?" she asked, leaning forward and trying to make out the words he was still scrawling across the page.

"Resentment is a fine motivator for criminal acts, Miss Cadwalader," Officer Huntington replied as he continued writing. "I'm beginning to get a clearer picture of what transpired, and I do believe what we're looking at is a disgruntled employee who was trying to frame her employer for theft."

"I beg your pardon?"

"You wanted to be more of a daughter figure to this Mrs. Davenport, and yet she saw you as nothing more than an employee."

"That's ridiculous," Gertrude said, wincing just a touch when she heard the slight bit of doubt in her tone, that doubt giving her pause.

Had she been holding resentment against Mrs. Davenport?

With her fingers once again drumming a rapid tattoo against the table, she considered that idea, fighting the urge to fidget when truth reared its ugly head.

It could be a distinct possibility that Officer Huntington wasn't completely off the mark.

She'd convinced herself over the past few years that she continued working for a woman who possessed very peculiar and obviously arrest-worthy pursuits because she needed to earn a wage. But in all honesty, companions in possession of good breeding were difficult to find, so she could have left Mrs. Davenport's employ at any point in time and found other employment easily, but for some reason, she'd stayed.

Why *had* she stayed?

"You mentioned you lost your parents at a relatively early age, Miss Cadwalader," Officer Huntington said, dragging Gertrude from her thoughts. "That right there, if I were to hazard a guess, is what is behind your resentment toward Mrs. Davenport. You wanted her to embrace you as more of a daughter figure than an employee, although I'm sure you were also hoping she'd make you the beneficiary of her estate if she is, indeed, without much family. How old were you when your mother died?"

"Ten," Gertrude said as Officer Huntington began writing again, far more words than it should have taken to record her age. "I do hope you're not adding that nonsense about my wanting Mrs. Davenport to make me an heiress."

Officer Huntington ignored her, writing a few more sentences before he began looking through his pages and pages of notes. "You mentioned Mrs. Davenport suffers from melancholy. May I inquire as to whether that melancholy has increased since you've been in her employ, and if so, could you possibly be the reason behind that increase?"

If Officer Huntington wasn't in possession of a lethal-looking weapon attached to his belt, Gertrude might have contemplated stalking out of the interrogation room. However, since he was in possession of a gun, and she was all but certain he didn't believe in coddling a prisoner who happened to be a lady, she settled for remaining silent, earning a grunt from him in response before he applied himself to his notes again.

The very idea he'd broached the topic of her purposefully drawing Mrs. Davenport into increased melancholy was laughable. If anything, she'd done everything in her power to lessen the depressed state her employer frequently embraced because, by doing so, she was hoping to find a bit of redemption, as well as relief, from the regret she harbored because of the circumstances surrounding her mother's death.

The moment that idea took hold, Gertrude realized it was nothing less than the truth, but before she could contemplate the idea further, there was a brisk knock on the door. A second later it opened, revealing Harrison, who immediately strode across the room, clear temper in his eyes.

Bracing herself for the anger she knew was about to be directed her way, and not blaming him for that anger because she'd been caught red-handed on board his ship with his sister's possessions and had gained entrance to that ship by spouting a lie, she could only blink in stunned surprise when he sent her a small smile and then turned his attention to Officer Huntington.

"I'm here to see Miss Cadwalader released."

Officer Huntington pushed back his chair and stood up. "Who are you?"

"I'm Mr. Harrison Sinclair of Sinclair Shipping."

Officer Huntington seemed to size up Harrison, and as he did so, Gertrude did the same. What she saw caused a laugh to bubble up in her throat, one she forced right back down again.

Harrison was dressed in one of the most outlandish outfits she'd seen him wear to date. A pink jacket brought attention to the darkness of his face, while the most unusual trousers she'd ever seen on a gentleman were done up in blue with tiny little clovers marching all over the fabric. His hair was pulled into a knot on the very back of his head, tied with a piece of frayed rope. Knee-high boots splattered with mud and in need of polishing completed his outfit.

Even though he didn't possess an ounce of what those with any fashion sense would call style, to her, he was the most stylish and handsome gentleman in the entire world at this particular moment. And . . . she realized, even if she'd never admit it out loud, that she'd fallen ever so slightly in love with the man.

Releasing a smidgen of a sigh, Gertrude forced all thoughts of what would only be unrequited love aside right as Officer Huntington gave a telling tap on his gun.

"Forgive me if I don't simply release Miss Cadwalader into your company, Mr. Sinclair, because, forgive me again, but I highly doubt you're related to the Mrs. Sinclair who caught this woman stealing. You're more likely one of Miss Cadwalader's associates, presenting yourself as a carnival hawker if I were to hazard a guess, unless you're truly a carnival hawker, which goes far in proving my theory you're another confidence artist."

Harrison narrowed his eyes on the officer. "Where in the world did you get the idea I'm a carnival hawker?"

"No self-respecting gentleman I know would be caught dead in pink, let alone wear pants like that. But I've seen carnival hawkers in my day wearing flashy items to drum up business."

"I originally thought my jacket was orange, and I'll have you know, I bought these clothes over in Paris a few months back. Granted, they were highly discounted, but the salesman told me this look was still slightly in style."

Officer Huntington's brows drew together. "If I thought that was the truth, I'd say you were swindled, but since I don't, do know that telling me you traveled to Paris isn't exactly enough evidence to convince me you're Mr. Sinclair."

Harrison threw up his hands in clear frustration and walked Gertrude's way. He reached her side before she could blink, and then she found herself pulled out of the chair and straight into his strong arms.

Wonderful warmth spread through her as her knees went a little weak, a direct result of having a gentleman come to her rescue for the very first time in her life, if she discounted the time Harrison had swept her up into his arms because she hadn't truly been a damsel in distress at that particular moment, simply winded from a tightly laced corset.

Burrowing her nose into the fabric of his shirt, she breathed in a scent that reminded her of lime mixed with the sea. Releasing a breath, along with a good deal of the tension she'd been carrying, she closed her eyes and enjoyed the feeling of safety she'd not felt in a very, very long time.

When unexpected tears stung her eyes, she drew in a shaky breath, but when she tried to step away from Harrison, he tightened his grip on her and bent his head.

"Are you all right?" he whispered in her ear, the feel of his breath caressing her cheek causing her knees to go weaker than ever.

"I'm fine," she managed to whisper back, her words muffled because her face was still pressed into the hardness of his chest. "Especially now when it doesn't seem as if you're furious with me."

What sounded exactly like a growl was his first response and then he eased her away from him and looked at her. "Why would I be furious with you?"

"Because your mother caught me with

items I think might belong to Margaret."

Harrison's lips curved into a smile. "Which is troubling to be sure, but I know there's a completely reasonable explanation as to what you were doing with those items, and not an explanation that ends with you admitting you're a thief."

"How do you know that?"

For what seemed like an eternity, Harrison simply looked into her eyes, the kindness resting in his unusual blue eyes drawing her closer. Another sigh escaped her lips, and then his gaze drifted to those lips, and everything faded away.

She was no longer standing in the middle of an interrogation room, but standing on the deck of one of his ships, feeling the breeze wash over her and anticipating what it was going to feel like when she received her very first kiss, given to her by the man she now knew . . .

A loud clearing of a throat had her stepping away from Harrison even as he blinked, blinked again, then turned his attention to Officer Huntington once more, temper flashing through his eyes again.

"I don't mean to interrupt what looked like a most touching moment, but now is hardly the time and place for gestures of a romantic nature," Officer Huntington said.

He nodded to the door then looked back at Harrison. "Now then, if you'd be so kind as to wait outside until I'm done questioning Miss Cadwalader, I will allow you to say a proper good-bye before I escort her off to a cell because I'm not completely heartless."

Harrison reached out, drew Gertrude closer, then settled his hand at the small of her back, almost as if he'd known her knees were trembling over the very idea she might soon be carted off to a cell.

"I'm not waiting outside, nor is there any reason for you to hold Miss Cadwalader, let alone cart her off to jail. My mother, Mrs. Sinclair, has sent me here with a letter to have all charges dropped against Miss Cadwalader, because my mother has come to the conclusion she's made a horrible mistake."

Officer Huntington arched a thick brow Harrison's way. "Not that I believe you, but how did Mrs. Sinclair arrive at that decision?"

"I explained to her that Mrs. Davenport, Gertrude's employer, has a peculiar habit of picking up items that don't belong to her. She's a little —" Harrison tapped a finger against his forehead — "touched in the head if you get my meaning, that condition brought about because of her age. She's quite elderly."

"Not so elderly she apparently wasn't capable of pulling off a heist of a considerable amount of jewelry."

"She's wily, I'll give you that."

Shaking his head, Officer Huntington pointed toward the door. "And I'll give you credit for having a glib tongue, but I don't believe your story."

As Harrison opened his mouth to obviously argue that point, the door opened with a resounding creak, and another gentleman entered the room.

"Agent McParland!" Gertrude exclaimed, smiling at the Pinkerton detective she'd met a few months before, and one who'd helped save her, Harrison, Asher, and Permilia from a madman intent on a killing spree. "Good heavens, it's wonderful to see you. Harrison and I are in desperate need of your assistance again."

To Gertrude's confusion, Agent McParland did not return her smile. Instead, he inclined his head to Officer Huntington. "What seems to be the problem?"

By the time Officer Huntington was finished explaining, Agent McParland was looking somewhat frightening, the normally pleasant attitude of the detective nowhere to be seen as he kept sending downright chilly glances her way. Taking a moment to shake Officer Huntington's hand, Agent McParland then stepped up to Harrison and shook his hand, but failed to offer even the slightest courtesy to Gertrude.

"He really is Mr. Harrison Sinclair?" Officer Huntington asked.

"He is," Agent McParland returned. "Which means the letter from his mother that Harrison turned in to the officer at the front desk is acceptable for having Miss Cadwalader released. All of the charges against her have been dropped."

"Wonderful," Harrison said, turning to Gertrude. "Shall I see you home?"

"I'm afraid that while Officer Huntington is done with Miss Cadwalader, I'm going to need her to stay for a little longer because I have some questions for her," Agent McParland said. He then walked Officer Huntington to the door, thanked him for his time, then firmly shut the door.

"What's this about, Agent McParland?" Harrison asked.

Agent McParland turned to Gertrude. "Do you want me to tell him, or shall I have him leave the room so you and I can continue this in private?"

Apprehension stole through Gertrude's veins. "Harrison is more than welcome to stay with me, Agent McParland, although I

311

have no idea what you believe I need to disclose."

Instead of answering her, Agent McParland gestured to the chairs, waited for Harrison to help her into a seat, then took the chair Officer Huntington had been using. Sitting down beside her, Harrison reached out and took hold of her hand, giving it a good squeeze.

"I'm a man with a reputation of being a good judge of character, Miss Cadwalader," Agent McParland began, "but I must say, you had me fooled. Why, with those delicate looks and that charming attitude of yours, I truly believed you were a lady above reproach. However, you fooled us all, didn't you?"

"I'm afraid you have me at a disadvantage" was all Gertrude could think to say.

"I believe it's the other way around, Miss Cadwalader," Agent McParland countered. "From what I can surmise, *you've* had everyone at a disadvantage, duped into believing you're simply a retiring wallflower, companion to an elderly lady whom everyone knows is odd." Agent McParland leaned forward. "But that's not the truth, is it, Miss Cadwalader? You and Mrs. Davenport are in league together, performing heists all over the place, while muddying the waters by returning some of the items but not all."

Harrison rose from the chair, a tic throbbing on the side of his cheek. "You go too far, Agent McParland. I demand you apologize at once as well as cease this ridiculous interview. It's past time Gertrude was allowed to leave."

Instead of responding to Harrison, a risky move in Gertrude's opinion because Harrison wasn't the type of gentleman most men would want to go up against when he was in a temper, Agent McParland leveled cool eyes on Gertrude. "You're good, Miss Cadwalader — very, very good. But you shouldn't have stolen from the Manhattan Beach Hotel. One of the victims identified you and Mrs. Davenport as suspicious characters, and to be clear, this victim is a credible one. She told us that you and Mrs. Davenport showed an inordinate amount of interest in her tiara only an hour or two before it went missing out of her room after she'd retired for the night."

Gertrude drew in a breath, fighting to keep the panic that was now flowing freely through her veins at bay.

Mrs. Davenport had shown a marked interest in the tiara the woman who'd joined them on the veranda had been wearing, but . . . she couldn't have taken it, because . . .

"What I'd like to know is how this woman identified Mrs. Davenport and Gertrude," Harrison said, his voice filled with steel. "There were hundreds of guests roaming about that hotel the night we were there."

Gertrude watched as Agent McParland gave a sad shake of his head. "While I do understand your reluctance to accept Miss Cadwalader's duplicity, I knew the moment the victim described an elderly, somewhat eccentric lady, that it could very well be Mrs. Davenport. We at the Pinkerton Agency have heard rumors about her odd behavior for years, but we've never been able to figure out exactly what she's been doing. However —" he turned his attention to Gertrude — "the second I learned this lady was in the company of a woman described as *wholesome* and possessed of an innocent face and charming demeanor, I realized she was speaking about none other than you, Miss Cadwalader."

"How would you have deduced it was Gertrude from that less than exact description?" Harrison demanded.

"Because I was fool enough to be taken in by Miss Cadwalader's appeal — a foolishness that we apparently share, Mr. Sinclair." Agent McParland sat back in the chair.

"She's not a young lady whom gentlemen neglect to notice, especially because wholesomeness is a quality we gentlemen prize. But it's now become clear she's nothing more than a chameleon, her charm and delightfulness a cover for the deceitful and manipulative woman she truly is. Add in the fact that Miss Cadwalader was discovered earlier today with possessions that did not belong to her, and . . . I rest my case."

Swallowing past a throat that was remarkably dry, Gertrude leaned forward. "I'm not a thief, Agent McParland. And, while I willingly admit I was in possession of items that did not belong to me today, I was simply returning them on behalf of Mrs. Davenport. She never keeps the items she takes, although I can't tell you why she takes them. It's a mystery to me. But I'd be more than willing to bring you back to search her house, which will prove both mine and Mrs. Davenport's innocence once and for all."

Agent McParland pulled out a small pad of paper from his jacket pocket and flipped it open. "So I won't find a ruby hair comb, sapphire ring, diamond brooch in the shape of a turtle, three strands of pearls, four watch pins encrusted with jewels, three pocket watches, and a tiara?" he asked.

"Goodness, all that has gone missing?"

Gertrude whispered.

"Stolen, Miss Cadwalader, not missing. Which means there's now been a full investigation ordered by the Pinkerton Agency because we're paid a substantial amount of money to keep the guests at the Manhattan Beach Hotel safe, and yet —"

"You did an abysmal job of that," Harrison finished for him. "And you're doing an abysmal job now because Mrs. Davenport did not have a reticule on her while at the Manhattan Beach Hotel, nor did I hear her jingling at all once she returned to the ship, where I personally helped her on board the *Cornelia.* As for Gertrude," he continued, sending her the smallest of winks, which seemed rather brave of him considering the situation, "I know she did not have any room to stash those items on her person, having suffered an unfortunate incident with her original gown that then forced her to accept a gown from my sister, who is not nearly as . . . wholesome in the figure department."

He moved directly beside Gertrude and held out his hand. "I'll be taking her home now, Agent McParland. If you happen to uncover any credible proof that warrants a search of Mrs. Davenport's home, feel free to seek me out and I'll accompany you to proceed with that search."

"Now see here, Sinclair," Agent McParland said, but before he could do more than get to his feet, the door to the interrogation room burst open and Temperance rushed in.

With a flutter of skirts and a flapping of her overly large hat, she stopped right beside Agent McParland, drew in a gulp of air, then nodded to Gertrude.

"I'm so sorry it took me so long to get here, but I'm afraid we don't have time to linger." She gulped in another breath. "I went to fetch Mrs. Davenport after I had the hansom cab follow you when I saw you being escorted away from the *Cornelia* by all those men. I didn't know what else to do when I realized they'd taken you to jail. But then —" She stopped talking and drew in another breath, almost as if she needed a moment to collect her thoughts. When she'd apparently gathered those thoughts, she looked to Gertrude again.

"I had no money if you'll recall, so I had no choice other than to hope Mrs. Davenport would lend me the money for the fare to pay for the hansom cab. However, matters took a turn for the concerning when I arrived at her house."

"She refused to give you money?" Gertrude asked.

Temperance waved that aside. "No, she gave me money immediately, but after she discovered you'd been arrested, she turned rather peculiar. Instead of agreeing to travel with me back to the jail to see you released, she dashed out of the house, saying she'd never be able to forgive herself, and then . . . I lost her as I tried to chase after her, and . . . I'm very much afraid that something horrible is about to happen."

CHAPTER NINETEEN

"I don't believe I thanked you for threatening Agent McParland with bodily harm when he wouldn't step out of my way as I was attempting to leave the interrogation room."

Harrison gave Gertrude's hand a squeeze. "And here I was concerned you'd be annoyed with me for threatening the man with physical violence."

Gertrude turned her head and peered out the narrow window of the hansom cab they were riding in, looking past where Harrison's horse, Rupert, was attached by his reins to the back of that cab. "I'm sure Agent McParland is suffering quite nicely in the cab following us." She grinned and turned front and center again. "I never imagined Temperance possessed a fiery nature underneath that meek attitude she's presented to the world over the past few years. It certainly was a fortuitous circumstance for us that she turned that nature Agent McParland's way. He was so taken aback to find himself bearing the brunt of her temper that he stepped right out of my way, which then provided you with an excuse to refrain from punching the man."

"I'm somewhat disappointed about losing that opportunity. He was behaving completely untoward, and don't get me started on that nonsense he spouted about you being a wholesome young lass. That is an observation the gentleman should have kept to himself."

Gertrude blinked. "I thought he meant that as a compliment."

"Well of course he did, but a gentleman simply cannot go around tossing compliments out at his leisure, especially when those compliments are directed to a young lady's . . . charms."

Gertrude's mouth dropped open. "Agent McParland was referring to my charms?"

"Indeed, but then he threw in that bit about you being a chameleon who is deceitful and manipulative, and I knew he'd hurt your feelings." Harrison squeezed her hand again. "You might recall that I was with you when we arrived at the Manhattan Beach Hotel and witnessed you practically leaping out of the carriage to ascertain if Agent Mc-

Parland was on duty that evening."

To Harrison's surprise, instead of agreeing with that, Gertrude wrinkled her nose. "On my word, Harrison, that almost sounds as if you think I hold Agent McParland in great affection. I assure you, nothing could be further from the truth. In all honesty, I was panicking after learning Pinkerton detectives were employed by the Manhattan Beach Hotel. As you've recently learned, Mrs. Davenport has a few issues when it comes to helping herself to items that don't belong to her. Knowing she could very well be up to her usual shenanigans, and not wanting her to draw the interest of the detectives, I had no choice but to rush to find her. Although given what Agent McParland disclosed, the detectives were already suspicious of Mrs. Davenport and had been for some time."

"Because she's been acting suspiciously for years," Harrison said, leaning forward to look past Gertrude and out the window, settling back against the seat when he saw they were still some minutes away from their destination. "You're certain we'll find Mrs. Davenport at Grace Church?"

Gertrude nodded. "Relatively certain. Grace Church is the one place Mrs. Davenport travels to on a regular basis. Since Temperance said she was distraught, I have to imagine she'll seek out a place that's very familiar to her."

"Then I hope we *do* find her there because I have to imagine the peaceful atmosphere at Grace Church will soothe her distraught nature."

"As I mentioned to you a few days ago, I don't believe Mrs. Davenport attends church because she's looking for peace. If you'll recall, I think she's looking for someone instead."

Harrison frowned. "I do recall you mentioning that. But tell me this, why are you so convinced she's looking for someone instead of searching for God?"

Gertrude returned the frown. "Because she'll visit Grace Church numerous times per week, but barely attends any services when we travel to her cottage in Newport. That's not a decision a person embracing her faith would choose to make. She also sends her butler to Grace Church while we're in Newport, demanding he send written reports to her regarding the members of the congregation who attend each service we miss."

"That does seem to suggest she's looking for someone."

Nodding, Gertrude added, "It worries me

to think about what she'll do when she finally decides that certain someone is never going to be at Grace Church, which is why I wish there wasn't so much traffic crowding the streets today. As the minutes tick away, I can't help but agree with what Temperance said — that something horrible is about to happen."

Harrison raised Gertrude's hand and placed a kiss on it. "What are you afraid we'll find?"

For a moment, Gertrude didn't answer him, but then her eyes brimmed with tears, and to his very great concern, those tears spilled down her cheeks.

"I'm afraid we'll find her with no hope left, which might very well encourage her to do what my mother did and end her hopeless state once and for all."

Abandoning the expected proprieties because he couldn't bear the idea of Gertrude suffering, Harrison turned on the seat, then pulled her straight into his arms. To his surprise, she didn't balk at the embrace, but burrowed right into his chest, releasing what sounded like a sigh. Gathering her closer, he rested his chin on top of her head and simply waited, allowing her the time she evidently needed to regain her composure.

When she shifted, he drew back, brushed the tears from her face, and placed the lightest of kisses against her forehead, knowing that was hardly proper, but unable to resist. When she sent him the wobbliest of smiles, he leaned closer.

"What happened with your mother?" he asked gently.

"It's not a pleasant story."

"I believe I once encouraged you to use my strong shoulders to unburden yourself, Gertrude. That offer is still good, and one I believe you should take advantage of right this very second."

"But you won't want to remain my friend if I tell you the sordid secrets of my past."

"I'll always be your friend, no matter what you're about to disclose."

She pushed away from him and smiled another wobbly smile. "I won't hold you to that promise after I've revealed all the nasty details of my story, but it's kind of you to say that." She drew in a breath, released it, then drew in another before she looked out the window, as if telling her story was so uncomfortable she couldn't do it while looking at him.

"My mother suffered from melancholy, quite like Mrs. Davenport suffers from, and she was prone to dramatic acts during her bouts of melancholy. That drama eventually led to her death, which happened in the home of my father's mistress."

"Your father's mistress didn't murder your mother, did she?"

Gertrude turned from the window. "No, there was no murder that day, although I believe my mother was hoping her death would be laid at the feet of that woman." She bit her lip. "From what I've been able to gather from the investigation that followed, although I was only ten at the time, my mother burst into that woman's house, ranting about the shame she'd been made to suffer because of the woman's involvement in my father's life. Then, after she was done ranting, she pulled out a pistol and shot herself."

Harrison rubbed Gertrude's arm, his heart all but breaking when he felt her trembling. "How horrible."

"It was, although I was spared the shame of how my mother died when my influential Cadwalader relatives stepped in, paid my father's mistress to not spread tales, and even managed to keep the manner in which my mother died out of the papers." Gertrude shuddered. "Her death could have been avoided, though, if only I'd been more diligent in her care." She shuddered again, drew in a ragged breath, then lifted her chin. "She was being overly dramatic on the day she died, and because of that, I didn't immediately go after her when she flew into one of her rages and raced out of the shabby rooms we were renting. Because of that decision, there was no one to stop her from taking her life."

"You were all of ten years old, Gertrude. Surely you must know there was little you could have done to influence your mother's decision."

"I'll never know for certain, and besides, my not going after my mother is not the worst thing I'm guilty of."

Brushing back a strand of hair that had come undone from its pins, Harrison wiped away a tear that was running down her cheek. "Perhaps you should start from the very beginning so I have a clearer picture of the situation."

"I really don't enjoy elaborating on that time in my life."

"Clearly, but I'm afraid I'm going to have to insist."

"Are you ever this insistent with your sisters?"

Harrison smiled. "I should think not since they'd then take to banding together to thwart me, but since you don't have an entire posse of ladies to band against me right now, I feel perfectly safe being insistent with you."

Shaking her head, Gertrude settled back against the seat. "Oh, very well, I'll elaborate, but do remember you're the one insisting on this after I disclose all the gory details."

"I'll keep that in mind."

Crossing her arms over her chest, Gertrude looked out the window again for a long moment, then returned her attention to him. "As I mentioned, my mother suffered from melancholy, but it's next to impossible to explain exactly how deeply a case of melancholy can affect a person, let alone a family," Gertrude began. "She'd always been prone to dramatics even when my father was alive, but after he died — and because he'd died under what can only be described as unsavory conditions — my mother's dramatics took on a new and concerning turn. She'd not speak for days on end, and then when she did, hurtful words would escape from her mouth, like how disappointed she was with me, her one and only daughter, but a daughter who possessed only passable looks and no great charm to speak of."

She held up a hand when he opened his

mouth, stopping the argument that was on the very tip of his tongue.

"There's no need to be offended on my behalf, Harrison," she said. "I was an incredibly shy child, which made it next to impossible to display much charm, although the criticisms my mother leveled at me were devastating and difficult to accept at the time."

"Did you ever consider in hindsight the idea that your mother might have been so critical of you because she was disappointed in herself? It's been my opinion that many a cruel word has been tossed an innocent person's way to distract from the deficiencies of the person spouting those words."

"While I've often been of that opinion as well, I'm afraid that in my mother's case, she meant every word. She was never happy with the books I chose to read to her, or the meals I tried to prepare. To this day, I'm not what anyone could call proficient in the kitchen, but I did try, although my attempts were never quite good enough for her."

"She sounds like a deeply unhappy person."

"She *was* unhappy, and spent the three years after my father's death trying to find meaning for all the disappointments she'd been made to suffer. That's why we spent an excessive amount of time on our knees in church, praying that God would bestow on us, or at least on my mother, a semblance of peace, but that particular prayer was never answered."

Harrison braced himself when Gertrude's gaze turned distant and fresh tears clouded her eyes before she continued her story in a voice no louder than a whisper.

"We'd finally run out of money, you see, on that day so many years ago, and Mother was wringing her hands and bemoaning her fate. I made the very great mistake of suggesting she seek out one of our many wealthy relatives and ask for some assistance, which turned out to be the suggestion that finally had her losing all sense of reason."

Gertrude raised a finger and traced it along the window of the hansom cab. "She screamed horrible accusations my way before she turned physically violent. She broke an umbrella over my head, then continued to hit me with the bits that were left, shouting words of disgust at me when I wouldn't fight back. When the umbrella had nothing remaining to it except the handle, she flung it aside, grabbed her reticule, then stormed out of the room."

She turned from the window. "That was

the last time I saw my mother alive, and as I said before, it's my fault she died. I could have stopped her. It wouldn't have been that difficult, but I chose to stay behind, unaware of my mother's plight until the police came looking for me."

An image of a young Gertrude sprang to Harrison's mind, one that had her covered in bruises and huddling all alone in a derelict room, wondering when her mother might return to rain more abuse down on her.

Closing his eyes for a single second, Harrison drew in a breath, and then reached out and drew Gertrude straight back into his arms. Pressing his lips against the top of her head, he breathed in the scent of her hair, blinking away the moisture that was now clouding his vision.

"You must know, Gertrude, that your mother's death was not your fault. She chose to end her life instead of fighting for it — and fighting for you. You were a child, she was the adult, and even though it does sound as if she suffered from severe mental anguish, she should have never allowed you to believe you were responsible for that."

Gertrude pulled away from him. "While I appreciate your outrage on my behalf, what I'm about to disclose will give you a clear glimpse into my true character, one that does not show me in a favorable light, which will then have your outrage dissolving straightaway."

Harrison frowned. "I highly doubt whatever you disclose is going to change my attitude about your character, but you've piqued my curiosity, so disclose away."

"I was not all that sorry my mother was dead. In fact, the honest truth is that I was relieved."

"Which is perfectly understandable given that she'd abused you both physically and mentally."

Gertrude ignored his response. "I barely mourned her death, relishing instead my new circumstance of being sent off to a fancy boarding school, paid for by the very relatives my mother refused to approach after we'd run out of money. Once settled into that school, I pushed almost all thoughts of my mother aside, appreciating that I could enjoy a peaceful life there, one where no one screamed at me, assaulted me, or left me riddled with guilt."

"It seems to me as if you're still riddled with some measure of guilt," Harrison said slowly.

"Of course I am. I failed to mourn the loss of my own mother." Gertrude shook her head. "What type of daughter does that except the most callous of creatures?"

Harrison leaned toward her. "Have you ever considered turning this guilt over to God? From what I understand, you attend church regularly, which makes me wonder why you've harbored such a devastating emotion for so long."

Gertrude gave a dismissive flick of her wrist. "My behavior in regard to my mother would have certainly disappointed God, which explains exactly why He never bothers to answer any of my prayers. He knows I have a selfish heart, one that is not worthy of His time, grace, or love."

"I beg to differ. Your heart is more than worthy of love and grace. If it wasn't, you wouldn't have been so considerate of Mrs. Davenport and her unusual pastimes over the years."

Another flick of her wrist was her first response to that. "Don't give me more credit than I deserve, Harrison. In all honesty, I've been hoping my care of Mrs. Davenport will allow me to make amends for my neglect of my mother. I thought that if I could prevent another woman who suffers from melancholy from experiencing the same sad end as my mother, God might forgive me for my transgressions, especially the one pertaining to not feeling overly burdened by her death."

Harrison took her hand in his. "Surely you don't think Mrs. Davenport is intending to harm herself, do you?"

"I'm afraid I do. I tendered my notice to her after she told me about leaving her reticule on board the *Cornelia,* stuffed to the gills with items that belonged to your sister." Gertrude released a sigh. "I could tell she wasn't expecting me to do that. Then, after Temperance told us how Mrs. Davenport reacted to the news of my arrest, I'm worried that news was too much for her to bear." She glanced back to him. "Even if Mrs. Davenport is not intending to harm herself, I do think my abandonment of her has proven to God once and for all that I'm unworthy of His attention."

"Have you actually listened to any of those sermons you've apparently been privy to while you've been in Mrs. Davenport's employ and attended services with her?"

"I listen well enough to where I can quote Scripture with the best of them, although like most people, I don't listen to every word of every sermon."

"You've obviously missed the sermons I'm sure have been delivered at Grace Church that center around the truth that everyone is worthy of God's grace and forgiveness."

"I haven't missed those sermons, Harrison. I simply don't believe them, but . . ." She stopped talking and looked out the window right as the hansom cab began to slow. "We're here."

As the cab came to a stop directly in front of Grace Church, Gertrude, exactly like she'd done at the Manhattan Beach Hotel, did not wait for him to get the door for her. Instead, she jumped out of the cab, then bolted toward the church, moving at a pace that would certainly earn her another painful stitch in her side and a definite bout of wheezing.

CHAPTER TWENTY

Whatever scenario Gertrude was expecting to discover in Grace Church paled in comparison to what she actually encountered. Stumbling to a stop, she felt her mouth drop open as she simply gawked at Mrs. Davenport.

That lady, for some unknown reason, was standing on a rickety ladder, wiping the panes of a stained-glass window with what appeared to be a cleaning cloth, muttering something under her breath as she wiped.

"Miss Cadwalader, thank the good Lord you've shown up," a quiet voice said from Gertrude's right, drawing her attention.

Moving up the side aisle was Reverend Benjamin Perry, an associate minister at Grace Church, and a gentleman who'd often tried to engage Gertrude in conversation, although she'd done her very best to dodge his attempts over the past few years.

The reason behind that dodging revolved

around the idea that Reverend Benjamin Perry was a gentleman possessed of a good and honest heart — a man of the cloth who clearly believed God was attentive, loving, and most of all, forgiving. Because of that, she'd kept her distance from the reverend, as had Mrs. Davenport, probably because Mrs. Davenport sensed the same goodness in him Gertrude did and felt somewhat lacking in his presence.

Pushing those uncomfortable thoughts away when Reverend Perry reached her side, Gertrude soon found her hand tucked into the crook of his arm as he nodded to where Mrs. Davenport was now applying herself more diligently than ever to her curious task.

"Any thoughts as to why Mrs. Davenport is cleaning a window that was cleaned only this morning?" he asked in a hushed tone.

"I'm afraid not."

"Is she perhaps one of those women who feels compelled to pick up a dustcloth when she doesn't believe a job has been completed to her satisfaction?"

"I've never seen her pick up a cleaning cloth before, and I've certainly never seen her apply herself so diligently to any domestic task."

Reverend Perry nodded. "How very curious, although her diligence in this matter must obviously have something to do with her telling me she's decided it was time to make amends for some grievance she didn't elaborate on." He gestured to the ladder. "After hearing that, I offered to fetch her a cup of tea. Imagine my surprise when I returned, and instead of finding her sitting on a pew, she'd helped herself to that ladder and . . . she's been up there ever since." He leaned closer. "I suggested she return to the ground, but her only response to that suggestion was a sniff. Maybe you'll have more success at getting her off the ladder."

Tilting her head, Gertrude considered Mrs. Davenport for a long moment, having no idea how to go about the feat of getting Mrs. Davenport off the ladder, especially when it was becoming clear the lady was in one of her determined moods. Taking a single step forward, Gertrude froze when Mrs. Davenport suddenly stretched to reach the very top of the shepherd's head she was polishing, the stretching sending the ladder tilting to the right.

Before Gertrude could call out a warning, Mrs. Davenport hurtled through the air, right as Harrison raced past her as the ladder began to fall.

An *umph* sounded a second later when

Harrison caught her in a way that seemed all but impossible. Staggering under Mrs. Davenport's weight, he lurched out of the way as the ladder crashed to the ground, splintering into pieces.

Gathering Mrs. Davenport against him, he turned toward Gertrude, sending her a wide-eyed look that clearly suggested he was as surprised as anyone that he'd actually been able to catch Mrs. Davenport before she'd hit the ground. Walking over to join Gertrude and Reverend Perry, who seemed to be whispering a prayer of thanksgiving, Harrison lowered Mrs. Davenport to her feet, then took her hand in his, placing a kiss on it.

"Honestly, Mrs. Davenport," he began when Mrs. Davenport simply stared back at him with unblinking eyes. "You just took a good ten years off my life. What say you and I agree you'll leave feats such as attending to stained-glass windows to the people who actually know how to go about it?"

Mrs. Davenport managed a nod in response before she raised a trembling hand and pushed aside a strand of black hair that was escaping its pins. "Excellent advice, my dear Harrison, although allow me to say that there aren't many gentlemen who'd have been up for the task of saving me from what might have been a very nasty death." She shook her head. "I've always heard people say they see their entire life pass before them when hurtling toward death, and I can now attest to the fact that that is nothing less than the truth, and . . ." She stopped talking as her gaze settled on Gertrude. "Goodness, Gertrude, you've been released from jail. But what are you doing here, and . . . you must loathe the very sight of me after what I've put you through."

Even though she'd been beyond put out with Mrs. Davenport of late, Gertrude simply didn't have it in her to continue holding ill thoughts for a lady she cared about more than she'd admitted. Taking a step forward, she pulled Mrs. Davenport's hands into her own and smiled. "I'm here because I'm worried about you, and no, I could never loathe you. I certainly don't want to ever spend time in jail again, but because Mrs. Sinclair has dropped all charges against me, I can now hope that unpleasantness is firmly behind me."

"There's still the matter of the missing items from the Manhattan Beach Hotel," Agent McParland called from somewhere in the back of the church.

Gertrude turned, but before she could respond to that, Temperance stalked into view, marching her way to join Agent Mc-Parland, who was standing in the middle of the aisle.

"Do be quiet, Agent McParland," Temperance said, stopping by the man's side. She pointed to a pew, then when he didn't move, took him by the arm and towed him rather forcefully into that pew before she turned back to Gertrude and gave a cheery wave. "Not to worry. I'll keep Agent Mc-Parland well in hand while you settle matters between you and Mrs. Davenport. And it's so lovely to discover you looking so well, Mrs. Davenport. I was certain we were going to discover something dreadful had happened to you, although that tumble you took was dreadful, but thank goodness Harrison was here to save the day." With that, she plopped down on the pew next to Agent McParland, where she began whispering furiously to him behind her hand.

"Goodness, but what has happened to Miss Flowerdew, and . . . do not say that is a Pinkerton detective with her, the one who I believe was hired a few months back to assist Asher Rutherford when he ran into some trouble," Mrs. Davenport said in a voice that was no louder than a whisper.

Gertrude pulled her attention away from where Temperance was now arguing with

Agent McParland and found that while she'd been distracted, Harrison had taken Mrs. Davenport's arm and was helping her into a pew.

"Temperance has apparently decided to come out of her wallflower shell," Harrison explained, taking a seat right next to Mrs. Davenport and pulling her hand into his. "As for Agent McParland, there's no need for us to delve into what he's doing here quite yet. You're still looking a little peaked, a direct result of that nasty plunge you took from the ladder. Because I've some experience with ladies who've landed in all sorts of nerve-wracking adventures, I know just the remedy to set you to rights again." He smiled a charming smile. "Stories are the best ways to recover one's composure, and luckily for you, I've been told I have a flair for storytelling, especially those concerning pirates."

Mrs. Davenport reached up and patted Harrison's cheek. "I do love a good pirate tale, but I'm afraid I have no idea why you'd offer to help me regain my composure with a story. I'm certain you're aware by now that I treated myself to possessions that didn't belong to me on board your *Cornelia,* abusing the hospitality you extended me in the process. Why, I'm surprised you didn't simply allow me to drop to the ground instead of catching me. At my age, such a fall would have been almost guaranteed to do me in, but . . . you saved me, and at great personal risk. That ladder could have cracked you right over the head, rendering you senseless."

Harrison completely ignored all of that as his eyes crinkled at the corners. "Since the idea of pirates seems to have sent your thoughts dwelling on matters I was hoping to distract you from, allow me to return to my comment about Temperance abandoning her shell." His lips curved. "Did I mention I believe she's done so because of that unexpected encounter with Mr. Gilbert Cavendish at the Manhattan Beach Hotel? From what little Gilbert told me, he and Temperance were fast friends growing up and even spent holidays together because their parents were fast friends as well."

Mrs. Davenport blinked, her eyes turning suspiciously bright again. She drew in a deep breath, and then squared her shoulders and smiled somewhat wobbly. "You're a kind man, Harrison Sinclair, which is incredibly rare in a gentleman as attractive as you. And because I'm not yet ready to discuss what I need to discuss, that being my horrible behavior of late and, well, forever, I'll join you in a discussion of Mr. Gilbert Cavendish. Although —" she tilted her head — "isn't he rumored to be in line for a title of the aristocratic sort, and isn't he the gentleman Miss Clementine Flowerdew began making eyes at while we were sailing back to the city on the *Cornelia*?"

"I thought Clementine only had eyes for me," Harrison said before he released an exaggerated sigh. "Just goes to show how one can never believe all of those rumors swirling about town."

Mrs. Davenport, who was beginning to regain some of the color in her cheeks, grinned. "Don't let your guard down, my boy. Clementine Flowerdew is the type of lady to pursue more than one option when it comes to what she wants for her future. She's probably making a list right this very moment, comparing your attributes with those of Mr. Cavendish."

As Harrison and Mrs. Davenport launched into a discussion about the peculiar natures of women and how Harrison didn't believe he understood the intricacies of dealing with feminine intrigues, Gertrude found herself completely mesmerized by the man. Here he was, doing his very best to distract a woman who'd caused more than her fair share of trouble as of late, and he was actually achieving success with that distraction.

There was no longer any denying her fascination with the gentleman, especially because it was next to impossible to *not* be fascinated with a man capable of catching a woman in midair. That he'd done so with barely a grimace only added to the impressiveness of the gesture and gave additional credence to the idea that he was certainly an extraordinary gentleman. Granted, he was still far above the reach of an ordinary lady like herself, but it wasn't a crime to dream, and in all honesty, Harrison Sinclair had been spending more than his fair share of time in her dreams of late.

He'd been born with a face that caused ladies to swoon, but he was in possession of something much more significant than a handsome face — a caring and compassionate heart.

He was kind, gentle, and sympathetic, and was perfectly willing to show empathy toward a woman who'd stolen from him, instead of judging her and demanding explanations about why she'd done what she'd done.

It was as if he instinctively understood the needs of those around him, even though he made the claim time and again that he was incapable of comprehending the feminine mind.

As she continued to watch him, Gertrude realized that while she'd admitted to falling slightly in love with Harrison Sinclair, the reality was it might be more than slightly. And even knowing there was relatively little hope he'd ever return that love, she could not, or would not, regret falling in love with him because . . .

"And while I enjoy delving into the mysteries of the feminine mind," Mrs. Davenport said, rising to her feet and pulling Gertrude directly back to the situation at hand, "I believe it's time I explain myself to the one person I've abused most assiduously over the past few years." She turned to Gertrude, her eyes bright with unshed tears. "I know I have no right to ask you to hear me out, my dear, but I'm hoping that by telling you a little about my past, it might allow you some insight regarding why I've subjected you to so many unusual schemes throughout the years."

When Harrison got to his feet and moved out of the pew to make room for her, Gertrude didn't hesitate to take his place. Joining Mrs. Davenport, she sat on the hard pew, waiting for the older woman to get settled before she raised an expectant brow her way.

Mrs. Davenport smoothed out the folds of her skirt. "I'm not certain where I should begin."

Gertrude nodded to the stained-glass window. "Why don't you explain what significance that window holds for you, or why you'd bother cleaning it when you and I both know domestic tasks have never appealed to you."

Looking at the window for a long moment, Mrs. Davenport's lips thinned. "My husband purchased that window for the church to honor the birth of our daughter. He was very particular about how it was to be cleaned, once going so far as to reprimand me when he noticed smudges on it, making the ridiculous claim those smudges were due to negligence on my part. When he then suggested I take over the care of the window, I refused, and I've not lifted a finger until today to so much as brush a speck of dust away from the glass."

With questions already crowding her thoughts, Gertrude asked the first one to pop front and center. "But why lift a finger today?"

Mrs. Davenport bit her lip. "I'm not sure. It just seemed like something I needed to do to begin making amends for the actions of my past."

Reverend Perry suddenly stepped from the shadows, moving to stand directly in front of the pew they were sitting in. "Forgive me for chiming in, Mrs. Davenport, but I've been considering your actions with the window. It occurred to me that you may very well have been trying to dust away something unpleasant from your life, using a window you once refused to clean as a symbolic way to cleanse you of the guilt you obviously feel about that unpleasantness."

Blowing out a breath, Mrs. Davenport tilted her head. "Perhaps, or it's more likely I was hoping God would be a touch more forgiving of the careless disregard I've had for the life I've been given if I began trying to be less selfish." She folded her hands in her lap. "I've never once considered doing a menial task, and while I know that polishing a pane of glass seems like an absolutely ridiculous way for me to earn some forgiveness, it was the only gesture I could think of after I arrived here today." She nodded Gertrude's way. "I was a little distraught, you see, after learning my demands had finally seen you arrested, but I wasn't brave enough to come after you — yet another flaw in my character I'm certainly going to need to address."

Reverend Perry smiled. "I doubt you're as flawed as you've come to believe, Mrs. Davenport. And since it does seem as if you've missed a good majority of the messages we address here on any given Sunday, even while you've attended services frequently, do know that God forgives easily. All you need to do is ask Him for that forgiveness."

"You're a good man, Reverend Perry," Mrs. Davenport said. "But I'm afraid I don't believe God forgives that easily, which means I need to make amends for the many, many grievances I've caused over the decades, brought about because of my spoiled and willful attitude."

"Admitting one's faults is said to be the first step into accepting responsibility for them," Reverend Perry said with a small smile. "As for God's forgiveness, that's a subject we'll certainly return to when you're in a different frame of mind, but do know that He'll forgive you anything."

"Will He forgive me for ruining my marriage even if the man I married was not the man he projected himself to be before I agreed to marry him?"

Reverend Perry nodded. "He will."

Instead of seeming relieved about that, Mrs. Davenport turned her gaze to the stained-glass window, pursed her lips, then nodded, just once. "Since this does seem to be the time to disclose my many past misdeeds, allow me to begin by saying that while my husband was a dictatorial beast, it was my choice to pursue him and convince him to marry me. Roy, that's my husband's name, was a very handsome gentleman. And after I noticed him at a ball, and arranged to become introduced to him, I then pursued him somewhat determinedly, allowing him no room to misinterpret my desire to become his wife."

Mrs. Davenport's eyes turned distant. "I didn't know for quite some time that he was more interested in my father's money than he was in me. I was blinded by first love, and because my father never refused me anything, he offered Roy a proposal he couldn't refuse. Before I knew it, I was married to the gentleman of my dreams, or so I thought, looking forward to a lovely life, one where my husband and I would, of course, rule society one day and enjoy a romance that would earn me the envy of all my peers."

A distinct rustle of paper from behind them drew Gertrude's attention. Turning, she found that while she'd been listening to Mrs. Davenport, Agent McParland had stolen closer and was now sitting directly behind them, eavesdropping on their conversation no less while he perused the small notepad balanced on his knees, pen in hand. Lifting his head, he looked unconcerned that he'd been caught in the act, as he sent the briefest of nods Gertrude's way.

"At least we know where she came by her money" was all he said before he bent his head to his notes again and added something to the page.

Not wanting to distract Mrs. Davenport, who didn't appear to realize Agent McParland was listening, Gertrude sent the detective a narrowing of her eyes, an action he missed because he was still looking through his notes. Returning her attention to Mrs. Davenport, Gertrude cleared her throat.

"Did your husband have *any* type of fortune to speak of?" she asked.

Mrs. Davenport released an unladylike snort. "Roy barely had two pennies to rub together, although no one knew that at the time. The Davenport family was well respected in New York and had some tenuous ties to wealthy relatives in England. But I later learned the New York Davenports were always short on cash, which meant they were always on the lookout for ways to plump up the family coffers."

She picked a small piece of lint off her sleeve. "I was exactly the plump pigeon Roy was looking for: a woman from a society family, although not one of the more established society families since our money was relatively new due to the ingenuity of my father, who married my society mother to become respectable. Roy was perfectly happy to help himself to that new money, though, even if he was disappointed to discover my father made the bulk of his fortune through trade."

Lifting her head, Mrs. Davenport frowned. "Roy was very attentive at first, showering me with presents, although he always seemed to buy items for himself at the same time. But then, after we'd been married for about six months, he began to distance himself from me, spending his time at his gentlemen clubs, or sailing the boats he bought with the money my father settled on us after our vows were spoken."

"I imagine his inattentive attitude didn't sit well with you," Gertrude said.

The barest hint of a smile flickered across Mrs. Davenport's face. "Indeed, and I admit I began to act rather outlandishly to gain his attention, my bad behavior drawing him back to the city to save the good Davenport name time and time again. Roy eventually decided I needed a child to settle me down, and about a year after he made that decision, my darling daughter Jane entered the world."

"But her birth didn't save your marriage?" Gertrude asked when Mrs. Davenport stopped talking, obviously lost in memories as her eyes turned bright with unshed tears.

Blinking, and then blinking again, Mrs. Davenport shook her head. "I'm afraid not. Roy didn't care for babies, finding the crying annoying, so even though we had nannies to attend to Jane whenever she turned fussy, he soon found excuses to quit our house whenever he could. Before too long, he'd returned to his neglectful ways, while picking up some unfortunate habits, most of those habits keeping him in the company of women who did not travel within society. Whispers soon began winding their way through town, and I decided that to draw him back to me, and have him abandon his many mistresses, I'd have to begin misbehaving again to attract his attention."

She dashed a tear from her cheek. "I'd decided Roy was truly attracted to ladies who didn't mind their manners, and because of that, I'm afraid I began to dress in unusual fashions, drank to excess, and adopted a flirtatious attitude with the gentlemen I encountered at society events. Unfortunately, none of that drew Roy's attention, but unwilling to admit defeat even though I wasn't certain I even wanted Roy back with me at that point, I turned to using Jane as a pawn in the game I was determined to win."

"This game didn't involve a murder, did it?" Agent McParland asked over the pew, his question causing dead silence to settle over the church as Gertrude, along with Mrs. Davenport, turned in the pew and found Agent McParland casting a hard look Mrs. Davenport's way.

Before Mrs. Davenport could answer, though, Temperance, who'd somehow managed to take a seat right next to Agent McParland without Gertrude noticing, swatted him on the arm, and then swatted him again. "Honestly, Agent McParland, what in the world is the matter with you? Mrs. Davenport does not have the look of a murderer about her, and your question was completely beyond the pale. Why, if you ask me, I think the disappointment you've recently experienced over the Manhattan Beach Hotel being robbed while the Pinkerton Agency was on the case has clouded your common sense."

Agent McParland turned the intensity of

his glare on Temperance, who didn't so much as flinch. "While I will admit the Pinkerton Agency has suffered embarrassment over allowing a thief to get the better of us that night, I'm not acting beyond the pale by questioning Mrs. Davenport in such a direct manner. She's behaved suspiciously for years, and because of that, I feel justified in asking her what happened to her husband, and wondering if that husband could have come to a sticky end at the hands of his admittedly disillusioned wife."

"Did I miss the explanation as to *why* we have a Pinkerton in our midst?" Mrs. Davenport suddenly asked.

"We'll get to that later," Harrison said as he stood, moved into the pew where Agent McParland was sitting, took a seat directly next to the man, then sent the agent a rather dangerous look. That look, unsurprisingly, didn't appear to bother Agent McParland in the least, although he did settle into silence.

"I didn't kill my husband," Mrs. Davenport said, turning front and center again. "For all I know, he's alive and well, living a life of leisure on the money he took from me."

Gertrude leaned toward Mrs. Davenport. "I'm not certain I understand how it came

354

to be that you lost track of your husband, and forgive me for being so forward, but did you lose track of Jane as well?"

For a moment, Mrs. Davenport stiffened, but then released a sigh. "I vowed years ago that I would never speak of what happened to my family. However, because you've borne the brunt of my more than mercurial moods at times, moods that were a direct result of my past, I owe you an explanation. In sharing the pathetic reality of my past, I hope you'll finally be able to understand that you were far more tolerant of me than you should have been, and far kinder than I deserve."

"I have my reasons for being tolerant of you and your peculiar habits, Mrs. Davenport, not all of which are a result of my needing the wages you afford me."

"And while I would love to distract everyone with questions about those reasons, I believe it'll be for the best if I simply spit out the whole horrible truth, making a clean break of matters once and for all."

Straightening her spine, Mrs. Davenport began to speak, her words tumbling out of her mouth one right after another.

"As I mentioned, I'd begun behaving badly to attract Roy's attention, but what I have yet to disclose is I enjoyed behaving that way. I absolutely adored shocking the staid members of society and reveling in the attention the designs I created and then wore around society attracted. As Jane grew older, I turned my styling efforts in her direction, dressing her in clothing that mimicked mine, never noticing the poor child was miserable being trotted around to all my events, then put on display like a performing pony."

"I imagine your daughter enjoyed the time she was able to spend with you," Gertrude countered. "I was not fortunate enough to have a mother who wanted me around, and I've always been envious of the girls who were blessed with attentive mothers."

"I don't believe Jane considered me a blessing, dear. She hated the way I'd try to style her hair, hated all the 'fussiness,' as she called it, that I'd add to her gowns, and hated knowing her friends were whispering about the rumors swirling around town, especially regarding my drinking. I never paid her complaints any mind, though, probably because my drinking was increasing every day back then and my thoughts weren't exactly clear."

Mrs. Davenport looked up at the ceiling for a long moment, then turned her attention to the stained-glass window again.

"Well, Roy got wind of what I'd been up to — he'd been off sailing, you see, with one of his many lady friends, and he wasn't pleased with me when he returned home." She shook her head and smiled rather sadly. "I can remember the exact day he returned — it was Jane's tenth birthday, and because I'd invited numerous little girls to our home to celebrate, I insisted Jane wear one of my creations, one that exactly matched a dress I'd designed for myself."

"Oh . . . dear" was all Gertrude could think of to say.

"Indeed, especially since our dresses were covered with rows of bows, and then I put more bows in our hair, lending both of us the appearance of tiered cakes. Jane tried to get me to relent, but I would hear none of her arguments."

"You forced your daughter to attend her own party looking like a birthday cake?" Gertrude asked.

"That's not the worst of it. Because I heard a few of the mothers mocking my outfit that day, I helped myself to all their pin money, and anything else of interest in the reticules those women had given over to our butler to store."

"Good heavens."

"Quite. Even though all those ladies

believed the thefts had been perpetrated by someone on my staff, because that's what I told them, and told them I'd dismissed that person, Roy knew exactly who the thief was when he showed up at the house after the party." She shook her head. "We got into an enormous row, not helped by the fact that I'd been drinking steadily since morning, and at the very end of it, Roy told me he'd had enough. He also told me that since Jane was no longer a young child, it was time for him to take over raising her. And when I put up a loud fuss, he stalked out of the room, telling me I was an unfit mother and couldn't be trusted with Jane another day."

She shook her head sadly. "I didn't realize how determined he was to get our daughter away from me. So, instead of immediately going to make certain Jane was fine, I helped myself to a bottle of wine first. By the time I finished that bottle and made my way up to her room, she was gone, as was Roy. All they'd left me was Jane's horrid birthday dress and a Bible I have to imagine Jane purposely left for me to see, one with the ancestry pages shredded into a pile on the floor and a ribbon marking Scripture that implied I'd forsaken her."

"It's no wonder you looked like a ghost

when I brought down that trunk," Gertrude said.

Mrs. Davenport nodded. "I hadn't seen that trunk since I threw the dress and Bible in it and had one of my footmen cart it up to the attic the very day Roy and Jane left."

"But they eventually came back, didn't they?"

"No, I've never seen either of them again. Roy emptied our bank account, although I had several my father had set up for me he didn't know about, and then he and Jane disappeared." She nodded to the stained-glass window. "Jane used to be enraptured with that window, having been told her father purchased it to honor her birth. She idolized him and blamed me for his never being around, which only added to the fantasy she created about him being so perfect." She dashed a tear from her cheek. "I imagine Roy turned her completely against me over the years, but I still hold out hope that Jane will someday want to come back to New York, if only to see her special window again."

"Jane's who you've been searching for all these years, isn't she, and why you insist on attending so many services," Gertrude said.

Mrs. Davenport nodded. "I know she'll never forgive me for how I treated her all those years ago, but I would like to have an opportunity to tell her I'm sorry." Tears sprang to her eyes again as she caught Gertrude's gaze. "I need to tell you I'm sorry as well, my dear. I've behaved horribly with you over the years, what with the outfits I've made you wear, the hairstyle horrors, and the expectation that you'll return all the items I pick up here and there that don't belong to me. You've stuck by me no matter what, and because of that, I must beg your forgiveness and express how deeply sorry I am to have expected so very much from you while giving you nothing in return. I don't expect you to forgive me. I do hope, however, that you'll eventually understand that what I asked of you was done to see how far I could push you. I've recently realized I did that pushing because I didn't believe I was worthy of your companionship. It's a great testimony to your character that you took every push I aimed your way with such grace, never pushing back at me as I'm sure you wanted to do at times."

Gertrude reached over and took hold of Mrs. Davenport's hand. "Working for you was not always a trial, Mrs. Davenport. I enjoyed the attention you spent on me, which filled a part of the void my mother left when she died."

Mrs. Davenport gave Gertrude's hand a squeeze. "May I dare hope that you might be able to forgive me someday then?"

"Of course I forgive you, and you don't have to wait for someday since I forgive you today."

"And may I also dare hope that you'll reconsider tendering your notice and continue working for me?"

"Of course Gertrude isn't going to continue working for you."

Turning toward the voice, Gertrude blinked when she discovered Miss Henrietta Huxley standing directly beside the pew, in the company of her sister, Miss Mabel Huxley, along with Edwina, Harrison's sister, peering over Miss Henrietta's shoulder, her eyes alight with curiosity.

Before Gertrude could greet anyone, or Mrs. Davenport could raise the argument that was clearly on the tip of her tongue, Miss Henrietta held up a hand, effectively keeping everyone silent.

"You, Mrs. Davenport, have clearly been running amok for far too long, and while I have proclaimed myself interested in taking a few of the wallflowers in hand —" she shot a glance to Gertrude, then to Temperance, then returned it to Mrs. Davenport — "after hearing your confession, of which I'm not ashamed about listening to, if that was in question, I've decided that your needs are greater than theirs. That means Mabel and I are going to intervene in your life, and I'll hear no arguments about that, if you please."

CHAPTER TWENTY-ONE

Given how his day was unfolding, Harrison couldn't claim to be surprised by the arrival of Miss Henrietta Huxley and her sister, Mabel, although why Edwina was accompanying those ladies, he couldn't begin to hazard a guess.

Rising to his feet, he stepped out of the pew, contemplating how best to go about the tricky business of intervening in the argument that was now in full bloom between Miss Henrietta and Mrs. Davenport. Before he could get much further than that, he was distracted by the sight of Agent McParland, who was now also standing, looking somewhat dazed as he stared at Edwina, his mouth slightly agape.

To Harrison's concern, his sister was looking somewhat dazed as well as she stared back at the Pinkerton detective, but then she smiled and took a step forward.

"I don't believe I've been introduced to

your friend, Harrison," she all but purred, the purring taking Harrison so aback that he felt *his* mouth drop open as he simply stood there at a complete loss for words.

Thankfully, Mrs. Davenport did not seem to be suffering from a loss of words as she discontinued her argument with Miss Henrietta and spun around, her attention immediately settling on Edwina.

"Goodness, Edwina, how delightful to see you, although I'm sure I have no idea how it came to be that you and the ever-troublesome Huxley sisters are at Grace Church at this particular moment in time."

"Miss Henrietta and Miss Mabel plucked me right off the sidewalk in front of Rutherford & Company as I was leaving that fine store after doing a bit of shopping for our Newport trip." Edwina shook her head. "They then proceeded to tell me the most outlandish tale, one that centered around the rumor that Gertrude was seen being escorted off to jail." She scratched her nose. "I have yet to understand all the particulars of that story, but as we were tooling past Grace Church, I spotted Rupert tied to the back of a hansom cab, so on a hunch, we decided to stop and investigate why Harrison was visiting a church our family doesn't belong to, and . . . well, here we are."

"Who, pray tell, is Rupert?" Mrs. Davenport asked.

"Harrison's horse," Edwina returned as she sent a frown Harrison's way. "I should mention that Rupert was giving the hansom cab driver a difficult time and might have been trying to relieve the man of his arm, although —" she held up her hand when Harrison took a step toward the door — "no need to worry about that now. I gave the driver an apple from my reticule, and that settled Rupert right down."

"I forgot all about poor Rupert," Harrison said.

Edwina smiled. "I'm not surprised considering the unlikely events you've apparently experienced today. But . . . getting back to that introduction I requested . . . ?" She directed her smile to Agent McParland, who immediately returned that smile, one that held entirely too much warmth in it, at least in Harrison's humble opinion.

"On my word, Edwina," Mrs. Davenport began, stepping right up to Edwina and taking her by the arm. "This gentleman is not what I had in mind for you when I agreed to sponsor you within society. And he's not a friend of your brother, but a member of the Pinkerton detectives."

Edwina's eyes sparkled. "Oh, I've always longed to meet a Pinkerton man."

"No, you haven't," Mrs. Davenport argued. "Pinkerton agents, as everyone knows, are overly suspicious sorts. And they're notorious for accusing completely innocent ladies of illegal activities, even when those ladies, such as myself and Gertrude, have absolutely no idea how such nasty accusations came to be leveled at our good names."

Edwina wrinkled her nose. "I'm afraid you have me at a disadvantage, Mrs. Davenport."

"Agent McParland seems to be unusually keen on seeing me and darling Gertrude arrested for crimes perpetuated at the Manhattan Beach Hotel."

"I didn't realize you were paying attention to all that," Agent McParland said, reaching into his pocket and extracting his notebook. "But since you evidently heard far more than I thought you did, tell me this . . . what do you know about the theft of various pieces of jewelry from the Manhattan Beach Hotel, specifically, one tiara worn by a woman who clearly recalls you being overly interested in it before it went missing?"

Mrs. Davenport drew herself up, but before she could voice what was certainly going to be her displeasure with Agent Mc-Parland, Edwina untwined her arm from Mrs. Davenport, stepped around Harrison, and moved to stand in front of Agent Mc-Parland.

"Do not tell me that you truly believe Mrs. Davenport, along with Gertrude from the sound of it, tried to make off with a tiara the night we attended an engagement celebration at the Manhattan Beach Hotel."

Agent McParland, even though he was obviously still a little dazed by Edwina's beautiful face, managed to finally give a nod before he cleared his throat. "Mrs. Davenport and Miss Cadwalader were identified as persons of interest by the lady now missing her prized tiara."

Edwina waved that aside. "That's ridiculous. I was with Mrs. Davenport almost the entire evening, and I assure you, sir, I would have noticed if she'd snatched a tiara straight off some lady's head."

Agent McParland cleared his throat again. "I never said Mrs. Davenport snatched the tiara from this lady's head. It went missing later that night from the lady's room."

"Which proves Mrs. Davenport isn't the culprit since, again, she was with me for most of the night," Edwina argued. "We had much to discuss between us, so there was not time for her to slip away undetected to perpetuate one theft, let alone numerous thefts from numerous victims."

Agent McParland consulted his notepad, frowned, then raised his head. "Can you provide an alibi for Miss Cadwalader as well?"

"Miss Cadwalader spent a good majority of her night in the company of Mr. Harrison Sinclair," Miss Henrietta said, stepping forward. "And when she wasn't on Mr. Sinclair's arm, she was graciously keeping me and my sister company." She let out a sniff. "Young ladies who choose to spend their time with members of the more elderly set are not the type of ladies to pull off swindles."

"Miss Cadwalader admitted she frequently returns items Mrs. Davenport helps herself to," Agent McParland argued.

Miss Henrietta sent Gertrude a fond smile. "Because she's obviously been trying to please Mrs. Davenport, a woman I've come to believe is somewhat of a mother figure for Gertrude. The good Lord knows Gertrude's true mother did not fulfill her responsibilities of caring for Gertrude as a child, and that right there explains much about why Gertrude is so very loyal to a woman who took advantage of that loyalty, although . . ." Miss Henrietta turned a knowing look on Mrs. Davenport. "Do know that my sister and I are fully aware you've been misbehaving over the years. You clearly do not believe you're worthy of any affection a person may want to give you. That, my dear Mrs. Davenport, is exactly why you've done everything in your power to push Gertrude away, even attaching a birdcage to her behind that you clearly should have known was not meant to be used as a bustle in the first place."

Mrs. Davenport raised a hand to her throat. "On my word but you do seem overly familiar with personal information pertaining to delicate matters. Forgive me, but am I mistaken in believing you and your sister spent the last several decades as little more than hermits?"

Miss Henrietta gave an airy wave of her hand. "It's always been a misconception, in my opinion, that hermits are believed to be oblivious to matters in the world outside their habitats. My sister and I, while unwilling to mingle with people who snubbed us most assiduously throughout the years, were perfectly willing to perfect our proficiency in observation by turning that proficiency toward the very society set that neglected us."

"You spent decades spying on all of us?" Mrs. Davenport demanded.

"Quite, but before you begin to take me to task, ask yourself this — am I right about why you behaved so outlandishly toward Gertrude? And, if I am, you might consider thanking me for bringing that to light, which will then allow you to adjust your behavior from this point forward. You are not alone, my dear Mrs. Davenport, nor will you ever be alone since Mabel and I have decided to invite you into our lives."

Mrs. Davenport lifted her chin. "While I have no intention of accepting that invitation, Henrietta, it might not even be an option at this point since that Pinkerton man —" she tossed a glare Agent McParland's way — "seems determined to arrest someone today. Because I certainly will not allow him to arrest Gertrude, I'm offering up myself to soothe his quest for justice." She thrust out her hands, exposing her wrists. "You may now feel free to cart me off to jail, Agent McParland. I have certainly helped myself to possessions that did not belong to me over the years, and while those possessions were returned to their rightful owners, I still took them. However, I will not allow you to charge me for the crimes committed at the Manhattan Beach Hotel.

I did not help myself to a single trinket there, although I will admit I did find that tiara almost irresistible."

"But you didn't take it," Gertrude argued.

"Of course I didn't," Mrs. Davenport said before she smiled ever so slightly. "Since I'd already stashed my reticule in that drawer on board the *Cornelia,* I had nowhere to stow a tiara."

"This is not the time for your odd sense of humor," Gertrude said before she looked Agent McParland's way. "It would appear as if your case is crumbling around you, Agent McParland, no matter that Mrs. Davenport has offered herself up as some type of sacrifice. As was stated before, Edwina can provide Mrs. Davenport with a credible alibi, and Miss Henrietta has offered to do the same for me. With that said, I can't help but wonder if you've now concluded we are not the prime suspects you imagined us to be, and are now willing to turn your investigation in a different direction."

For a long moment, Agent McParland simply considered Gertrude, until he stuffed his small notepad back into his jacket and nodded. "I'm not an unreasonable man, Miss Cadwalader, and admit that the evidence I have against you is not as strong as

I originally thought. For now, I will allow you and Mrs. Davenport to maintain your freedom, but do not plan on leaving the country any time soon." He turned and was suddenly smiling at Edwina again. "Your alibi has been most helpful to me, but I will still need to get a more detailed accounting of the events of the night in question, if that would be acceptable to you, Miss . . . ?"

"She's Miss Edwina Sinclair, my sister," Harrison said, drawing himself up to his full height. "And I don't believe there's any need for you to get a more detailed accounting than you've already received, nor is there any need for you to smile quite that way at my *baby* sister."

Edwina, being the annoying baby sister she obviously was, wrinkled her nose at him. "Stop embarrassing me," she mumbled before she began batting her lashes at Agent McParland in a way Harrison had never seen before.

"Where did she learn how to do that?" he asked to no one in particular.

"Agent McParland at your service, Miss Sinclair, but do feel free to call me Samuel," Agent McParland said before he took Edwina's hand, raised it to his lips, and placed a kiss on her fingers that had Harrison's hands clenching into fists.

"And here I was so hoping to add Edwina to the top of our list of ladies to take in hand," Miss Henrietta suddenly said with a sad shake of her head. "But I've seen that look before, which means our assistance won't be needed in her case."

"It's a shame," Miss Mabel agreed, speaking up for the first time. "But we still have Gertrude, and do not forget Miss Temperance Flowerdew."

Miss Henrietta and Miss Mabel turned their attention to Temperance, who was even now trying to edge ever so discreetly backward down the aisle, her escape effectively thwarted by the notice now directed her way.

"There's really no need for you to take me in hand," Temperance began. "Not that I don't appreciate the interest, Miss Henrietta and Miss Mabel. But since I'm soon going to have to secure employment, along with finding a room to let, I'm afraid I won't have time to be taken in hand, no matter how *delightful* that idea sounds."

Miss Henrietta and Miss Mabel exchanged looks before Miss Henrietta turned her gaze back to Temperance. "Mabel and I have known it was only a matter of time until your reprehensible relations kicked you out into the street. That is exactly why we decided to add you to our take-in-hand list. However . . ." She leaned closer to her sister, they began whispering furiously, then Miss Henrietta lifted her chin and smiled.

Because Harrison wasn't used to seeing Miss Henrietta smile all that often, he found the smile to be somewhat frightening, and when Miss Mabel began to smile and nod Temperance's way as well, he couldn't say he was surprised when Temperance began edging backward once again.

"You'll be pleased to learn that Mabel and I have already come up with the perfect plan as to what to do with you, Miss Flowerdew."

Temperance's backward momentum increased. "While that does sound most exciting, you'll have to tell me about it later. I really must be getting back home — lots of packing to do and all."

Miss Henrietta's smile widened. "Indeed, because you'll need to move immediately, especially to take up your new position at Miss Snook's School for the Education of the Feminine Mind. That position, you'll be simply delighted to learn, comes with room and board on the school's new premises, otherwise known as Mabel's and my former home."

Temperance's edging came to an immediate stop. "Why do you believe Miss Snook would be interested in bringing me on as a teacher? It's not as if I have any experience in a classroom."

"You may not have any experience teaching," Miss Mabel said, stepping forward, "but Henrietta and I are well aware that you were studying painting in Paris with some of the renowned painters of the day at the time of your parents' deaths. We also remember, although that memory just sprang back to mind, that you possess quite the talent with musical instruments, having performed in Boston when you were only a child, and stunning the audience with your ability to play not only the piano, but any string instrument you were handed."

"And because of those talents," Miss Henrietta added, "and because Miss Snook recently remarked that she wants to expand the classes offered at her school to include the arts, well, I would have to imagine this is one of those curious instances when God has aligned everything just so in order to bring about His will."

"But how do you know about my artistic nature?" Temperance asked.

Miss Henrietta smiled rather smugly. "I wasn't exaggerating our abilities to observe and collect information, dear. We've even been known to reach out via letters to people in all different parts of the world."

"Goodness," Temperance whispered, earning another smile and a nod from Miss Henrietta in the process.

"Indeed, but to dispel any doubts you may have as to whether you should accept this position at Miss Snook's school, who, by the way, is a most charming lady, let us turn to the expert in all matters of God and His unusual ways." She gestured to Reverend Perry, who'd moved closer toward the altar and hadn't entered this recent conversation, but seemed to be content with simply observing the scene unfolding in front of him.

Smiling, Reverend Perry stepped forward and cleared his throat. "How unusual to have such rapt attention directed my way from everyone in the congregation at the same time," he began. "Attention I'm hoping I'll see again the next time I'm delivering a sermon, especially since it does seem as if a good majority of the sermons I've delivered have not been listened to over the years." He nodded to Mrs. Davenport and then Gertrude.

"However, having said that, allow me to elaborate on Miss Henrietta's excellent point. Over the years, I've seen God arrange lives in the most curious of ways, and I do believe all of us have witnessed God's will and grace today." He gestured to Temperance. "You are obviously in need of employment and a new place to live, and a solution has been presented to you most unexpectedly. But not only will you be benefiting from this, Miss Snook's students will be given an opportunity to experience the arts, something most of her students would never dream they'd be given the opportunity to do."

He turned to Gertrude. "You, my dear, have obviously been trying to make amends for what happened to your mother — a situation you've never been open to discussing with me before, but I do know the circumstances surrounding your mother's death. What I believe you've been given today is a way to understand that God never held you accountable for her death, because it was her choice to leave you. I've come to think you've been trying to make amends for something over the years, but know that God forgives you."

"I don't think it's that easy," Gertrude argued.

Reverend Perry inclined his head. "Then allow me to point out something to you. When Mrs. Davenport asked for your forgiveness, you didn't hesitate to give it to her, did you?"

"Of course I didn't. I care about her."

"And you believe God doesn't care about you, one of His children?"

Gertrude blinked. "I suppose I didn't consider it in quite that light."

"Well, now you can," Reverend Perry said before he turned to Mrs. Davenport. "And we know God drew you here today because you needed to release the hurt and fear you hold of being abandoned, which will now allow you to move forward and seize your life, hopefully in a more productive and less illegal way." He then turned to Miss Henrietta and Miss Mabel. "As for the two of you, I may be reaching with this last bit, but I imagine God wants to encourage you to use that keen proficiency with observation to help others, such as you just helped Temperance."

"You could work with the Pinkerton and other agencies of the law," Edwina piped in as she smiled at Agent McParland. "Wouldn't the Huxley sisters be a *wonderful* source for you and your fellow agents?"

Harrison felt a tic begin throbbing on his forehead when he realized that Agent McParland had completely missed the question Edwina posed, probably because he'd returned to gazing at her with eyes that were once again decidedly unfocused.

"Beg pardon?" Agent McParland finally asked, which had Edwina smiling far too brightly back at him before she took hold of the man's arm and steered him to an empty pew where they both sat down and began chatting as if they'd been fast friends forever.

"And here I was so longing to bring her out," Mrs. Davenport said.

"No need to fret, dear," Miss Henrietta said. "We still have Gertrude."

As all eyes, except for those of Edwina and Agent McParland, turned to Gertrude, Harrison stepped forward, wanting to distract everyone from a topic that was clearly embarrassing Gertrude, whose cheeks were now looking overly heated. Before he could draw everyone's attention, though, Mrs. Davenport began *tsk*ing in a way that turned all eyes *her* way.

"We don't still have Gertrude because —" she lifted her chin — "using *my* keen proficiency with observation, I've observed that matters are progressing nicely between her and Harrison, which means she has no need of being taken in hand."

Finding himself the center of attention a mere second later, attention that came with an air of expectation, Harrison drew in a breath, then paused when an unexpected thought sprang to the forefront of his mind.

He could, right here and now, appease them all by proclaiming his very great affection for Gertrude while standing in the midst of God's house.

Since that idea might have come directly from above, and because he was a man who believed in following where God led, he knew it was an idea he should act upon.

Drawing in another breath, he opened his mouth, but then he glanced to Gertrude and found her not looking back at him in an anticipatory way, but with an expression on her face that seemed to be one of . . . horror.

Not understanding the horror in the least because he'd been under the impression she held him in some esteem, Harrison struggled to understand the look, breathing a sigh of relief a second later when a perfectly reasonable explanation sprang to mind.

Gertrude had been without the attention of a mother figure forever, and yet now not only Mrs. Davenport but Miss Henrietta and Miss Mabel as well were anxious to take her in hand, smothering her in feminine attention if he was understanding their intentions correctly.

That was why she was obviously not

anxious for him to declare his intentions, because that would deprive her of fulfilling a need she'd been longing to experience most of her life.

Realizing he'd evidently misunderstood God's subtle nudge, he inclined his head Gertrude's way before smiling at Mrs. Davenport.

"While I willingly admit that Gertrude and I have been progressing nicely as I do believe you mentioned, we're progressing nicely as *friends.* She has become one of the most important ladies in my life. As such, I wouldn't do her the disservice of discouraging you, Mrs. Davenport — or Miss Henrietta, or Miss Mabel — from taking her in hand. My greatest hope is that you'll see her well-settled with her very own happily-ever-after in the not-so-distant future."

For a brief moment, silence settled over the church, until Mrs. Davenport let out a completely unexpected snort, took Gertrude by the arm, and then marched her way up the aisle, muttering something about what an idiot he was when she brushed past him.

He was not reassured when Temperance sent him a sad shake of her head before she followed Mrs. Davenport and Gertrude, nor did it bode well for the situation when Miss

Henrietta and Miss Mabel cast pitying looks his way before they, too, marched up the aisle. Edwina and Agent McParland left next, although they didn't bother to even acknowledge him, apparently having missed everything he'd said because they seemed interested only in each other.

Before he knew it, he was standing alone in the sanctuary save for Reverend Perry, a gentleman who tossed what might have been a commiserating glance his way before he bowed his head and began to quietly pray aloud, his prayer seemingly centered around the topic of misunderstandings.

CHAPTER TWENTY-TWO

Two days later
Miss Snook's School for the Education of the
  Feminine Mind

Gertrude walked the length of the long dining table, checking each place setting to make certain everything was laid out properly for the class she was preparing to teach on table etiquette.

Miss Snook's school was not yet back in session, but because Gertrude was no longer Mrs. Davenport's companion, and had accepted the offer of becoming a full-time instructor in all matters of decorum, she had hours and hours of time on her hands. Those hours needed to be filled with tasks that kept her busy, especially since when she was at her leisure, thoughts of Harrison snuck into her mind and left her feeling somewhat morose.

Spotting a knife that wasn't polished as well as it should have been, Gertrude picked it up and moved to a serving cart situated by the door to the dining room, smiling when she saw someone had snuck in while she'd been occupied with her lesson planning and left a little snack of cookies and milk for her on the cart.

Gertrude picked up one of the cookies, gave it a nibble, and wondered if she'd ever get used to being fussed over.

Not only was Mrs. Davenport hovering over her at all hours of the day and night, but Miss Henrietta and Miss Mabel were hovering as well, their obvious determination to distract her from Harrison's disappointing response to how he viewed their relationship going far in keeping her from descending into too many bouts of wallowing.

It wasn't that she'd truly believed Harrison would fall on his knees and extend her a proposal of the most romantic sort smack-dab in the middle of Grace Church. However, his staunch rejection of the idea that his relationship with her was progressing in a romantic fashion left her with a somewhat aching heart.

That she'd known falling in love with Harrison was a great risk didn't ease the disappointment now settled deep in her soul, especially since she'd thought she'd seen something interesting in his eyes after Mrs. Davenport's initial remark, something that —

"I simply do not understand why I'm being required to enter Miss Snook's school as a student. Clearly I have designing skills those poor women who attend the school could find very useful in getting them out of their domestic jobs and into more satisfying ones."

Swallowing the piece of cookie she'd just put into her mouth, Gertrude looked up and found Mrs. Davenport standing in the doorway, holding what seemed to be a large amount of horsehair in her hands.

Gertrude smiled. "Miss Henrietta believes it will benefit you to hone some of those skills by working with a real designer, one who designs clothing for the socially elite on a regular basis."

"But *I* can design for the elite as well," Mrs. Davenport argued before she held up what might have been her attempt at another bustle. "Take a gander at this. Perfection, if you ask me, and I didn't resort to dismantling a single birdcage to obtain this large size."

Gertrude eyed the lump of horsehair, proud of herself when she didn't so much as shudder. "It's impressive to be sure, but I don't believe that's going to persuade Miss Henrietta to change her mind."

Mrs. Davenport released a sigh right before she flung herself into the nearest chair, discarding her creation on a neighboring chair. "Henrietta's a nightmare."

Gertrude smiled. "You two adore each other."

Mrs. Davenport returned the smile. "True, but she's still a nightmare." She flicked aside the lacey curtain and peered out the narrow window directly beside her chair.

"Expecting someone?" Gertrude asked, picking up a new knife and returning to the place setting she'd been working on.

"I keep wondering when Harrison will stop in to call. We haven't seen that gentleman since the *incident* at Grace Church."

"Edwina told us yesterday that Harrison had to leave town because their father needed assistance again with one of their more difficult customers over in Boston."

"If you ask me, I think Harrison frequently abandons the city for the high seas when he's facing disgruntlement from the feminine set," Mrs. Davenport said.

Gertrude pulled a ruler out of her pocket, made certain the knife was exactly aligned with the other silverware, then repocketed the ruler. "*I* am not disgruntled with Harrison."

"Well, I certainly am," a new voice said from outside the doorway. A second later, Edwina strode into the room, stopping directly in front of Mrs. Davenport. Bending over, she gave her a kiss on the cheek, then straightened and grinned. "I couldn't help but hear your dulcet tones, Mrs. Davenport, as I was walking down the hallway. You appear to be in a feisty state today."

Mrs. Davenport returned the grin. "Your brother's fault, dear, and why have you begun addressing me as Mrs. Davenport again instead of Hester?"

"Because Gertrude can't seem to get comfortable with calling you Hester, even though you finally came to your senses and suggested she do exactly that. I'm simplifying the situation for everyone."

Mrs. Davenport inclined her head. "Very thoughtful of you, dear. However, returning to your brother, is he truly out of town, or is that excuse simply a ruse that is sparing him an unpleasant encounter with ladies such as myself, Miss Henrietta, and Miss Mabel?"

Edwina plopped into the chair next to Mrs. Davenport. "Oh, he's definitely out of town, and you may add me to the list of ladies who long to have an unpleasant encounter with him." She released a dramatic breath. "He had the audacity to tell my mother I was batting my lashes at Agent McParland, and . . . behaving in what he described as an untoward fashion with a man I'd only just met."

The corners of Gertrude's lips curved. "That sounds exactly what I would expect an older brother to do, and you *were* batting your lashes at Agent McParland."

"Well, quite, but he's the most delightful gentleman I've ever laid eyes on, and what good is having long lashes if I don't ever get to bat them? As for Harrison, he may have been acting like a ridiculous older brother, but in my mind, he's nothing but a traitor. Did I mention he also told my mother that I began speaking in a very sultry voice *and* that I was calling Agent McParland by his given name?"

"It's somewhat sweet when you think about it," Gertrude said, trying her best to swallow the laughter that kept bubbling up in her throat. "He's just looking out for you."

"I'm almost a spinster. And while Adelaide and Margaret seem perfectly content to embrace that unfortunate condition, I'd rather not spend the rest of my days surrounded only by women — no offense to the two of you — and a brother who I swear was put on this earth to torment me."

Mrs. Davenport suddenly sat forward, her eyes sparkling. "We could always attempt to convince Miss Henrietta and Miss Mabel that it would be in your best interest to travel to Newport for the summer as we originally planned. Why, I'd still be more than happy to sponsor you into society. I would imagine you'd have offers from some of the most delectable society gentlemen the very second you're presented."

Edwina slouched deeper into the chair. "You're forgetting your agreement with Miss Henrietta, one that has you on a probationary period, so to speak. During this period, you're barely allowed to take a walk down the sidewalk, let alone enjoy any society events."

Mrs. Davenport sat back in the chair again. "They believe I could still be tempted by items of a shiny nature."

"And it's best not to take any chances with that type of temptation," Gertrude said, nodding at the table setting that was now perfect. Walking to join the other ladies, she pulled up a spare chair next to Mrs. Davenport and sat down. "The good news is that you and I were planning on an uneventful summer before you met Edwina, something I know you weren't looking forward to. However, with us moving into Miss Henrietta and Miss Mabel's old house, our summer is now anything but uneventful, so there's no need for you to bemoan the loss of a season in Newport. And because there's still so much organizing to do in this old house before classes resume in a few weeks, you'll be distracted from all thoughts of shiny objects for the foreseeable future."

Mrs. Davenport's brows drew together. "I'm not certain organizing a house filled with the treasures Miss Henrietta and Miss Mabel collected over the years is really the best way to dissuade me from old habits."

"You know you'll never take anything from them, and you know it's a reach to use that as an excuse to get you and Edwina off to Newport."

"It was worth a try," Mrs. Davenport mumbled. "Newport is so very lovely in the summer."

Edwina released a sigh. "I'm sure Newport is oh-so-lovely, but even if you weren't on a probationary period, I'm afraid it wouldn't be possible for me to join you at your cottage." She rolled her eyes. "Besides squealing on me about Agent McParland, Harrison also made a point of telling our mother about my society aspirations. Pair that with the fact that she caught Gertrude with items you, Mrs. Davenport, admitted to stuffing in your reticule, and I'm afraid, even after I explained the perfectly logical reason behind your peculiar habit, she's not exactly keen to see me deepen my association with either you or Gertrude."

Gertrude sat forward. "Does she know you've come to call on us today?"

"She knows I've come to call at Miss Snook's School for the Education of the Feminine Mind, a school my mother finds quite acceptable given her progressive attitude." Edwina grinned. "She might not be aware of the fact, though, that you and Mrs. Davenport have taken up residence within the walls of this particular school."

"And you're not concerned your mother might find out that less-than-secret information?" Gertrude pressed.

"I'm hoping by the time she does, she'll have come to her senses. She's not a very trusting woman, quick to judge if you must know. Although, after poor Margaret got taken in by two fortune-hunters, as did my mother, who thought those fortune-hunters were aboveboard, one can't blame her these days for being overly cautious about anyone unfamiliar trying to get close to our family." Edwina blew out a breath. "She's also currently in a bit of a dismal mood because she's missing my father."

"Then why didn't she go off to assist your father instead of Harrison?" Mrs. Davenport asked. "Am I mistaken in believing she's an integral part of Sinclair Shipping?"

"She and Father have always been equal partners in the business, although Harrison has been assuming more of a leading role these days. Mother and Father intend to eventually hand everything over to Harrison, me, and my sisters." She released a dramatic sigh. "I might have mentioned to her that I have no interest in continuing on with the family business, which explains why she didn't travel to Boston but sent Harrison instead."

"So Harrison didn't sail out of the city because he's avoiding all of us?" Mrs. Davenport pressed.

"Oh, I'm sure that was one of the reasons he agreed to go to Boston to assist my father, although I'm also certain he didn't bother to explain that to my mother. No, he, being annoying, made certain to point out the errors of my recent ways, thus encouraging my mother to stay behind and keep watch over me." Edwina turned to

Gertrude. "I feel I should explain that Harrison takes to the sea when he's troubled, and I do believe you'll find it comforting to learn he's definitely troubled about you."

Gertrude's spirits began to improve just the slightest little bit. "Why would he be troubled about me? He made a most emphatic argument about us being strictly friends, an argument I couldn't help but notice he truly seemed to believe."

"He doesn't believe that. He's simply confused, a condition Harrison suffers frequently in this messy business called life. However, you mark my words, by the time he returns to the city, which will hopefully be today, he'll have sorted through that confusion and come up with a plan to make amends." Edwina's eyes twinkled. "That's when it will get very interesting around here."

Gertrude's brows drew together. "I do believe you're in for a disappointment, Edwina, because Harrison has been rather firm that he doesn't have time for a romantic relationship."

"That's because he's never met a lady he wants to become romantically involved with — until you."

Not caring to dwell on that since she wasn't fond of her heart aching all the time, and she certainly didn't want to experience another disappointment like she had at Grace Church, Gertrude got up from the chair and casually strolled back to the table, pulling out her ruler in the pretense of rechecking her perfectly set table.

"I do wonder how Harrison will go about the tricky business of making amends for that fiasco he caused," Mrs. Davenport said.

Gertrude moved her ruler to the next place setting, edging a crystal water goblet a fraction to the right. "There's no reason for Harrison to make amends. He was simply being truthful, and while I may have allowed my affections for him to travel in a direction they never should have traveled, one can't force a gentleman to return affections he doesn't care to return."

"She's very stubborn, isn't she?" Edwina asked Mrs. Davenport as she abandoned her chair and moved to join Gertrude. "However, because you're my friend, and I'd like for you to remain my friend, I'll stop harping on the subject of my brother." She leaned forward and began counting the forks that were now perfectly aligned. "I do hope this isn't a typical table setting, because, on my word, the forks alone are overwhelming."

Relieved to have a change of topics, Gertrude smiled and gestured to the table. "I've set this table for an eight-course meal because I want the students to become comfortable in any social setting. One never knows when you might be asked to attend a dinner at Delmonico's, but you should know that many society matrons serve a twelve-course meal. And, unfortunately, I do believe the number of courses will steadily increase, what with so many competitions sprouting up amongst the society set — each society matron trying to outdo the last society event attended."

"But . . . how can a person be expected to eat so much?" Edwina asked.

"You merely *taste* the courses, dear," Mrs. Davenport said, walking up to join them. "Society is all about appearances. The more courses you serve, the more gold and crystal you have on your table, the more exclusive the wine, well, the more you've proven you've arrived. That is what society believes to be all important these days."

Edwina glanced down the table again, then shook her head. "Perhaps I'm not meant for society after all. I don't know if I'd be able to witness such pretentious attitudes and still be able to hold my tongue." She smiled. "Having admitted that, it's probably fortunate I've *almost* decided to pursue a completely different avenue these days for my life."

"You're giving up on the idea of becoming a society lady?" Mrs. Davenport asked.

Edwina nodded. "I believe I'm meant to live a more adventurous life, Mrs. Davenport. And I believe I might just find that life by learning skills that will allow me to embrace a position investigating crimes." Her eyes sparkled. "Samuel, I mean Agent McParland, told me there are a few ladies employed by the Pinkerton Agency. I'd like to become one of those ladies, especially because, after living with Harrison all these years, I've decided that men do not think like we do, which means a feminine mind might very well prove useful when dealing with cases involving lady confidence artists."

"You didn't come up with that idea because of my past misdeeds, did you, dear?" Mrs. Davenport asked.

Edwina gave an airy wave of a hand, her only response to Mrs. Davenport's question.

Narrowing her eyes, Mrs. Davenport tapped a finger against her chin. "I don't believe your mother is going to be very keen about this latest development."

"My mother's always been a bit of an odd duck. I imagine she'll be far keener about me becoming a detective rather than spending my days at events she believes are frivolous — no offense."

"None taken," Mrs. Davenport returned. "And while you may be correct in that your mother might not balk about this new idea, I highly doubt Harrison is going to readily accept it."

Edwina's lips curved. "I'm not planning on telling Harrison, and by the time he figures out what I'm up to, it'll be too late."

Gertrude tilted her head. "I don't believe Harrison is as oblivious as you seem to believe, especially when it concerns his sisters."

"How very astute of you to realize that, Gertrude, but I'm hoping he'll be so consumed with trying to make matters right with you, he'll neglect to notice me for a while."

Before Gertrude could argue with that, even though the thought of Harrison making amends with her sent her heart pitter-pattering, Miss Mabel popped her head into the dining room.

"Oh good, here you are, Gertrude, but . . . where's my sister?"

"Miss Henrietta took a carriage over to the Flowerdew residence. She wants Temperance to move out of her cousin's house posthaste and get settled here before classes begin," Gertrude said.

Miss Mabel stepped into the room and smiled. "It is lovely to see this old house filling up with delightful young ladies. I would have never imagined it would become a place of hope instead of the despair and secrets Henrietta and I endured for so long. However, enough about that maudlin time. I've just come from Rutherford & Company, having a small lull from managing the crowds in the tearoom, to deliver a message from Permilia." She nodded to Gertrude. "Your friend would like to see you at the store at your earliest convenience, which I believe means within the next hour."

"Did she say why she needs to see me?"

For a second, Miss Mabel looked somewhat shifty, but then she was smiling again. "I'm afraid not."

"Ah, a trip to Rutherford & Company," Mrs. Davenport exclaimed, distracting Gertrude from Miss Mabel's now beaming face. "I adore that store, and how very convenient it's only right down the block. It's a lovely day for a stroll, so we don't even need to call for a carriage."

Miss Mabel stopped beaming, walked directly over to Mrs. Davenport, and shook her head. "Nice try, dear, but you're still on probation from stores, and before you begin arguing, did I mention that I've brought by Miss Betsy Miller, designer extraordinaire, who might just happen to be down in the design room waiting to show you how to make paper patterns?"

"How marvelous," Mrs. Davenport said, and after barely bidding good afternoon to Gertrude and Edwina, telling them to enjoy themselves at the store, Mrs. Davenport hurried out of the room with Miss Mabel.

"It was brilliant of Miss Henrietta and Miss Mabel to insist Mrs. Davenport allow them to take her in hand," Edwina said. "As well as insist she move here for the foreseeable future. It's only been two days, but she seems happier." Edwina came and took hold of Gertrude's arm. "Did I mention I've decided to help you with Harrison?"

Gertrude blinked at the rapid change of topic. "I don't believe you mentioned a thing about that at all. But, if I need remind you, Harrison was quite forceful in his denial that he and I were involved in a relationship. Because of that, and because I truly don't enjoy rejection from a man I *might* have held in high esteem, I'm going to simply accept the idea that Harrison and I are only meant to be friends."

"Where's the fun in that?"

"There's no fun in that, but it'll save me a world of hurt in the end."

"But it won't give you your very own happily-ever-after, something I can help you to achieve."

Gertrude frowned. "How would you go about doing that?"

Pulling her toward the door, Edwina smiled. "I'll tell you on the way to Rutherford & Company."

CHAPTER TWENTY-THREE

"Are you quite certain this is the best way to go about making amends with Gertrude?" Harrison asked, taking the reins from a groom in the Rutherford & Company stable as Asher nodded back at him from where he was already sitting astride his horse.

"Time is of the essence, Harrison," Asher returned, waiting until Harrison swung himself into his saddle before continuing. "From what I understand, you're now of the belief your affections for Gertrude have changed to something a great deal more than friendship. However, for a reason I have yet to comprehend, when you were presented with a prime opportunity to divulge your true emotions, you apparently lost all good sense and made a complete muddle of the situation instead."

"I don't know why you're having a difficult time comprehending the idea I made a muddle of things. We've been friends for years, Asher, and because of that, you should be able to understand that I simply misinterpreted Gertrude's facial expression."

Asher arched a brow. "I'm not sure what type of expression a lady can actually make that would lead you to believe she wanted to be taken in hand by Miss Henrietta and Miss Mabel, two of the most frightening ladies I've ever met."

"She was looking horrified."

Asher's other brow rose to join the first one. "Of course she was looking horrified. Ladies do not enjoy being placed in a position where the gentleman of their affections is put on the spot to declare his intentions."

Harrison frowned. "Which does make perfect sense now that I consider it. However, you were not around to lend me such valuable insight, and as such, I blundered . . . badly."

"I'm in full agreement with that, but now find myself curious as to how you managed to conclude you'd made a grave error."

"I had an epiphany once I reached the high seas when I was sailing toward Boston to meet my father."

"And it didn't cross your mind to turn your ship around so you could make amends with Gertrude directly after you had this epiphany?"

"I'm afraid not. I needed to mull the matter through to satisfaction."

Asher clicked his tongue, sending his horse into motion. "On my word, Harrison, you've grown up surrounded by women. Surely you know by now that it's never a good idea to allow ladies any great amount of time to dwell on their disappointments. In all honesty, I wouldn't be surprised to learn Gertrude's now decided you're an idiot and that she's better off without you."

"Again, information that would have been useful before I landed myself in this mess."

"We'll get you out of this mess, one way or another, and —" Asher turned in the saddle — "we'll also get to see if our theory is correct regarding over-the-top romantic gestures. As you know, I've compiled a list of just such gestures from some novels I had my secretary pick up for me at the bookseller. Why, I have to imagine if enacting a few of them allows you to get back in Gertrude's graces, we'll be held up as heroes to our gentlemen acquaintances, once word gets around about our success."

Harrison steered Rupert after Asher and out of the stables, blinking as bright sunshine practically blinded him. "I don't remember agreeing to share our results, Asher."

"It would be selfish of us not to if we do, hopefully, succeed." He lifted his face to the sun. "I can feel success within our grasp, and I'm going to take it as a positive sign that it's stopped raining, although we did need that rain in order for you to enact number two on the list I created."

Digging his hand into his pocket, Harrison fished out his copy of the list. Written across the top in Asher's fine hand was *Romantic Gestures to Win Gertrude's Heart.*

Scanning the page, he frowned. "Number two suggests I place my jacket over a puddle and then encourage Gertrude to walk over that jacket." He gestured to his jacket. "Did you not hear me when I mentioned I only recently picked up this jacket on an obscure island, drawn to it because I think the color suits almost every pair of trousers I own?"

"You should have left the jacket on that island because it's the most lurid shade of green I've ever seen, and I doubt it suits a single pair of your trousers."

"I thought the jacket was slightly orange."

"How many shades of orange do you think are out there?"

"Obviously too many, but . . ." Harrison returned his attention to the list. "What if we're completely off the mark and Gertrude decides I've taken leave of my senses?"

"You took leave of your senses when you didn't declare yourself and the affection you hold for her at Grace Church. However, because you told me she seemed to enjoy you sweeping her up into your arms the night of my engagement celebration, I think romantic gestures are the best place to start for you. Besides, this was the only thing I could come up with on such short notice."

"I suppose it can't make the situation worse."

"That's the spirit! So onward we go. Miss Mabel has had plenty of time to deliver Permilia's request. That means you need to ride Rupert past Miss Snook's school, then wait until Gertrude's moving down the sidewalk before you whisk her right up on your horse, delivering her to Rutherford & Company in style. I'll keep an eye on the situation from afar, and if I think you're floundering, I'll ride to your rescue."

Harrison glanced down Broadway, blowing out a breath when he noticed how crowded the street was. "I don't know, Asher, perhaps I should leave the whisking her up on my horse for another day. If you'll recall, I mentioned my concerns about that gesture. There's every chance she'll have a different reaction than we're expecting, one that won't leave her feeling overly fond of me. Besides, the only whisking scenes I've read are centered around the heroine's life being in danger because of bandits or an approaching train. It seems somewhat odd to use this particular gesture when Gertrude's life isn't in danger since she's simply walking to your store."

"I've found seven instances of the hero whisking the heroine up onto his horse in those novels. In every one of them, the heroine was suitably impressed by the masculinity displayed by the hero because of the strength it takes to pluck a woman from the ground and get her situated just so on a horse." Asher smiled. "Because you're an expert rider, there's no question in my mind that you'll be able to accomplish this feat with great skill, suitably impressing Gertrude in the process. Why, I'll bet she'll be so impressed, there won't be a need to make use of the other suggestions on the list." With that, Asher spurred his horse forward, leaving Harrison trailing after him. Gesturing him forward a short time later, Asher pulled his horse to the side of the street and sent Harrison a nod.

Realizing there was nothing to do but see if this harebrained idea might work, Harrison urged his horse forward, keeping hidden behind all the carriages on the street until he'd passed Miss Snook's school. Turning Rupert around, he blinked when he saw Gertrude a little ways down the sidewalk, the cream-colored walking dress she was wearing accenting her charming figure to perfection. Taking a deep breath, and not allowing himself time to reconsider what might very well be yet another blunder, he set Rupert into a gallop, coming up behind Gertrude far quicker than he'd anticipated. Leaning over Rupert's side, he reached out, then almost pulled back when he noticed Gertrude was not alone but with his sister, and . . . they'd entwined their arms together.

Before he could fully grasp what that meant, his hand closed around Gertrude's arm, and then she was flying up in the air in front of him and onto his horse, her legs flailing about as she began to scream at the top of her lungs.

Unfortunately, Rupert was not a horse possessed of a mild manner, so the second the screams began — and an unexpected weight landed on him — he was off like a shot.

Turning his head when Gertrude's hat flew by, Harrison spotted Edwina sitting on the sidewalk, apparently having been knocked to the ground when he snatched Gertrude. Unable to do anything about that troublesome situation because Rupert was galloping faster than ever, Harrison tightened his grip on Gertrude, who was screaming so loudly his ears were beginning to ring.

She was also practically falling off his horse with her skirt flying every which way, exposing a good deal of petticoats and a nicely turned feminine leg in the process.

Calling himself every type of fool, he pressed his knees into Rupert, but instead of having the desired effect of bringing Rupert to a stop, the horse continued bolting down the street, causing people who'd been trying to cross the street to leap out of their way.

Wincing when a gentleman dove onto the sidewalk, losing his hat in the process, one that Rupert then trampled under his very large hooves, Harrison shouted an apology right as the sound of someone blowing a whistle met his ears. Glancing over his shoulder, Harrison didn't know whether to laugh or groan when he recognized none other than Agent McParland racing after them.

"I think I'm going to be sick!" Gertrude yelled.

Harrison immediately tried to reassure her they'd be stopping soon, but her hair was now coming undone from its pins and the long strands were whipping him in the face, making it next to impossible to speak or to see much, for that matter.

All he could do was keep a tight hold on Gertrude and pray that his stallion would become winded before they reached the next state.

It took three complete blocks before Rupert began to slow, and then, when he finally stopped, Harrison could not think of a single thing to say to the woman who shoved her hair out of her eyes, struggled upright, turned the upper half of her body toward him, then pinned him with a furious glare.

"Harrison! Good heavens, it's you." Her eyes narrowed. "Have you taken leave of your senses? What could you have been thinking, abducting me like that?"

Disappointment slid through him. "You only now realized it was me?"

Her eyes narrowed another fraction. "How could I have known it was you before this very moment? We were traveling at break-neck speed, and far be it from me to point out the obvious, but my skirt was practically flying over my head, making it somewhat difficult to see. Add in that you caught me completely unaware, and . . . no, I didn't realize it was you."

He summoned up a smile, hoping it was the one he'd heard ladies found charming. Unfortunately, it did absolutely nothing to diminish the fury in Gertrude's eyes. "May I assume you're not even a smidgen impressed by how I was able to accomplish the feat of getting you up on my horse?"

"You almost killed me in the process, so if you're ever planning on trying this particular feat again, you might want to practice — and not with a living lady as your subject."

"I thought you might enjoy arriving at Rutherford & Company in . . . what was that again . . . oh yes . . . style."

"I enjoy arriving at fine stores in one piece, thank you very much, but now, if it wouldn't be too much of a bother, you need to get me off this horse."

Harrison frowned. "I'm not certain how to go about that safely."

"Because my safety is obviously such a concern for you today."

Before he could reply to that telling statement, the sound of horse hooves sounded behind them.

"I say, Miss Cadwalader, are you quite all right?"

Turning his head because there really wasn't anything else for him to do, Harrison found Agent McParland drawing his horse to a stop directly beside them. There appeared to be a touch of satisfaction in his eyes — the reason for that becoming clear when Harrison realized Edwina was sitting securely behind Agent McParland, her arm wrapped around the man's waist. She was smiling in clear satisfaction as well, even though she did scowl at him for just a second and roll her eyes.

"You're supposed to pull a lady up and then behind you," she whispered in a voice that still carried. "Which you would know if you applied yourself more diligently to those novels you pretend you don't read, although given this disaster, you've clearly been skimming your way through them."

Gertrude leaned over him to look at Edwina. "What novels?"

Edwina opened her mouth, but then closed it again, shaking her head. "You'll have to ask Harrison, Gertrude. I may be annoyed with him, but we do share a sibling bond, one that prevents me from exposing all his secrets."

Gertrude returned her attention to him. "What novels?"

To Harrison's relief, Asher suddenly galloped into view, his hair distinctly disheveled, and his expression relieved once he caught sight of them. Pulling his horse to a stop, he got to the ground and moved to Rupert's side. "That didn't go quite as planned, but allow me to help you down, Gertrude."

"How did it not go as planned?" Gertrude demanded. "And what exactly were the two of you planning in the first place?"

"That's a little difficult to explain," Asher said. "But if you would be so kind as to give me your hand, we can then continue our conversation when you're safely on the ground."

Sticking her hand out, even though she seemed to do so somewhat grudgingly, Gertrude slid less than gracefully from his horse. Thanking Asher, she stalked a good five feet away from Rupert, probably because Rupert was now tossing his head and pawing at the ground.

Harrison swung his leg over the saddle, dropped to the ground, told Rupert to behave, then blinked. To his utter disbelief, Agent McParland was not getting off his horse to assess the situation, something Harrison thought the Pinkerton agent would have done. Instead, he was already galloping away on his horse, Edwina waving cheerfully back at Harrison before she turned around, the sound of her laughter drifting back to him on the breeze.

"At least someone knows how to go about orchestrating a dashing gesture," Asher muttered to Harrison as he took hold of his horse's reins, then nodded to Gertrude, who was looking remarkably grumpy. "What say all of us walk back together to Rutherford & Company? I'll buy you a nice cup of tea from the tea shop."

Gertrude smoothed her hair. "There's no need for either of you to accompany me, Asher. I'm perfectly fine — and some might say safer — walking by myself."

Asher smoothed back his hair as well. "This area is known to have pickpockets lurking about. Best not to chance your well-being."

"Because pulling me on top of a rabid beast wasn't a risk to my well-being," Gertrude replied before she lifted her chin and started forward, limping every other step.

"Are you hurt?" Harrison asked, hurrying to catch up with her.

"Lost a shoe."

Harrison winced. "I am sorry about that . . . and about your hat."

"I've lost my hat?"

"Indeed."

"Not to worry," Asher said cheerfully as he trailed behind them. "I happen to know we have numerous lovely hats in our millinery department, and you may choose a new one. My treat."

Gertrude stopped walking and turned. "Why would you treat me when it's Harrison's fault I lost my hat in the first place?"

Asher winced. "Umm . . . because I enjoy extending my soon-to-be wife's favorite friend a treat?"

Gertrude's brows drew together. "Was it your idea for Harrison to snatch me off the street?"

"I must say I can't remember a time I've seen Edwina looking so delighted, but she certainly seems to have enjoyed being pulled up on Agent McParland's horse," Asher said, ignoring the question. "That sparkle I noticed in her eye is exactly what I'd like to capture in an advertisement for my store." He nodded to Harrison. "Do be certain to remind me to broach the idea of her modeling for me if she ever returns from her adventure with Agent McParland."

"I'll do no such thing," Harrison argued. "Edwina's enough of a handful as it is. The last thing we need is for her face to be all over the city, because that'll encourage more men like Agent McParland to come calling.

And don't even get me started on what my mother will do if she learns I've encouraged your mad idea to use Edwina for advertising copy."

Asher began *tsk*ing under his breath. "There's no need to be so argumentative. If you haven't noticed, I'm trying to help you."

"Perhaps you should stop helping him, Asher, before you both get into more trouble than you're already in," Gertrude said. "But speaking of Edwina, I do hope she hasn't suffered an injury. If either of you didn't notice, she tumbled to the ground after Harrison ripped me right away from her." Gertrude rubbed her arm. "She and I are fortunate to still have our limbs attached."

"How are matters progressing at Miss Snook's School for the Education of the Feminine Mind?" Harrison asked, earning a nod of clear approval from Asher but a frown from Gertrude.

"It's going very well, thank you," Gertrude said, and even though her response was perfectly pleasant, Harrison thought he detected a trace of an edge to her tone.

He refused another wince. "Have you been enjoying being taken in hand by all the ladies?"

When Gertrude spun on her heel and stomped away from him, and Asher began shaking his head somewhat vigorously, Harrison realized he'd once again allowed the wrong words to escape. Breaking into a stride, even though his stride was somewhat limited because Rupert wasn't cooperating and Harrison had to practically pull him down the street, he finally reached Gertrude's side.

"May I assume you don't care to be taken in hand?"

"You shouldn't assume anything about me." Sending him a look that practically scorched the skin right off his face, she lurched ahead, and he wasn't quite brave enough to catch up with her just yet.

"What are you doing?" Asher demanded, joining him. "Why would you broach the idea of her being taken in hand? That's what got you into this mess in the first place."

"Forgive me for being a little rattled, but if you missed it, my dashing gesture wasn't remotely dashing, and I'm afraid my mind has yet to snap back into place."

"Then allow me to snap it back for you, because there's a puddle up ahead, and it's time to try out romantic gesture number two."

"Do you honestly believe I should continue on with the list?"

"What possible harm could come of the

next gesture? The worse that can happen is she'll feel sorry about you ruining your jacket, although" — Asher met Harrison's gaze — "that's exactly what we need her to feel for you now: sympathy. So, off you go again. I'll hold Rupert's reins. But you'd best break into a bit of a run or she'll pass that puddle before you have an opportunity to act the gallant."

Handing over the reins, Harrison started forward, breaking into a run. Shrugging out of his jacket as he passed her, he fished the list out of the jacket pocket, tucked it into the pocket of his trousers, then stopped directly in front of the large puddle Asher had pointed out. Spinning around, he stepped right in front of Gertrude, blocking her way.

He was not reassured when she lifted her chin and narrowed her eyes.

Taking a second to make a big production of shaking out his jacket, he turned and threw the jacket over the puddle, turning back to her and gesturing her forward.

"You're not suffering from a fever, are you?" she asked slowly.

Thinking it would be a little much to tell her he was feverish with affection for her, Harrison cleared his throat and gestured forward again instead. "I'm fine. I simply want to help you cross over this puddle without getting your dainty little feet wet."

"I have larger feet than the average woman."

"If you don't walk over that jacket soon, your feet, whether they be large or small, will get soaked because the water seems to be absorbing somewhat quickly into the fabric of my coat."

The very corners of her lips twitched. "I don't think I'm up for arguing with logic like that."

Feeling slightly more confident because her lips had most definitely twitched, Harrison bowed her forward, watched her take her first step over the jacket, then another, and another, and then . . . she dropped like a stone into what turned out to be not a puddle, but a rather deep hole.

CHAPTER TWENTY-FOUR

The second her feet finally hit solid ground, Gertrude looked down, relieved to discover she'd only fallen up to her waist in what felt like a vat of mud. Raising a hand, she took a swipe at her face, shuddering when clumps of something of a questionable nature became firmly attached to her glove. Peeling off the glove, and then the other, she flung them away from her, lifted her gaze, and found Harrison, along with Asher, standing frozen in place, their expressions so horrified she couldn't help herself . . . she laughed.

Once she started, she couldn't stop, until the muck attached to her face began to dribble down her cheeks, and not caring to have it slide right into her mouth, she pressed her lips together, swallowed another laugh, then held out a slimy hand, which Harrison immediately took.

"On my word, Gertie, I don't know how

to go about even asking you to forgive me for this one," he said, pulling her up effortlessly and keeping hold of her as she caught her balance, even though doing so stained his linen shirt with mud.

"It was my fault," Asher said, stepping forward, pulling one of his ever-handy handkerchiefs from his jacket and handing it over to her. "I'm the one who convinced Harrison you'd be impressed with romantic gestures, but here we've scared you half to death, and then consigned you to an almost bottomless pit of mud."

Gertrude wiped her face with the handkerchief, trying to ignore the fact her pulse was now beginning to race through her veins, a direct result of Harrison having called her Gertie.

She'd always longed to be familiar enough with a person where they'd adopt a special name for her, and that Harrison was the first person to ever call her Gertie — an adorable adaptation of her name if she'd ever heard one — well, it was enough to send her heart pitter-pattering in her chest.

That pitter-pattering hitched up another notch when Harrison took the handkerchief from her and started wiping mud from her forehead.

"I'm afraid I'm now responsible for ruining your dress, and I don't know how to tell you this, but . . ." He stopped wiping her face and looked down. "It appears you've lost your other shoe."

Gertrude waved that aside. "It's of little consequence, Harrison. I'm much more concerned about what you're trying to accomplish today. Forgive me, but the only instance I'm aware of where a gentleman willingly ruins what I thought was a very fine coat, even with its peculiar green color, is when said gentleman is trying to, again forgive me, woo a lady." She caught his eye. "If you'll recall, you stated quite emphatically only a few days ago that you and I were strictly friends, and . . . you encouraged me to allow the ladies to take me in hand. Now, I'm not certain if you're aware of this, but *being taken in hand* more often than not is simply a different way of saying it's time to find a gentleman for a lady to marry."

Harrison blinked. "Is it really?"

With those three little words, Gertrude felt her spirits lifting. "Yes."

"I had no idea," Harrison said, dabbing at her forehead again before he turned and handed Asher back his handkerchief. "It seems as if this is a day of discovery for me, and looks as if it needs to be a day of disclosure as well."

"What kind of disclosure?" Gertrude asked, not wanting to allow herself to hope too much, but unable to stop the anticipation now racing through her.

"All in due time" was all Harrison said as he nodded to Asher. "I need to get Gertrude back so she can change out of these wet and muddy clothes. I may not have intended her to take a dousing today, but that's exactly what happened and I certainly don't want to see her catching a chill because of my less than dashing gesture. Will you see to Rupert while I see to Gertie?"

Asher inclined his head. "Of course." He looked to Gertrude. "I cannot apologize enough, Gertrude, for my part in the distress that we caused you today."

She smiled. "I'm fine, Asher. There's been relatively little harm done, so do stop looking so solemn. Why, the events of this day will make great stories to tell my children someday, if I ever have any, so there's no need for either you or Harrison to continue fretting. But do pass on my apologies to Permilia, since clearly I'll not be able to meet with her now."

"I will, although knowing Permilia, she'll be over at Miss Snook's before you have time to change."

Sending her a smile, before seeming to wince at Harrison, Asher walked away, leading the two horses behind him. Oddly enough, even Rupert was looking a little solemn and didn't bother to so much as toss his head when he passed Gertrude.

Taking hold of her hand, Harrison placed it in the crook of his arm, giving it a pat and refusing to listen to Gertrude's protests about his not getting close to her because she was ruining his clothing.

"Asher's of the belief this is an outfit best confined to the ragpickers anyway," he said. "And I'm certainly not going to allow you to slip and slide all the way back without benefit of a steadying arm. You've now lost both of your shoes, which is going to make navigating down the sidewalk tricky."

"I'll be fine," Gertrude said. "Although I am sorry you lost your jacket as well."

Harrison smiled. "Asher was offended by the green, although I have to admit I was of the belief the jacket was orange."

She returned his smile. "Asher is very fussy when it comes to fashions, but if you tell him I said that, I'll deny it. However, as for the green, it was a somewhat bright green. There aren't many men who can wear that color, but you were certainly one of the exceptions."

Giving her arm another pat, Harrison leaned closer to her, his eyes turning slightly . . . dangerous.

As all her breath got caught in her throat, he leaned even closer, but then, before his lips could touch hers, something she truly thought might happen, he blinked, shook himself ever so slightly, then straightened.

"Do forgive me, Gertrude. I have no idea what just came over me. Here I promised to see you directly home, and yet I'm dawdling."

Opening her mouth to tell him she was perfectly happy to have him dawdle all he'd like, and that she now preferred him addressing her as Gertie, her words died a rapid death when he suddenly began walking, his long legs eating up the sidewalk so rapidly she found herself practically having to gallop to keep up with him.

It came as no surprise that she soon developed a stitch in her side right before she started wheezing.

Slowing, Harrison turned his head and frowned. "Another stitch?"

"Just a small one."

The very next second she was back in his arms, her dress soaking the fine linen of his shirt as he strode down the three blocks toward the school. With laughter rumbling from his throat when she suggested he was going to hurt himself if he didn't put her down soon, Harrison flipped open the latch of the wrought-iron gate that separated the school from the sidewalk. He then continued up the path leading to the front door, nodding to the Huxley butler, Mr. Barclay, who was already holding the door open for them.

"I wasn't expecting to see you still manning the door, Mr. Barclay," Harrison said, stepping past the butler, then stopping with Gertrude still in his arms when he reached the marble entranceway.

"I find it much more exciting back here than at our new residence," Mr. Barclay said. "The sisters do enjoy the house by Gramercy Park, but it gets a little quiet there for me, what with Miss Henrietta and Miss Mabel occupied with so many different matters these days." He smiled. "That's why I asked to be reassigned here at the new school when the sisters know they won't be at the other house, because . . . well . . ." He looked at the puddle of mud pooling under Gertrude. "Adventures seem to happen often these days, and I'm sure that will only increase once we get the school up and fully operational."

"Was that someone at the door, Mr.

Barclay?" Mrs. Davenport asked, poking her head around the corner of the hallway before she let out a small shriek, then barreled directly toward them, wearing what appeared to be pattern pieces attached to her clothing. Skidding to a stop in front of them, the skidding a direct result of her being in stockinged feet, she raised a hand to her mouth as she looked Gertrude over.

"Goodness, what happened? Why is Harrison carrying you, and what are you doing with Harrison in the first place?"

"I'm carrying her because she got another stitch, Mrs. Davenport, and she's also missing her shoes."

Mrs. Davenport turned a sharp eye Harrison's way. "How, pray tell, did that happen?"

"Peculiar as this is going to sound, she lost the first one when I made the mistake of pulling her onto my horse, which didn't turn out exactly as planned. And then she lost the second one when she took a dip in an unexpectedly deep puddle that was, unfortunately, filled with a great deal of mud."

"You're right, that does sound peculiar, but because Gertrude is dripping all over the entranceway marble, perhaps it would be for the best if we saved the rest of this conversation for later." Mrs. Davenport nodded toward the stairs. "Because I'm certain you don't want the poor dear to suffer from another stitch, you may carry her to her assigned suite of rooms, up on the third floor no less." She smiled. "I'll act as chaperone."

It took a great deal of effort for Gertrude not to roll her eyes. "There's no need for Harrison to carry me, and aren't you in the middle of a design lesson with Miss Betsy Miller?"

Mrs. Davenport looked down at the paper patterns attached to her, then gave a dismissive flick of a wrist. "I'm sure Miss Miller has more important matters to attend to for the rest of her day than continuing on with me. She's agreed to give me weekly instruction, and since I certainly don't want to neglect you at this troubling time, I'll just have Mr. Barclay tell Miss Miller something of an urgent nature has come up."

Knowing it would be futile to argue because Mrs. Davenport was looking far too determined, Gertrude soon found herself being carried up three flights of incredibly steep steps. Mrs. Davenport matched Harrison step for step up the flights, chattering on about her pattern lesson as they climbed.

She shooed him away once they reached

Gertrude's suite of rooms. Setting her down, he sent her a charming smile, then headed down the steps again, leaving her a little weak at the knees.

"Goodness, dear," Mrs. Davenport exclaimed. "This is beyond my wildest hopes for you, but do know that you must proceed carefully. It's been my observation that gentlemen such as Harrison, or rogues if you will, tend to enjoy pursuing a lady, so don't make it too easy on him, especially after he delivered such a cruel disappointment to you just the other day."

Walking into her little sitting room, Gertrude moved to the bathing chamber, turning once she reached that door. "Harrison, no matter his appearance, Mrs. Davenport, is not a rogue, nor is he a typical gentleman. And while I truly have no idea what he's up to, I think he may very well have regrets about what happened. I'm intending to hear him out, no matter if you believe that's being easy on him or not, but do know that I appreciate your concern and welcome your support."

Unfortunately, Mrs. Davenport didn't appear to hear a single word of Gertrude's speech since she was already walking out of the room, muttering something about making plans.

Realizing it would be less than prudent to allow Mrs. Davenport too much time to organize what would surely turn into yet another fiasco, Gertrude stripped off her ruined clothing, hurried through a bath in a marble tub that was so enormous a person could practically swim in it, then towel-dried her hair. Slipping into blissfully clean and dry clothing, she arranged her still wet hair into a knot on top of her head. Slipping her feet into the first pair of shoes she found, she bolted for the door and dashed out of the room.

By the time she reached the main floor, she was somewhat winded. Not wanting to draw everyone's attention to that sad state of affairs, she drew in a few deep breaths, and once her breathing returned to normal, she walked down the hall at a pace that wouldn't leave her wheezing again, entering the library a moment later.

What she found inside the library stopped her in her tracks, her gaze traveling over what appeared to be a least a hundred different articles of clothing, all hanging from racks with wheels on them.

"Surprise!" Permilia exclaimed, stepping out from behind one of the racks and beaming at Gertrude. "I hope you don't mind, but after hearing what happened to you, I decided to change my surprise of having you and Harrison sit down to tea with me and Asher to . . ." She gestured to the racks.

"But what is all this?" Gertrude asked as Asher stepped from behind a rack that seemed to be filled with clothing for gentlemen, and then Edwina, in the company of Agent McParland, popped up from where they'd been hidden behind a lovely fainting couch done up in blue.

"Harrison is treating you to an entirely new wardrobe to make up for the fact he almost gave you a heart attack earlier and lost you a most charming outfit of your own in the process," Edwina said.

Gertrude turned and found Harrison sitting on a settee, looking mildly confused while Mrs. Davenport poured him a cup of tea.

"I can't accept such an extravagant gesture" was all Gertrude could think to say.

"Of course you can't," Mrs. Davenport surprised her by saying. "Which is why I'll be picking up the bill for today's fun to make amends for all the embarrassment you've suffered over the years on my behalf."

"And I'll be picking up the bill for the clothing I'm sure all of you have noticed I just happened to have chosen for Harrison,"

Asher said as he rubbed his hands together in glee. "I've been itching to be presented with an opportunity to freshen up Harrison's wardrobe."

"I don't really think I need to be freshened up," Harrison argued.

Asher completely ignored that statement, turning toward the door instead and letting out a whistle, which had several members of the staff from Rutherford & Company walking into the room.

Before Gertrude could voice even the smallest of protests, she found herself led to a screened-off section of the library that had been erected for her use, while Harrison was led to a smaller room that connected with the library, muttering protests as he was led, none of which Asher addressed.

It quickly became clear that the staff from Rutherford & Company knew their business. They had her out of her garments and into new ones so quickly, she barely had time to blink before they gave her a gentle shove and she found herself standing on the other side of the curtain, where Edwina, Agent McParland, and Mrs. Davenport sent her nods of clear approval. Permilia and Asher, on the other hand, eyed her critically.

"I think the blue one next," Permilia

called. "It'll go well with her hair."

Gertrude looked down at the lovely green she was wearing. "The green doesn't go well with my hair?"

"Of course it does, but blue will be striking, and . . ."

Everything else Permilia said got lost when Harrison suddenly stepped out from his dressing area, looking stylish in gray trousers, a white shirt, a gray jacket with pinstripes, and a tie that Gertrude was certain she'd seen bankers wear at her bank.

Even though he looked devastatingly handsome, something about his appearance was wrong.

Marching across the room, she stopped in front of the rack that held the clothes marked for Harrison and began riffling through them, smiling when she spotted the perfect jacket and waistcoat for him. Pulling them down, she turned and displayed her choices to the room at large. "I think this is more to Harrison's tastes."

Silence was the first reaction, before Asher cleared his throat.

"I only brought that jacket, Gertrude, because it was the only one I could find that had a thread of orange to it. And then I found that waistcoat, which is definitely orange, but it's merely a sample from a vendor, and a color I rejected because, well, it speaks for itself."

Gertrude lifted her chin. "I love it, and I want to see him in this, along with . . ." She turned back to the rack, found a pair of charcoal colored pants with a bit of a plaid, then marched her way over to Harrison and handed him her choices. "Off you go."

Sending her a warm look and a smile that made her knees go weak again, Harrison inclined his head and disappeared from sight. Not caring for the knowing looks she was getting from Edwina, Mrs. Davenport, Permilia, and even Agent McParland, who was now enjoying a cup of tea, Gertrude headed back to her dressers, finding herself redressed in the blink of an eye in the blue gown Permilia had suggested.

Stepping into the room again, she found Harrison already standing there, looking rather pleased with the outfit she'd chosen for him as he looked in a floor-length mirror Asher had evidently brought over from his store. Given that Asher didn't appear completely horrified by the outfit she'd picked out for Harrison, she smiled and moved farther into the room.

Any thought she may have had about commenting on Harrison's appearance, though, disappeared straightaway when he turned from his reflection and saw her. His mouth dropped open, and then he was striding across the room toward her. Stopping directly in front of her, he reached for her hands, lifted them, then placed a kiss on each one.

"How extraordinary you look, Gertie. Quite possibly the most beautiful woman I've ever seen in my life."

For what seemed like forever, Gertrude could not get a single word past her lips, until she managed an impressive "Oh my" right as Harrison kissed her hand again, then cleared his throat and suddenly began to look rather nervous.

"There's much I need to say to you," he began. "And while this is not exactly how I planned this, I need to . . ."

"Hold your tongue before you make the biggest mistake of your life."

CHAPTER TWENTY-FIVE

"Oh, this is unfortunate," Harrison heard Edwina say right as his mother marched her way across the library, her eyes darting about the room, and her color turning more concerning with every step she took. Coming to a stop in front of Harrison, she sent a pointed look at Gertrude's hand that he'd been lingering over, then thankfully, leaned to the right, and let out a sound like an angry cat when she spotted Edwina sitting directly next to Agent McParland on the fainting couch.

"It would seem as if I got here in the nick of time," Cornelia began, stepping around Harrison to march her way over to Edwina. "If memory serves me correctly, dear, you allowed me to believe you were off to this school to better acquaint yourself with the programs offered here." She drew herself up. "However, you neglected to mention Miss Cadwalader was to be present, or —"

she shot a look to Agent McParland, who'd now risen to his feet and was watching Cornelia warily — "a gentleman I've yet to meet but who seems far too comfortable in your company, or . . ." She spun around and pointed a finger to Mrs. Davenport. "If I'm correct in my assumption, and given the unusual manner in which that lady is dressed, that's Mrs. Davenport, a woman, Edwina, I distinctly recall telling you to steer clear of."

Harrison winced when Edwina pushed herself up from the fainting couch and narrowed her eyes at her mother.

"You've been unreasonable with your opinion of Mrs. Davenport and Gertrude," Edwina said. "And while I do apologize for not being more forthcoming about this gentleman —" she paused to smile fondly at Agent McParland — "I wasn't certain you'd be accepting of my spending time with a Pinkerton detective, especially when I've decided my new goal in life is to join their illustrious ranks."

"Agent Samuel McParland at your service, Mrs. Sinclair," Agent McParland said, impressing Harrison in spite of himself when the man executed a perfect bow toward Cornelia even though she was obviously seething with animosity.

"While I'm sure that under different circumstances, I'd be just delighted to meet you, Agent McParland, I'm far too annoyed with my daughter for purposefully withholding information from me to appreciate making your acquaintance." Cornelia spun around and pinned Harrison with a furious scowl. "Why were you holding Miss Cadwalader's hand?" she demanded.

Realizing this was not the moment to divulge what he'd been intending, because that would diminish what should be a moment Gertrude could cherish for the rest of her life, Harrison forced a smile. "What are you doing here, Mother?"

"I came to find Edwina because I've recently experienced a most disturbing situation that I needed her assistance with, a situation that coincidentally concerns Miss Cadwalader and Mrs. Davenport." She cast a glare Edwina's way. "I had no idea I'd find you and your brother cozying up to the enemy."

"Enemy?" Harrison repeated.

Cornelia gave a jerk of her head. "Exactly. Which is why I suppose it is a fortuitous circumstance I stumbled on you here, and before you were able to do something ridiculous such as declaring your affections for the oh-so-scheming Miss Cadwalader, a declaration I'm afraid you'd live to regret for the rest of your days."

Gertrude pulled the hand he was still holding back, and even though her color was now leaching out of her face, she lifted her chin and nodded to his mother.

"I'm afraid you have me at a disadvantage, Mrs. Sinclair," Gertrude began. "I've done nothing that could be considered disturbing of late, although you seem to believe otherwise."

Cornelia crossed her arms over her chest. "You're very good with the innocent act, dear, but I've found you out. Margaret told me the other day about your interest in my painting, an interest that was disclosed to her by some well-meaning lady from what I understand." She shook her head. "Imagine my disbelief when I traveled to the *Cornelia* today to have her readied for a trip I need to take this week, and discovered that my painting is no longer hanging on the wall in the library, nor is it to be found anywhere on the ship."

"Oh . . . dear," Harrison heard Gertrude mumble before she lifted her chin another notch. "I'm sorry to hear about your painting, Mrs. Sinclair, but I assure you, I did not take it."

"Nor would she have had any time to take

it, Mother," Edwina said, stepping up next to Gertrude and entwining their arms together. "I've been in Gertrude's company often since she was released from jail, and she's spent the majority of her time over the past few days moving her belongings, as well as Mrs. Davenport's belongings, here to the school."

"An obvious ruse to muddy the waters," Cornelia said with a wave of her hand.

Harrison stepped closer to his mother — a risky move if there ever was one, but one that needed to be taken. "Mother, I know you've been worried of late with all the changes that seem to be happening so quickly, but you're wrong about Gertrude and Mrs. Davenport. Yes, Mrs. Davenport did have a little . . . er . . . problem with helping herself to items that did not belong to her, but there's a perfectly reasonable explanation behind her peculiar habit, and never once did she keep any of the items she helped herself to." He reached out and gave her arm a squeeze. "I was under the impression after our talk before I left for Boston that you understood the circumstances surrounding Mrs. Davenport's idiosyncrasies. And that you were sympathetic toward her because of the pain she'd suffered in her past."

Cornelia lifted her chin. "I *was* sympathetic to Mrs. Davenport's plight, and remorseful as well about having Miss Cadwalader carted off to jail. However, that sympathy and remorse died a rapid death the moment I discovered someone — and let us not dither about who that someone is — stole my painting."

Asher suddenly cleared his throat, drawing everyone's attention. To Harrison's confusion, his friend was fishing his copy of the list — the one with all the romantic gestures written on it — out of his pocket. After perusing that list for a second, Asher looked to Harrison. "Forgive me for interrupting, but could this missing painting perhaps be gesture number five?"

For the briefest of seconds, Harrison simply stared back at his friend, having no recollection of what gesture number five was, but knowing full well he'd not made his mother's most treasured painting disappear to perpetuate that gesture.

"I don't recall what gesture number five is, but do know that none of the gestures can be used to explain how my mother's painting went missing."

Asher stuffed the list back into one of his many pockets. "That's too bad, and number five was solving a mystery, if you wanted to know, however . . ." He turned back to Mrs. Sinclair. "I've forgotten my manners." Walking over to Cornelia, he took her hand and kissed it. "You're looking lovely today, Mrs. Sinclair. The color in your cheeks is very becoming."

"Put there by my children no doubt, but thank you, Asher. And this must be your lovely fiancée, Miss Griswold. I neglected to see her as well, being so consumed with all the many intrigues floating around this room and all."

Permilia moved forward, and to Harrison's relief, she took hold of his mother's hands, smiled, and then drew Cornelia into a hug. She stepped back a moment later. "Do call me Permilia, Mrs. Sinclair, since I'm certain we'll eventually turn into fast friends, given how close Asher and Harrison are. Because of that closeness, and because of my closeness to Gertrude, I feel I must speak up and defend my friend since you're a bit off the mark about her. Gertrude is one of the kindest, sweetest, most generous ladies I know, and I don't think you'll want to continue discouraging Harrison from . . . well, whatever it was he was about to do."

Harrison was not reassured when his mother took a step back from Permilia. "I'm afraid I cannot give my blessing to a woman

I feel has fooled everyone she encounters. My painting is missing, one of my daughters has been encouraged by Miss Cadwalader and Mrs. Davenport to lead a society life, although it now appears she's also been encouraged by someone to pursue a career as a detective, which —" she nodded to Edwina — "is a far better choice than entering society, but still." Cornelia drew in a breath. "Miss Cadwalader has somehow slipped through my son's defenses and wormed her way into his heart. That is not an easy challenge to undertake nor find success with, and that right there has convinced me she's a charlatan of the worst sort."

She swung her attention to Gertrude. "While I was willing to forgive you for lying your way onto the *Cornelia* to replace the items Mrs. Davenport helped herself to, I won't forgive you for deceiving my son or for beginning to build a friendship with Edwina."

"And yet I imagine Gertrude will easily forgive you, Mrs. Sinclair, for casting aspersions on her good name after I prove to you you're completely mistaken about her stealing your painting."

As everyone turned toward the door, Harrison found Miss Henrietta walking into the room, her pace less than hurried.

"Who, pray tell, are you?" Cornelia demanded. "And how in the world do you know my name since I know full well we've never been introduced?"

"I'm Miss Henrietta Huxley. You may call me Henrietta, though, which means I'll feel free to address you as Cornelia. As to how I know you, let me simply say I make it a point of always being well informed." Miss Henrietta smiled. "I must admit I've spent many an hour admiring that fine-looking husband of yours from afar, and might have even been known to admire your rascal of a son a time or two as well."

Cornelia arched a delicate brow. "I'm sure I have no idea how anyone expects me to respond to that."

Miss Henrietta arched a brow right back at her. "I would suggest you say 'thank you,' since I was obviously complimenting you on your wonderful taste in gentlemen as well as complimenting the stellar good looks of your son. But enough of the pleasantries. You've leveled an accusation at our dear Gertrude, which I can understand, given Gertrude's rather suspicious situation on board the *Cornelia.* However, because I've concluded you're normally a very rational lady — because how could you not be, being the mother of such upstanding children

— I'm going to simply present you with evidence of Gertrude's innocence and allow you to form your own conclusion."

"Is that presentation of the evidence going to result in my arresting anyone?" Agent McParland suddenly asked.

"I should say not, although how delightful to find you here, Agent McParland," Miss Henrietta said with a knowing look sent to Edwina. "May I assume matters are progressing nicely between the two of you?"

Edwina's eyes widened, and she sent a not-so-subtle nod in the direction of her mother, which had Miss Henrietta sending Edwina a bit of a wink in reply. "Ah yes, too right you are. Probably not the best time to broach that particular topic. So, moving right along, allow me to present my evidence." She turned toward the door and gestured to it with a flourish of her hand, frowning when nothing appeared. Clearing her throat, she gestured again. "My evidence," she repeated a little louder than before, but still, nothing.

Releasing a sigh, she marched toward the door, stopping a mere foot away from it. "Temperance, you're ruining the moment by not appearing on cue," she practically bellowed.

A second later, Temperance appeared in

the doorway, slightly out of breath, and looking decidedly disheveled as well as a little wild about the eyes.

"Goodness, Temperance," Gertrude said, stepping forward. "What happened to you?"

Temperance lifted a hand, patted down hair that could only be described as having a fly-away look, and shuddered. "I was just given the supreme pleasure of careening down the streets of the city in an open buggy with Miss Henrietta at the reins." She looked at Miss Henrietta and shuddered again. "What a thrilling adventure that was, especially when Miss Henrietta decided we weren't traveling fast enough because of traffic and took me on a tour of the side streets, traveling at breakneck speed and taking turns that almost saw the buggy wheels leaving the ground."

Miss Henrietta smiled somewhat smugly. "But we did make it back here in one piece, and it seems fortunate indeed we made such excellent time or else Gertrude and Mrs. Davenport would continue suffering from nasty accusations being directed their way." Her smile dimmed. "Forgive me, Temperance, but I just noticed you don't seem to be in possession of our evidence."

Temperance smiled. "Mr. Barclay wanted

to be included in the process of revealing it."

"You mean the butler who answered the door when I arrived?" Cornelia asked slowly.

"Indeed, although he's been branching out from his butler duties these days," Miss Henrietta said. "Just as I've been branching out from my established role as recluse." With that, Miss Henrietta looked to the door. "Mr. Barclay, we're ready for the big reveal if you please," she called.

Mr. Barclay immediately appeared in the doorway, his eyes twinkling as he presented the room at large with a bow. Straightening, he rubbed his hands together and smiled as he gazed fondly around at everyone.

Miss Henrietta wrinkled her nose. "Forgive me, Mr. Barclay, but I believe we may be at sixes and sevens here. Was it not your intention to bring *the package* in with you?"

"I thought it would lend the situation a more dramatic air if I were to come in, then depart again to retrieve the package, increasing the level of suspense for everyone."

"Ah, prolonging the moment. A most excellent way to increase the drama of the situation," Miss Henrietta said with a nod. "We'll now direct our full attention to you as you depart to retrieve the package."

"Very good, Miss Henrietta," Mr. Barclay

said with such a tone of seriousness that Harrison couldn't help but think the man had missed his calling on the stage.

"Is it only me, or has the entire world suddenly gone mad?" Cornelia asked to no one in particular.

"Shh," Miss Henrietta returned. "You're ruining the moment."

As his mother descended into silence, even though she didn't look happy about it, Mr. Barclay moved toward the door ever so slowly, as if he wanted to keep prolonging the suspenseful moment for as long as possible. When he disappeared through the door, Harrison felt his lips twitch when everyone simply kept their attention centered on that door.

At long last, Mr. Barclay returned, carrying a package wrapped in brown paper that Harrison was fairly certain had been wrapped in that paper in another attempt to increase the theatrics of the moment. Walking directly up to Cornelia, Mr. Barclay handed her the package. "For you, Mrs. Sinclair."

"Thank you," Cornelia said, setting the package on the floor. "Although I have to say this is quickly becoming over the top in more ways than one." With that, she tore open the paper then frowned. "On my word, it's my painting."

Miss Henrietta nodded. "Indeed, which means you now owe darling Gertrude a most heartfelt apology, since clearly she did not take your painting, nor did Mrs. Davenport."

"I'm afraid I don't understand," Cornelia said.

Gesturing around the room, Miss Henrietta nodded again. "Perhaps it would be for the best if everyone were to find a seat, because this might take some time to explain."

As Permilia and Gertrude sat down on a settee, Temperance moved to sit between them. Everyone else began to look for places to sit, a tricky business since all the hat boxes and other accessories that Asher and Permilia had brought with them were scattered about the room. After all the ladies found a seat, Harrison moved to stand next to Asher by the fireplace.

They were soon joined by Agent McParland, who pulled his notepad out of his pocket and glanced around.

"I'm hoping some of the disclosures about to be made might help with the investigation still going on regarding the thefts at the Manhattan Beach Hotel," Agent McParland said to the room at large.

"I'm afraid the mystery of Mrs. Sinclair's painting is unrelated to the mystery you're attempting to solve," Temperance said, drawing everyone's attention. "Especially since the culprit seems to be my oh-so-vindictive cousin, Miss Clementine Flowerdew."

Gertrude's mouth dropped open. "Really?"

"I'm afraid so, although I doubt she did the deed herself. Clementine wouldn't want to dirty her hands with theft, but she wouldn't be opposed to hiring someone to do it for her." Temperance shook her head. "It was only a lucky happenstance that I stumbled on the painting, finding it in the attic when I went up there to fetch a trunk I'd stored there. I found the painting tucked behind a stack of blank canvases I'd also stored in the attic, tucked there no doubt under the assumption it would never be found. I'm sure when my relatives left rather suddenly for Newport, it never entered their minds that I would stumble on the painting because I'd decided to move out of their home earlier than expected."

"Your relatives went to Newport and left you behind?" Gertrude asked.

Temperance waved that aside. "I highly doubt Clementine wanted me tagging along since she's more than put out with me at the moment. And considering how rapidly they left town, I do think that they might have done so to provide Clementine with the alibi of being out of town if any suspicions were ever to be cast her way about the missing painting."

"But why would this cousin of yours steal the painting to begin with?" Agent McParland asked.

"Because she's vindictive and wanted to get back at Gertrude since Gertrude refused to advance Clementine's pursuit of Harrison," Temperance said. "My cousin is not the type of lady to ignore what she clearly believed was a slight, even though she now seems determined to win the affections of Mr. Gilbert Cavendish, a gentleman who foolishly accepted an invitation to join my Flowerdew relations in Newport."

Gertrude's eyes widened. "Good heavens, Temperance. Perhaps we should plan a trip to Newport to rescue Gilbert. His future could be doomed if Clementine convinces him she's a lady he should consider pursuing."

Temperance shook her head. "Gilbert's perfectly capable of taking care of himself, Gertrude, and besides, his mother is more frightening than Cornelia." She shot a look

450

to Cornelia. "No offense, Mrs. Sinclair."

The very corners of Cornelia's lips curved. "None taken, dear, although I don't believe you and I have ever been introduced."

Harrison stepped forward. "She's Miss Temperance Flowerdew, Mother. Temperance, this is my mother, Mrs. Sinclair."

"Charmed," Temperance said, rising to her feet. "And while you and I have just met, Mrs. Sinclair, I do hope you'll agree that Gertrude is obviously innocent of any wrongdoing in regard to your painting, and in all honesty, she incurred the wrath of Clementine simply because she was trying to protect your son from my cousin's vindictive nature."

Cornelia considered Gertrude for a long moment, and then, to Harrison's relief, she nodded. "It would seem as if I've made a very grave mistake, Miss Cadwalader, for which I apologize. Do know that I certainly don't expect you to forgive me anytime soon, given the nasty accusations I kept throwing your way."

Gertrude rose to her feet and smiled. "Of course I forgive you, Mrs. Sinclair. You mustn't think on that for another moment."

As Gertrude gave his mother an unexpected hug, and then encouraged her to join them on the settee, Harrison moved back to where Asher and Agent McParland were still standing, shaking his head as he turned and regarded the ladies again.

"They're curious creatures, aren't they?" he asked in a low voice.

"Indeed," Agent McParland agreed. "Although speaking of curious, how would you think these Flowerdew relatives will react if I track them down to Newport and question them about the matter of the now-recovered painting? And do you think it may be possible that Clementine Flowerdew might have played a part in the thefts at the Manhattan Beach Hotel?"

Harrison shook his head. "Clementine spent a great deal of time with me while we were at the hotel and was also one of the first guests to reboard the *Cornelia* once everyone left the hotel. She wouldn't have had time to enact a heist of any great size. As for questioning Clementine and her parents, I don't think you'll find much success with that. Clementine's father, Wayne, has lofty connections in the city that he'll use if he feels the need. In all likelihood, the most they'll admit to is proclaiming that the painting was taken as a lark, so I would say a trip to Newport won't be worth your while. And since the painting has been returned to my mother, I don't believe she'll want to press charges in the end."

Agent McParland sighed, tucking his notebook away. "I suppose the only way I'll solve that mystery now is to return to the Manhattan Beach Hotel. Although, given the time that has elapsed since the thefts, I'm not sure we're going to be able to uncover any additional evidence."

Asher stepped closer to Harrison. "We could use the mystery at the hotel to set the stage for what I'm sure you were about to do with Gertrude before your mother burst in. If you'll recall, solving a mystery is number five on our list."

Harrison blinked. "I'm not sure we should continue on with that list, Asher. The two gestures I've tried so far have not worked out exactly well for me. In all honesty, I've been thinking it might be for the best if I pull Gertrude aside in the next few minutes and simply get this over with once and for all."

Asher shook his head. "Absolutely not. A gentleman should not approach matters of such a delicate nature with an attitude of *getting it over with once and for all.*' Gertrude has proven herself to be an extraordinary lady, and as such, she deserves a romantic gesture from you, one she'll remember for the rest of her days." He glanced at Agent McParland. "If you've no objections, and with your full cooperation, I'm going to suggest we repair to the Manhattan Beach Hotel. We'll say we're traveling there to assist you with your investigation, and then, after the ladies have snooped around a bit, discovering nothing with their snooping, of course, we'll then gather on the beach. It's to be a full moon tonight, and with the moon shining down on you, Harrison, and the waves lapping against the beach, that will be just the romantic setting you need to extend Gertrude the most romantic gesture of her life."

"But what if their snooping turns up more than we're expecting?" Harrison asked slowly.

Asher smiled. "Since the Pinkerton detectives have uncovered nothing of worth, I'm more than confident the ladies' paltry efforts of poking around will turn up nothing as well. There's absolutely nothing for you to worry about because I'm quite sure nothing can possibly go wrong."

CHAPTER TWENTY-SIX

"While it certainly is lovely being back at the Manhattan Beach Hotel," Gertrude began, her arms linked with Edwina's and Temperance's as they strolled down the boardwalk with the ocean to their left and the hotel to their right, "don't you find it somewhat curious we find ourselves here on what seemed to me to be a spur-of-the-moment decision?"

Edwina smiled. "My family has always embraced the idea that adventures are best enjoyed when they're the spur-of-the-moment kind. Although I do think the haste in which we found ourselves here is likely because Samuel, or rather, Agent McParland, seems to be somewhat anxious to have us assist him in solving the mystery of the missing jewelry." She nodded to Gertrude. "I know I mentioned before that we ladies think differently than men, and I have to imagine that is why Samuel requested our help in his investigation, unless . . ." She frowned and met Gertrude's gaze. "I'm completely off the mark and this is Harrison's curious way of making matters right with you for the disappointments and embarrassments you've suffered at the hands of my family lately."

Temperance drew in a sharp breath. "Perhaps Harrison has arranged all of this as your very own version of a *Northanger Abbey* mystery, one complete with an actual mystery and a setting that, while not gothic, is still somewhat mysterious since the hotel is so grand and sits right up next to the ocean."

Gertrude smiled and shook her head. "I don't think Harrison is the type of gentleman to read Jane Austen, although that would be a lovely gesture for a gentleman to make if he needed to make amends. Not that Harrison needs to make amends, mind you."

"He completely made a mess of matters with you in Grace Church, and he's yet to be given an opportunity to correct that," Edwina pointed out.

Gertrude's smile dimmed. "I believe he might have been trying to explain his actions right before your mother burst in, but since he has yet to try again, he might have had a change of heart. That means it might be time for me to simply embrace the idea that Harrison and I are going to remain strictly friends."

"Don't be daft," Edwina said. "Harrison adores you, and I believe he's simply waiting for the perfect moment to act. However, until we reach that moment, I suggest we enjoy our unexpected adventure, and see if we can't go about solving the mystery of the missing items from the Manhattan Beach Hotel." She smiled. "If we could do that, I do think my interest in joining the Pinkerton Agency would be taken seriously, and I could very well impress Samuel in the process, which . . . wouldn't that be lovely?"

Forcing her thoughts away from Edwina's comment about Harrison adoring her, and ignoring the weakness her knees had acquired, the second the word *adores* entered the conversation, Gertrude cleared her throat. "That would be lovely, but I don't believe you need to work too strenuously to impress Agent McParland since, in my humble opinion, he seems more than impressed with you without you solving any mysteries."

"He is adorable," Edwina returned. "And speaking of adorable, did I mention how adorable I found it when you dismissed all the expected clothing choices Asher provided for Harrison, instead choosing the one jacket that was not what anyone would consider a fashionable choice, but one that suited Harrison's sense of style perfectly?"

"Harrison has a sense of style — a curious sense of style, but one he's made all his own."

Edwina beamed a smile back at Gertrude. "And that is exactly how I know you're the lady specifically meant for my brother. You don't see him as others see him: dangerously attractive but in need of fixing. You see him as simply Harrison — a man with disheveled hair more often than not, who mixes plaids with stripes, and a man who seems completely oblivious at times when faced with what he obviously finds to be the bewildering world of women."

"I enjoy his air of bewilderment," Gertrude said with a smile.

"Whose bewilderment are you discussing?"

Turning, Gertrude found Harrison right behind them, accompanied by Agent Mc-Parland who was, of course, smiling Edwina's way. A few yards behind them were Miss Henrietta and Miss Mabel, who'd refused to be left behind, claiming they were taking on the position of chaperone for all the unmarried ladies traveling to the hotel.

"We were discussing how bewildering it was to us when Mrs. Davenport didn't put up a fuss about not being able to travel to the hotel," Edwina said without a single bat of an eye. "Although I do believe any indignation she might have felt over missing this adventure was put to rest when Permilia offered to take Mrs. Davenport back to Rutherford & Company with her."

"The treat of seeing where Miss Betsy Miller designs her creations was certainly brilliant on Permilia's part," Temperance said, speaking up. "Hopefully Permilia and Asher won't be too long finishing up their business at the store, or else they might not be able to sail with Mrs. Sinclair when she finishes up whatever business it was she needed to finish before joining us here."

"My mother won't leave the city without Asher and Permilia," Harrison said. "But since I know all of you promised Permilia you wouldn't delve into too much investigating until she arrived, what say we enjoy ourselves with a nice game of croquet?"

As Miss Henrietta and Miss Mabel finally reached them, Harrison took hold of Gertrude's arm, and having no reason to protest a game of crocquet, she soon found herself

459

holding a mallet and having the time of her life.

"Did you just miss Gertrude's ball on purpose?" Edwina demanded after Harrison took a turn and missed Gertrude's ball that had been lined up directly in front of his.

"Have you ever known me to miss on purpose?" Harrison asked, sending Gertrude a wink before he turned back to his sister.

"Well, no, but you've also never missed such an easy target before, which is telling," Edwina said before she took her shot, knocking Miss Mabel's ball out of the way, and after that, it was war.

By the time the game was complete and Miss Mabel declared the winner, Gertrude's sides were aching from laughing so hard and she'd once again fallen into the easy relationship she'd enjoyed with Harrison before he'd turned a little peculiar that day at Grace Church. The only thing different about that relationship seemed to be in the way Harrison watched her.

His eyes, always filled with one emotion or another, appeared to hold a new level of warmth she'd not encountered before, and that warmth was what was giving her hope — hope that he'd reconsidered and truly was contemplating declaring his intentions in the not too distant future.

"Wonderful game," Miss Mabel said as Miss Henrietta nodded in clear agreement. "But now I'm going to suggest we ladies go and freshen up in our assigned rooms." She looked to Harrison. "What time would you like us to meet you for dinner and where?"

Harrison smiled. "We'll be dining on the beach this evening after we've taken an evening swim, so do make certain to wear the appropriate bathing costumes, because swimming in the sea at twilight is an adventure that shouldn't be missed."

"We've been assigned rooms?" Gertrude asked. "I assumed we'd be returning to the ship at some point and sailing back to the city."

Harrison took her hand and tucked it into the crook of his arm. "We're here on holiday, Gertrude, for an unplanned number of days, courtesy of my mother, who is feeling beyond guilty about what she put you through and is attempting to make it up to you by providing you with a bit of a treat."

"I can't accept such generosity."

Harrison smiled. "Did my mother not have you carted off to jail?"

"Well, yes, but that was understandable. I did have Margaret's belongings in my possession."

"Stop being contrary and simply enjoy my mother's generosity. You'll have to get used to it eventually, so there's really no time like the present to accustom yourself to accepting gifts from my family."

Before she could get a single protest out of her mouth, Harrison passed her off to Miss Henrietta. Saying something about going with Agent McParland to see if any leads surrounding the mystery had turned up, Harrison then quirked a brow at McParland when that man started grinning, the action having McParland turning somber in a split second right before he and Harrison strode away.

"I must say I'm looking forward to a swim in the sea," Miss Henrietta said as she prodded Gertrude into motion, but not in the direction Harrison had just gone. "And not to fret, ladies, because I've arranged with the concierge of the hotel to have bathing costumes delivered for all of us, ones that should be waiting in our rooms by now. To save time, feel free to change into those costumes, but do put a change of clothing into a bag. This hotel has numerous bathing huts they make available to their guests, so we'll take our swim, then enjoy what will most likely be a charming dinner served on the beach."

Entering the hotel through a side door, Miss Mabel produced keys from her reticule, handed them all around, and once they located their assigned suites, the Huxley sisters reminded everyone not to dawdle, then told them they'd all meet down by the beach in the next fifteen minutes.

Following Temperance, who'd unlocked the door of the suite Gertrude would be sharing with her, Edwina, and Permilia, when she finally arrived, she found the traveling trunk her friends had packed for her stored in a corner, while the garments that had been inside those trunks were already hanging in a large wardrobe on the other side of the room.

Moving across the main sitting room, Gertrude's gaze traveled over the plush furnishings done up in a frothy pink, the light from the small chandelier made of sparkling glass casting a welcoming glow throughout the room.

Opening the wardrobe door wide, she found all the garments Permilia had chosen for her hanging in a line, her friend obviously having decided Gertrude would keep all of them, and thinking her friend might have need of an entire wardrobe for a holiday that seemed to have no set end date.

Reaching out to touch the soft fabric of a

blue walking dress, the dress Harrison had enjoyed so much, Gertrude felt tears spring to her eyes as she was suddenly overwhelmed by how many people truly did seem to care about her.

She'd felt so alone for so long that now, when faced with the idea she wasn't, her heart was filled almost to bursting, and a sense of peace she'd not realized she'd been missing was simply becoming a part of her everyday life.

It was as if after finally realizing God didn't hold her responsible for her mother's death, she was now able to move on with her life — a life that God expected her to make extraordinary and had shown her how to go about doing exactly that.

"I found the bathing costumes!" Edwina called from another room in their suite.

Dashing away a tear that had slipped out of her eye, Gertrude lifted her head and found Temperance watching her closely, but then, instead of questioning her, Temperance simply took hold of her hand, quite like Gertrude imagined good friends had done for centuries, and without saying a word, pulled Gertrude with her into the room where Edwina was holding up a bathing costume.

"These are quite different from what I'm

used to wearing when I swim," Edwina said as she wrinkled her nose.

"What do you usually wear?" Gertrude asked.

"Lightweight trousers and shirts we steal from Harrison."

"What does Harrison wear?" Gertrude asked.

Edwina grinned. "He's quite scandalous. He cuts a good portion of the legs off his old trousers, leaving them all tattered and torn. He pairs those short trousers with shirts he cuts the sleeves from, which is why his arms are so dark, something that drives poor Asher mad."

"I'm sure the sight of your brother in short trousers and exposing his arms would drive society ladies mad as well," Temperance said with a grin of her own. "But since Gertrude is now turning bright pink, allow me to change the subject to another dashing young gentleman — Agent McParland."

"Since I'm sure I'm going to marry that man someday, Temperance, you're going to have to start referring to him as Samuel."

Temperance and Gertrude exchanged looks before Gertrude stepped forward. "I don't mean to be so forward, Edwina, but don't you think your family might caution you against rushing into a marriage with a man you just met?"

"Oh, I won't marry for at least a year, if not longer," Edwina said, shaking out the bathing costume before she kicked off her shoes. "I'm in no rush to get married so the idea of a long courtship, if Samuel actually holds me in affection, is very appealing to me."

"That will allow Harrison to sleep better at night," Gertrude said.

Edwina nodded. "Indeed it will. As you've seen, he can be annoyingly overprotective at times, but I really wouldn't want it any other way, although . . ." Her eyes widened. "Don't tell him I said that. He'll be impossible to live with if he knows my sisters and I appreciate him."

"Mum's the word."

After that, the conversation turned to bathing costumes, Miss Snook's school, how large bustles really were expected to get, and all the other nonsensical subjects friends enjoyed chatting about. Before too long, they were dressed in their bathing costumes — long pants that were slim at the ankle and wide everywhere else, stockings, shoes, and shirts they agreed might be called smocks, which were not as uncomfortable as expected due to the scooped neckline and generous cut of the fabric.

Grinning as they twirled around for each other, proclaiming themselves looking very sharp indeed, they threw on the cloaks the hotel had provided for them, then headed out. Walking down the hallway, they soon reached the door that led outside and moved through it, the warm breeze still drifting the heat of a summer day over them.

"There's the veranda that leads into the ballroom where Permilia and Asher's celebration was held," Edwina said with a nod, right before she stopped in her tracks and tilted her head.

"Is it my imagination, or does it seem as if someone's lurking at the very edge of that veranda, and . . ." She turned to Gertrude with eyes that were now incredibly wide. "One of you needs to go and find Harrison and Samuel."

"Why?" Gertrude asked slowly.

"Because whoever I just saw climbed over the railing of that veranda. I'm going to hazard a guess and say it's our thief because that's suspicious behavior, no doubt about it."

Without saying another word, or listening to the protest Temperance immediately began voicing, Edwina bolted forward, leaving Gertrude and Temperance behind.

"I'll go help Edwina, you go find help," Gertrude said before she dashed after Edwina. Sprinting toward the ocean, she felt her pulse hammering through her veins, and even though a sliver of fear was creeping up her spine, she'd never felt more gloriously alive in her entire life.

CHAPTER TWENTY-SEVEN

Shrugging out of the cape she'd thrown over her bathing costume, Gertrude dropped it to the sandy ground and raced on, using the distant sound of yelling to guide her way.

Reaching the beach, she tumbled to the ground when she tripped over two ladies who were now engaged in what seemed to be a bout of wrestling — one of those ladies none other than Edwina.

"Have you gone mad? Let go of me this instant!" the woman Edwina was wrestling yelled, but before Edwina could respond, the woman rolled on top of Edwina, slapped her soundly across the face, then sprang to her feet. Letting out a bit of a growl when Gertrude rose from the sand, she then charged directly at Gertrude, knocked her to the ground again, then turned on her heel and raced off down the beach.

Indignation had Gertrude up and chasing after the woman, although what she'd actually do if she caught up with an obvious member of the criminal sort, she couldn't hazard a guess.

Trying to keep an eye on the woman, who was putting more and more distance between them, Gertrude drew in a much-needed gasp of air right as someone ran up beside her and then passed her.

"Stay there!" Harrison yelled over his shoulder as he continued to run, followed a few paces later by Agent McParland.

Knowing there was little point in continuing on with the chase since Harrison and Agent McParland were far faster than she was, and because she was now experiencing a most painful stitch in her side, Gertrude slowed to a walk, but didn't stay put. Moving after the gentlemen, she was soon joined by Edwina, who was bristling with temper and shrugging out of the cape she was still wearing.

"She hit me," Edwina said.

"I saw that."

"She knocked you down."

"I *felt* that."

Edwina flashed a grin. "How extraordinary, though, that we may have found the culprit behind the thefts, which will clear your name once and for all, as well as Mrs. Davenport's."

"We don't know this woman is the thief, Edwina. She might simply be fleeing because she thinks you and I are madwomen for chasing after her."

"I saw her climb over the railing on the veranda."

"Suspicious behavior to be certain, but it's not proof she's a criminal."

"Why would she hit me then?"

"I might be going out on a limb with this one, but if she isn't a criminal, she might have hit you because you tackled her."

Edwina rolled her eyes. "You might have a point, but I've always wondered if that tackling business Harrison taught me years ago would work in a tricky situation, and . . . it did."

"Harrison taught you how to tackle?"

"He wanted to ensure his sisters could at least have a chance if we were ever attacked." She smiled. "I can't tell you how many times he's ended up with black eyes when he gave us lessons, but he believed it wouldn't benefit us if we didn't fight as hard as we could, even if he was the one who bore the brunt of our efforts."

Gertrude returned the smile. "He's a very protective sort, isn't he?"

"He is, and he's one of those men who doesn't draw attention to his protective attitude. It's just who he is."

"He's like one of those heroes in a novel come to life," Gertrude said, earning an arch of a brow from Edwina she didn't understand. However, before she could ask, fresh yells erupted in the distance.

Without needing to say a single word, Gertrude and Edwina increased their pace, Gertrude's pace coming to a rather abrupt halt when a large, very male form stepped directly into her path. Looking up, she found Harrison standing in front of her.

"Didn't I suggest you stay put?" he asked.

Gertrude wrinkled her nose. "Where's the fun in that?"

For a second, Harrison simply considered her, and then he grinned. "Where indeed?"

The very sight of that grin caused her soul to sing.

He was such an easy gentleman to be around, even with his being so devastatingly handsome. But more importantly, he seemed to understand her in a way no one had ever understood before, and . . . she felt safe with him. When he reached out and took hold of her hand, not to kiss but to simply hold, she felt not only safe but cherished.

She'd never expected to find a gentleman who'd cherish her, protect her, and allow her to embrace an extraordinary life instead of a merely ordinary one.

While she wasn't certain just yet he returned the very great esteem she held for him, she was beginning to embrace the idea that maybe, just maybe, Reverend Perry had the right of matters and that God was far more present in a person's life than was known. Maybe He'd been responsible for bringing Harrison into her life, having known she needed a gentleman of the most chivalrous sort.

With that thought taking a firm hold, Gertrude felt a glimmer of hope run through her that perhaps her life was —

"Is something wrong, Gertie?" Harrison asked, his question bringing her directly back to the situation at hand, although his use of the name *Gertie* was making her heart race just a touch.

"I'm fine. Simply trying to recover my breath. Those pesky stitches do have a way of making themselves known whenever I seem to travel at a pace faster than a plod."

"Shall I carry you to make certain you don't suffer additional stitches?"

While the mere thought of being swept up into his arms again was enough to make her sigh, although silently, Gertrude forced herself to shake her head. "Thank you, but no. Since I don't believe I'll be expected to dash off after another . . ." Her eyes widened. "Goodness, I've forgotten about the woman I was chasing. Did she get away?"

Harrison tucked her hand into the crook of his arm, a gesture she was beginning to expect of him, and pulled her forward, not in the direction of the Manhattan Beach Hotel, but in the direction the suspicious woman had fled.

It didn't take them long to run across that woman, who was now sitting in the sand, her hands secured behind her back while Agent McParland stood in front of her, his notebook at the ready, and Edwina gesturing wildly with her hands as she apparently explained what had happened.

". . . snuck down off the railing, then took off like a flash when she realized I was on to her, aiding my suspicions that I might have uncovered the culprit behind the Manhattan Beach Hotel thefts."

Agent McParland sent Harrison the smallest of smiles before he returned his attention to his notes, mumbling something about "who would have thought this would happen" under his breath as the woman sitting on the ground scowled.

"You recognize her, don't you, Gertrude?"

Edwina asked, drawing Gertrude's attention.

"I can't say that I do, although I haven't had time to give her a proper look, not even when she was inches away from me when she knocked me to the ground."

"She knocked you over?" Harrison asked.

Gertrude pressed her lips together and nodded, stepping closer to where the woman was sitting, stopping though when the woman let out another growl.

"I'll have to teach you how to defend yourself," Harrison said as he joined her.

Not allowing herself to turn into a mass of blubbering jelly over that ridiculously sweet offer, she turned her gaze on the woman again, studying a face that was looking downright menacing. Blinking, she leaned forward.

"On my word, you're the lady from the veranda who was wearing the tiara that supposedly went missing — and who threw suspicion on my good name and that of Mrs. Davenport's."

"She was wearing a dark wig that night," Edwina pointed out. "You'll notice she's not wearing one tonight, although I do wonder how it came to be she picked you and Mrs. Davenport to take the fall for her apparent misdeeds."

Agent McParland stepped forward. "How wonderfully observant you are, Edwina. I thought this woman looked familiar, and now, yes, you're exactly right. She is the woman who first reported a theft from that night, claiming someone had stolen her valuable tiara. And —" he narrowed his eyes on the woman in question — "she must have been wearing a wig to disguise herself." He jotted down a note and then returned his gaze to the woman. "You're evidently not new to the confidence artist business since it was somewhat brilliant to claim you'd been a victim of theft when you apparently were the thief. I am curious, though, as to how you decided to cast suspicion on Mrs. Davenport and Miss Cadwalader."

The woman, unsurprisingly, remained silent.

"It'll go easier for you if you'll only confess to your crimes," Agent McParland continued.

Getrude's lips twitched when the memory sprang to mind of hearing almost those exact same words when she'd been questioned about her own misdeeds. She cleared her throat. "Not that I want to be the voice of doubt, but having recently been wrongly accused of theft myself, I would like to ask if there's any evidence to prove this woman is a thief, because running away from a hotel is hardly substantial proof."

Edwina held up a bag Gertrude hadn't noticed. "I pulled this off her when we were engaged in our little brawl, and as you'll see, it's filled with loot." Pulling open the drawstring, Edwina pulled out a diamond brooch and pearl necklace, then rattled the bag. "There's a small fortune in this bag alone, and who knows what she's stashed away elsewhere."

Talking the pearl necklace Edwina handed her, Gertrude frowned and caught the woman's eye. "Could it be possible that you eavesdropped on the conversation I was having with my friend that evening on the veranda — the one where I might have mentioned I was concerned about Mrs. Davenport slipping away because I'd learned there were Pinkerton detectives roaming around the grounds that evening?"

The woman shrugged. "You weren't exactly being quiet, and considering it was a most enlightening conversation, I couldn't have been expected to ignore it. Everything would have worked out perfectly if you'd actually been arrested and jailed, and if I wouldn't have made the very great mistake of returning to the scene of the crime. I thought the coast would be clear for one more little foray into, well, mischief, if you will, since it was so easy the first time around. Unfortunately, I was mistaken, and barely got anything at all because . . ."

The woman glared at Edwina, then pressed her lips together, refusing to say so much as another word, seeming to realize she'd allowed too much to slip as it was.

Pulling her up to her feet, Agent McParland nodded to Harrison. "If you'll excuse me, I need to see this woman properly arrested and processed." He turned to Edwina. "May I say how impressed I am with how you were able to puzzle this out. Why, I truly did not expect this mystery to be solved in the near future, but you, after being at the Manhattan Beach Hotel for mere hours, puzzled out a mystery that has stumped our most senior agents, myself included. You then chased the culprit down and helped me secure her in the end."

"I believe Harrison is actually the person responsible for securing her," Edwina said.

"It was a group effort," Harrison said, exchanging a smile with his sister.

"Perhaps both of you should consider a career as a Pinkerton," Agent McParland said before he smiled at Edwina. "Would you care to accompany me to see how we go about processing a person accused of theft?"

"I would be delighted."

With the suspect between them, Edwina and Agent McParland walked away, leaving Gertrude alone on the beach with Harrison.

"Why do I have the distinct impression my family is someday going to have a Pinkerton in the family — or perhaps two, if one is by marriage?" Harrison asked.

"Because you're astute that way," Gertrude returned.

Smiling, he took her hand and kept it in his as he pulled her forward, leading her back toward the Manhattan Beach Hotel.

"Now that the mystery has been solved," Gertrude began as they walked, "will our holiday be cut short here?"

Harrison gave her hand a squeeze. "About that . . . would you be disappointed to learn there was never any intention to actually . . ."

Whatever else he'd been about to say got lost when they crested a dune and laid out before them was the most amazing sight Gertrude had ever seen.

Torches were lit around a most elaborate picnic setting, complete with numerous picnic blankets and cushions for the many guests who were gathered there.

Those guests, she was stunned to discover, were Asher, Permilia, Temperance, Mrs. Davenport, Miss Henrietta, Miss Mabel, Mr. Barclay, Mrs. Sinclair, Margaret, Adelaide, and an older gentleman Gertrude had never met before, but given his resemblance to Harrison, she assumed he was Harrison's father.

"Surprise!" Mrs. Davenport called.

With tears now clouding her vision and a sense of anticipation running through her, Gertrude held tightly to Harrison's hand as he pulled her into the midst of everyone. After introducing her to his father, greeting his sisters with a kiss to each of their cheeks, and then kissing his mother, Harrison led Gertrude into the very center of the picnic setting, took her hand in his, and then . . . dropped to one knee before her.

CHAPTER TWENTY-EIGHT

The sight of Harrison on his knee in front of her caused Gertrude to lose the ability to breathe, an unfortunate circumstance if there ever was one, because the lack of breath made her light-headed, and then . . . the wheezing began.

Unable to catch her breath, Gertrude couldn't say she was surprised when Harrison was back on his feet a second later, giving her a resounding pounding on the back, a pounding that soon had her breathing almost back to normal.

Giving one last wheeze, while raising a hand to stop additional pounding, Gertrude raised now watering eyes to Harrison. "I do beg your pardon, Harrison, for ruining what would have been a lovely moment. Do feel free to continue since I'm now no longer struggling for air."

"Don't forget number seven on the list," Asher called.

Harrison blinked, stuck his hand into the pocket of his trousers, ones she'd just noticed were meant for swimming and were paired with a striped shirt, the stripes a bright shade of purple. Before she could fully appreciate the look, though, Harrison pulled out a piece of paper, glanced at it, frowned, then lifted his head and looked to Asher.

"Are you certain about this?"

Asher nodded. "Remember when our friend Gilbert claimed that ladies enjoy special gestures to commemorate special occasions? Well, rest assured, I daresay Gertrude will never forget the gesture of you reciting Lord Byron's 'She Walks in Beauty,' especially if you do it properly."

Harrison drew in a breath, looked at the paper again, then returned his attention to Gertrude. He took her hand in his again, frowned, and then leaned closer. "Would you be offended if I paraphrased? I must admit I did not memorize it properly, and . . . well, I'm afraid I'm about to make a muddle of matters since all I can recall is a line pertaining to a woman walking in beauty and something about mellowed skies, or mellowed nights, or . . ."

Gertrude placed a finger over his lips. "Forgive me, but why are you and Asher so convinced that you need to recite poetry to me, and what exactly is that list the two of you keep consulting?"

Harrison handed her the list, but before she could glimpse more than the title — something about romantic gestures — he was releasing a breath and looking slightly nervous.

Taking her hand in his, he squeezed it. "I know I've blundered badly with you, Gertie, and I need to make that up to you. Asher and I thought compiling a list of the best romantic gestures we'd found in romance novels might be exactly what was needed for you to see how sorry I am for not declaring my very great affection for you that day in Grace Church. The only way I can explain why I denied my affection was because you were looking so horrified after Mrs. Davenport suggested we were progressing nicely together."

Gertrude frowned. "Of course I was looking horrified. No lady wants the gentleman she holds in great esteem to be pressured into declaring himself. That leaves all manner of doubt about why he would declare himself at all, but tell me, why did *you* think I was looking horrified?"

"I thought you wanted an opportunity to be taken in hand by ladies who truly care about you. You'd just admitted to me you did not share a warm relationship with your mother, that she was less than maternal with you when you were a child. When Miss Henrietta declared she wanted to take you in hand, with her sister agreeing, I decided it would not be fair of me to deny you their motherly attention. With that said, I then made the very grave error of allowing you to believe I wanted to maintain a friendship with you, when that was not even remotely close to the truth."

The sweetness of that gesture warmed Gertrude all the way to her toes. "And the horse incident and subsequent almost drowning in a puddle — were those supposed to be romantic gestures?"

"They were, but didn't turn out quite so romantic, nor did the pretend mystery holiday work out well either since we certainly didn't intend to really solve a mystery."

"We'd just noticed so many instances of mysteries in romance novels, you see," Asher added. "We thought it would be a great way to set the stage for . . ." He gestured to the scene around them.

"I knew it," Edwina said, striding into the light to join them. "Did I miss anything?"

"Harrison was about to recite a poem by

Lord Byron, although I believe he mentioned something about paraphrasing it since he neglected to memorize it," Miss Henrietta said.

"How delightful," Edwina said. "Although I do think Samuel would enjoy hearing this recitation, but . . . he won't be back for some time, so . . . you might as well get on with it."

"Who is Samuel?" Harrison's father suddenly asked, earning a whispered reply from Cornelia and an innocent batting of Edwina's lashes before Harrison cleared his throat.

"Getting back to my poem," he began, but before he could get more than that out of his mouth, Gertrude stepped closer to him.

"I don't know why you feel the need to enact romantic gestures, Harrison. You're romantic without even trying, and do know that I've noticed and adored the little romantic gestures you extend me all the time without apparently even realizing it."

"What gestures?" Harrison asked slowly.

"You swept me up into your arms to get me off your ship, but it wasn't the sweeping that was the most romantic part of that gesture — it was that you'd done so because you'd noticed me wheezing. You then sat down to dinner with Clementine, a nasty woman if there ever was one, simply because I asked it of you, and . . . you call me Gertie."

Harrison blinked. "You find that romantic?"

She smiled. "I always wanted to have a pet name, and I find it absolutely delightful that you're the gentleman to finally give me one."

Harrison returned the smile. "Are you certain you don't want me to have a go at reciting the poem?"

"I'd rather you just use your own words."

As everyone around them went completely silent, Harrison took the list she was still holding from her, stuffed it back into his pocket, shoved a strand of hair that was now blowing in front of his eyes aside, then smiled. Taking hold of her hand, he dropped to his knee again.

"I knew from the moment I met you that you were an unusual woman," he began. "Probably because you were dyed an unusual shade of orange, and you didn't seem all that concerned about it. As I got to spend more and more time with you, though, I realized you are the most extraordinary woman I've ever known. You're beautiful, certainly, but more importantly, you have a most generous heart and a thirst for adventure I believe you're only just now beginning to understand. If you would agree to share the rest of your life with me as my wife, I promise I'll do everything within my power to feed that thirst of adventure and love you as no man has ever loved a woman for the rest of my days."

Gertrude blinked to clear the tears that were clouding her vision as all the ladies surrounding them immediately began dabbing at their eyes and sniffling ever so quietly, although Miss Henrietta and Mrs. Davenport took to practically howling as they cried into handkerchiefs Asher provided to them.

"I would be honored to share a life of adventure with you, Harrison. You've captured my heart quite like I imagine a pirate would capture a ship, and because of that, I'll not be content to live my life without you. I'll love you for the rest of *my* days, days I know will no longer be merely ordinary, but extraordinary."

The moment she finished talking, Harrison was on his feet, pulling her close as he cupped her cheek in his hand, leaned toward her, and then . . . he kissed her.

Everything in her world settled to rights as she slipped her hands around Harrison's neck and relished the feel of his lips on hers.

When he pulled away from her, though sooner than she would have liked, he then surprised her by scooping her up into his arms and striding with her directly toward the sea.

Before she could grasp what he was up to, he tossed her into the air, and shrieking with laughter, she hit the water, unsurprised to feel his arms lift her up against him a moment later. Exchanging grins, they dove into the waves, Gertrude knowing this was only the first of what would certainly be more adventures. Looking up to the sky, she grinned and lifted up a prayer, thanking God for blessing her with the love of an extraordinary gentleman.

EPILOGUE

Three months later

Taking a step back from the dress form, Mrs. Davenport regarded the latest dress design she'd been working on, nodding in satisfaction at the draping she'd managed to create.

"How lovely, Hester," Miss Henrietta said as she walked across the completed design studio at Miss Snook's School for the Education of the Feminine Mind. "In all honesty, I've come to believe you're almost ready to teach a class on your own."

Mrs. Davenport shook her head. "While that's very kind of you to say, I don't believe I've learned quite enough to start teaching just yet. Although . . ." She smiled. "I have been enjoying my new position as house mother, and thank you again for offering me such a position."

"You're very good with the young women," Miss Henrietta said, stopping beside Mrs. Davenport before she ever so casually fanned her face with a fancy piece of ivory vellum. "And speaking of one of our young ladies . . ." She held out the vellum. "Look what was just delivered from our social secretary."

Drawing in a sharp breath, Mrs. Davenport held out a hand that was trembling ever so slightly and took the piece of vellum, blinking a few times to clear the tears that were now clouding her vision. Bending her head, she began to read.

The pleasure of your company is
requested at
47 Broadway
To celebrate the engagement of
Miss Gertrude Cadwalader
to
Mr. Harrison Sinclair
Monday, October the Eighth
at Ten o'clock.
Responses delivered to
47 Broadway
Miss Snook's School for the
Education of the Feminine Mind
Mrs. R. Davenport, Miss Henrietta Huxley,
Miss Mabel Huxley

"I am still all aflutter Gertrude agreed to

allow us to host her engagement celebration here," Miss Henrietta said after Mrs. Davenport raised her head. "Mabel and I are simply tickled our old home has had such new life breathed into it. Mr. Barclay has declared he's going to personally see to the renovations of the third-floor ballroom to ensure Gertrude will not be disappointed on her special day."

"He is a dear man and so willing to take on extra responsibilities when he's not needed as the butler," Mrs. Davenport said. "He's very attentive to the students here as well, even stepping in when we need a gentleman to partner them in the dance classes we've just begun teaching."

"Unless Permilia happens to be visiting," Miss Henrietta said with a shake of her head. "I do not believe that young lady will ever be proficient with all the steps, but one must give her credit for enthusiasm. But speaking of visiting and visitors, I've actually come to tell you there's someone here to see you."

Mrs. Davenport frowned. "I thought you came to show me the invitation."

"Well, that too, but then I was supposed to tell you that you have a visitor waiting for you in the library."

"Is it Gertrude? Have she and Permilia

returned early from Paris, and if so, has she told you anything about a wedding gown she might have found over there?"

"It's not Gertrude or Permilia."

Mrs. Davenport tilted her head. "It must be Edwina then. She sent me a note earlier asking if she could sit with me, a woman with proficiency in petty larceny, and ask me questions that may help her understand the criminal mind."

Miss Henrietta wrinkled her nose. "That's somewhat disturbing, but no, it's not Edwina."

"Temperance then?"

"Since Temperance lives here, she'd hardly be a visitor. Besides, she's taken a group of young women down to the docks to paint. But no need to look so concerned, she's taken Mr. Barclay with them, and he, I'm happy to report, is armed with more than one pistol and has gotten very skilled with using them, thanks to the efforts of our darling Harrison."

"I'm beginning to run out of people who might be here to visit me."

"It's Reverend Perry."

"Oh, of course, he must be here with the final plans for the new stained-glass window I purchased for the church — one that's in honor of all the people who've entered my life, yourself included of course, who've become my family."

"What a lovely gesture," Miss Henrietta said before she offered Mrs. Davenport her arm, and together, the two ladies left the studio and made their way to the library.

To Mrs. Davenport's surprise, once they reached the library door, Miss Henrietta excused herself, leaving Mrs. Davenport all alone.

Walking into the library, she found Reverend Perry waiting for her, and after accepting his kiss on her hand, she took a seat on a fainting couch where he joined her a second later.

A trace of unease settled over her when he didn't bring out plans for the new window, but took hold of her hand instead.

"Is something amiss?" she asked.

He shook his head. "Not exactly, but there's a story I've been asked to tell you, one that concerns your past, and one you might find a little distressful."

"May I inquire as to who might have asked you to relate this story to me?"

"Miss Henrietta and Miss Mabel."

"Which does explain why Miss Henrietta made herself scarce after she told me you were here."

"It does, but do know that the sisters have

your very best interests at heart, which is exactly why they hired the Pinkerton Agency to investigate the mystery of your past — or more specifically, to investigate what happened to your husband and daughter."

Mrs. Davenport raised a hand to her throat. "But I hired investigators years ago. They were never able to uncover a single clue as to where my husband had taken Jane."

"I'm not certain the resources of those investigators were the same as what the Pinkerton Agency has at its disposal these days."

"But why would Miss Henrietta and Miss Mabel go to such bother on my account?"

Reverend Perry smiled. "Because you're their friend, and they obviously cherish that friendship and want to do what they can to make your life more fulfilled."

Mrs. Davenport pulled a handkerchief out of her sleeve and dabbed her eyes. "I am fortunate indeed to have been blessed with such wonderful friends, a gift I'm sure you'll agree was given to me after I made my peace with God."

"You always possessed the ability to form fast friendships, Mrs. Davenport. You simply didn't believe you deserved them, but it's wonderful to see you adopting a more accepting attitude. But now, before I continue, you must decide whether you want to know what the detectives found, or if you'd prefer for your past to remain in the past."

Mrs. Davenport lifted her chin. "I need to know."

Patting her hand, Reverend Perry nodded. "I thought you'd say exactly that." He drew in a breath and slowly released it. "The detectives learned that Roy Davenport left the country after he disappeared with your daughter, Jane, and he settled on a country estate in England."

"England? Why in the world would he settle in England?"

"He apparently had a cousin there, one with a large family. That, to me, says that even though Roy was wrong to steal your daughter away from you, he was trying to provide her with a family of sorts, albeit a distant one."

"He wouldn't have had to provide Jane with a family at all if he'd simply stayed in New York, worked on our marriage, and allowed me to be a mother to Jane."

"Well, quite, but you must remember that you were not the woman you are today. You've admitted to drinking heavily, stealing, and even using your daughter as a pawn to draw Roy's attention. In all fairness to your husband, he probably saw you as a distinct threat to Jane."

Mrs. Davenport blew out a breath. "I was a threat to Jane, and in all honesty, I was a horrible mother. However, since no good will come of dwelling on my past deficiencies, may I dare hope Roy and Jane are still over in England?"

Reverend Perry squeezed Mrs. Davenport's hand. "This is the part you may find distressful, because, you see, not long after getting settled in England, Roy became very ill. And while he was fighting a fever, he apparently told that cousin of his that you were . . . dead."

Mrs. Davenport's mouth dropped open. "He killed me off?"

"I'm afraid so, and that's not the worst of it."

"How could that not be the worst of it?"

"Because before Roy could rescind that statement, he died, but only after he got his cousin's promise to take Jane in and raise her as his own. That cousin then adopted Jane, which changed her last name, making it next to impossible for you to uncover her whereabouts."

Mrs. Davenport simply sat there for a long moment, stunned. "But . . . is she still over in England, and if so, do I dare travel there and try to explain why I'm not dead?"

"There's no need for that, because I decided to travel here to New York and see for myself if the mother I've believed dead for decades was still very much alive."

Turning toward the door, Mrs. Davenport suddenly found it next to impossible to breathe because standing in that doorway was . . . Jane.

She was obviously no longer a child, but Mrs. Davenport would have recognized her anywhere.

An eternity seemed to pass between them, but then Mrs. Davenport was on her feet, rushing to her daughter's side. Drawing Jane into her arms, she held on for dear life as tears flowed freely down her face.

"I never thought I'd see you again," she whispered.

"I never thought I'd see you either since I truly did believe you were dead."

Stepping back, although she kept a firm grip on Jane's hand, Mrs. Davenport managed a wobbly smile. "From what I understand, your father was in the midst of a fever when he told you that, but I know why he told you I was dead. As I've just recently admitted to Reverend Perry, I was a horrible mother."

Jane smiled. "Since I have children of my

own, I'm of the belief that we mothers do the best we can with what we have available at the moment. Father was not an easy man, which I'm sure contributed to the situation at the time."

"I kept hoping you'd return someday, maybe not to see me, but to revisit the window your father purchased for you at Grace Church." Mrs. Davenport smiled. "You were always fascinated with that window, which is why I've attended almost every service there for decades."

"I remember that window, but because I believed you gone, there was never a reason for me to return."

Walking back to the fainting couch as Reverend Perry sent her a nod before he departed, Mrs. Davenport took a seat directly beside Jane, delighted when Jane immediately took hold of her hand again.

"We have much to catch up with, Mother," Jane said. "Did I mention I'm married to an earl — the Earl of Ossulton — and that I have five children?"

Mrs. Davenport raised a hand to her chest. "I have five grandchildren?"

"You do, and they're scamps, each and every one of them." Jane smiled. "Do say you'll accept my invitation to come and stay at our castle in Northumberland so you can get to know me again, as well as my family."

Brushing away a tear that was trailing down her face, Mrs. Davenport smiled. "I would be delighted to accept your invitation, although I will need to stay in the city until October." Her smiled widened. "A very good friend of mine will be celebrating her engagement then, and I truly cannot miss that occasion." She reached up and touched Jane's face. "She is a most compassionate sort, stubborn at times, quite like you were as a child. And, she's an extraordinary woman, one who is certain to have an extraordinary life — a lady who goes by the delightful name of Gertrude."

ABOUT THE AUTHOR

Jen Turano, a *USA Today* bestselling author, is a graduate of the University of Akron with a degree in clothing and textiles. She is a member of ACFW and RWA. She lives in a suburb of Denver, Colorado. Visit her website at www.jenturano.com.